B P Walter was born and rais[...] childhood and teenage years rea[...] bookshops then went to the Uni[...] Film and English followed by an MA in Film & Cultural Management. He is an alumnus of the Faber Academy and formerly worked in social media coordination for Waterstones in London.

B P Walter Thrillers

Written as Barnaby Walter

THE TREEHOUSE

B P WALTER

One More Chapter
a division of HarperCollins*Publishers* Ltd
1 London Bridge Street
London SE1 9GF
www.harpercollins.co.uk
HarperCollins*Publishers*
Macken House, 39/40 Mayor Street Upper,
Dublin 1, D01 C9W8
This paperback edition 2025
2
First published in Great Britain in ebook format
by HarperCollins*Publishers* 2025

A catalogue record of this book is available from the British Library

ISBN: 978-0-00-875017-6

Printed and bound in the UK using 100% Renewable Electricity
by CPI Group (UK) Ltd

For Molly and Ash

Prologue

The boys watch her die. For the younger of the two, there is panic, horror even, mingled with curiosity. In the other, a more reserved, focused fascination. This is what they had planned. Discussed. Waited for. What their whole summer had been building up to. A summer they will remember forever.

Then things start to go wrong.

Just when they're convinced she's slipping away, crossing the great gulf between life and death, she moves.

'I don't feel well,' she murmurs. 'I need to go home.' She makes an attempt to stand. Falls back down. 'I feel awful,' she says.

'Lie back down,' says the older boy.

'Perhaps we should—' the younger starts to say, but his older brother silences him with a look.

'Lie down,' the older one says again.

'I think I should go home,' she says. The older boy steps forwards then, blocking her path. Does she know, wonders the younger, does she know what they're doing? Why they've brought her here? The planning involved. The waiting. The betrayal.

She keeps moving.

She's still alive, trying to get up again, hands and legs scrabbling and scraping.

Something has to be done.

The older boy goes forwards and holds a bowl to her lips, tilting it backwards, trying to force her to drink.

She splutters and gasps.

Trying to get away, she falls back, smacking her head on the wall of the treehouse. She doesn't move. He gives her a little push. Just a nudge. But because she's weak and sleepy, she falls backwards easily. The thud of her head on the back wall of the treehouse sounds like a canon going off, the momentous impact of it rippling across time, touching their past, present and future.

The younger brother is sure of that. He feels it within him. It's impossible for this *not* to affect their future. To remake it and reshape it. Send them both spinning down a new path, transforming them into different people.

'Has her soul left her?' the younger boy asks.

'Yes,' says the elder. 'It's floating away now. I can sense it.'

The younger brother suddenly feels a rush of reality – it's like the façade of the whole sacrifice and the theory behind it are starting to feel ridiculous, and the true horror of what's happening is becoming clear.

'Oh God,' he says. 'Oh God. What have we done?'

Chapter One

ROBERT

It's not often Robert has a truly amazing day, but today he knows for sure this is one of them. Everything's gone right. He is a naturally careful person and often worries the best laid plans will hit some sort of snag along the road. But not today.

He heads home to his flat, alighting at Knightsbridge underground station, barely noticing the crowds of people pushing and shoving. His mind is still back at the office, where the CEO of the charity he works for personally named him in an international memo to the whole company. His mind is also on Laura in the legal department, who WhatsApped to congratulate him and ask if they could both 'grab a drink' after work the following week. Two bits of good luck in one day. He's never thought of himself as a fortunate person. His older brother, Kieran, is usually the lucky one. They both had their own ways of navigating the choppy waters of adulthood. They'd needed to carve out paths that suited them, that fit their personalities. They both have their demons to deal with. Shared demons. Things they've had to wrestle with as the years have gone by. But he doesn't want to think about any of that. Not today.

Robert walks down through Lowndes Square, heading for his Wilton Crescent flat, taking the slightly longer route. He fancies extending his time outside. It's a beautiful evening, the sun bathing the streets of London in a golden glow. The city has been in the grip of a heatwave for the past few weeks and up until now he's been complaining about it like everyone else who regularly takes the Tube, but not today. Today he is basking in the heat, loving the warm breeze that blows along the streets, the frazzled leaves falling and scattering around the parked cars. A fool's autumn, he's heard it called. The colours of the next season brought forward due to dried-out leaves. Whatever the technical name for it is, he thinks the effect is beautiful.

He arrives home to find his flatmate, Albie, filling a tumbler glass with crushed ice, fruit juice and vodka.

'Good thinking,' he says. 'Make one of those for me.'

Albie grins. He is only staying with Robert as a favour to his older brother, who had been Robert's friend at school. Albie is twenty-nine, an actor in West End shows, and the Central London location of the flat means he can walk to work, with Robert charging him a low rent for the area. They had clicked immediately when he moved in the previous year, and the arrangement, which had initially been intended to last only a few months until he found another flat-share with fellow 'theatre types', has become indefinite. Robert doesn't mind. Though he doesn't exactly need the money, he quite likes feeling like an older brother in the friendship. He's always been 'the young one' in his family, and treated like it, as though he is a naïve soul who will one day find out how the world works. With Albie, however, he can be the experienced man in his thirties guiding the inexperienced youth in the ways of the big city – or something like that. And being single in one's mid-thirties can be a lonely existence, so he welcomes the company.

'I thought you started in *Phantom* tonight?' Robert asks as he sets down his laptop bag and picks up the drink.

'That's next week,' Albie says. 'Been in rehearsal today. Want to go out somewhere?'

Robert considers for a moment, then declines. He enjoyed the evening walk from the station, but now he is home he wants to spend a night in the cool, peaceful new cinema room he's had installed in one of the converted spare bedrooms. So with a few taps on his phone, he organises an Ottolenghi delivery and he and Albie spend a pleasant few hours chatting over most of the movie until conversation peters out and Albie nods off to sleep. When the credits roll, Robert nudges him and says it's over and Albie mumbles that rehearsing all day has tired him out and wanders off in the direction of the bathroom and then bed.

Robert stays in front of the screen, feeling too awake to contemplate sleep. He switches to general TV and sits through the end of a late-night news bulletin. After that is a repeat of the first episode of a new drama series that started earlier in the week.

'*With scenes some viewers may find distressing right from the outset of the programme,*' the continuity announcer says, '*here's another chance to see the first part of our new thriller* The Treehouse.'

The title of the drama causes a pang deep within him. It is a sound, like a far-off siren, signalling unease. He is used to this, although it doesn't make it any less unpleasant. There are reminders all the time of what happened all those years ago.

But what follows is more than a reminder. By the time the pre-title sequence is finished, Robert's world is in a spin.

Two teenage boys, standing in front of a girl.

Their backs to the camera as a girl lies on the floor in front of them.

A silver goblet rolls to the floor.

The frame cuts to the faces of the two boys, watching.

'Has her soul left her?' the younger of the two asks.

'Yes,' says the older boy. *'It's floating away now. I can sense it.'*

Robert turns off the TV, rushes from the room and vomits into the kitchen sink.

His hands grapple at the sides, sending some pots on the drying rack clanging to the floor. The sound hurts his head; his thoughts are in a mess, his vision blurring, his heart beating.

'What's going on?' says a voice from the doorway. Robert pulls himself up shakily, turning on the tap. He glances over at Albie standing in the doorway, his brow furrowed, concern on his face. 'Woah, you look awful. You OK?'

Robert nods, unable to form words. He's still wearing his work shirt and undoes the top few buttons, wishing he'd changed earlier – in fact, he wishes everything earlier hadn't happened. He wishes he'd taken up Albie's offer to go out somewhere, or that he'd gone to bed straight after the film. Anything that would have kept him from turning on the TV and seeing what he's just seen.

Albie comes over to him. 'Are you sick? You look really hot.'

Robert says nothing for a few seconds, just trying to calm his breathing.

'Yeah,' he says, eventually. 'It's… I think it's just the heat. That's all. Maybe the food and the drinks and… I'm fine. I'm fine.'

Albie fills a glass of water from the cooler unit in the refrigerator and holds it out.

'Thanks,' Robert gasps, taking a few sips.

'Do you need, like, a doctor or hospital?' Albie says, eyeing him warily. 'You really don't look well.'

Robert shakes his head. 'No, no, I'm fine. Or I will be. Just a funny turn, I suppose.' He's never used the words 'funny turn' in his life, doesn't even know what it's supposed to mean. He just wants Albie to go back to bed so he can try to get his thoughts in order.

Eventually, after tapping him on the shoulder and telling him to find him if he needs help, Albie pads back to his bedroom, leaving Robert still breathing heavily, his face burning. But he's finally able to come to a cold, clear conclusion. The only conclusion that could explain what he's just seen on the TV.

Someone knows what he and his brother did twenty years ago.

Chapter Two

ROBERT

As soon as he feels able, Robert leaves the kitchen and heads to his bedroom. He sheds his clothes in a distracted rush, ripping a button off his shirt in his haste and knocking over a stack of books on his bedside table. He doesn't care. He's just thankful the noise doesn't cause Albie to come and ask more questions and distract him from what he knows he has to do. He needs to speak to his brother. Kieran will have the answers. He'll know how to sort this.

He grabs his phone, taps Kieran's name in his contacts and waits for the call to connect. But it doesn't. It just rings. Kieran doesn't even have his voicemail turned on. *If someone really needs to talk to me, they'll call me back* he's said in the past.

'Fuck's sake,' Robert mutters to himself as he hits his brother's name again. 'Pick up, Kieran. Please pick up.' Nothing. He wonders if he's asleep in front of the TV at home and tries his mum's mobile to ask her but gets no answer from that either.

He flings his phone across to the bed and feels a twinge of pain in his arm. These aren't uncommon; his right forearm and wrist often give him pain though doctors have never been able to explain why. Instinctively, he opens the drawer in his bedside cabinet and takes out a box of codeine and ibuprofen. After he's taken two pills, he tries Kieran again. To his surprise, he answers.

'What's up, Rob?' he says, his voice slow and slurred.

'Kieran … there's something awful—'

His words are interrupted by a distorted sound, followed by muttered expletives.

Robert feels a rush of fury. 'Kieran, listen to me!'

He thinks he hears his brother laugh.

'Christ!' Robert snaps. 'Are you drunk, off your face or getting laid? Or all three?'

There's a muffled sound of breathing clouding the line, then he hears another voice, a man with a Scottish accent, say quite clearly, 'Do you want another line, pal? Or some ket?'

Then the call goes dead.

Robert is gripping his phone so hard it's a miracle it doesn't crack. He tries dialling again, but it rings out. Not that he'd get much sense out of Kieren even if he did pick up again.

After a few seconds, the screen lights up showing an incoming call. He answers without properly taking in the name on the screen and for a moment is confused to hear his mother's voice.

'Sorry I missed your call, Robert. This is very late for you to be phoning. Are you all right?'

'Er … Mum, yeah… I…' He instantly regrets calling her, especially since he knows Kieran is getting wasted somewhere else. He has to try to be calm, try to act normal.

'Hey, Mum,' he says, his attempt to make his voice sound light coming out oddly high pitched. 'I wanted to speak to Kieran. I wondered if you were with him, but I think he's out.'

'Am I with Kieran?' she repeats back, the confusion immediately clear in her voice. She's talking quietly and he wonders if his father is sleeping nearby. 'No, no, he's gone out? What's wrong?'

'Nothing's wrong,' he says, wincing at how unnatural the words sound. Evidently, something is. Although he's not about to tell her that. He sits down on his bed with a thud, cursing himself for not just telling her he'd phoned her by accident. 'Just wanted to speak to him about something. Sorry to wake you.'

'You didn't wake me. I just popped in to check on your father, but I'm out of his room now. I was busy cataloguing books in the library. It's been a while since I've done a proper inventory. You sound odd, Robert. What's wrong?'

'Nothing … muscle pain. I'll take some painkillers. I'll be fine.'

His mother sighs. 'You don't need to take a painkiller. Just stretch before and after you go to the gym or run, do some exercises when you wake up and you'll be as right as rain.'

'It isn't as simple as—'

'But I suppose, if you want to keep funding those big pharma companies, that's up to you. But if you ask me—'

'I'm not asking you, Mum, as you don't have a great track record when it comes to medical advice.'

There's a tense silence.

Then his mother says, 'As I said, Kieran isn't here. You'd better try tomorrow. Presuming his hangover isn't too intense. Good luck getting much sense out of him. He's often out all hours of the night. When he said he was going to move home to help me deal with your father's care, I had hoped for a bit more commitment and attentiveness.' She sniffs disapprovingly. This isn't the first time his mother's mentioned this, but he can't deal with her complaints about Kieran now. He needs to focus on the matter at hand. 'But I dare say the lure of alcohol and womanising is too strong,' she continues, warming to her topic.

'I'll try him later,' he cuts in. 'Or tomorrow. It's … nothing urgent.' Again, he worries it's obvious he's lying. 'I've got to go, Mum. I'll call or visit very soon. Goodnight.'

He cuts the call before she can delay him further. Dropping the phone, he lets himself fall backwards onto the mattress and stares at the ceiling. He has a vague idea that he'll be able to think properly in the morning. Come up with a plan. A strategy. Yes, that's what he needs, a strategy. Of the kind he comes up with at work. He does this sort of thing all the time – managing situations, crises, surprises, changes of plan, adaptability, pivoting, diversifying ideas... All these words bring a strange sort of solace to his spinning mind. The sense of order they create helps carry him off into an uneasy sleep.

Over the years, they've reached an agreement not to talk about that night. It was a request Robert made, not long after it happened. No, not a request. A demand. He can remember it like it was yesterday. Him sitting in a hospital bed. Kieran coming to visit him. Robert telling him that he never wanted to speak about what had happened. And Kieran, to his credit, has stuck to that. He's never been the one to bring it up in conversations. There has been the occasional allusion to it in the intervening years, but mostly they've just carried on with their lives. Pretended none of it ever happened.

But this is different, Robert thinks as he reaches for his phone. Then something makes him pause. Is this different? Or is Robert just doing what he sometimes does: catastrophising? There have been some instances over the years that have sent him into a spiral, made him fall into dark periods of anguish over the part he played in what happened back in 2004. But nothing like this, says a small voice in his head. Nothing this ... unusual.

'Are you OK?'

Albie's in the doorway. Robert must not have closed the door when he'd come to bed. He realises he's at an odd angle, half out of the bed, half in, a foot on the carpet, a hand outstretched holding his phone. The picture of indecision.

'Yeah,' Robert says, putting his phone back down and arranging himself in a more normal position, sitting on the side of the bed. 'Yeah, I think so.'

Albie is looking at him in much the same way he had the night before. Then Robert notices his eyes are focused on the floor, where empty sheets of the painkillers have fallen.

'Perhaps you shouldn't go to work today,' Albie says, his eyes still on the medication.

Work. Robert had completely forgotten about anything as ordinary as work. He reaches out and taps his phone screen, and for a second he thinks he's about to discover it's ten o'clock and he's hours late, but it's only 7am. He has time. He gets off the bed and stretches, reassuring Albie he's perfectly fine to go into the office.

He hardly remembers his journey. His feet carry him to all the right escalators, platforms, train carriages and exits, but he barely acknowledges where he's going. By the time he's at his desk, he knows he's made a mistake coming in. His mind is elsewhere. Doing work seems inconceivably complicated. Pointless, even. He should have feigned illness or contrived a family emergency. Anything that would have excused him from having to be a fully functioning, normal human being. People say things to him and the information doesn't go in. He nods, trying to act normally but aware he isn't doing anything of the kind. Laura comes over to his desk, says how she's looking forward to their drinks the following week. Suggests Tuesday as an option.

'Tuesday?' he says vaguely, frowning at her.

She looks instantly offended. Mutters something about how she 'understands if he's too busy' and how they'll catch up later, glancing back at his desk, confusion on her face.

An afternoon of meetings stretches ahead. He isn't sure he can face them. The thing that finally pushes him back into the realms of panic is a conversation he overhears.

Two young women from the accounts team are talking in the kitchen by the coffee machine.

'I'll need to watch that,' one of them says as she fills her mug. Robert is putting a plate into the sink when he hears the other woman, who he thinks might be called Steph, say, 'Oh definitely. It's called *The Treehouse*. My husband and I watched it all in one night. That whole bit where the boys sacrifice the girl in a treehouse… That's not a spoiler – you know that's going to happen; you see it within the first few minutes. But anyway, it's so creepy. The lads are, like, total psychos.'

This is too much for Robert. He leaves the kitchen. Leaves the office. Walks out of the building onto the streets of Southwark. He walks and walks until he gets to a random café on Great Suffolk Street, far enough from the office to make it unlikely he'll bump into any colleagues. In there, he takes out his phone and googles 'The Treehouse TV series'.

He reads reviews, reads synopses, reads social media reactions. People seemed to have found the three-part series 'gripping', 'compelling', 'disturbing', and some key lines stand out; key details he wishes he'd never read, but he can't deny their significance.

Poisoned by two boys.

Her torn body found in the woods.

Ripped to shreds.

Deciding there is no way he can ignore this, no way he can carry on as normal, he navigates to his contacts on his phone and taps *call* once again.

'Kieran, it's me. Something weird has happened. Something awful.'

Chapter Three

KIERAN

Kieran's phone wakes him. The harsh, mechanical sound of it vibrating under his cheek makes him start and look up. Where is he? He isn't sure, but can feel that he's outdoors. He can see buildings. Not skyscrapers, though, so this isn't London. He's on a balcony – his hangover-fogged brain acknowledges that much. But where?

The phone continues to buzz. He looks at the screen and sees it's his brother's name.

'Hey, what's up?' he says, yawning.

'Kieran, it's me. Are you… Can you talk now?'

'Talk now? What do you mean?' he mumbles, his mouth feeling dry and scratchy.

'You sounded off your face last night. I needed to speak to you and you sounded like a smackhead.'

Kieran remembers now. He'd been out in Soho with his mates and one of them, Matt, had encouraged him to go to a particularly seedy establishment on Greek Street called Club Pleasure, then back to an even seedier flat next to it with a group of girls. He remembered getting off with one of them on the sofa and her complaining that the jeans around his ankles kept vibrating with incoming calls.

'Oh yea … I think I spoke to you,' Kieran says. 'Wasn't a good moment. I was wrecked.'

'Yes, I know. You often are these days, and it's fucking annoying when I need to speak to you.'

'What's got your knickers in a twist?' Kieran groans.

'Something's happened,' Robert says, sounding increasingly stressed. 'Something awful.'

He snaps awake. 'What? What's wrong? Is it Dad?'

'No, no, something else.'

Kieran gets up and stretches. He feels a twinge in his right arm. He thinks he may have pulled something on the rowing machine in the gym the other day and sleeping in a weird position on what appears to be a two-seater garden chair hasn't done it any favours.

'Can I phone you back?' he murmurs. 'I've only just woken up.'

'It's *lunchtime*,' Robert says, the frustration, tinged with judgement, clear in his voice. 'On a *weekday*. Are you still in London? Can I see you?'

'No… I think I'm in Colchester, at Matt's flat. Christ, I don't even remember getting back here.'

He picks his way along the balcony, avoiding the discarded beer bottles. Inside the flat, he sees a girl he doesn't know asleep on the sofa in just her underwear and no top. Matt's younger brother, Jesse, is lying facedown on the carpet next to her.

'Ah. You've finally arisen,' Matt says. He's by the kitchen island looking as rough as Kieran feels, a large glass of water in his hand.

'Yeah. Slept on the balcony. Must have passed out.'

He then hears a distant tinny sound and looks down at the phone in his hand. Just about audible, Robert is barking 'Kieran! Kieran!' down the other end of the phone line.

'Give me a sec,' Kieran mutters to Matt, walking through the

16

flat to the bathroom. He perches on the edge of the bath and says, 'Calm down, I'm here. So what's up?'

'It's … complicated… Maybe I… I'm not sure how…' There is reluctance in Robert's tone now and he seems to be regretting calling Kieran, or at least is likely to suggest they talk at another time when Kieran's more with it. Sure enough, Robert says, 'I think I should phone you later.'

'Why? What's all this about?' Kieran says, sounding more irritable than he intends to. He nudges the pale blue bathmat with his toe, creasing his brow, wondering if he should start raiding the cabinet above the sink for paracetamol to aid his growing headache.

'Did you happen to see a drama on TV this week called *The Treehouse*?'

The two words at the end of the question make Kieran go very still. 'Called the what?'

'*The Treehouse.*'

A slight prickle runs down the back of his neck – a small little shiver that makes him shift his shoulders. 'No, I haven't. What's this about, Rob?'

Robert pauses at the end of the phone line. Kieran hears someone shout 'Caramel latte for Elaine!'

'This isn't the right place to talk about this. I'm sorry,' Robert says. 'I should get back to work. Or I might go home. I'm not feeling too good. Just … when you get home, go online and type in "The Treehouse ITV series" and watch it. All the episodes are there. I think… I think we have a problem. But watch it first, then we'll talk. You'll see what I mean.'

Then the line goes dead. Disoriented and now with a pounding headache, Kieran stands up and goes looking for the painkillers he'll need to take before driving.

An hour and a half later, Kieran skids his car to a halt outside his family home. His mother is at the front of the house, watering can in hand, tending to the dry and wilting plants at the front of the large Regency-era property.

'There's been a hosepipe ban,' she announces as Kieran steps out of the car, as though it's an important fact he should know. 'I didn't think we still had those. Probably pressure from those eco-protesters. An overreaction, in my view. Though part of me admires their determination and commitment.'

'Great,' he grunts back, swaying a little as he heads for the front door.

'Good morning to you too. Or perhaps I should say, good *afternoon*.'

'Don't have a go,' he says, raising a hand to his temple. 'I've got a headache.'

'You mean a hangover,' she says sharply. He continues to walk away from her and through the open door. He hears the clang of metal behind him – presumably the watering can has been dispensed with at the entrance – followed by a curt 'Kieran.'

'*What*?' he says, turning around.

'You're drunk.'

He lets out an exasperated laugh. 'Drunk? A hangover isn't the same as being drunk.'

'You shouldn't be driving in this state,' she says, her voice icy, low in volume, but still impactful. She's always been able to do this – to make it feel as if she's shouted when her voice has only been a few notches above a whisper. 'You could lose your licence and hurt someone. And not just that, I'm worried about your place here.'

He pulls a face. 'My *place* here?'

'Your place here, at home. And in life in general.' She took a step forwards and placed a hand on his shoulder. 'Darling, this sort of behaviour may have been acceptable when you were young, if one were being generous. But it's growing a bit pathetic now.'

Kieran's eyes widen. 'You think I'm pathetic?'

She lets out a sigh. 'Well, you are nearly forty. Irresponsible hangovers should have been left behind a decade ago.'

'I'm still years off forty, so don't age me because it suits you. And I'm only living here to help you out with Dad.'

She raises a pointed eyebrow. He knows what she's saying, even without her vocalising it. He hasn't been much help with his father. He thought he was being so selfless, moving back home at the age of thirty-seven to live with his parents in order to help ease the burden of his dad's decline. When he had first been diagnosed with lung cancer two years ago, the outlook had been positive – he seemed to respond well to initial treatment and although he had to take prolonged sick leave from work, he generally seemed in good spirits. But things got worse, and then much worse, until an acceleration in the wrong direction became very apparent to both his wife and sons. Constant care has been needed ever since. Although Kieran has been back in the house for a few months now, he's mostly left anything practical to either his mother or the carer, Maude, who comes in every day.

'OK, I'm sorry. I'll try to do more,' he says, now feeling awkward standing there in front of his mother in yesterday's clothes, sunglasses still on, head crying out for more pills and rest.

'I know you haven't had to think about money, and I'm not saying your father and I haven't been grateful for your help in the upkeep of this place. But I'd hate for you to be one of those lottery winners who becomes rich too young then goes through life with a bolstered bank balance but builds up a deficit in other ways.'

'OK, OK,' Kieran says, waving his hands in a dismissive way.

'I'll help out more about the house and … stuff. I just need to lie down for a bit. My head…'

'There are painkillers in the cupboard in the kitchen if you need some,' his mother says, turning on her heel and going back outside, picking up her watering can as she leaves.

Kieran locates the ibuprofen, pours himself a glass of water and collapses onto the sofa in the library. It's so unfair, he thinks to himself, that he's basically been *blamed* for winning the lottery at a young age and being able to spend his adult life not working. Although his family had been well-off beforehand by anyone's standards, keeping a house the size of theirs running costs a lot and he knows his parents' lives have been made easier thanks to him writing cheque after cheque for roof renovations and wall improvements and rewiring and God knows what else. Not to mention buying a Central London flat for his brother to live in rent-free.

He thinks about Robert then and his mind winds back to that strange phone call earlier. And two words: the treehouse.

He jabs the remote at the television on the wall at the far end of the library and selects the ITVX app. He doesn't have to look long to find the TV programme. It's blazoned across the homepage, with a quote from the *Daily Mail*, saying it's apparently 'Chilling, compelling, unsettling'. He clicks *play* on the first episode.

Just under three hours later, he's still sitting on the sofa, the afternoon sunlight visible from the tall windows taking on an early-evening quality. He picks up his phone.

'Hi, it's me. I've watched it. I'm not saying we need to panic, but I think you might be right. We need to meet.'

Chapter Four

ROBERT

Robert is walking in Hyde Park when he gets Kieran's call. He has decided not to go back to the office, knowing he wouldn't be able to concentrate. At the same time, though, he doesn't want to go back to his flat. Suddenly, his comfortable SW1 sanctuary feels small and cramped, like a suffocating prison. But now that he is out in the hazy early evening sun, dappled light filtering through the trees and making the water sparkle, he feels numb to the beauty of London in summer. He feels hot and uncomfortable and can hardly believe just twenty-four hours ago he was heading home on a high, appreciating the intoxicating hum and heat of the city in the midst of a heatwave. People around him seem to be doing just that right now, cheerfully talking, walking towards Hyde Park Corner tube station, their weekends stretching out before them. Whereas he has a sense of doom hanging over his head. His dark rain cloud, invisible to everyone, is felt by only him.

The phone call from Kieran is like a confirmation of his worst fears. His big brother, usually so calm, laid-back, unfazed, has a note of concern that makes Robert feel suddenly cold.

'You're right. Something weird is going on.'

You're right isn't what Robert wants to hear. *You're overreacting. This is nothing to worry about.* That's what he's been hoping Kieran would say. And then Kieran continues to talk and the rest of what he says does nothing to alleviate the sinking feeling of dread Robert now has in his stomach.

'The scene in the treehouse. It's … weird. What the boys say to each other…'

'I know,' Robert says. 'I'll never forget that moment. It's…' He swallows, trying to find the words. 'It's something that's imprinted on my mind and I don't understand how anyone can know what we said. What we *did*.'

'Slow down,' Kieran says. 'Let's not go back over that again.' He speaks as if he and Robert regularly discuss the details of what happened nearly twenty-one years ago, even though they hardly ever do. Robert has sometimes wondered if it lingers on Kieran's mind as often as it does on his, like a fly you can't brush away. Or a wasp with a very sharp sting.

'I can't believe it's been twenty years,' Robert says quietly, coming to a stop under a tree near the edge of the Serpentine.

'Let's not,' Kieran says. 'Let's not place too much importance on this.'

Robert feels a rush of anger then. 'It's you that called me,' he says. 'You wouldn't have phoned me if you didn't think I was right.'

'No, Rob, you're the one who started this, who brought this to my attention. And I agree with you, it's weird. I'm just saying let's not fly into a blind panic and start becoming paranoid. Weird things happen.'

Don't they just, Robert thinks. The phoneline is silent for a few seconds, then Kieran says, 'Have you watched the whole thing?'

Rob shakes his head, even though his brother can't see him.

'No, I haven't. Just the first bit of the opening episode. But I read some reviews and I saw other details…' There's nobody around him but he still lowers his voice. 'Details like … about the condition of the body. The fact she was attacked by dogs.'

Kieran makes an odd sound like he's sucking in air through his teeth. 'Yeah, that bit … is concerning too.'

'Christ, this is awful,' Robert says, struggling to keep his voice steady. 'I'm going to go home and watch the whole thing. I need to know what we're dealing with, fully. I've been scared to. I think that's why I didn't go straight home.'

'Where are you now?' Kieran asks.

'In Hyde Park.'

'Well, go home and watch it. Then we'll talk some more. But please, when you're watching it, try to keep a clear head. We'll get through this. Things will work out fine. They always do.'

Robert says goodbye to his brother and puts the phone in his pocket, thinking. Thinking about the past. About problems now infecting the present. About how he and his brother seem to have a different idea about the definition of 'fine'.

After a slow walk back through the park, Robert cuts through Belgrave Square in the direction of home. He's grateful Albie's out on a date tonight, although Robert desperately hopes he doesn't bring the girl home. He can't bear the thought of being polite and nice to a visitor, not when he feels like this. As though on cue, his next-door neighbour, a woman in her sixties named Cassandra, pulls her car into her parking space and gets out carrying a Harrods bag.

'Hello, Robert, so nice to see you,' she says. Wishing he'd managed to slip into the flat undetected, he smiles and says hello, coming to a stop on the pavement. She's nice enough, Cassandra, and reminds him a little of his own mother in a cool and detached sort of way. Friendly and well-mannered but with a steely undercurrent he can't quite put his finger on.

'How's Kieran?' she asks, putting the cardboard bag down in order to fish out her keys. 'Still helping out with your parents?'

Robert confirms he is. Kieran knew her son at school and it was him who'd tipped him off to the news a flat in the house next to his mother had become available for purchase. Because of this, she regularly asks after him and Robert never quite knows what to say, aware his brother's life hardly changes from month to month and year to year.

'Such a kind boy,' she says, unlocking her front door. 'I think some people are always destined to do the right thing in life and he's one of them.'

She bids him goodbye with a smile, leaving Robert wondering if there was a dig somewhere within her words. Perhaps she thought Robert should have moved back to his Essex family home when his father had become ill. This pattern isn't unusual, with people thinking well of Kieran, amplifying any good decisions he makes and ignoring his faults. He is lucky in this way. Only his mother seems to see through it all.

He lets himself into the flat, thinking of a recent conversation where his mother had mentioned her worries about Kieran's drinking and how he was still acting like he was in his twenties. Robert had wanted to tell her none of this was new, feeling like she was only bothered now that it was happening under her roof. But he'd tried to reassure her, promising that he'd have a word.

'He's always been a very lucky person in many ways,' his mother had said, 'but I do wonder if that will one day be his downfall.'

Robert pours himself some wine and plants himself in the cinema room. Allowing the alcohol to soothe some of his nerves, he forces himself to rewatch the opening scene of *The Treehouse*. It's just as startling as he remembers from the night before. It then leads into an eerie title sequence with a grungy, echoey remix of a well-known pop song as a theme tune, pieces of splintered wood flashing onto the screen interspersed with the names of the actors. All the various pieces of wood eventually come together into the shape of a tree, with a treehouse nestled in its jagged branches, the title of the drama above in big, block font.

This is insane, Robert thinks to himself as he sits through the first episode. *This is literally insane*.

He watches all three parts. With adverts removed, they amount to less than fifty minutes each, although over three hours have passed by the time he feels mentally and emotionally able to get up and leave the cinema room. In the kitchen, he grabs his laptop and opens up Chrome. He pauses for a second or two, thinking about the best way to go about this, then goes to IMDb, finds the page for *The Treehouse* and clicks on the name of the director, Jim Strike. Robert hasn't heard of him but he seems to have directed a lot of well-known TV series for the BBC and ITV, along with a couple of minor British films and a few pilot episodes of American cable dramas.

He then clicks on the screenwriter.

R.R. Dread.

The name makes him shiver. There isn't a picture on IMDb, and *The Treehouse (2025)* seems to be his only credit. Robert tries Google and after a scan of the limited relevant results, ends up on the website of a literary agency based in Hammersmith that represents authors and screenwriters. A photo comes into view as he scrolls down the page for R.R. Dread, alongside a short bio, which explains that it is the screenwriting pen-name for a fiction writer named Sean Smith. He looks ordinary enough, probably early to mid-thirties, but it's hard to tell. The photo's black and white but it looks like he has light hair, and very deep, dark eyes.

Robert reads the bio. He is a writer from the southwest of England, working on novels and screenplays, with *The Treehouse* his debut commission. It doesn't look as though his novels have been published, or at least there's no listing of them that Robert can find. He looks at the words 'southwest of England' again, then back at the man's face.

The more he looks, the more there's something about him that makes Robert feel uneasy.

Chapter Five

KIERAN

Compared to his brother, Kieran has never normally struggled to attain mental equilibrium. Or at least, it's never been that far out of reach when he finds himself being tested. Robert has always been the productive brother, the conscientious brother, trying his best at everything from school exams to his career, but he's also been the worrier of the two. Kieran has always quite liked the fact that he doesn't have the sort of personality that defaults to anxiety when a problem arises. That said, he'd be lying if he didn't admit this situation involving the TV series has shaken him. That calm, serene surface of the waters of his mind is now rippling. And he prefers a life with no ripples.

After he'd finished watching the series, Robert had WhatsApped Kieran to say he was coming to the house so they could talk face to face. Waiting for him now, Kieran makes himself a small dinner from things he finds in the fridge, having previously turned down his mother's offer of chicken casserole, then goes to see his father in his bedroom at the back of the house. The room was converted into a downstairs bedroom when his father's illness made it hard for him to use the stairs. A stairlift was debated, but in the end it was decided that the room Kieran's mother had used for reading and sewing – as it receives better sunlight than the library – should become his bedroom. Or rather, a hospital room at home.

Kieran hovers in the doorway, watching as his mum spoons casserole into his dad's mouth.

'I can still do this myself,' his father says, trying to lift his hands, but they drop back onto the surface of the mattress.

'No complaining,' she says, giving him the last spoonful, then puts the bowl down on the side table that also holds TV remotes, golfing magazines and dense hardback biographies of Winston Churchill and David Cameron, along with an equally weighty book about the rise and fall of Concorde. All of them would be difficult for him to lift now. 'I still haven't forgiven that hospital for letting you starve.'

His father swallows and lets out a rasping sigh. 'That's because it was 2020 and we were in the midst of the first Covid surge. And anyway, they didn't let me starve.'

'You said you were hungry when you were in there,' she says. 'The virus was just an excuse. A wild overreaction, though very convenient to those big pharmaceutical companies, of course. Now, if I was in charge of the NHS or the Department for Health—'

'Well, you're not, are you.'

'More's the pity,' she says. 'I knew the British public were gullible, I just didn't realise *how* gullible—'

'I don't want to get into all that again. You know we have a difference of opinion on it. And that was years ago now, and I'm still clinging on.'

'Well, I think that's more to do with mindset, that and your willpower, than the pharmaceuticals they insist on giving you,' she says, tersely.

Kieran finds he can't stay silent any longer. 'You do realise it's your anti-medication nonsense that's driven Rob to pop pills for every little ache and twinge. Doesn't that bother you?'

His mother narrows her eyes at him. 'Do you want to talk about drug misuse, Kieran? Do you really?'

Kieran closes his mouth and swallows. He chooses not to respond, just frowns back at her. His father's coughs fill the silence, then he says, 'Please don't fight. Why are you lingering anyway, Kieran?' There's an irritable edge to his voice. Keiran has noticed him becoming more irascible and unpredictable with each passing week. The physical changes have been even more profound each time he sees his dad, which is usually most days, even if it's only to say a quick hello. Although his mother is quite a bit older than her husband, his dad now looks very much the senior of the two. He is a shell of the youthful, strikingly handsome man he had once been.

'No reason,' Kieran says, then adds, 'Robert's visiting. He's on his way.'

His mother turns around to look at him. 'Robert? Why?'

Kieran shrugs, 'Does he need a reason?'

'No, of course not,' she says. 'But it just seems a bit sudden, that's all. If he visits, it's usually for a weekend.'

'It is the weekend ... just,' Kieran says, turning to go. 'But I don't think he's staying. He didn't say that he was.'

His mother looks even more puzzled by this. 'Surely he's not driving all the way from London to Rettendon tonight and then going straight back? Why on earth would he do that?'

Kieran shrugs again, regretting even alerting her to the impending visitation and wishing he'd just left it to Robert to explain.

His mother tuts and walks past him. 'Well, I'll put a fresh set of sheets on his bed just in case.'

'I don't think he cares, even if he does stay,' Kieran mutters, but his mother's already out of sight and earshot.

'She misses it,' his father says with a half-smile. 'She misses being the efficient mother, especially now she doesn't work. I think…' He struggles for breath for a moment, then tries again. 'I think she feels she worked too much when you were younger. Relied on the housekeeper too much.'

Kieran frowns. 'She was always efficient, even when she was working.' He wasn't quite sure of his father's point and didn't want to revisit the tense and uncomfortable atmosphere that sometimes inhabited the family home when he was a child and a teenager. School holidays had often been a difficult time, with Kieran aware his mother and father's relationship was strained; he'd never really wanted to unpick the reasons behind the tension. It's true, his mother had sought solace by taking on a lot of work, translating large German books into English and English books into German. He was impressed that, considering she'd moved to England from Berlin at age nine, his mother's grasp of the language had never left her, kept sharp by constant reading, and watching of German-language films, keeping abreast of the evolution of words and phrases. Kieran had once asked his mother, who had been born to an English mother and German father, both killed when she was eleven, resulting in her being shipped off to relatives in Hampshire, if she now considered herself to be English or still thought of herself as German. After all, there was barely a trace of a German accent to her speech – most people wouldn't know she'd grown up anywhere other than amongst the upper classes of English society. She'd thought about it for a moment, then said with apparent complete sincerity, 'Well, darling, I suppose that depends on how recently I've been to Ascot.'

Kieran mooches about his dad's room for a minute, not speaking, aware of the eyes following him. Eventually, he turns to his father and says, 'Dad … do you ever…' He pauses, thinking if he's wise to give voice to what he's about to say.

'Do I ever...?' his father prompts.

'Do you ever think about the past? About ... bad things in the past?'

He tries to hold his father's gaze, but it becomes difficult. He feels awkward and unsettled, conscious that going down this conversational route may be a bad idea. His dad coughs, then says in a slow, rasping voice, 'Take this advice from a dying man, son: no good can come of it. Just let things rest.'

When he leaves his father's room soon after, Kieran wonders if his father knew what he was talking about – or at least the period of the past in question. Or perhaps he was thinking back to his own misdeeds. His own mistakes. Things he's wrestled with himself over the years.

They have many regrets in this family. All four of them. And they each have to find a way of living with them.

His dad's are almost certainly to do with women. Ill-judged affairs. Foolish dalliances when he was younger. He'd probably be mortified if he knew Kieran is aware of them.

His mother is no stranger to guilt either. He saw that when she sat in a hospital chair at Robert's bedside when his brother nearly died because of a choice she'd made.

Robert's deepest regret is obvious and, to him, monumental. He probably believes Kieran has the same shame and guilt over what they both did, but he's wrong.

Kieran's one true regret is involving his little brother in the plan in the first place. How simple things might have been if he had just acted alone. But it's too late to think about that now.

Chapter Six

ROBERT

Robert arrives while it's still just about light, and positions his car neatly next to Kieran's untidily parked Lamborghini. He clocks Kieran watching him from the window and attempts a smile in greeting but is aware it probably looks more like a tight grimace.

'Darling, how lovely of you to drop in,' his mother says smoothly as she kisses her youngest son on the cheek. 'Although Kieran tells me you're not staying the night. Is that the case?' She looks over at Kieran, who shrugs. His mother tuts. 'Shrugging is becoming your trademark response these days.' Looking back at Robert, she says, 'Is everything all right? You don't look very well.'

'Don't worry,' Kieran says, stepping forwards. 'She says the same to me when I walk in too.'

'It isn't the same thing,' his mother responds icily, 'because Robert hasn't arrived drunk.'

'Kieran and I are going for a walk,' Robert says. The sentence feels sudden and jarring to Kieran, not fitting with the flow of the conversation.

'Don't you want to see your father first?' his mother says.

Taking the point, Robert nods and the three of them journey to the room at the back of the house. Robert exchanges a few awkward sentences with his father. He briefly describes how work is going well, but doesn't go into details, and before long his father says he needs his sleep and they leave him in peace. His mother settles down in the living room for an evening of German cinema, telling her disinterested boys that she's going to continue her 'Volker Schlöndorff retrospective', and requests Robert comes to say goodbye before he leaves.

'Come on,' Kieran says to Robert, nodding in the direction of the back door. They walk through the kitchen and out into the garden. It's just gone 9pm and is still just about light, with hazy layers of residual heat still hanging around in the air. They amble across the lawn and walk amongst the mulberry trees at the bottom of the garden.

'So what did you think of the whole series?' Kieran asks. Robert's surprised by how calm his brother sounds, as though he's genuinely asking his opinion on a new TV show rather than a potential existential crisis.

'What did I *think*?' Robert says. 'I was fucking horrified! Weren't you?'

Kieran doesn't say anything for a few seconds. Then he says, 'Horrified isn't something I feel very often. Let's just say I can understand your concern.'

They have been ambling amongst the darker parts under the trees, but Robert comes to an immediate standstill. 'Understand my *concern*?'

'Stop repeating things back to me,' Kieran says. 'Look, I get why you're worried. I'm … uncomfortable about it. But let's look at the big picture. The story in the series is fictional. The whole police team, which is clearly the main thrust of the story is, for all we know, entirely made-up. The family of the boys is so different from

34

ours; the peripheral characters are colourful archetypes you often get in that sort of melodramatic potboiler.'

Robert swallows, trying to find order amongst all the things he's feeling. 'I'm worried you're trying to dismiss this,' he says, his eyes seeking out Kieran's. 'This isn't something you can brush away. I just know it. And just because there are some other things that are different within the fictional part of the story doesn't mean there aren't parts that are true.'

Kieran has a pinched look, as though he's chewing the inside of his cheeks, thinking. 'There wasn't any "based on real events" notice at the start or end of each episode. It could just be a very strange coincidence.'

'Then why did you tell me you thought something weird was going on?'

Kieran is silent.

'I looked up the screenwriter,' Robert adds, taking out his phone. 'I found him on IMDb and then went to his agency's website. This is him.'

He holds out the phone, the harsh light of the screen making the area around them seem suddenly much darker. Kieran stares at the face on the webpage, then scrolls down to read the biography.

'Southwest England,' Robert says, injecting clear meaning into his voice.

Kieran scoffs. 'That's a pretty big area.'

Robert stares back at him.

Kieran returns his eyes to the phone. Robert watches him scroll again, then zoom in on the man's face.

'Something about his face…' Robert says. 'Do you see it?'

Kieran continues staring at the screen. The more the seconds go by, the more Robert thinks he sees something in his brother's eyes. Something worryingly like recognition. As though he's working something out. As though pieces are clicking into place in his mind, out of sight. But he just shakes his head. 'No, I don't recognise him.'

Robert studies Kieran, trying to work out what's going on.

'You *don't* recognise him?'

Kieran shakes his head.

'Think, Kieran. Maybe…' He lowers his voice. 'Maybe you told someone. At school? Or at university? Was there a boy you confided in, and perhaps now that he's older he looks a bit different? Could he have come to visit, perhaps, and that's why I might recognise him too? A friend you've lost touch with? Someone who was interested in writing or screenplays, anything like that?'

Still Kieran says nothing, just shakes his head.

Robert senses their conversation has reached a dead end. 'Well … if anything comes to you—'

'You'll be the first to know,' Kieran says. 'Come on, let's go back into the house. I don't think we should talk about this anymore. I'm not sure it's helping anything.'

Robert is tempted to argue with this but finds he no longer has the energy to push back on whatever resolve Kieran's determined to uphold. As they walk back up to the house, Robert can't shake off an uneasy feeling, one he isn't used to. The feeling that his brother is lying to him.

Chapter Seven

JUNE

June pauses her film when it's only part of the way through. She can't concentrate for some reason. She feels both tired and restless, though unsure about what has unsettled her. Of course, her husband's declining health and the effects of the terrible illness take their emotional toll on her, but she's quite sure that isn't it. She thinks it has something to do with Robert's visit. The suddenness of it. It's unusual. And June doesn't like unusual things. She likes her world neat and tidy.

Her youngest son isn't one to keep away, and she's glad he takes the time to come down from London, but impromptu evening trips like this are certainly out of the norm. And then there's the sudden twilight walk in the garden with Kieran – another odd thing. The two have always been fairly close, as brothers, but evening walks in the garden aren't exactly their thing.

There is an atmosphere between them, she can sense it.

Turning the TV off completely, June gets up from the sofa and goes to the window. For a few seconds she can't see her sons in the growing gloom. Then she spots them. They're around the mulberry trees at the end of the garden. They seem intent in their discussion, although she's too far away to make out their faces or get a sense of what they're saying. She watches for a few minutes, then turns away and walks over to her husband's bedroom. He's sleeping. She thinks about how different he is now – how he's been through various stages in his life: the handsome fiancé she'd married; the disenchanted and chaotic husband he's become. A disappointment.

If she is being blunt about it, he is – and has always been – a weak man. And now he is a weak man for a whole different reason, his body ravaged by illness, someone to be pitied. In spite of everything, he'll be a man she'll grieve when the end finally comes. It makes her sad to think of this, but she also feels something else: a touch of annoyance. Because a younger husband is supposed to die *after* his much older wife, not before. Things haven't gone to plan. And June doesn't like that. It makes her feel out of control.

As she looks at him, he opens his eyes.

'Anything wrong?' he asks.

'I don't know,' she says, thinking. 'I feel like there could be trouble ahead with the boys. Something's happening. I can feel it.'

Chapter Eight

ROBERT

Robert declines his mother's suggestion that he stay the night. He says he'd prefer to wake up in his flat.

He barely remembers the drive back to London, the M25 now much emptier than his journey down, and it feels as if no time has passed when he manoeuvres into his parking space on Wilton Crescent. When he gets inside, he's surprised to find Albie in the kitchen, snacking on a rice cake and looking distinctly crestfallen.

'I thought you'd still be out with your date?' Robert says as he pours himself a glass of water.

'Yeah, well, that didn't progress how I planned.'

Robert raises an eyebrow at him as he drinks. Albie launches into an explanation about how he 'overshot things' by booking a romantic getaway for the two of them in the Lake District and surprising her with it during their dinner.

Robert nearly spits out his water. 'You booked a holiday for the two of you before you'd even had your first date?'

Albie looks sheepish. 'Well, yeah, but it wasn't as if we didn't know each other. I've done a bunch of shows at the theatre she works at. Quite a few. And we've been out for drinks with friends.

So it wasn't as if it was totally out of the blue. I just got carried away when I saw this deal online and there were these little chalets – well, cabins, really – by this tranquil-looking lake and I thought it would be romantic if we went back to hers tonight and set off in her car tomorrow.'

'*Tomorrow*? That's … intense.'

'I know. I think it rather put her off.'

Robert nods. 'I can understand why. Probably a bit soon.'

Albie nods, sadly. Then his face changes, as though a thought has occurred to him.

'Robert,' he says, 'I've had an idea.'

Robert only agrees to go with Albie to the Lake District so he has something to do. The weekend is stretching out ahead of him like a desert wasteland of anxiety and unease, and the immediate opportunity to fill the time feels like a bit of a life raft. He's conscious Albie only wants him to go with him because he doesn't want to lose money on his non-refundable booking but isn't keen on going on his own. Robert also has a car, whereas Albie doesn't have a licence.

Robert has always liked driving and doesn't mind spending hours on a motorway with Albie talking away. It serves as a good distraction for his troubled mind, listening to his friend talk about anything and everything, pushing away thoughts about television dramas, screenwriters and uncomfortable memories. It mostly works, but also gives him the feeling that he is delaying something, playing truant, or procrastinating a significant task.

It's during the last stretch of the journey that he has his first wobble. Albie's talking to him about his sister, who works with pregnant women on their birthing plans and choosing private agency midwives. Robert is nodding along and making sounds of interest, when Albie says something that sticks in his mind.

'Her partner's a screenwriter, so bit of an unstable income. He's a bit older than her. Recently had something commissioned by ITV. First thing he's ever done.'

Robert's steering slips. The car starts to stray across into the middle lane, causing a large people carrier to swing into the right lane in order to avoid a collision.

'Watch out!' Albie yells, just as the blare of a horn shocks Robert back into focus. He sees a parking area coming up on the left and steers the car into it too fast. He has to brake hard so as to avoid ploughing into the trees that line the motorway.

'Woah! What was that?' Albie says, clutching the sides of his seat.

'Who is this screenwriter?' Robert barks at him.

'What?'

'Who is this screenwriter? The one your sister's dating? What's his name?' Robert is aware he probably sounds mad, especially after just nearly killing them both on the road, but he has a feeling. A feeling like there's been something under his nose all this time and perhaps, just perhaps, he is about to find a missing piece of whatever unusual puzzle he is trying to solve. 'What have you told him about me?'

'Why?'

'Just tell me.'

'Leo,' Albie says. 'His name's Leo Simonds.'

Robert feels both relief and disappointment sweep across him.

'He almost got an episode of *Vera* but that didn't work out as they decided to end the series for good, so now he's working on an adaptation of a crime novel set on the Isle of Wight.'

Robert nods. 'Great. That's, er, that's great.'

'Why does it matter? Is there something wrong?' Albie is staring at him as if he's worried for his sanity. Robert can't blame him.

'No,' Robert says, taking a deep breath. 'Nothing's wrong. I... I was interested, but I lost my grip on the steering. I just panicked.' This doesn't all add up, of course, but he hopes Albie doesn't press him further.

'You asked what I've said about you. Why would it matter what I've said about you to my sister's boyfriend?'

Robert doesn't reply at first. He busies himself with putting the car back into drive and manoeuvring it straight. He drives slowly along the end of the parking strip then says, as casually as he can, 'Did I? I must have got my words mixed up.'

Albie doesn't reply and Robert feels a twinge of guilt. Albie must know Robert is lying to him, and with that must come a sense of hurt or betrayal, similar to how Robert felt when he suspected Kieran had been lying the previous night as they walked back to the house across the lawn in the warm night air.

The situation on the motorway has a profound effect on Robert's mood for the rest of the weekend. Even though he had initially welcomed the distraction of Albie and the change of scenery, he finds himself immune to the beauty of the Lake District. The idyllic cabins and lakeside view at the luxury holiday park they are staying at are closed off from him, as though he is viewing everything through dusty, cracked sunglasses, aware the world is there but unable to appreciate any of the finer details. Albie's constant talking ends up becoming annoying in a way it never was before. In the flat, Robert usually welcomes the constant hum of Albie telling him things he wouldn't normally have found interesting. There is a comfortable companionship to their living relationship – or at least there was back in London. Here, on the decking out front of their little cabin, overlooking the vast body of water, the sunlight beating down upon them, Robert fantasises about telling Albie in no uncertain terms to shut the hell up and leave him in peace. Within the past half an hour, Albie's shared his views on topics as numerous and varied as the price of food in London, new-build houses, donkey sanctuary advertisements, *The Walking Dead*, the best brands of suntan lotion, sexism within the performing arts, his favourite Doritos flavours, his sister's online campaign against taxes on women's hygiene products such as tampons, mink farming, Jude Law, the rise of the long-form podcast, ankle pain, his first alcoholic drink, Nike running shoes, Scottish independence, and the discontinuation of his favourite meal-deal multibuy offer.

Since the trip was originally intended as a 'romantic couple's holiday', Robert and Albie have to share a bed. Although not averse to sharing a bed with a platonic friend of the same sex, he isn't impressed to discover Albie's default sleeping position is like a splayed starfish, leaving precious little mattress space not claimed in some way by one of his limbs. At about 4am on Sunday morning, Robert gives up on sleep and goes out onto the deck. He finds himself staring out at the water as the dawn starts to break. The moon is still visible in the sky and he thinks back to a night over twenty years ago when he and his brother had planned a moonlight swim. A plan that involved a girl. He forces himself not to think about her. Tells his brain not to focus on what she looked like, wading through the water, swimming over to them. In spite of their plans, they hadn't even waited for the moonlight, deciding to head into the water when it was still just about daylight, the evening twilight lending a heady, almost magical feel to the evening. He remembers how he felt. A mixture of nervousness and fear and a feeling life was about to change forever.

'No,' he says out loud, pressing his hands to his eyes.

That's in the past, that's gone. Leave it all behind.

It had been stupid to come on this weekend trip with Albie. A summer excursion involving woodland and water is a prime situation to drag up old memories, even if it is at a different end of the country.

When Albie wakes up and wanders out of the cabin in his pants, hair sticking up, yawning widely, Robert has returned from his walk around the circumference of the lake. He's sitting in the corner of the seating area, facing away from the water, thinking. It feels like that's all he does now. Think. Or try not to think.

'Sleep well?' Albie asks, apparently oblivious to the fact Robert exited the bed four hours before.

'Hmm. Not very,' he says.

Albie sits down and looks at Robert, the same worried expression on his face of a few nights ago when he found Robert vomiting in the sink.

'I'm getting a bit worried about you,' he says. 'You don't seem … right.'

Robert thinks a moment. For a few seconds, he's tempted to tell Albie everything. His whole story. Every terrible part of what happened nearly twenty-one years ago, hundreds of miles away in a little Cornish village named Port Bowen. The mistakes he made, the choices that were having deep, life-changing impacts on his future, and how he is still living with those demons to this day. But he knows he can't.

It isn't fair to put Albie in that position.

It wouldn't be fair to make him choose. Choose between keeping a secret to protect a friend or reporting a murder.

'I'm fine,' Robert says.

He might have got away with it – not telling Albie anything at all, not having to make up something to keep him quiet – if it hadn't been for the radio programme on the journey home. Finally growing tired of Robert's lack of participation in his various topics of conversation, Albie settles back for a nap. Two hours later, Robert is tired of the music choices pumped out by the radio stations he's been flicking between. As he slows behind some built-up traffic on the approach to London, he decides to listen to Radio 4 for a bit and comes in on a programme discussing ethics in the television industry.

'*Take the ITV drama*, The Treehouse, *for example*,' says a TV journalist on the show. '*That was presented to audiences as entirely fictional, but later tonight on his YouTube channel, Piers Morgan will interview a woman who says she thinks her daughter's death inspired the drama.*'

If the vehicle had been moving, Robert would have crashed the car and he and Albie may well have been killed. He feels so alarmed by what he's just heard that part of him can't bring himself to believe it's real. This has to be a joke, he thinks. A wildly elaborate stunt, created to drive him mad, to reduce him to a quivering wreck. It's too insane, too awful to be real.

But real is exactly what it seems to be.

The conversation continues on, with further discussion about what the conversation between Piers Morgan and his guest might include. It's mentioned the chat will begin at 10pm on YouTube.

The sound of multiple car horns blaring around him jolts him back to awareness. The sound wakes Albie and he nudges Robert's arm.

'Traffic's moving,' Albie says.

Robert nods distractedly, forgetting which foot goes on which pedal. The car lurches forwards and then stops, then starts up again. This earns him another prolonged beep from the Land Rover behind him.

'God, I wish you'd tell me what's going on,' Albie says quietly.

'What, me being a poor driver?' Robert says with a half-laugh that doesn't sound the least bit convincing.

'You're not a poor driver. Not usually.'

Robert says nothing and Albie doesn't press the issue.

Once home, Albie says he's going to go and chat to his mum on the phone and then catch up with some emails as he's back at the theatre tomorrow early for final rehearsals. Robert barely hears him. He goes to his own room and spends a terrible, fraught hour googling more details about the woman who is appearing on Piers Morgan's chat show. He finds an Instagram post saying he's interviewing a woman who claims ITV have 'exploited her daughter's death for entertainment'.

Oh God.

He tries to phone Kieran but gets no answer. He leaves his brother several messages but the clock moves closer to 10pm with no response. When it's time, he goes onto the YouTube channel and starts to watch.

Piers Morgan introduces the woman as Magda Bradley, a woman whose eighteen-year-old daughter died during a brutal dog attack nearly twenty-one years ago. The camera cuts to a woman sitting in the studio. She looks to be in her fifties with very long blonde-grey hair and a stony expression on her face.

Piers says, '*So Magda, tell me why you're here today talking to me.*'

Magda's expression grows angrier and she replies with a tremor in her voice.

'*Well Piers, I don't think enough people know the truth. So that's why I'm here. To tell everyone about my daughter's death.*'

Chapter Nine

ROBERT

Robert doesn't think he's been this terrified for over two decades. Not since that night when he turned to look at his brother in horror at what they had done. When they sat through a conversation with the police the next day. When their parents asked them if they knew anything the police should know. And they lied.

He watches through wide, tired eyes as Piers Morgan asks Magda to give an outline of what her issues are with the TV drama *The Treehouse*.

'Well, my issues are with the fact that it's so obvious what's been done. My beautiful girl, Chloe, was savaged to death by some maniac's dogs, back in 2004. It was awful. People might remember it. It was in the papers back then. Got politicians talking about dangerous dog laws.'

'This was at your home in Cornwall?' Piers clarifies.

'Yeah. We lived in a village, a very ordinary place, but there were these luxury holiday homes nearby on the other side of the woods – lodges they called them, although they were more like huge houses. And a farm. It was that farm where those dogs came from.'

'Now, this is quite similar to what happened in the TV series,' says Piers. 'Let's take a look at this clip.'

The studio is replaced with footage taken from the drama, the screen ratio changing to accommodate the wider, cinematic footage. The clip shows the two main detectives lifting crime scene tape. One is a short, red-headed heavily built male in his middle age and the other is a young blonde female in her twenties.

'*So what have we got?*' grumbles the male.

'*A nasty one, guv,*' says the young woman. '*But possibly an accident. Well, not a murder.*'

The man is handed forensic gear by a non-speaking, white-plastic-wearing extra. He passes some to the other person and they kit up.

'*I heard something about dogs,*' he says.

Another woman comes into the frame and introduces herself as a forensic pathologist new to the area.

'*You are correct about the dogs,*' she says. '*From what I can make out, more than one. On the parts of the limbs that remain whole, there are different teeth indentations. But most of her is gone.*'

The male detective frowns. '*Gone?*'

The pathologist nods. '*Yes. Eaten, or so chewed up that it's hard to tell immediately which bits are what. It's very grisly.*'

The camera cuts to a mass covered in a white sheet on the ground.

'*Prepare yourselves,*' says the pathologist, about to pull the sheet back.

The clip ends.

'*We won't show the gory details, there,*' Piers says, '*but it gives viewers an idea of what's happened.*'

'*Well,*' says Magda, with the emphasis of someone gearing up for a speech, '*I've read people online saying that the forensics were pretty rubbish, there are tonnes of mistakes there, but anyway, yeah, it's the dogs at first in the show, but they make up this nonsense about these boys.*'

'*Yes, I was about to come to that,*' says Piers. '*So there are two boys in the TV series.*'

A promotional still from the show appears on the screen showing two teenage boys, one slightly taller and older than the other. They're standing in the sea, wearing just swimming trunks, with the setting sun behind them, water around their knees, their expressions moody. The whole photo is very atmospheric, giving the sense that these boys have done things. Bad things.

'*Total rubbish,*' interjects Magda.

The screen returns to the studio again.

'*Rubbish in the sense…?*' prompts Piers.

'*Rubbish in the sense that in the series they make out that she was visiting this weird little treehouse, getting up to God knows what with them. My daughter was a bit of a free spirit, I accept that. Probably my fault. I had my issues. I was an alcoholic and on pills and took my eye off the ball, I fully accept that. She may well have been out seeing people. I caught her bringing blokes home sometimes, but as far as I know, these two boys didn't exist. So to make out like the dogs didn't actually kill her, that it was some awful murder in a treehouse, a weird like ceremony thing, you know? Well, that's just awful. Didn't happen. I mean, if anyone can produce these two boys, I'd be interested to know. Who are they? Where are they? What are they doing now? If they exist, let them put their hands up. Though of course they won't.*'

'*Because that would incriminate them,*' Piers says.

'*More because they don't bloody exist, if you ask me. They're figments of the warped mind that thought all this up. To use the real situation of my daughter's death and … and … to twist it into something messed up like that … well, I find that bloody offensive.*'

Robert watches the interview to the end and breathes a tentative sigh of relief. Other than a statement read out from the drama's production company about the series being entirely fictional and any resemblance to any persons living or dead being entirely coincidental, the conversation becomes a bit cyclical. Despite Piers's expert attempts to get the most out of Magda, she continues to repeat the same thing, with words like 'offensive' and 'gutter television' used multiple times.

He reaches for his phone and rings Kieran. No answer. He tries again, then again, feeling angry at the sense of déjà vu, at how he's always the one trying to get through to his brother, always trying to get his attention when it matters.

It takes five attempts before he eventually gets an answer.

'Fuck's sake, Rob, I'm busy!' Kieran barks into the phone.

Robert has to stop himself smashing a clenched fist into his bedside table in frustration. 'Oh, I'm sorry to interrupt your drug-addled nymphomania or whatever shit you're up to, but in case you've forgotten, we have a rather pressing situation here. A situation that concerns both of us.'

'Drug-addled? Piss off, you bloody hypocrite.'

The line goes dead.

Rob spends the next few minutes almost shaking with rage and the leftover intensity that burned within him throughout the whole YouTube interview. He lies on his back, his eyes closed, trying to calm himself. He thinks he feels the familiar pain in his right arm and wonders if it's enough for him to take some pills. Maybe one wouldn't hurt, he thinks. As he slides out a new sheet of tablets, the word 'hypocrite' echoes around his brain. But this isn't the same thing, he thinks to himself as he pops out a tablet. He has muscle pain, that's all. He's not inhaling lines off coke off a woman's back or knocking back MDMA mid-orgy. It's not the same thing. He's not the same as his brother.

Before long, his phone buzzes.

'I'm sorry, Rob,' Kieran says at the end of the line. 'What were you trying to tell me?'

Rob sits up and tells him what's happened. Tells him about the

TV interview that's just finished. How he thought it was going to be the end of everything, their final undoing, but it actually wasn't. Amazingly, it sounds like they're fine.

'I think we might be in the clear,' he says, feeling lightheaded with relief. 'It wasn't the disaster it could have been. I just hope that's it and there isn't more to come.'

After the call, he lies back down and tries to relax. Tries to tell himself this is a full stop to the whole horrible situation. But the relief he felt just minutes earlier is short-lived. Magda's words come to him, echoing around his head, like a recording on repeat.

If anyone can produce these two boys, I'd be interested to know.

Stop it, he tells himself. Stop thinking about it.

Who are they?

Nobody can identify them.

Where are they?

Nobody knows where he and Kieran live.

What are they doing now?

Living in a nightmare, he thinks to himself. And try as he might, he finds it impossible to convince himself that the nightmare will be over any time soon.

Chapter Ten

KIERAN

'Who's a hypocrite?' the young woman next to Kieran asks. He's lying back on the bed, his mind many miles from the London hotel room he's currently in.

'Nobody,' Kieran says.

'That's not a nice way to talk about your brother,' Jesse comments, followed by an extended sniff as he inhales the last of the cocaine on the bedside table. He turns to the woman between them. 'The hypocrite is his brother Rob,' he explains to her. 'He and Kieran don't get on.'

'Brothers are tricky,' she says. 'I've got one. He's a brute. Nearly strangled someone once. Awful man.'

Kieran rubs his face. 'It's not true. I do get on with him. And anyway, you're a fine one to talk, Jesse. You and Matt bicker all the time. Where is Matt anyway? Thought he could never resist a night of vice if I'm picking up the tab.'

'He thinks we should all slow down a bit,' Jesse says, sitting up. 'I don't agree. But then, I'm still in my twenties. Matt says he's too old to be getting off his head three nights a week. He says you are too.'

Kieran makes a noise of disbelief. 'That's his guilt talking. If he wants to screw around and have fun, he shouldn't have lumbered himself with a girlfriend.'

He watches as the woman gets off the bed with a sigh, apparently bored by the conversation between the two men. She picks up a clutch bag from the side of the bed and takes out a little bag of white powder. 'Shall we, gents? I think we need a touch more.'

Kieran ignores her. He turns onto his side so he can see Jesse properly. 'What does he say about me?'

Jesse pulls himself up onto his elbows, frowning at Kieran. 'I shouldn't really say. I mean, I'm not really part of you and Matt and Hugo and all the other guys in your little gang. I'm just the younger brother. I'm a hanger-on, I suppose. I mean, it's nice of you to invite me to do shit like this, but...' He shrugs.

'But you have an opinion,' Kieran says, looking at him.

Jesse has his eyes on the naked woman, now on the other side of the room, bending to sniff a line of the cocaine she's just tipped onto the glass coffee table. 'I mean, I don't want to spoil a good thing. I like wild nights with Russian call girls in five-star hotel suites as much as the next bloke.'

'I'm not Russian,' the woman says, letting out a sharp laugh and brushing at her nose with the back of her hand. 'Don't even remember my fucking name,' she mutters, more to herself.

'Sorry,' Jesse says, without feeling, then turns back to Kieran. 'But what I'm saying is, do you plan on doing this for the rest of your life? Matt's the only one of your school friends who still hangs out with you. Most of the time, at least. Everyone else has settled down. I think he'd like to. He's been talking about having kids, even.'

Kieran gets up off the bed with a groan. 'That's because he's limited by what he *thinks* he should want. And so are you, mate.'

He's suddenly feeling awkward. They'd been having a good time, but now Jesse's gone and ruined their fun with his moralising and second-hand disapproval. It reminds him of how he used to feel as a child when he'd be enjoying a visit home during the holidays, perhaps watching TV or playing in the garden, then his mother would make a dig about him not doing homework. And even if he'd done his homework, there was always 'extended study', a task which often seemed inexhaustible in its range and length.

'No, no,' Jesse says. 'Honestly, I'm not judging. I think you have an awesome life. I hope I'm still doing this kind of thing when I'm thirty-eight.'

He's about to correct Jesse, tell him that he's thirty-six, not thirty-eight. But instead he says, 'You could, you know. You can have anything you want in life. There is a way.'

'Oh yeah,' Jesse says, but he sounds distracted. He's watching the young woman as she walks towards him. She has an index figure stretched out and for a moment Kieran thinks she's pointing at something. Then he sees the little mound of powder balanced on the top of it. She stops in front of Jesse and presses the edge of the finger below his nose. He grins at her and inhales sharply.

'I guess I should call my brother back,' Kieran mutters, picking up his phone and crossing the room. Once inside the en suite, he closes the door and sits on the sizeable edge of the marble bathtub and puts his phone to his ear.

'I'm sorry, Rob. What were you trying to tell me?'

He listens to his brother's words. How he thinks disaster might be averted. About how things might be OK. Of course it is, he tells himself. Of course it is.

When he finishes the call and comes out of the bathroom, he finds Jesse kissing the woman on the bed again. 'Round two,' he says, laughing, taking his lips away from hers for a few seconds before she pulls him back.

Kieran shakes his head and starts looking for his clothes on the floor.

'I left you some coke,' the woman says, flicking a wrist over at the table.

'No … no, I'm going to head off.'

'You sure?' Jesse says. 'Sorry, I didn't mean to piss you off earlier.'

'No, it's fine,' Kieran says. 'The room's paid for the night, with late check-out, so you can stay until the afternoon.'

'Well, if you're sure,' Jesse says, turning his attention back to the woman's lips.

'Yeah, I'm sure,' Kieran says, pulling on his jeans. 'I should get back. There's something I need to watch on YouTube.'

He's walking through the entrance hall at home when he becomes aware of some commotion going on at the back of the house near his dad's room.

'I'd advise an ambulance, but it's up to you.'

He recognises the voice of his father's carer, Maude. He goes a bit closer to the doorway and sees her coming away from his father's bed, his mother standing with her hands on her hips. There's another carer, a younger one, adjusting his father's pillows. Maude sometimes brings a younger carer for the day, especially if she's got one in training.

'No. I think we'll just get a doctor out in the morning,' says Maude. 'I don't see there's any benefit from him waiting in a corridor of a packed A&E, picking up an infection. I think we'll keep him here for now.'

Kieran quietly slips back down the corridor in the direction of the living room. He doesn't fancy joining in the discussion about where his father should be cared for or where it would be best for him to die. This isn't a discussion Kieran feels he needs to join in with. Not when his head is still buzzing from his night of hedonism.

He settles down on the sofa, opens up his phone and scrolls through social media, looking at the reactions to Piers Morgan's show.

She's just trying to get the limelight. Clearly after her fifteen minutes of fame.

It's disgusting if what she's saying is true, they shouldn't make shows about people's dead kids without checking with them.

Yeah it's exploitation, defund the BBC, cancel the licence fee.

It was on ITV you twat.

There isn't anything very alarming. He opens up YouTube and watches the interview, trying to work out if he recognises Magda from all those years ago. He isn't sure if he ever actually saw Chloe's mother. He thinks he heard her once, calling out from her room in the bungalow where they lived, but he doesn't remember them meeting face to face. Like so many moments from that time, it's like a hazy memory, a faded photograph of the mind, the kind of blurry warm-tinged shots you find in old family albums, even though it all happened in 2004, not 1974.

'Thank you for your help, Kieran,' his mother says from near the doorway, watching him sit there.

He hurries to pause the video and put his phone down. 'Sorry?'

'Your father had another of his difficult moments.' She says the last two words with razor-sharp emphasis, as though Kieran is responsible for such a moment. As though he is to blame for the cancer that is ravaging his father's body. He doesn't appreciate the sense of disapproval or resentment that emanates from her words.

'What did you want me to do? The room was crowded enough as it was.'

'Show some interest. Try to care. Either of those would be a good start. Sometimes I feel Robert is more conscientious in asking after your father than you are, and he doesn't even live in the same house as him.'

He stands up, glaring at her. 'I'm the one who moved back here.'

'Yes. You're unemployed and don't have the need or motivation to work. I had hoped you moving here was a positive sign, but apparently not. Just can't resist London's night life, can you, even when you're thirty miles from it.'

'I came home tonight,' he protests. 'I could have stayed out.'

'Judging by the size of your pupils, you might as well have.'

'You're not being fair,' he snaps, starting to walk away.

He's halfway across the room when she surprises him. 'You're right. I'm not being fair. I'm sorry.'

It isn't often his mother admits she is at fault and he's both surprised and impressed.

'What?' he says, wondering if he misheard.

'I said I'm sorry. It's... It's been a stressful day.'

He stands where he is, now feeling awkward, similar to how he felt when she pulled him up on his hangover. He doesn't like how he still feels like a child in front of her. Perhaps if he'd succeeded in finding a wife and having a family, he wouldn't feel like this, would have had something of a foundation. Perhaps it would make him more of an adult. But tonight isn't a night for 'what ifs' and 'should haves'. He just wants to get into bed.

At a loss as to what else to say, he just says, 'Goodnight, Mum.' But at the door, she makes him stop again. 'If there was anything … odd … going on, you would tell me, wouldn't you?'

He looks at her. 'I'm not sure what you mean by "odd",' he says, dropping his eyes to the carpet, 'but there's nothing going on. Night.'

She doesn't reply. Doesn't say 'goodnight' back. She just watches him as he leaves the room and heads for the stairs.

In his bedroom, he sits in the chair by the window. He tries to return to the scrolling of reactions to the interview, but he feels like he's read it all.

As ever, he's been lucky. Things will all blow over now. Things will go back to normal. This will prove, he thinks, as he goes to brush his teeth, to be one of those weird moments that just fizzles out and people will just forget. Something that feels important when it's happening but ultimately comes to nothing.

Twelve hours later, he finds he can no longer think this.

The next morning, he has to accept, despite his naturally relaxed approach to life, that he can still get things very wrong.

Chapter Eleven

ROBERT

'F uck!'

Robert shouts the word without meaning to.

One night. That's all he was able to have. One night of feeling like things might be OK, that things might calm down, that he and his brother were safe.

But not now. The first thing he saw when he unlocked his phone that morning were the reactions to Piers Morgan's interview. They all seemed fairly predictable and he skimmed through most of them, occasionally lingering on the ones that took a more verbose approach to saying what essentially everyone was saying – that TV programmes should be careful when fictionalising real cases as it's not nice for the families involved. This was a fairly reasonable conclusion to reach, and he had been about to close his phone and start to get ready for work.

Then he'd seen it.

The post on the official Piers Morgan Uncensored account.

*A new twist in the tale: screenwriter R.R. Dread will be on my
show this coming Thursday to answer Magda's claims that he used
the story of her daughter's death for his controversial and much-
debated TV drama The Treehouse.*

It is after reading this that he yells. Then his phone goes black
and the empty battery symbol in the centre of the screen mocks
him. He exclaims again.

Albie barges into the room. 'OK, I've had enough of this,' he
says, looking uncharacteristically angry. 'I swear not a day goes by
now when there isn't some weird crisis. Why are you shouting
"fuck" like a madman?'

Robert hasn't got the time or brain space to counteract this.
'Where's my charger?' he says, feeling down at the plugs to no
avail. Then he remembers that he hasn't unpacked from their trip
to the Lake District. His bags are in the hallway.

He thuds past Albie out of the room.

'Where are you going?' Albie says, following.

'I need my charger.' He crouches on the floor and starts
unzipping his small overnight bag with such vigour that the zip
sticks. Swearing again, he begins tugging things out through the
small gap until his hands close around the wire cord. Pulling it out,
he heads for the kitchen counter and stuffs the plug in, connecting
his phone. While it starts to charge, he spots his laptop on the
kitchen table, though after a whole weekend unplugged he's sure
that's likely suffered the same fate as his phone.

He raises his hands to his eyes.

'Why is everything awful?' He says it to himself, not expecting
Albie to respond.

But his flatmate does, saying tersely, 'I don't know, probably
because you don't trust me to listen.'

Robert doesn't respond. A few minutes later he hears Albie leave the flat without saying goodbye, closing the front door more forcefully than is necessary.

Growing impatient for his phone to become usable, he connects his laptop and sees it spring into life almost immediately. He heads straight to the Piers Morgan Uncensored Instagram account and rereads the post he saw, slowly and carefully, as though he expects to see something new, some mitigating factor, some glimmer of hope that says very clearly, 'Robert Palmer doesn't need to worry about this as he won't be mentioned.' Of course, there's nothing of the kind. The comments are horribly excitable. People seem to be relishing a new twist in the story, keen to see the writer of the show being challenged for appropriating a real-life case for the purposes of entertainment. If he weren't so panicked and suspicious, Robert might have felt sympathy for the writer. After all, hasn't he just done what writers have done for centuries – turned to real life for inspiration, changed a few of the details to make it 'fiction' and packaged it up as a piece of entertainment? Which, of course, it is. Only in this instance, to Robert's dismay, it happens to be a case in which *he* played a significant role. Significant, but up until literally a few days ago, completely out of sight.

The Magda interview wasn't a disaster for him, but he knows this definitely could be. He wonders with mounting horror what secrets could be broadcast to a YouTube audience of millions. What might this man tell people? How will he try to explain himself?

All this, Robert feels, hinges on a central question: Who is R.R. Dread and how much does he know?

He tries a social media search for Sean Smith, forensically going through as many of the results as he can, but there are hundreds of Sean Smiths. He has to accept he may never find him, or perhaps more likely, he isn't on social media at all. The major social networking sites show the username or handles for R.R. Dread, with or without dots, as unclaimed.

Time ticks by. His phone pings from behind him. He glances at it, wondering if it's his brother, but it's just a colleague asking if he's coming into work today. The idea of going to work, to focus on anything else other than this feels completely preposterous to him. How could he work on reports and attend meetings when there's this maddening mystery to solve?

In the end, he returns to the literary agency page he discovered a few days ago. Feeling a rush of frustration and determination, he phones the number on the website. A cool, professional female voice answers the call. Stumbling over his words and wishing he'd come up with a carefully planned script, Robert says that he is after the contact details of the screenwriter R.R. Dread.

'May I ask who is speaking?' says the woman.

Robert omits mention of his name but says he's a film director trying to get in touch with the screenwriter. With a note of suspicion, the speaker at the other end informs him that they're unable to give out contact details over the phone and the best thing to do would be to discuss with the agency the opportunity and they could let their client know and take it from there. Recognising that he's reached a dead end, Robert thanks her and says he'll be in touch, cutting the call before she can respond.

A thought then strikes him. He heads to the gov.uk website and does a search through the Companies House database.

At last, a breakthrough.

A business was registered two years ago under the name RR Dread Entertainment.

And it's registered to an address in a village in Cornwall.

This can't be a coincidence.

He thinks back to the reference to southwest England on the

man's bio online. He told Kieran it couldn't be a coincidence. Now he has proof – at least in his eyes – that it isn't.

He thinks about phoning his brother but instead decides this deserves a face-to-face chat. He has an address. The question now is what he should do with it.

This is going to involve a lot of deliberation. They need to come up with a plan.

Chapter Twelve

ROBERT

Robert's bedroom hasn't been decorated since he was a teenager. Film posters for *The Lord of the Rings: The Return of the King* and *The Matrix Reloaded* are still evident, the sun-faded faces of Aragorn and Neo staring down at him from the walls. He's never seen the point of taking them down. He only spent time here in school holidays, then he was straight off to university. The books on the shelves are the same, the DVDs in a vertical stacking unit like relics from a bygone era.

Robert and Kieran had ended up in this room as the garden had proved too hot, and although their mother is out at the shops, the downstairs rooms are being noisily hoovered by the weekly cleaner. Robert feels all the memories of the past weighing heavily on his shoulders. As he sits on his bed, he fantasises about taking a flamethrower to everything around him.

'What is it exactly you want to do?' Kieran asks, leaning back on the chest of drawers, his arms folded.

'Throttle the guy,' Robert says.

Kieran raises his eyebrows.

'I'm not serious,' Robert clarifies. Then adds, 'I'd question him first, then throttle him.'

Kieran continues to look at him. 'I take it you're joking.'

'Well, of course I am. I just want to know *how* he manages to know so much about what happened back then. That, coupled with his location, suggests he was there. Like, actually there. Watching us.'

'Not necessarily,' Kieran says. 'I accept it seems someone knows more than we thought, but this guy might not be that someone.'

Robert frowns. 'How do you mean?'

'Someone else could have watched us and told someone else what happened. Or someone could just have an overactive imagination. They could have hit on the truth without realising it.'

Robert scoffs. 'Pretty unlikely. And please don't try to start convincing me this is a coincidence again. I can't bear it.'

'Well, I hate to sound like a stuck record, but I would once again suggest leaving this alone. Let the man make his revelations during the interview. There's nothing he can prove. To the police, the crime is solved. It was manslaughter. The drunken farmer was a solid and easy candidate and, crucially, *pleaded guilty*. If there was anything about the body that linked back to something else going on, it was either impossible to determine after the dog attack or we were lucky enough to have a helpfully incurious set of detectives and forensic people. Regardless of which of those it was, there'd be nothing to test now. There wasn't much left of her at the time, so even if she had been buried, I doubt anything would remain that they could usefully use to test or investigate.'

Robert listens to his brother's words.

Kieran, apparently reading Robert's silence as a sign of making progress, walks up to him and kneels down, bringing their eyes in line.

'The police never arrested us. Never even suspected us, for all we know. We just happened to be there. That is, and always will be, the official version of events. So we just need to calm down and let that truth remain the truth. The *only* truth.'

Robert looks at his brother. 'But it isn't the truth, is it?'

Kieran holds his gaze. 'There's nothing more we can do.'

Robert directs his gaze down at the floor for a bit. Then he says, keeping his voice even, 'We could … go and see him.' He takes out his phone and reads aloud the address he's screenshotted. So easy, he thinks to himself. He could just put the postcode into his car's sat nav and he would be there in a matter of hours.

A few beats of silence pass between them. Then Kieran says, 'Something tells me, when you say, "go and see him", you mean something more than a cup of tea and a chat.'

More silence. Then Robert eventually says, 'What if I do?'

Kieran gets up and moves over to his brother's side, lowering himself onto the mattress.

'I hope you don't mean what I think you mean.'

This makes Robert turn his head sharply. 'Well, that's a bit rich, coming from you.'

'What's that supposed to mean?'

Robert gapes at his brother. 'Are you seriously telling me you've suddenly become squeamish about murder?'

He isn't sure if he's made Kieran angry or upset. There seems to be something complicated happening behind his eyes. Eventually, he said quietly, 'That was different.'

'Perhaps,' Robert concedes. 'But we're not exactly inexperienced.'

'I know,' Kieran says. 'But it's not the same as cold-blooded murder.'

Robert stands up. 'That's exactly what it was. Whatever spin you put on it, however you try to dress it up, that's what we did. Or at least tried to do.'

Kieran is motionless, sitting on the bed, looking at him. Then he says coolly, 'Gosh, you do surprise me. All this time you've made me feel like the evil one. Like I'm one who led my little brother astray. Led the sweet innocent boy into sin.' He shrugs. 'Guess we all have a ruthless streak. If you back a cuddly creature into a corner, the fangs will eventually appear.'

Robert feels himself growing cold. 'I'm not a cuddly creature. And there's no need to get nasty.'

'I'm not the one contemplating murder.'

A noise makes them stop. Robert looks at Kieran in alarm. Have they been speaking too loudly during their heated exchange? Said things that, to anyone else, could sound both confusing and – depending on how much was heard – deeply disturbing?

Then there are voices. A conversation, more than one person, although too far away to hear what is being said.

'I think it's just the cleaners,' Kieran says in a near-whisper.

Then they hear a voice that's unmistakably their mother's. 'But how did it get broken?'

Robert opens the door and they hear more fully their mother's irritated voice. 'Well, I suppose there's nothing to be done. Leave the pieces on the side table there.'

After sharing a look, the two of them leave the bedroom and go out onto the landing. Further discussion would feel odd after such a trivial interruption – a slice of real life intruding on whatever dark precipice they had been nudging towards. In some ways, Robert is pleased that their mother's anger over something – a broken vase, as it turns out – took him and Kieran away from their strange moment. A moment of retrospection and introspection from which Robert would usually run a mile.

'Oh, boys, can one of you find a box for me to put these pieces in?' their mother says, glancing up at them. 'Just a shoebox or something. I don't want to throw it away. I think it could still be salvaged. They can do all kinds of invisible mending these days.'

Kieran disappears off on this errand and Robert starts to descend the stairs. 'Was it valuable?' he asks her as he reaches the bottom step.

'Not very, but I rather liked it,' she says. 'It was a present from Isabelle and Patrick Moncrieff and since they're now both, well, deceased, it would be nice to keep it.'

Not wanting to get into any subject involving death, Robert starts walking towards the door. 'I should be getting back to London,' he says.

'Oh, well, see you soon then,' says his mother, sounding surprised. 'Where are you going?'

Robert pauses, frowning. 'I've… I've just told you.'

'You have?' she says, looking at him.

'Yes, I'm going home. Back to London, to my flat.'

She frowns. 'Good. Yes, that's good. I take it you looked in on your father earlier?'

'Yes,' Robert lied.

'Good. We've been seeing a lot of you lately,' she says.

'I… I know,' Robert says, nodding, still looking at his mother, a pang of worry forming. There is something off about this goodbye. Something not quite right. 'I'm trying to be more… Well, I thought I should be here more. Because of Dad. I think I've thrown myself into work because of it. But I realise I shouldn't keep my distance, even though I find it hard to see him … as he is. I know it … won't be long now.' As he says this, his guilt for running off before even going into his father's room rises within him.

'No,' says his mother quietly. 'No, it won't be long.' There's another pause, then she says, 'Well, you'd better get off back to London.' She steps forwards and lays a hand on his shoulder.

'Yes, I'll be back … soon. Tell Kieran I've gone.'

He leaves before any more strangeness can arrive, wondering if his mother is OK. A mother with dementia or early Alzheimer's is all he needs, he thinks, as he starts his car and heads off in the direction of London.

Robert's glad to find Albie still out when he gets in. His conversation with Kieran has helped crystalise something for him. He needs to act alone with this. He needs to stop letting on to others that there's anything wrong; stop looking for support, for a plan to materialise from somewhere. For someone to give him permission. He knows if he takes his brother's approach, he'll go mad waiting for his doom to be realised. Waiting for the axe to fall. He needs to take control of the situation.

The next morning, he messages work saying he's still ill and needs to spend the day at home once again.

But he doesn't stay at home. He sets off early, before Albie is awake. Before he can change his mind.

He's not going to hurt anyone.

Just have a talk. A friendly chat, to see what he knows.

Or at least, that's what he tells himself as he drives out of Central London and begins his journey towards Cornwall.

Chapter Thirteen

ROBERT

He doesn't think about turning back. Even though Robert is filled with nerves and concerns about what a confrontation with R.R. Dread might entail, he doesn't reconsider the journey. It means he's moving forward. Getting closer to the truth. And finding out how this terrible, stressful mystery might end. One way or another.

He stops for a break three hours in at Crossover Services. He didn't have breakfast because he wanted to leave before Albie could ask him where he was going, and he's now aching with hunger. But as soon as he's got a breakfast wrap, doughnut and coffee from McDonald's, he struggles to eat. His mouth is dry, his teeth seem unsure how to chew, and his throat protests each time he tries to swallow. He throws half of it away and heads back to his car.

It takes another two hours to reach his destination. Thornton Business Centre looks just how it did on Google Maps when Robert checked it out the night before. A skip filled with old office chairs is the only difference to its frontage. He parks his car two streets away and walks to the building. He sees there's an intercom and a list of businesses.

R.R. Dread Entertainment is the fourth on the list, sandwiched between Shelly's Accounting Wizards and The Cornish Confectionary Guild. Robert is about to press the buzzer when the door opens and a young man wheeling an office chair comes out. The legs snag on the step and Robert reaches forwards to help him.

'You here for the rest of the stuff?' he asks, clearly thinking Robert is someone with a more legitimate reason for being there.

'No, I'm… I'm looking for R.R. Dread Entertainment. Do you know it?'

The man shakes his head. 'Nah, sorry, but the names are on the doors. Just go down that corridor.'

Robert nods his thanks and steps inside. There is no reception, just a table of plastic plants with a layer of dust coating their dark green leaves. Some piles of leaflets sit next to them that appear to advertise services matching some of the companies Robert saw on the intercom labels.

He walks down the corridor as instructed, the dim lighting and lack of windows making it hard to see the names on the doors. Some have more professional and expensive-looking bespoke signs and logos; others have business names printed in capital letters in Times New Roman on sheets of A4 paper. On one door, 'Rick's Bike Chains' is scrawled on the actual wood with what looks like a felt tip marker.

R.R. Dread Entertainment falls somewhere in the middle of these. The name of the company is presented on a little framed sign which looks professional enough at first glance, but closer inspection shows it to be printer paper glued to a cleanly cut piece of card.

A noise behind him makes Robert jump. He turns around to see a woman coming out of the door opposite, a stack of ring binders balanced under her chin as her hands grapple with a bunch of keys.

'Sorry,' she says, smiling, as she bumps up against him, the width of the corridor too restrictive to accommodate them both. Robert steps to the side so she can turn to lock the door she's come out of. He spots the 'Shelly's Accounting Wizards' sign on it and presumes this is Shelly. One of the folders clatters to the floor and Robert bends to pick it up.

Passing it to her, she beams wider and says, 'Thank you so much. Always have too much to carry. You here to see Sean?'

The name instantly makes him alert. 'Yes. I'm… Yes. I'm a friend of his. Well, a business acquaintance, really. I don't have an appointment, but I wondered if there's anyone in or if you knew if there would be … um … soon. Today, hopefully?'

She pulls a face. 'Oh it's just him. There isn't a team in there or anything. He uses the room for writing. There's not much behind that door, I assure you. Most of us here are just one-person businesses. Does he know you're coming?'

Robert is intrigued to hear that not only has she spoken to this man – this person who has become a demonic spectre in his head over the past few days – she also knows he's a writer.

Robert opts for honesty. He remembers seeing in a film that spies are told to keep their stories as close to the truth as they can. It's more convincing that way. And he is, after all, spying.

'No, he doesn't, but I've been wanting to talk to him about a screenplay of his.'

He is ready to add details if he has to, some made-up accreditation or TV company, but she doesn't seem suspicious.

'Well, he works from here sometimes. He says he likes the enclosed space. Helps with his focus.' She rolls her eyes, as if in her view this is the very apex of artistic eccentricity. 'But I haven't seen him in ages. He's probably up at the house.'

Robert is about to risk asking her for the address. But then it hits him, with a nauseating sense of inevitability. It's suddenly obvious. And the rest of her words start to sound as though they are being spoken underwater. Distorted and echoey. Not quite real. Part of a terrible dream.

'He's having an extension built, but the builders keep blocking the country road up to it and it's caused a falling-out with the posh neighbours. They're a funny lot, up in Hill Valley.'

He doesn't respond. He can't. All the available bandwidth of his mind is taken up processing the revelation. The revelation that this man – this mysterious screenwriter who has haunted practically every waking and sleeping moment over the past few days – has not only fictionalised a real-life murder that took place at Sunshine Lodge, but he's actually living on that property right now.

Chapter Fourteen

ROBERT

When Robert gets in his car, he sits back and closes his eyes. He should have guessed, he tells himself. Should have realised where all this was leading. He should have known that the past would somehow pull him back. And now here he is, about to drive to a place to which he swore he never would return.

He could just stop, he tells himself. Could just drive home. He could leave this town and not drive the short trip to Port Bowen and the little community of Hill Valley. But he knows, as he starts the engine, that such a thing is impossible. That would be like waiting for an important letter only to refuse to open it. Even if the contents were painful, it would be better to know. Better not to have it hanging over you.

So he drives. At first, he foolishly thinks he might be able to remember the way and just drive there using twenty-year-old knowledge, or even instinct. But he's never been to the small town where the office block resides and the roads all look the same, impossible to pull from his faded teenage memories formed before he could drive or even take much notice of road signs or routes or anything like that. The road signs he passes now aren't much use, being both infrequent and vague, and in the end he has to resort to his sat nav once again. He uses Google to find a postcode for another property in Hill Valley that's for sale and taps it into his sat nav with trembling fingers. Then he steers out of the layby and drives on.

Even though he's had trouble remembering aspects of his journey to the little community of houses, crawling down the winding country lane towards Sunshine Lodge brings so much of it back. It's like he's sweeping away layers of mental dust to reveal a vivid picture of him and his family in their Range Rover, driving down this road. He had a cassette of Greek myths he was listening to on his old Sony Walkman. He liked to borrow cassettes from the library, liked how he could stop them and pick the story back up in the same place. How ancient that all felt now – but vivid, too. His mother had said something to him – he can't quite remember what – just as he got to the end of one of the sides of his tape and she'd become frustrated that he couldn't hear her with his headphones on. He'd ignored her, looking out of the windows until the gates of Sunshine Lodge had come into view. They had been a strong black metal, back then. Any sniping with his mother had quickly vanished from his mind when he saw them, wondering if he'd been brought to a castle in a fairytale. It hadn't been a castle though, and the gates, as it turned out, had been wildly out of place in terms of design and tone. Sunshine Lodge had come into view moments later, proving to be a vast, newly built wooden lodge.

Robert sits in his car in front of it now – or at least in front of the gates. They haven't been completely replaced, but modernised somewhat, with brick pillars on either side and an intercom that certainly wasn't there before, built into the one on the left. He can see the building through them. There's a garage to the side that wasn't there before, along with evidence of building work around the back, but aside from that it still looks the same: a large, impressive wooden building, promising a family from Essex a taste of the Cornish countryside.

Only now, it doesn't house holidaying families. Now, it seems, it has a sole occupier: R.R. Dread.

Seeing the house, Robert is increasingly appalled by the significance of that man choosing to buy it. The whole thing feels like a crass, aggressive statement. He thinks for a moment about what he's going to say. How the confrontation – if it is to be a confrontation – is going to go. He rehearsed it on the way down, but now all the words and potential opening lines seem muddled in his head. He just has to go for it, he thinks. He takes a deep breath and then presses the button on the intercom.

After a few seconds, a voice says with remarkably crisp clarity, 'Yes?'

Robert clears his throat. 'I… Um … is that … Mr. Smith?'

'Yes,' comes the curt reply.

'I'm here to deliver a package. It's from Carrington & Stoke Literary Agency. I can't leave it outside – I need a signature. Would you be able to—'

A buzz sounds and the gates in front of him start to open, barely making a sound as they swing inwards, removing Robert's obstacle to the front drive.

'Thanks,' Robert says.

He's in. He's back at Sunshine Lodge. And as he drives closer to the house, part of him wonders if Sean Smith buying this place and writing a fictional account of what happened here might be less an act of aggression, and more akin to setting a trap. And like a naïve insect, he is walking straight into its web.

The man who opens the door is instantly familiar to Robert. He felt a sense of this from the photograph but half convinced himself this was down to his own paranoia, fuelled by studying it at every opportunity as if to decode some hidden secret buried amidst the pixels. Seeing him in the flesh, he's now certain of it: he has definitely seen this man before. He just can't place where. Like his photograph, his hair is short and sandy blond, and he has a jawline that's a little round and boyish but still defined. Robert imagines women might find him good-looking, though he isn't classically handsome in the way people have always considered himself and Kieran. More wholesome than handsome, Robert thinks, then finds it strange he could ever think of the world 'wholesome' to describe a man he's made into a monster.

Robert's silence, as he stands there staring at the figure in the doorway, clearly puzzles the man.

'Hello?' he says again, though this time there is a trace of irritation.

Robert's surprised that Sean Smith doesn't immediately know who he is. At the moment, he genuinely seems to think Robert's a courier bringing a parcel. The man takes a closer look at him, then at the car Robert has just parked. It's quite obvious what he's thinking: couriers don't normally drive gleaming new Porsche Cayennes.

He leans forwards, squinting, then his eyes widen and he says, 'My god. It's you.'

A cold chill floods across Robert's back. It's as if he's been plunged headfirst into an ice bath, the warm heat of the air around him vanishing within seconds.

'I can see it – you look practically the same,' the man says, tilting his head to the side, making that squinting expression again. 'Extraordinary. It really is you.' His voice has a refined quality, reminding Robert of old BBC news broadcasts from the days of strict Received Pronunciation.

'Yes,' Robert says. It's all he can manage. It serves as confirmation of many things.

Yes, this is extraordinary.

Yes, he may well look very similar to how he did at sixteen.

And yes, it is really him.

'Well, well, well. I imagine you have a lot you want to ask me. You'd better come inside.'

He steps back into the house. Robert stays where he is for a moment, then follows, lifting his legs over the front step, feeling as though his limbs have been replaced with concrete slabs. Perhaps it's his unconscious mind warning him not to follow this man into his lair. But follow he does.

Sean Smith has changed the interior of the property – or at least changes have been made since Robert was here last. The floor is white, tiled and gleaming, as is the kitchen, which is visible as soon as he enters the building. It takes him a moment to realise a whole partition has been removed, giving the house a more open-plan feel.

'It's probably strange for you to be back here,' the man says.

'A lot about this is strange,' says Robert, still looking around.

After a few seconds of silence, the man steps forwards and says, 'I assume you know my name, if you've managed to track me down here.'

Robert nods. 'Your name is Sean Smith. Although you also use the name R.R. Dread.'

'Correct on both counts,' Sean says and smiles. 'If I were being pedantic, I'd say I used to be Sean Smith. I changed it through deed poll. But yes, essentially you're right. I went through a phase of wanting a complete change of identity, but I just couldn't shake the name Sean. So I don't mind.' He shrugs. Although he doesn't seem exactly relaxed, Robert gets the feeling this man isn't finding this painful or frightening. He may even be enjoying himself. There's excitement in his eyes, a glint that suggests this is all rather thrilling for him.

'Come through into the kitchen,' he says. 'By chance, I've just put the kettle on.'

Robert follows him through. The kitchen is entirely new, with a white marble surface and island, upon which are a food mixer, a blender and a knife set, along with a bag of flour and a block of cooking chocolate.

'Sorry for the clutter. I was going to do some baking.'

Robert has no idea what to reply to this so says nothing.

Sean is taking mugs out of a cupboard above his head. 'I don't want anything,' Robert says.

He sees Sean grin. 'Are you worried I'm going to poison you? That's more your approach, isn't it?'

The chilling effect is back on Robert's neck. 'No,' he says, his mouth clenched. 'It isn't.'

Sean looks at him, arching an eyebrow. 'I wouldn't bother if I were you,' he says, smoothly.

'Wouldn't bother what?'

He sees amusement in Sean's face. 'Denying it.'

'I'm not denying anything,' says Robert, 'because there's nothing to deny.'

Sean rolls his eyes. 'Oh, here we go.'

The remark makes Robert feel a jab of anger. 'Who even are you, anyway? You're talking as if you knew me and knew some secret about my life, and I don't even know who you are.'

Still, that expression of amusement remains in Sean's face. 'Are you sure?'

Robert stares at him, willing himself to make a connection that he's sure is there, somewhere in his mind, if only he can find it.

Then, at last, it comes to him.

'Oh … shit…'

He smiles wider. 'It's clicked, hasn't it.'

Robert watches. He looks at the face, the movement of the lips, the shifty eyes with the beginnings of creases at the corners. There were no lines there, of course, back when he first laid eyes on that face. He's only properly seen the man twice, but now he's made the connection, it seems blindingly obvious.

'You're that awful boy.'

Sean frowns, but the smile is still there. 'Awful? Now that's a bit harsh. I barely hurt you that day. I think you and your brother did more harm to me than I did to you.'

He goes over to the fridge and takes out the milk. 'You sure I can't get you a drink?'

Robert shakes his head. 'Could you just … stop for a minute? I'm trying to get this straight. You were … nothing like what…'

'Nothing like what I am now? Well, that's a fair point. I realise, when you met me – if we can call it meeting – I was a bit different. It's the lack of glasses, now, isn't it? Or the weight? It took me a while to lose it, I must say. A lot of dedication in my early twenties. Gym, crunches, swimming, the lot. I've always loved my food – as I said, I like my baking. I could offer you a cupcake. No? Not hungry?' He smirks. 'No matter. Well, I don't know if you want to hear my whole life story or just the highlights…?'

Robert stays silent, overwhelmed and disoriented.

'I'll go with the highlights,' Sean continues. 'Well, in short, I know what you did. I followed you that night. I climbed up the ladder. I saw everything. Heard everything.'

Although Robert knows this must be the case, it is still terrible to hear it. Up until this moment, he has still been holding out for an explanation that comforts rather than appals. Now, all hope is lost, it seems. The worst is swiftly coming true.

'I wasn't keen to involve myself in the investigation at the time. I was frightened of the police due to some experiences I went through as a young child, though I won't be sharing those with you. They're not relevant to all this. And besides, I don't want you thinking you've got any hold over me. I'm the one holding all the cards, my friend.'

Robert tries to keep his breathing steady. 'I am not your friend.'

He walks slowly over to Robert, holding his gaze. 'No. And you weren't my friend back then, were you? You made that very clear.'

Robert frowns. 'It was twenty years ago. I barely remember you. But I think you were the one who—'

'Oh, come on. This isn't why you're here. Not really. We're not here to discuss whatever happened between *us*. You're here to talk about what happened down there.' He points to the garden that's visible from the sliding glass doors. 'In the treehouse.'

A tense pause passes between them.

'Well, that's easy enough,' Robert says, worrying his voice sounds unnaturally high and panicky. 'Nothing happened in the treehouse.'

Sean looks at him, clearly disbelieving, then laughs. It is a horrible, cold laugh that makes Robert's stomach turn.

'Jesus, who do you think you're fooling?'

He walks forwards so he's standing right in front of Robert. He's so close that Robert can see every stitch on his checked flannel shirt and smell the harsh, fresh spicy scent of his aftershave.

'Because if nothing ever happened in that treehouse, you wouldn't be here, would you?'

Chapter Fifteen

ROBERT

Robert opens his mouth, then closes it again.

'Ah, memory issues,' Sean says, tapping his head. 'I understand. You're stressed. This must be a stressful time. Ever since you saw my TV series, I presume? Do you know, I've wanted to be a writer for so long. I never thought I'd have people traipsing miles across the country to come and talk to me about my work.'

The two men stare at each other, neither blinking. Then Sean seems to relax, his shoulders going down, his smile returning. 'Tell you what, follow me.' He starts walking to the wide glass wall at the end of the kitchen – another change to the property since Robert was here – and pulls the handle at the end, sliding a panel across so the transparent wall separating the kitchen from the garden is gone and Sean can step out into the summer sun.

'Come on,' Sean says, looking back at Robert.

Robert hesitates for a moment more, then follows.

Sean leads the way across the lawn and through the garden. It's obvious where they are heading and Robert has to fight an instinct to run – from the garden, from the house, from this neighbourhood, from Cornwall. From this land of ghosts he thought he'd laid to rest many years ago.

Eventually, it comes into view. Right at the bottom of the garden, where it curves around, backing onto the woodland, is the tree. The large oak tree. And situated in its branches is…

'Behold your darling treehouse,' Sean says, opening his hands in the manner of a magician who has completed a conjuring trick.

'It's just as it was,' Robert says, stepping nearer and nearer, feeling both drawn to it and repelled.

'Are you sure?' Sean says.

The closer Robert gets, he sees Sean is right to question his comment. It isn't the same. In his tense, uneasy state, he filled in the picture with his mind before truly appreciating what's before his eyes.

'It's a newly constructed, state-of-the-art treehouse. It even has solar panels, working lights, two beds – it's a dream. I'm having an annexe built and thought it could be a draw when I rent it out to people on summer holidays – city types, or just families wanting to visit Cornwall. You're familiar with the concept, of course.' He smirks.

'Why did you get rid of the old one?' Robert asks, his voice weak, his mouth dry.

'I didn't,' Sean says. 'It was gone. When I bought this place, whoever owned it before me must have decided to dispense with it. I inherited a load of cash from a relative abroad. Alaska, of all places. Weird. For a bit, I considered going to live over there so I could make a clean break from this place. It messed me up, you know. Keeping that secret. That *massive* secret … of what I saw, right here, on that day, over twenty years ago. I had a lot of problems after that. But I worked hard, really hard, got into a good university, made my mother proud. It was only through reinventing myself that I was able to let go of the past. But you never really let go, do you? You just put it in a box. And that box started to go rotten. The sides started to split. The gory contents started to seep out. So I decided the only way not to let it control me was to confront it.' He nods to the treehouse above them. 'This is the confrontation. In more ways than one, I suppose.'

Sean puts his hands on his hips, continuing to look up at the small but nonetheless impressive building nestled in the branches, then looks over at Robert.

'Want to go inside?'

Robert shakes his head.

Sean laughs. 'I don't blame you. It took me a while to pluck up the courage, even though this one's a bit more comfortable than the one you and your brother used to play in. Of course, that one was sturdy and impressive in its own way. Especially for back then. Such a shame it's gone. Good for you though. Puts paid to any investigations that might be … inconvenient.'

Robert turns sharply. 'What's that supposed to mean?'

Sean shakes his head. 'Oh do come on. I already told you. I *saw* you. I *saw* your brother. And I saw Chloe. Don't say her name much, do you? I bet you avoid it as much as you can during your day-to-day life, right? But yeah, I dare say there may have been some DNA evidence in the treehouse's previous incarnation.' He shrugs. 'Then again, I'm not an expert. But I've watched quite a lot of those cold-case dramas. It's amazing what they can find. Do you know, I might even do a cold-case mystery as my second screenplay? I'll have to make one up, though. Haven't got a first-hand account of a crime to recycle for that one. I've played my ace already.'

Robert tries to get himself together.

'This is a very nice treehouse. You've done impressive work on the property. I think I've seen and heard all I needed to see and hear. I'll leave you in peace.'

Sean looks surprised for only a second or two, then shakes his head.

'No, no, we're not finished. If you don't want to climb up there, let's go inside and get out of the sun. Unless you'd like a walk in the woods?' His eyes have a malicious glint to them that Robert doesn't like. 'Back in the house then,' Sean says.

Once they've reached the kitchen, Robert again makes another attempt to bring their discussion to an end. He feels confident – more than he has throughout his whole visit. Sean Smith has nothing. Nothing on him at all. The treehouse has gone. He saw something as a kid, but that's just hearsay. Perhaps he should have listened to Kieran and allowed this guy to do his worst – to do whatever interviews he wanted. It's all smoke and mirrors, after all.

'Before you go,' Sean says, folding his arms, 'there's just one more thing.'

Robert waits, the sense of dread he hoped he'd vanquished now rising within him once again.

'I'm happy to cancel my interview this week. Happy to never say a word about this again. Whatever buzz my TV series has created will die down. It might get a bit of interest if it shuffles onto a streaming service for its second-run rights, but I'm happy to quash any rumours. Happy to say it's all made up.'

Robert looks at the man in front of him, trying to read his expression. 'Er … thank you?' he says awkwardly, wondering if this is it. Or if there's a catch.

'But,' Sean says, confirming Robert's worst fears, 'I'm going to need something from you.'

'What?' asks Robert.

Sean shrugs his shoulders. 'I'm sorry, it's a cliché. I wish I could be more original, but it is what keeps the whole world spinning. The thing that motivates everyone, in the end.' He pauses, theatrically, watching Robert, then says, 'I want money. You see, my renovation works on this place have not gone smoothly. I've had trouble with the neighbours and planning permissions, and although progress has been achieved in that respect, each delay costs a fortune and now there's been a dispute about materials. I won't bore you with the intricacies, it's all very dull, but the long and the short of it is that I've got a fifty-thousand-pound hole in my budget. I don't know if you know much about screenwriters' royalties but, spoiler alert, it isn't enough. So yes, there's the pitch. I want money. Fifty thousand pounds. Every year, that is. To keep things ticking over. Consider yourself … a co-investor. You could be an angel investor in my little annexe holiday home project. Think of it as … penance.' He grins.

Robert stares at him. He feels a compulsion to both laugh and shout. It's ludicrous. The idea that he's come all this way just to be blackmailed makes him feel foolish and naïve. But of course, Sean is right. This is an obvious twist in the whole sorry tale. And blackmail feels like a very mundane, run-of-the-mill thing compared to the distorted horrors of the past that have been occupying his present. He is reminded of the scene in *The Wizard of Oz* where the great wizard in his Emerald City is revealed to be a very commonplace old man. Robert even ends up chuckling to himself at his strange connection, amused he's capable of thinking such a thing in these circumstances.

'What's funny?' asks Sean. 'Do you find my business proposition amusing?'

'No,' says Robert, 'but I'm not going to invest. Nice try. But I'm not interested. You've got nothing on me. Sure, you've freaked me out with your overcooked TV series and buying this place, but that's all it is. In the end, you're just a little creep. An opportunistic blackmailer. A pathetic nobody. Just like you were when you were sixteen. You tried your best at the tough talk back then, but you still can't quite pull it off, can you?' Robert shakes his head. 'I don't think we'll see each other again.'

He turns to go, determined to actually leave this time – leave and never come back. But just as his hand goes for the handle, Sean says, 'Except there are the recordings.'

Robert freezes, hand still stretched out. 'The what?' he says.

'The recordings. Three of them.' He raises a finger. 'One, a recording of a conversation between you and your brother. Two,' he raises a second finger, in the manner of an adult counting for a child, 'a recording I made of what you and your brother did that night. What you did to Chloe. And the conversation you had afterwards. And three,' he drops his fingers and pulls out a small smartphone from his shirt pocket. 'I've been recording you ever since we walked into the kitchen. You were rather entranced by the adaptations I've made to this place, so I had a good opportunity to tap my voice notes app. I usually use it to record writing ideas, but I think this will be the most inspirational recording on there yet.'

Robert steps forward. 'Go on then, show me. Let me hear it.'

Sean looks smug, pocketing the phone again. 'I don't think so.'

'Because I didn't say anything incriminating,' Robert says. 'I haven't said a single thing since I've arrived here that a police officer or crown prosecutor would give a moment's thought.'

Sean raises his eyebrows and leans back against the kitchen island in a calm way that Robert finds maddening. 'Are you sure?' Sean says. 'Are you absolutely certain about every word you've said? Because there's a really important incriminating detail hidden within there. Something you may have forgotten you mentioned.'

Robert starts to feel extremely hot, the back of his T-shirt pricking his neck and shoulders as if it were made of sprigs of holly rather than cotton. He absent-mindedly scratches his left shoulder, his eyes glazing over as he tries to think, to roll his memory back, hunting through everything they've spoken about since he crossed the threshold.

'Trying to remember, aren't you?' Sean says, tauntingly. 'Desperately thinking "Oh shit, what was it I said that gave the game away." Go on, you can work it out. I'll give you a few minutes.'

'You're making it up. This is a bluff. I've said nothing.'

'You tell yourself that.'

'Shut up,' Robert says.

'Why should I? It's my house. You're a visitor. Or rather, a prospective investor. I'll be very grateful for your generous fifty-thousand-pound input. I presume you've come to the decision to accept?'

'Show me that phone,' Robert says. 'Play me the recording. I want to know what I said.'

Sean still smiles and shakes his head slowly.

It's the smile that does it. The thing that sends a white-hot streak of anger firing through him. Robert has never thought of himself as naturally violent. He's always been one to discuss and reconcile rather than lash out. But right now, lashing out feels like the only thing that will stop his mind breaking apart from the sheer energy created by the sense of anger and hatred he's feeling.

The punch lands with force in the centre of Sean's face. He looks immobilised with shock at first, then he raises his hand to his face and yells. He lunges forward, and Robert hits him again, even harder this time.

It's a mistake. A huge, calamitous mistake. The distance gained in those few footsteps Sean took in the aftermath of the first punch causes the impact of the second to have far more devastating consequences. When he falls backwards, his head is at the perfect point to collide with the marble edge of the kitchen island. Within seconds, he is on the floor.

Sprawled.

Silent.

Motionless.

Chapter Sixteen

KIERAN

Kieran is exercising when he gets the call. When he was younger, he was able to stay fit very easily, but now he's edging towards forty, he finds he needs to work at it. Especially given his liking for alcohol. Seeing his brother's name on the screen, Kieran lets out a groan and comes to a halt. Out of breath and very hot, he lets the handle of the rowing machine clatter back into its holder and jabs at the phone.

'What's up, Rob?'

He's surprised to find his brother sounds more breathless than he is. Robert's panting hard – panic-attack style breathing, gasping, trying to get words out.

'Rob? You OK?'

'I… I…'

The line crackles and then there's more breathing, mingled with something else. Perhaps a sob? Is his brother crying?

'Rob, talk to me. What's going on.'

Then he says the words. The three words that make Kieran's world tilt.

'I've killed him.'

Kieran gets to his feet. He is unsteady, swaying a little, as he leaves the conservatory. He has the door open so he can hear his father's buzzer if he needs him.

'Please tell me you're not serious.'

This causes an explosion. 'Why would I joke about something like this?' Robert shouts.

Kieran has to stop himself shouting back at him in response. This is a disaster. A total disaster. If Robert had only listened to him and done nothing, like he said. He had been so certain everything would be fine.

'Where are you now?' Kieran says, sitting down on one of the garden benches near the flower beds.

'I don't know,' Robert says, sounding desperate, a sob rising in his voice again. 'I haven't got a clue where I am. I just left the place and drove. I drove for about an hour, I think. Until I couldn't do it anymore. So I stopped and phoned you.'

Kieran pinches his brow, thinking. 'So … you're where? In Cornwall?'

He hears a sniff. 'Yes. Or I presume I still am. He's living there, Kieran. Or …: *was* living there.'

'Where?'

'At the house. The lodge. Where it happened. It was so insane. He's literally had a treehouse built where the old one was. It was so awful being back there, so fucking awful, I think… I think I went a bit mad. He got to me. Started jeering at me, saying he's got recordings and shit like that and wanted money and I just lashed out and— God! I'm going to prison. I'm *actually* going to go to prison.'

'Stop talking so fast. I'm missing things,' Kieran says. 'You lashed out? What did you do? Punch him?'

'Yes,' Robert says. 'Twice. The second one made him hit his head on the countertop of the kitchen island. He fell. It was the phone… He said about … recordings. Fuck. Fuck, fuck, fuck.'

'Stop swearing and explain to me what you mean.'

'What?'

'Recordings. You said he has recordings.'

Robert's breath is rattling at the other end of the line. 'He said he had recordings of me. Of us, from back then. Ones that proved we … you know. Proves what we did. And he said he had been recording my conversation with him on his phone. Although I'm not sure about that, as when it fell onto the floor there was nothing on the home screen that made it seem like there was— I mean, there's normally a red dot or something to show it's recording, right? Shit, I don't know. I don't know if he actually— He may have been trying to wind me up. Well, it worked. I hit him.'

'Did you call an ambulance?' Kieran says, though he's pretty sure he knows the answer.

'No. I just left.'

Kieran takes a deep breath. There are many things he needs to ask, so many decisions he needs to make. Personal decisions. His brother has put him in a very difficult situation. He has turned his mistake into *their* mistake. Kieran wonders about the legalities of the situation. Phrases such as 'accessory' and 'conspiracy to murder' and 'joint enterprise' come to mind. He doesn't know which might apply here, but he's fairly sure that unless he's very careful, he will soon find out.

Then he reminds himself of something. Something he always does when he isn't sure what to do. It's an action he's performed ever since he was a teenager. He bends down and takes off his trainers and tugs off his socks. He can hear Robert calling his name from the phone but he ignores him. He places his bare feet on the grass, the ground dry and scratchy on his skin. Then he closes his eyes and breathes.

Yes. He knows what to do. The path he needs to follow is very clear to him. And he needs to guide Robert. His younger brother has never been able to do this himself, never been able to see his way through a situation without panicking, without wanting a helping hand or a nudge in the right direction, when the choices would be obvious if only he tried.

Kieran takes another deep breath and says, 'Just drive home, Rob.'

Robert had been midway through calling Kieran's name again, talking about everything being a disaster. He stops for a moment, then says, 'What?'

'It won't be a disaster. Just drive home.'

'What, to London?'

'Yes,' Kieran says. 'I can't come to you. Mum's out for the day visiting a friend and the carer's gone home with the flu. A replacement will be here eventually, but I don't know when that is, so I can't leave Dad. But regardless, just go home. You hear me?' He says all this as calmly and firmly as he can, willing his brother to accept it and obey. To not question it. Life will be so much simpler if he complies.

'I hear you,' Robert says. 'But what about forensics, like DNA and things like that? When I left I used my T-shirt to cover my hand to open the door handle, but they can get skin cells and stuff? And hairs? I've probably touched something else in the place. I didn't drink. Thank Christ I didn't accept the tea. And this phone call? The police could be listening right now.'

'No, they're not. Keep calm. Stop ranting and raving, it won't help anything. Only drive when you've calmed yourself down. In terms of DNA, just take your clothes off immediately when you get in and put everything on a hot wash. Don't let them touch anything else other than the inside of the washing machine. Tomorrow, take your car for a full clean and valet. Then get a taxi over to me. Do all of it methodically and calmly. If you panic, you'll make mistakes.'

There's a worrying silence on the other end.

'Rob, you still there?'

He hears a sniff, then a cough. 'Yes,' he says. 'Yes, I'm here. I'm just… It's a lot. This entire day has been a lot.'

'I understand that,' Kieran says. 'And it will be over when you get home. Do you think you'll be able to drive?'

'Yes.'

'Drive as normally as you can. Don't speed or make stupid mistakes. Just clear your mind and drive. Put some music on or something.'

'OK.'

'Good,' says Kieran. He feels like he's a boy again. He feels like he's trying to tell his crying little brother what to do when the older boys are mean to him, or offering comfort and perspective when a teacher has told him off for leaving his homework up in his dorm. 'Drive home calmly. Clothes in the wash. That's all for now. Phone me once you're in, no matter what the time is.'

'Yeah,' Robert says. 'OK.'

'It's going to be fine,' Kieran says. 'Believe me, it's going to be fine.' He pauses for a second, then says something he doesn't think he's said for years, but suddenly it feels important. 'I love you.'

There are a few seconds of silence. Then Robert replies. 'I love you too. And I'm sorry. I'm sorry for everything.' Then the line goes dead.

The end of the phone call unsettles Kieran, perhaps even more than the bombshell his brother has just unleashed. His sign-off felt horribly final and Kieran prays it's not the prelude to something.

Like handing himself in to the police. Or something even more self-destructive.

He remains sitting on the bench for a few more minutes, thinking about what the days ahead will bring.

'I know what to do,' he says quietly to himself, closing his eyes again. 'Everything's going to be fine.'

Chapter Seventeen

ROBERT

Robert does as his brother instructs. He drives. Just drives. He doesn't stop. Doesn't speed. He follows his sat nav to the letter. He calms his mind by focusing on every turn, every acceleration or braking, every indication and lane change. He is careful and methodical, just as Kieran said.

The most difficult moment comes when he reaches a large stretch of congestion and all the lanes are completely stationary. That's when his thoughts threaten to come for him, trying to terrorise him with images: him being handcuffed; him in a dock in a courtroom in a scene ripped from a movie, but real, with him there; him being checked into jail by stony-faced wardens, being searched and issued with a prison uniform and introduced to a knuckle-cracking cellmate. Then spending twenty-five years trying to survive being terrorised and brutalised by some of society's most dangerous, damaged and violent men.

When the traffic starts moving, he's able to pause his thoughts temporarily in his mind. He needs to stick to Kieran's instructions. He needs to keep a calm, clear head. Once he's back at his flat, he unlocks the door and is about to go straight through to his bedroom and collapse into a heap of fear, exhaustion and anxiety but then he remembers and instantly pulls off his T-shirt and holds it close to him while he bends to undo his shoelaces. He can't remember if Kieran mentioned shoes or if he should just wipe them clean – or if that was even necessary. Or maybe he should put them into the washing machine with everything else. They're only trainers, after all. People put trainers into washing machines, don't they? And Kieran had said 'everything', so surely everything includes shoes? Wishing he had paid more attention to crime-solving and forensics practices in films he's watched, Robert includes the trainers in his bundle and carries everything to the kitchen. The untidy ball of clothes and shoes is placed into the washing machine, then he pulls off his pants and socks and throws them in too. He sets the machine for a hot three-hour wash and then goes back into his bedroom. He can hear Albie in his room with the TV on – thankfully not in the lounge – and he hopes he can slip quietly over to the shower without any questions. No such luck. A knock sounds at his door and Albie's voice can be heard from the other side. 'That you, Robert?'

Well, who the fuck else would it be? He thinks about screaming this for a moment, then decides it would only lead to more enquiries and worried looks.

'Yes,' he says, pulling on some tracksuit bottoms. 'I'm going to go have a rest. Might have a shower, then call Kieran. Not feeling too good.'

'OK. How's your dad?'

'Sorry?'

'I… I presumed that's where you've been today. You weren't at work. There was a technical fault at the theatre, so I had the afternoon off. I dropped by your office to see if you wanted to grab lunch. They said you weren't in today, so I thought maybe there was some crisis with your dad?'

'No… I… Yes, that was it. He … isn't good … but he's OK now. Touch and go, but it's fine.'

Silence greets this, and Robert knows why. It's because he's talking through the door when normally he'd have opened it. It's because he's been acting strange for days now. It's because he's obviously lying.

'Robert … do you … do you have an addiction problem?'

This causes him to fling open his bedroom door. 'An *addiction* problem?'

Albie looks shocked by his sudden arrival in front of him. 'Sorry … but … I've seen the pills. And your behaviour lately. I'm just worried about you, that's all.'

'No, I don't have an addiction problem,' he says, but it's too loud and causes Albie to take a step back. 'My brother's the one with the addiction problem. All I do is—' He stops, unsure what he's trying to say. 'I just take perfectly legal drugs when I need them – when I feel unwell or have pain. That's what people are supposed to do with medication.'

Albie looks confused, and Robert can't blame him.

'I'm not saying you should talk to me about this, but I really think you should talk to someone,' Albie says. 'Maybe a professional.'

Even in his tense state, Robert can see the well-meaning concern in Albie's face. But right now, it's inconceivable that he should be worrying about how many tablets he knocks back after the events of the day. After what's he's done.

'I'm fine,' he says stonily, feeling anything but.

'Right. OK. Well, goodnight,' Albie says, turning to go.

'*Fuck's sake*,' Robert mutters to himself when he's alone again. Now he feels guilty, and that's something he doesn't have the mental space for, not right now. He grabs a clean towel from a pile of fresh laundry he hasn't had time to put away and heads over to the bathroom.

In the shower, he imagines with each gush of water that he can see blood splashing to the floor. It's as though he's drenched in the stuff, covered in thick, red, gory coatings, dripping off his flesh, dried into his hair and eyebrows and lashes and between his fingers. Everywhere, contaminated. Of course, there is no such evidence – nothing the human eye can see, in any case – but still he scrubs and scrapes.

Once he's out and dry, he returns to his room and phones Kieran. The call is answered almost immediately.

'Rob, you OK?'

'Yeah,' he says. 'I've done everything you said.'

Kieran lets out a breath that Robert takes as relief. 'I knew you would be fine.'

'Did you?' Rob says weakly. 'Because I didn't. I'm not sure how I managed to drive all that way without going insane. Perhaps I did. Perhaps I will.'

'Stop thinking like that,' Kieran says. 'This may not be as bad as it seems.'

'Jesus Christ, Kieran!' Robert hisses, trying to keep his voice as low as possible. 'I've just killed a man and done shit that makes me look guilty as hell. I didn't call an ambulance; I fled the scene; I've come home and washed all my clothes, scrubbed away any chance of him that might remain on me. I couldn't look more guilty.'

'Perhaps,' says Kieran, 'but proof is what matters. Clear, quantifiable proof. Not how things *look*. And besides, as I said before, he might not even be dead. Just knocked out.'

'That's worse,' says Robert, then checks his words. 'Well, no, not worse of course, but that means he'll phone the police. I'll be arrested for assault or attempted murder before the night is over.'

'Rob, you're panicking. I told you not to do that.'

Robert closes his eyes, lies back and wishes he could turn back time. 'How can you be so calm?' he asks.

'Rob, I do wish you hadn't forgotten.' His voice is strange. Still very calm, though with a tinge of frustration, or perhaps even regret.

'Forgotten what?'

There's a pause. Then Kieran says simply, 'Everything.'

Robert feels an uncomfortable prickle on his skin, not dissimilar to how he felt during his conversation with Sean Smith just hours before. 'You're not making sense,' he says to his brother. 'I'm tired. I need to sleep. I'll sort the car out in the morning, then I'll come and see you.'

'Good. Do that. It's going to be fine, Rob. It's all going to be fine.'

Robert ends the call, tosses the damp bath towel onto the floor, and crawls into bed, wishing he could believe his brother's words. Wishing he too could be so sure they were true.

In the night, he dreams. He can see Sean Smith. It's as if Robert is hovering in a space above him, watching him on the ground up against the kitchen island. He's waking up with a bit of a sore head but completely fine. He's walking out of the house and getting into a car that's waiting for him. A car that takes him at dizzying speed to a television studio. Robert can see this, from his bird's-eye view of the whole thing, as one scene slips into another, like watching seamless clips of a video that have been stitched together to remove the passing of time. Sean's going on to do his YouTube interview. He sits down in front of the cameras and starts speaking. He says everything he wrote in *The Treehouse* really happened. He watched the whole thing unfold, back when he was younger. And that isn't all. '*The younger boy tried to kill me. He beat me and left me for dead. And the police are closing in on him right now.*' Robert then hears them. Noises outside on the pavement. Lots of booted feet running. The door is smashed open, more footsteps, running down the hallway then sound bursts through the doorway as uniformed men pour in. Robert tries to burrow under the duvet, pressing his head under the pillows as though that will be enough to shelter him from what's happening. The men seize him by his wrists and his ankles, and carry him, thrashing and screaming, out of the room. One man, who vaguely resembles the old detective from twenty-year old memories, dressed in a suit and tie, walks calmly alongside him, saying, '*We'd better take him straight to prison. He should have gone there a* long *time ago…*'

He wakes up screaming. And there are hands – hands really are grabbing him – but not the hands of the police.

'Robert, can you hear me?'

Robert tries to focus. He forces himself to stop shaking, to keep himself still. Albie is staring at him, looking scared.

'Christ, that must have been some nightmare,' he says.

'Yeah,' Robert says, panting. 'Bad… Bad dream.'

'Well, it's over now,' Albie says.

It isn't, Robert thinks, as he sits up. It really isn't. He looks at the bedside table and sees that he hasn't refilled his water.

'I'm so thirsty,' he says, pulling himself out of bed and shakily getting to his feet.

'Are you sure you're not unwell? Did you, um, take something after we spoke last night? I'm not trying to be on your case, I'm just worried.'

'No, I didn't.'

'OK. Should I call someone?'

Robert shakes his head. 'I'm fine. I'll be fine. Kieran says so.' He's only vaguely aware he's said this last bit out loud, but Albie doesn't question him on it. He stumbles to the bathroom, splashes cold water onto his face and drinks greedily from the tap. He looks at himself in the mirror, expecting to see someone transformed and twisted by guilt, by sin, by the sheer evil of their actions. But his own, normal face stares back at him. Tired and stressed-looking, but still him.

When he eventually goes into the kitchen, dressed and feeling calmer, he sees his phone is on the kitchen counter where he left it after emptying the contents of his trouser pockets before putting them in the washing machine.

'That's been buzzing away,' Albie says from over at the kitchen table. He has the TV on the kitchen wall tuned to one of the breakfast news shows and a particularly loud burst of music comes on. He turns it down and says, 'Listen, I feel bad after what I said last night. I was worried you thought I was having a go at you or calling you a druggie or something.'

'I don't think that,' Robert says.

'I can make you some coffee or breakfast if you want before I head off?'

'No, no, I'm fine,' Robert says distractedly as he looks at the phone screen. He's thankful to see he hasn't run it dry this time – it's still got 45% battery – although he's alarmed at the amount of missed calls and messages from Kieran.

Albie says something about making a move. Robert nods, pleased his flatmate isn't asking too many questions – perhaps he's trying a new approach to dealing with his increasingly odd behaviour.

He pours out a mug of coffee and picks up his phone, planning to call Kieran and put him on speaker. He's just about to pick up the remote to switch off the TV when the newsreader says something that makes him drop his mug to the floor. The coffee isn't boiling – Albie must have brewed it a short while ago – but it's still hot and most of it coats his bare feet, along with sharp shards of porcelain. But Robert barely notices. He can't tear his attention away from the TV screen.

'Detectives have confirmed they are treating the death of a thirty-five-year-old man in the district of Port Bowen, West Cornwall as murder. Police were called to a large house in the affluent community of Hill Valley when builders working on the property found the body of a man in the kitchen area of the home. The police are yet to confirm the identity of the victim, although several online publications have reported that the deceased is a man named Sean Smith who works as a screenwriter under the pseudonym R.R. Dread.'

Chapter Eighteen

KIERAN

Kieran is trying not to become unnerved by the lack of contact with his brother. He has been trying to reach him since 7am, but each time he fails to get through he presumes Robert is tired from his terrible ordeal the day before. He just needs to be patient.

His patience is rewarded – although it doesn't feel like a reward – when he spots his brother's car heading up the driveway around mid-morning. He pulls to a halt and gets out. Kieran walks out of the front door and goes over to him.

As soon as Robert sees him, he says in a shaking voice, 'He's dead. He's fucking dead. I knew it. I've killed him.'

'Shut up,' Kieran hisses. He walks up to him and says quickly and quietly, 'Mum's out the back, in the garden. We can't talk inside. Let's just get away from here.'

He leads his brother down the drive, taking him back out onto the road from where he had just come, this time on foot, and chooses a route he knows will take them to the nearby estuary. They came along here many times as children, catching newts or caterpillars or just throwing stones into the water. Today, Robert looks as if he's ready to throw himself in. Kieran can't let that happen. He needs to get his brother under control. He is a liability.

Kieran says, 'I see you ignored my advice about the car.'

Robert looks at him as if he's mad. 'Why is it even worth bothering with that now? It's all over. I can feel it.'

They stay standing at the riverbank for a good few minutes, Kieran watching his brother's face, unwilling to press him any further.

Then Robert says, 'Have you seen the news report?'

'No.'

'You don't seem worried,' Robert says. It's a statement, rather than a question, so Kieran doesn't reply. But he can think of one. *I'm not the one who has committed murder. At least not today.*

Robert then says, 'I know you've worked it out. About it being that boy. From back then. You recognised him, didn't you?'

Kieran thinks for a moment, then nods.

'Fuck's sake,' Robert says. He kicks an empty Pepsi can into the water. It gets caught in some reeds at the edge and looks ugly amidst the natural greenery. 'You're always the one holding the cards, steering the way, aren't you?'

'Things work out better that way,' Kieran says. He's keen not to turn this into a fight. That won't help anything.

So they walk on. He's aware they'll talk about the past. The worries for the future. The problem they find themselves in now.

And so they do talk, with no easy answers coming to them on the light summer breeze.

The landmine explodes that evening. During their walk and an uncomfortable lunch in a village pub, Kieran wondered where everything was leading. Robert ate an extraordinary amount, as though it was his last supper. Wondering about the future and ruminating about events isn't Kieran's natural approach to a problem, and he's frustrated his brother has put him into this situation. He tries his best to retain a sense of control. He instructs Robert to stay the night. They need to see the coming days through together, whatever they have in store. But that evening everything changes.

The two brothers are sitting in the living room, waiting for the evening news report to see if there are any updates on the murder case that haven't yet been reported on the BBC news website. Robert stands up and says, 'I'm sorry. I really am. But I can't take this. I'm going to phone the police.'

Kieran had guessed they were heading in this direction, but it still pains him to hear it. 'That's a mistake, Rob.'

'No, it isn't,' he says, 'I've listened to you all my life and now I'm going to have to do this for myself.' He seems to sway a little on the spot. His face is pale – grey even – and Kieran wonders if he might be sick. 'I have to make my own decisions, face my own mistakes, and I'm not going to do that by hiding away here.'

Kieran shakes his head. 'None of that's true. You're not listening to me. You went off and killed a man against my advice, and now you're wondering why life is hard. And you didn't listen to me back then, did you? I know you went along with it all in the end, but that didn't stop you going rogue. Do I need to remind you of your little nighttime trip? You could have spoilt everything doing that. And you nearly died.'

'It was Mum's fault I nearly died.'

Kieran's still looking at him with that infuriating look – a mixture of pity and superiority. 'Keep telling yourself that,' he says.

The words seem to trigger something in Robert's face. He screws up his hands into fists and for a second Kieran wonders if his younger brother is going to try to hit him. But then he appears to deflate. His hands release and his shoulders sag. He doesn't seem to have enough force left within him.

'I don't want to go into all that,' Robert says eventually. 'And you're just confusing things, bringing that up. I can't cope with confusion right now. I really can't.'

Kieran leans closer. 'There's no confusion. Nothing's complicated. Nothing's beyond repair. Just sit back down and wait.'

Robert draws himself up and takes out his phone. 'I can't. I'm done. I won't mention you or that you know anything about what I did yesterday. I'll tell them everything was me. Every single thing. I have to do this. It's either this or … I don't know what. Something worse.'

That's when the door to the living room creaks open. Kieran turns at the same time as his brother and both look at their mother, standing in the doorway, watching them.

'Shit,' Kieran says quietly.

There's a moment of silence that feels so tense that it's as if the air around them is vibrating with it.

Then Robert says, 'Mum, I'm so sorry.' Tears start to form in his eyes and spill over onto his face as he looks at her.

'Enough, both of you,' she says, holding up a hand.

Kieran is confused by this. He expected his mother to demand to know what was going on or to be instantly furious with them. But instead, she walks into the room and takes the phone from Robert. She sets it down on the coffee table in front of Kieran and then looks at her hands.

'Before anyone phones the police – and believe me, the police will be called before this night is out – you both need to come with me.'

Robert says nothing. The mixture of confusion and emotion seems to make speech impossible for him. But Kieran frowns and says, 'Where are we going?'

His mother takes a breath, and suddenly Kieran's struck by how old she's starting to look. Tired, too. Tired like Robert. And just as troubled.

'We're going to your father's room. We're all going to have a little chat. There's something you both need to know. About what happened yesterday. And what happened twenty-one years ago.'

Chapter Nineteen

KIERAN

2004

K ieran sits in his history class, trying to work out if he's glad it's the end of term. On one hand, he's grateful he has parents who take them all away every summer for an extended holiday, to villas or hotels abroad or to the countryside in the UK. But he's reached an age where he finds the family unit more than a little suffocating. At sixteen, he feels he should be striking out on his own path, meeting interesting people, going to parties and discovering himself. All that's hard to do when cooped up with one's mum and dad and little brother.

That said, he likes his brother and misses him during term time. He says hello to him in the corridors and smiles across the school hall, but he's in a different year, a different dorm, a different friendship circle. And boys with brothers in other years don't usually socialise. It's seen as a bit of a social failing if you have to hang out with your own sibling during breaks or evening downtime.

'Am I keeping you from something more interesting, Kieran?'

He's been staring out of the window, and Mr Pertwee saying his name drags him back to the present. He blinks at his teacher, then realises what's happening. He's been caught daydreaming. Boredom is his general state at school and it isn't unusual for teachers to pick up on it. When he started his first term at boarding school when he was eleven, he'd actively looked forward to being away from home and the parents he'd started to find immensely irritating. But the novelty had worn off within that first term, and the years that followed felt more like a prison sentence than an escape.

'Kieran, hello?' his teacher says, still looking at him.

He isn't especially embarrassed. Kieran doesn't really do embarrassed. He doesn't see the point in it. But he finds an overt display of his naturally carefree approach doesn't usually result in a good response from others, especially those in authority, so he settles his expression into what he hopes resembles 'regretful and respectful' and says, 'I'm sorry, sir.'

Mr. Pertwee smiles at him, waving an unconcerned hand. 'That's fine, I know it's the end of term. Anyway, as I was saying, all this leads us up neatly to ritualistic sacrifice.'

Kieran shifts his frame so that he's properly facing the whiteboard. Ritualistic sacrifice sounds like it might actually be interesting. Mr Pertwee starts to give a summary of the history of the practice, talking about the difference between the methods of the Greeks, Romans and Celts. Kieran sits and listens to tales of communities throwing people off cliffs to try to protect the society from disaster. They had been looking at Greece as a quick preview of the next year's syllabus, when they would be focusing on the topic in a more 'rigorous way', according to Mr Pertwee.

After the bell has rung, signalling the end of the lesson, Kieran is about to leave with the others when a thought occurs to him.

'Sir, with ritualistic sacrifice, has anyone ever used that as a defence in court?'

Mr Pertwee raises his eyebrows. 'I… Do you know, I'm not sure, but it wouldn't surprise me. Many years ago, I would imagine. I doubt it's very common these days. I've certainly heard about demonic possession being used as a defence. There was quite a bit of that after *The Exorcist* came out in cinemas when I was a teenager. But I suppose ritualistic sacrifice is more of a *reason* for killing rather than a defence of it. I should add, too, that I've given a very brief and cursory nod to the topic here today. If you're interested, I could recommend a few books the library should have.'

He reaches across his desk for a filer card from a stack on his desk, picks up a pen and begins to write.

'Here you are,' he says, offering the card.

Kieran takes it, feeling like he's getting more than he bargained for, but thinks he might as well check the books out if he has time.

'It's good to see you showing an interest, Kieran. Let's hope we see more of this next year. Natural intelligence will only get you so far. You have to really apply yourself.'

Kieran makes a non-committal movement with his head and makes a show of glancing at the clock. 'I'd better get going, sir,' he says.

'Very well. But I'm serious, Kieran. Solid, hard work. Consistent study. I'm worried you think things are just going to land in your lap all your life without trying. It doesn't work like that. Just think about your priorities over the summer.'

Kieran can't be bothered to argue.

'Of course,' he says.

Then he exits the room before any more unsolicited advice could be sent his way. The last class of the day – and indeed the whole term – is PE, and although Kieran usually enjoys sports he is distracted by the conversation with Mr Pertwee and the books he suggested. He spends most of the time kicking the sun-bleached ground at the edge of the playing field, staring out at the buildings that lined Vincent Square and the glimpses of London visible beyond, thinking. The main school library normally remains open into the evening for the older boys of the school to revise for their exams, though it being the end of term and with a lot of boys going home that night, he isn't sure if there will be time for him to visit before closing. Thankfully, he finds he's in luck. After showering and changing in a rush, he nips down to the library to find the door still open. Late afternoon sunlight streams through the windows and the librarian Mrs Hill is calmly shelving books in the far corner. He's never been an avid reader, but there's something about the quiet tranquillity of the place that's very appealing. Perhaps he should come here more often, he thinks, as he takes out the filer card and begins his search for the books.

That evening passes in a blur. He finds two of the three books Mr Pertwee recommended and reads various chapters on the history of ritualistic sacrifice. Some of the writing touches on links to modern-day crime – or at least things from the twentieth century rather than things occurring before the birth of Jesus Christ or recorded time periods. He then moves over to one of the computers and begins googling, reading online about various cultures and countries, religions and sects, theories and ideologies, his interest growing the more he reads. He ends up on forums where people share details about cases – murder cases where ritual sacrifice seems to have been the driving motivator, and cases from locations as varied as Arizona, Munich and Edinburgh, along with many others. Then one comment from a forum user named TrueDCFollower1971 changes everything for Kieran.

Followers of the Dark Core concept understand the importance of ritual sacrifice more than any other community in the twenty-first century. Other religions and groups may pretend to understand, but they often get things wrong or don't really get the true power. If you really want to understand, you should watch the videos of The Raven. He's incredible. He's changed my life and I'm sure he'll change yours.

Underneath the comment is a URL that appears to lead to a video-sharing site. Kieran hasn't fallen foul of the school's internet firewalls so far, but he suspects this site might be a problem. Sure enough, when he clicks it, a message comes up with an internet security software logo and the words 'ACCESS DENIED' in big red letters.

Tutting, Kieran takes out Mr Pertwee's filer card and in the blank space at the bottom writes down the web address, taking care to get each letter and number correct.

'Time to power off, dear,' says Mrs Hill behind him. It makes Kieran jump, and his look of surprise is apparently mistaken for an indicator of guilt as Mrs Hill cranes her neck to look at the screen and frowns. 'Now, now, we're not looking at *things*, are we? I've been on this earth long enough to know what *things* you boys like to look up on the computers.'

'No,' says Kieran. 'It's … homework. Or research.'

'Is that so?' says Mrs Hill with the tone of someone immune to being fobbed off with such excuses. 'Well, I've seen it all here. Women in skimpy swimwear. Chatrooms where boys try to buy drugs from dealers over on the Vauxhall Bridge Road. I won't stand for it, I can tell you.'

'I wasn't on a chatroom buying drugs,' Kieran says, logging off the computer and putting his chair under the desk.

'I should hope not,' she says by way of a goodbye.

'Have a lovely summer,' Kieran says, grinning warmly at her, which earns him a confused frown.

Back in his dorm room, he finds his roommate, Hugo, packing. Both of them are being picked up tomorrow, though quite a few of their friends have gone home that night.

'Have you packed yet?' Hugo says, taking a handful of clothes out of one of the drawers to his left and tossing them into an open case on his bed.

Kieran shakes his head. 'No, not yet. I was wondering, you know you've cracked or tricked or hacked your study laptop to get past the school's security? So you can … you know … watch stuff?'

Hugo raises an eyebrow. 'Uh huh,' he says with a knowing grin.

'Well, could you do it to mine? Or let me borrow your laptop, just for this evening?'

His grin widens further. 'Can't believe you've gone all term without asking me.' He bends down to the bottom drawer of his bedside unit and pulls out a small black computer. 'Here you go,' he says. 'Just make sure you use your headphones. I'm being picked up early and you know me, I like my sleep. Can't be kept up all night with whatever *distractions* you're watching on there.' He hands it over with a wink.

Kieran nods and smiles. He doesn't bother to tell Hugo he won't be using it to look at girls; he wants it for quite a different thing altogether. Hugo's a nice guy, but he doesn't have depth. Everything is always very surface level with him. Kieran knows he wouldn't understand.

Aside from a break for dinner, Kieran spends most of that night on the same forum he was looking at in the library, reading intensely. Once Hugo has climbed into bed and said goodnight, Kieran pulls on his headphones, takes out the filer card and types in the web address he copied down earlier. The page that opens up is a video-hosting sight he's never heard of called VidShareGo, with a rather amateurish-looking logo. A video starts playing, with the text 'The Earth's Dark Core: An Introduction from The Raven' on a black background. Then it cuts to what looks like a forest glen, in black and white. There's the sound of the trees and noises of rustling – animals perhaps. There's a chair in the centre of the frame and a few seconds later a figure dressed in a long black cloak appears. That would be odd in itself, but it's the mask that makes a shiver run up Kieran's spine. A mask that looks, from its glinting surface, to be made of metal, but the edges are shaped like leaves – many leaves, piled on top of each other, with the outline of a face in the centre. There are holes for the eyes and a slit for the mouth, behind which lips are just about visible. He's fairly sure the figure is male, from his frame and build, and the brief side view of his head when he sits down. Kieran is holding his breath, waiting.

Then the man starts to speak.

'This is an introduction to the Dark Core movement,' he says. 'In this introduction, I will explain our central tenets and beliefs, share with you an outline of our origins and offer an idea of what will follow if you choose to join us on this journey.'

There's a rustling movement and the man reaches down to pick something up that's out of shot. It's a cage – a little metal cage with a handle at the top. Inside is a rabbit, its head looking through the bars, its ears twitching.

'First, though,' the man says, 'a practical demonstration.' Then he reaches into the folds of his black cloak and takes out a long silver knife.

By the next morning, Kieran has watched many of the videos uploaded by the user. He's also immersed himself in the comments, reading what people have to say about the man's interpretation of sacrifice and its benefits. Some say he's mad; others mention that they too have tried animal sacrifice but it hasn't worked. They don't feel their lives have changed or feel a connection to 'the deep core'.

A user called JackP1983W comments:

That's because, like he says, animal sacrifice is a very temporary measure. For it to be lasting, to be a life-long change, you need to go further. The subject of the sacrifice needs to be human.

'Time's up, mate,' Hugo says behind him. He looks around and sees Hugo has his bags all packed and is standing by his bed that's been stripped, ready for the laundry. He has his arms folded and for a moment Kieran's confused. Then he realises. 'Oh, you need your laptop back?'

Hugo nods. 'Is it worth me asking again what you've been watching all this time?' He walks towards him, but Kieran exits the browser before he can see.

'Just research for next term. Coursework stuff for History.'

Hugo has a similar expression to the one Mrs Hill had the day before, but doesn't argue. 'Well, so long as it's virus-free,' he says, picking up the computer. 'You around to meet up in the summer at all?'

Kieran flops down onto his bed, sighing. 'I doubt it. We were supposed to be going to Portugal, but Dad has some business meetings in Plymouth, so my parents have got a holiday lodge sort of thing in Cornwall. It sounds dull, if you ask me.'

Hugo makes noises of empathy and bids him goodbye, wishing him luck and saying he'll see him in September. Kieran hears him out in the hallway apologising for bumping into someone. Seconds later, his younger brother walks in.

'Hey, why are you still in your pyjamas? Dad's downstairs in the car.'

Kieran suddenly feels exhausted, and the upbeat sound of Robert's voice gives him an instant headache. He shouldn't have stayed up until 3am, but he found it nearly impossible to pull himself away from what he was learning. And the things he was seeing.

'Fuck. I haven't packed.'

Robert lets himself drop down on the bed, causing Kieran to bounce, which doesn't make his headache feel any better. Groaning and pulling himself up, he watches without enthusiasm as Robert goes over to his cupboard and starts taking out his brother's clothes.

'Hey, hands off! I'll do that.'

'Dad says Mum's preparing a lunch in the garden when we get back; she'll be cross if we're late,' Robert says, ignoring the instruction. 'All the boys in my dorm are already packed and gone. You're lucky it just being you and Hugo. I hate sharing with five others. Never any peace.' He opens up one of the top drawers in the unit next to the cupboard.

'Hey, get out of there,' Kieran says.

'Woah, are these condoms? And cigarettes, too? You know Dad will be furious if he knows you smoke. He'll mention that old uncle he had who died because of it. The one who coughed up his own lungs or something hideous.'

'I don't smoke,' Kieran says, rolling his eyes. 'And anyway, Mum used to smoke when we were kids.'

Robert tosses the packs of condoms and cigarettes into the open suitcase and then starts to take out handfuls of Kieran's socks.

'Hey, I told you to get your hands off my stuff,' Kieran says, nudging him in his side. 'Sit down over there while I pack,' he says, gesturing to his desk in the corner.

Robert sits down on the chair as Kieran packs, and a little while later he says, 'What's all this?'

Kieran glances over to see Robert holding the printed sheets from the library the day before.

'Oh, just something I was researching.'

Robert nods, then leans back in his chair.

He reads some more, apparently intrigued by what he is discovering.

Chapter Twenty

ROBERT

2004

The masked man wipes the knife clean on a folded piece of material kept to the right of the frame. The rabbit he has just stabbed lies twitching on a wooden table. Leaves fall. Branches of trees sway. The rabbit goes still.

Robert is disturbed by what he has spent most of the evening watching. He had discovered the videos of The Raven after googling the forum noted down at the top of one of the print-outs Robert found on his brother's desk. The links to them had been shared by a few users, saying that this guy is *hardcore but knows the truth*. So Robert had clicked on one of the links.

That was before dinner. During their evening meal, he hadn't felt like talking much. He'd watched one of the first sacrifice videos and felt troubled. Cutting into the chicken breasts they were having for tea made him feel sick and his mind kept filling with the images of the blood pouring out of the slit in the animal's fur. He kept missing things his mother and father were saying to him. He noticed his brother, too, seemed deep in thought. Both went to their separate bedrooms after eating and now, a few hours on, he has watched over half of the videos The Raven has uploaded. Some of them don't contain any animal killings. Some are just him talking to the camera, always wearing his metal leaf mask. He says things Robert isn't sure he understands, but also suggests things that make a lot of sense to him. That the taking of life, no matter whether someone feels it to be right or wrong, is an act of great power and has a deep effect on the person wielding the weapon. Robert imagines that's probably true, though he's never killed more than a wasp in his life.

'This is why I didn't want you boys to have computers in your bedrooms,' says his mother's voice from the door, making him start. 'You used to read loads of books during the holidays, and now look. Not a book in sight. Glued to a screen at 11pm. You should be in bed, not surfing the web.'

'I was watching a film,' Robert says, 'I'm allowed to do that. And it's the first night of the holidays; I've got time to read books and do lots of other things. I don't see the problem.'

His mother sighs, 'I have no idea why you'd choose to watch a film on a computer when there's a perfectly good television downstairs. Your father and I have just been watching a very interesting documentary about a man who breeds red squirrels in Inverness.'

'Well, that sounds thrilling,' Robert says, 'I'm going to brush my teeth.'

His mother bids him goodnight and leaves the doorway. Once he's certain she's gone, Robert leaves his room and heads to find Kieran. He's lying on top of the covers of his bed in his boxer shorts, the small desk fan on his bedside table on its highest setting. He has his new Apple laptop he got for his sixteenth resting on his knees and he tilts the screen away from view when he sees Robert.

'Hey, ever thought about knocking?' Kieran says.

'Sorry, you busy?'

'Depends what you want,' Kieran mutters, continuing to click on his computer.

Robert sits down on the edge of his bed. 'I thought you said you were tired? Why aren't you asleep?'

Kieran sighs. 'Too hot. And I got caught up watching some stuff.'

Robert nods. 'Can I show you something on the computer?'

Kieran looks and him, frowning. 'Why? What is it?'

Robert holds out his hand and after a few seconds' pause, Kieran gives him the laptop. Robert is about to go onto the video site when he notices the page Kieran's on. A very familiar page.

'Oh, you're on it now…' Robert says.

'What?' Kieran looks confused. 'You were going to show me this?' He takes the laptop back.

'No, don't go off it. There are links in some of the comments. There's this guy… Some videos. But I guess you may have…'

'I've seen them.' Kieran says it simply, seemingly unmoved. Robert's rather amazed by this, but he doesn't say so. Instead, he says, cautiously, 'What did you think of them?'

'Think of them?' Kieran frowns.

'Yeah … I mean … they're weird. The mask and the cloak and … well, what he does to the rabbits…'

Kieran thinks for a bit, then says, 'I suppose you could call it a bit…'—he pulls a face, apparently hunting for the right word—'theatrical. The get-up and stuff. I think masks and cloaks are a bit silly for a grown man. But what he says is very interesting.'

Robert nods enthusiastically. 'Do you think it's true?'

'Which bit?'

'About the Dark Core. The thing about the centre of the earth being kept hot by an energy. A dark energy that thrives on bad stuff happening, and how if you commit a sacrifice it pleases the Dark Core or makes it remove the negative energy from you.'

Kieran rolls his eyes, 'That isn't what he says.'

'Isn't it?' Robert says, 'I think it is; I've literally just watched loads.'

'I mean, that's all true except the last bit you said, about removing the negative energy from you. It's not that the negative energy is, like, sucked out of you or anything, because it isn't within you in the first place. It's that the negative energy that surrounds us is kept off our path in life. In one of the videos – it's one of the later ones – he explains it like… Oh, hang on, just a sec…' He turns the laptop properly towards him and taps away at it. A few seconds later, he says, 'Come round here' and Robert moves over so both of them are sitting on the bed leaning up against the headboard facing the computer screen. 'Here we go, I think it's about … here.' Kieran moves the cursor to about a third of the way through the video he's prepared. He clicks it and after a few seconds of buffering it starts to play.

In the video, the man – The Raven, as he styles himself – isn't outdoors this time, nor is there a rabbit, or rabbit corpse, in sight. It's just him, sitting in a darkened room, the wall showing tattered wallpaper peeling off in curled folds, the bottom of it showing evidence of water damage and mould. He's sitting on a rickety old desk chair with the material coming away from the seat. The footage is black and white, as usual, and The Raven is wearing his metal mask and cloak. He starts talking to the camera, outlining things – things Robert already knows, things the two boys have just spoken about. About how the negative energy of the Dark Core is affected by the act of sacrifice. Then something happens that surprises Robert.

'The Dark Core impacts our pathways in life. Infects it with difficulties, delays, and frustrations. But what if those frustrations just … weren't there.' He raises a hand and clicks his fingers.

Suddenly the image changes. The image is no longer in black and white. It's rich and full of colour: deep browns and dark reds. It takes Robert a moment to realise that the room is different. The peeling wallpaper has vanished. The walls are now burgundy with an ornate pattern and the chair The Raven is sitting in is now a comfortable-looking armchair with upholstered bold-brown material. The Raven himself has changed clothes, too – he is no longer wearing his flowing black cloak. He is now wearing a suit, a sharply-cut, three-piece suit. He looks very smart, with a thin black tie. In fact, the only thing that remains the same is his mask, but for the first time, now the footage is in colour, Robert is able to appreciate that it's not just metal; it's golden.

'This change you see,' The Raven continues, 'goes some way to illustrate the changes you could feel in your life if you allow the energy of the Dark Core to be diverted from your path. Think of it as a pathway leading through a forest. It's strewn with broken branches. Sticks, maybe logs or tree trunks that have crashed down in storms over time. Moss might grow at the sides, the path might even become hard, maybe even impossible to see. Many, many people lose sight of their paths as the years go on, or never even knew they were there in the first place. But just imagine that you were able to clear that path. Able to make every last piece obstructing or obscuring that path disappear. That is the power of sacrifice. It frees one path, makes it possible to see once more. Makes it possible to see your way ahead. See what you have to do.' The man then reaches down and starts to untie the laces of his shoes. As he does this, the side of his face is just about visible and Robert is surprised someone so wise appears to be quite young, or at least he looks it judging by his hair and jawline. He wonders who this man is really, how he's come to do this with his life. The man takes off his shoes and sets them to one side, and then pulls off his socks and sets them on top of the black leather shoes.

'You can get in touch with your pathway immediately by simply setting your feet on the ground,' he says. He places the bare soles of his feet on the ground and the camera moves back to show that the ground appears to be a thick, soft-looking cream carpet. 'Feel the energy vibrating, feel the peace growing within you. And in your mind's eye, you will see your pathway becoming clear. Every stick and stone, every branch and leaf, every item of clutter, every sign of decay or cause of delay, everything will be cleared from your journey onward. You can picture this in your mind. You can visualise it. See the negative energy being repelled from your central path as though pulled away by a magnet. For that is the power of the Dark Core and the impact of sacrifice upon the energy it gives out.'

After viewing, the boys look at each other. Robert has many thoughts, a lot of questions, but isn't sure he should say them. He's aware Kieran is still looking at the now black computer screen with a pensive expression, and Robert doesn't want to appear foolish by saying the wrong thing. Throughout growing up, Kieran has always kept his own counsel, rarely asked the opinions or permissions of others, often content to do his own thing in his own way, quietly and determinedly. Whereas Robert likes to talk to people, to work things out, explore ideas through lively conversations – and right now, he feels like that isn't something within reach with this new topic he'd fallen into. This is different. This subject, and the things The Raven told them, is a discovery unlike anything else he'd come across.

'I don't know about you,' Kieran says, slowly, 'but I can't think of anything better than a life without obstacles. Imagine not having anything in the way of the life you'd like.'

Robert can't help roll his eyes. 'You mean not having to do schoolwork and revision.'

Kieran's expression grows stern, indicating to Robert that he may be correct but was perhaps unwise to have mentioned it. Neither of them says anything for what feels like an age, and eventually Robert can't cope with the silence any longer.

'So ... have you tried it?'

A ghost of a frown creases Kieran's forehead. 'Tried what? A sacrifice?'

Robert shakes his head, 'Of course not. The thing about trying to feel the vibrations through your feet, trying to visualise your pathway, like he said.'

Kieran shakes his head. 'Well, no, because that's something you're supposed to do after a sacrifice. There wouldn't be much point, would there? If you haven't made a sacrifice to divert the negative energy, how would you be able to feel the energy moving and clear your pathway?'

Robert feels temporarily stupid for not realising this, shifting in his reclined position. Then, leaning up and turning around on the bed to face his brother, he says, 'Why wouldn't it work? Surely the pathway is always there, whether the negative energy – the obstacles – have been cleared from it or not. I don't see why we wouldn't be able to see it. Even if our pathway isn't clear.'

Kieran appears to think about it. Then he gets up off the bed. 'OK,' he says. 'Let's try it.'

Robert is taken aback. He'd expected Kieran to dismiss the point again. He gets off the bed, feeling a small buzz of excitement and says 'So ... we have to sit down?'

Kieran nods. 'Straight-backed. Feet on the floor. Eyes closed.' He looks around his room. Robert looks around too. There's Kieran's swivel desk chair, but that doesn't feel appropriate somehow. Then Kieran says, 'Let's go downstairs.' Robert agrees, the buzz of excitement increasing.

Quietly, they make their way to the living room. The house is in darkness, though light can be seen underneath their parents' bedroom doors. The stairs creak a little as they journey downstairs, but nobody comes out to interrupt them. In the living room, Robert instantly sits in the tall-backed single-seater armchair their mother sits in when watching television, while their dad usually lounges back on the sofa. Kieran clicks a lamp on, looks around, then says, 'I think I'll get a dining room chair.' He goes into the neighbouring room and comes back with a chair from the main table. He sets it next to the armchair and sits down.

'Now we close our eyes?' Robert says, eager to get started.

Kieran, who is already barefoot, points at his brother's feet and says 'Take your socks off. That's what he did in the video.'

Robert nods and reaches down to tug off his sports socks and tosses them onto the rug. Then plants his feet on the floor in the same deliberate way as The Raven had, rubbing the rough texture of the well-worn rug with his toes.

'How are we supposed to start?' he asks in a near-whisper.

'I don't know,' Kieran says, a note of irritation creeping into his voice. 'You're the one who thinks we can do this without a sacrifice.'

Robert thinks for a bit, then says, 'Let's close our eyes and…'

'Try to feel vibrations?' Kieran says, quietly. Robert can't work out if he's making fun of him or if it's a serious suggestion.

'I know it sounds weird; we don't have to do this,' Robert says, half-standing up.

'Sit back down,' Kieran says, firmly. 'We're doing it. It might not work, but let's … let's just find out.'

So the boys sit there, in the darkness, Robert feeling stupid, wondering at what point Kieran will declare the whole thing a failure and mock him for even suggesting it.

He tries as hard as he can to feel vibrations in the soles of his feet, trying his best to picture his pathway. For a few seconds, he wonders if he can actually feel something vibrating under him, but then thinks it might be just the electrics or plumbing or some other mundane thing with a clear rational explanation. He then decides to try and picture his pathway, conjure an image as vivid and detailed as the one The Raven suggested in his speech. He amuses himself picturing a path covered in sticks and leaves for a bit, then gets too caught up on whether it should be a winding pathway amidst trees, or a straight road cutting through them, dividing a wood in two. And is it still a wood if it's divided? Wouldn't it become two woods? This isn't working how it was supposed to, he thinks, as he finds other things crowding his brain, thoughts like *I need to give mum my laundry before we go to Cornwall* and *I forgot to get my PE shorts back from Edward before the end of term, I knew I shouldn't have lent them to him* and *I hope we have roast chicken for dinner soon* and *I wonder if I'll have time to finish the final Dawson's Creek box set before we leave*. All these unrelated thoughts cluster into Robert's mind, and with each one he feels, once he has dismissed it, as though he is failing at his own mission, unable to focus his mind. Or clear it? He isn't even sure which of these is correct. Nor is he sure how long he's been sitting there when he hears it.

The heavy breathing.

And the strange sound. The strange brushing, scratching sound.

Even though he knows he is in his own home, in the living room, he's suddenly afraid. He opens his eyes and worries for a moment that he's going to find The Raven standing there in his cloak and metal-leaf mask, breathing loudly, scraping one of his weapons on the floor, ready to slay him like he'd cut open those twitching, wriggling rabbits in the video.

But there is no stranger in the room. The sound is coming from Kieran. He's still in his chair, sitting straight-backed, but his shoulders are heaving, going up and down, his chest rising and falling, a gloss of perspiration starting to show on his collarbone.

'Kieran?' Robert says, quietly, rising slowly from his armchair and going over to him. 'Are you OK?' he says, crouching down. Even though Kieran's eyelids are closed, he can see his eyes underneath moving very fast. 'Kieran!' Robert says again, starting to panic now, reaching forward and seizing his brother by the shoulders. He feels hot to the touch, his olive-tan skin which so rarely flushes looks red in the lamp-light. Robert wonders if this is what a seizure looks like, or perhaps a heart attack. He sees movement down near the floor and he realises the scraping sound Robert can hear is Kieran's feet. They're still pressed onto the floor, but brushing the carpet from side to side as though they have been shot through with an electrical current. He's about to shout for his mum or dad when Kieran's eyes fly open.

'Ahhh… God…' He grunts, breathlessly. His feet have stopped but his shoulders are still heaving. He leans forward, his hands gripping the skin of his legs, his fingers white with the pressure.

'Are you OK?' Robert asks.

'What's going on?'

Robert turns to see his dad at the doorway of the lounge.

'Nothing,' Kieran pants, 'I'm fine… I'm … fine.'

His Dad comes over to them looking worried. 'You don't look fine,' he says.

'I am, honestly,' Kieran says in between breaths. His dad helps him stand, then looks back at him again, 'He hasn't taken anything, has he? You weren't down here doing … you know … something you shouldn't… Pills or anything like that?'

'*What*? No!' Robert says.

'Then what *were* you doing?'

'We were just … hot… Came in here to cool down.'

Kieran's standing now and his breathing is starting to become normal.

'Well, he's certainly warm,' Dad says, laying a hand on Kieran's forehead. 'It's hard to tell if he's got a high temperature in this heat… Perhaps we'll take him to the bathroom. Get a cold flannel on him.'

'Should I get Mum?' Robert says.

'No!' His father and brother say together.

'She'll just call out a private all-night doctor, disagree with what he suggests, and then spend the rest of the summer making digs about the expense,' Kieran says.

'That's a bit harsh,' his father says. 'But I think any talk of doctors can wait until the morning. Let's get you to bed, then we'll see how you are tomorrow.'

They help Kieran to his room, although by the time they are climbing the stairs he is batting them away, saying that he is completely fine, he just had a dizzy moment.

Robert wants to talk to him properly about what happened, but he's aware his dad is still there. Noticing him lingering, his father frowns and says 'To bed, Robert, it's midnight. And make sure you do your teeth. Just because you're on school holidays doesn't mean you can let these things slip.'

Robert wanders off reluctantly, muttering about his dad talking to him as if he's still ten years old. Once he has brushed his teeth and undressed, he gets into bed but knows there's no chance of sleep. Not now. On his way past his room, his dad opens the door and pokes his head around. 'Just checking you'd gone to bed.'

'Well, I have,' says Robert, then adds a fake yawn, hoping it will speed up any potential interrogation.

'Kieran's funny turn… He hasn't taken anything or drunk

anything, had he? I know you both said he hasn't – I'm not accusing either of you – but he looked … weird.'

'He was telling the truth,' Robert says. 'And so was I.'

His dad nods, slowly, watching him, then, 'OK. Goodnight.' He then leaves, closing the door gently. Robert waits for his footsteps to disappear and silence descends upon the house. He gives it another ten minutes, and after hearing no more noise, leaves his room as quietly as he can and goes over to his brother's bedroom once again. There's no light showing underneath the door this time, but he's betting Kieran's still wide awake. Very quietly he turns the handle and looks inside. 'Kieran?' he whispers.

The bed is empty.

For a moment, he's afraid. He's not sure what of or why, but he feels a shiver, as though something's wrong. Something's very wrong. Then he notices the figure by the window and he almost yells out.

Kieran is standing in a shaft of moonlight, looking out into the garden. He turns and looks over at Robert, then whispers, 'Close the door.'

Robert does so, then walks over to him.

'What happened?' he asks Kieran as he comes up beside him.

Kieran doesn't reply for a moment. He isn't looking at Robert but keeps his eyes on the garden and night sky beyond the window. Then he says, 'The things I saw, Rob…'

Even though the air is still very warm and close, with no breeze coming from the open window, he suddenly feels chilly, the hairs on his arms pricking up. 'What did you see?' he asks, quietly.

Kieran turns to look at him. Then says, 'Bad things. I saw my pathway. I saw it, just like The Raven said. It was stretching out, going further than I could see. And there were things on it. I can't quite say what all of them were, I'm not sure – I just knew they were bad. Some things I could make out, like barbed wire and old branches of gnarled trees and bushes made up of thorns and needles. But there was also blood. Bits of people. Broken glass. And I was having to walk down it while every piece cut into my skin, made me bleed. Made me scream with pain. The barbed wire was ripping at my legs…' He bends down for a moment and touches his right calf as though to check there were no visible wounds. 'It felt so *real*.'

Robert doesn't know what to say to all this. It's all so different from what he experienced during the exercise – his vague, meandering thoughts, filled with distractions – that he feels totally at a loss as to how to approach such a starkly different experience. 'Even though it felt real … maybe… Could it have just been your imagination?' He says it hopefully, keen to find a rational explanation for the unsettling turn the night has taken. But Kieran shakes his head immediately. 'No. It was more than that. It really was as though I was *there*. Walking down that pathway, feeling that pain. And it made something very clear to me.'

Robert frowns. 'What?'

Kieran pauses, turning back to look out of the window. 'That I'll do anything to clear that path of all of those things – all those terrible obstacles. All that pain. I want a clear path, like The Raven said. I want it to be like walking on a plush carpet for the rest of my life, not broken glass or thorns or needles. I'll do anything, Rob. Anything.'

Chapter Twenty-One

ROBERT

2004

'Some people just don't get it,' Kieran says to Robert as he types back a reply to an internet user named WoodlandNymph1989 who suggests the concept of visualisation doesn't work without taking hallucinogenic drugs beforehand. 'The whole point is that our pathway is there, plain to see – you don't need to put chemicals into your body to see what's already there. Anyone who thinks you need to isn't doing it right.'

Both of them have been spending a lot of time exploring the various forums and chatrooms relating to the 'Dark Core Society'. These sites are cluttered by ardent followers, sceptics and cynics, curious experimenters, along with the cautious and the confused. Robert isn't sure where he and his brother fall on this spectrum. He feels naturally cautious and confused, but as the days go on, he suspects his brother is fast becoming an ardent follower. He is bold in his responses to people, keen to ask questions and even put people right when they air misapprehensions or doubts that he feels sound naïve.

'I can tell a lot of these people don't know what they're talking about, or try to make out they're more advanced in the process than they are,' he says, closing his laptop with a snap. 'They're not like me. They haven't seen what I've seen. What *we've* seen.'

Robert thinks back to his failed attempts to visualise his 'life pathway' and feels a pang of regret. Later in the evening on that first night, Robert had exaggerated to his brother what he had seen during their attempts, saying he thought he could make out the obstacles on his pathway, but they weren't clearly visible. Kieran had told him to practise and eventually he would see what he had. But Robert's practices have not led to such a revelation. On multiple occasions now, in the forty-eight hours since their first attempt in the living room, he has sat in his room on his bed, or on the edge of the bath, or in his dad's empty study. Each time he has planted his bare feet on the floor and tried to feel the vibrations of the Dark Core, but every time he's done this, his mind has wandered off or he's felt irritated from the start, frustrated with himself that it wasn't coming as easily to him.

He feels he is failing some sort of test – a test his brother is passing with flying colours – and he feels a pang of shame each time he watches Kieran fire off a very superior-sounding comment to someone on one of the forums. So Robert continues to exaggerate – exaggerations that balloon into flat-out lies. In one instance, when Kieran was present in the room during one of his attempts, he purposefully holds his own breath and clenches his teeth so that once he opens his eyes he's able to do a convincing impression of the breathless after-effects Kieran apparently experiences after his visualisation. He even mimics the movements of Kieran's feet and the rising and falling of his shoulders. He both welcomes and dreads his brother's look of approval afterwards and the excited glint in his eye when he asks Robert to explain what he saw on his pathway. After such faked efforts, Robert's descriptions have remained vague, but he's now starting to feel Kieran is becoming disappointed in his lack of specifics. He's mentioned broken glass and thorns and the things Kieran purports to have seen, but he has a feeling he needs to think up something original – some horrible obstacle on his pathway that's particular to him.

At the end of his fifth attempt at visualisation, performed outside on a bench in the garden with Kieran sitting next to him, watching, Robert opens his eyes and decides it's time for a bit of creativity.

'Er … yeah, it was … powerful and … kind of scary,' he says, feeling like a pathetic fraud but hoping he's covering it well.

'What did you see?' Kieran asks, looking eager.

'I saw … severed limbs. Lots of them. Legs and arms, with rats eating the splintered parts of bone jutting out of the jagged ends.' He feels his imagination kicking up a gear, inspired by the grisly scenes he's inventing. 'And there were, like, these canals around the pathway, either side, but they were flowing with blood, with flesh and teeth and bits of hair floating on the surface. And skin, too. Like, folds of torn skin.'

He worries this sounds ridiculous and over-the-top, like something from a trashy horror film, but Kieran nods earnestly and remarks how he has read on the forums that someone else saw body parts on their pathways.

'RavenFollowerItalia33 saw partially decomposed hearts and lungs,' he says. 'Perhaps you should message him and compare what you've both seen.'

This level of deception makes Robert carry a sad feeling. He's hoping that by throwing himself into it all, he'll eventually 'click' with all the things his brother is saying, all the peculiar experiences the followers online claim also to have had. His lies are just him buying some time to get his head around it all, he thinks to himself.

It's Robert who spots the mention of the meeting. A user named

AdminDCR3 posts a simple message in the main Dark Core Followers forum, saying:

The Raven will be speaking to followers on 26th July at 2pm in London. Reply to this post to register your interest.

He takes the computer into Kieran's room immediately.

'There's something you should see,' he says, not trying to hide his pride in his find. 'I saw this – thought it could be interesting.'

He watches Kieran's face as he takes in the info.

'What do you think?' he says hopefully. 'Sounds like it could be fun, right?' He regrets saying 'fun' as soon as it's out of his mouth – he could have chosen his words better – but Kieran nods enthusiastically. 'Yeah … that it is interesting.' He pulls the laptop towards him so he can use the touchpad. Within ten minutes, they've registered their interest and are sent an address of a house on St George's Square in Central London. Kieran searches the postcode and opens up Google Maps. 'If only we were still at school. It's so close,' he says.

'Let's ask Mum or Dad to take us,' says Robert. Kieran looks at him as if he's mad. 'Why not? We won't tell them where we're actually going, of course. Just that we want to get a head start on our homework for the summer break before we head to Cornwall where resources are limited. Sounds convincing, right?'

Kieran frowns, then nods. 'Worth a try, I suppose. I'll tell them we can get the train. I've got enough money to pay for us both if they don't want to, but I reckon Dad will take us. He'll want to go to London before we go away.'

This strikes Robert as a curious comment but he doesn't follow it up, too wrapped up in the challenge of securing their trip to London. He's certain that if he can see The Raven in person – perhaps even talk to him – he too will be able to succeed in the visualisation practices, or at least be in a better position to than he is now.

Although Robert was hopeful, he is still surprised when their parents don't put too many problems in their way.

'Sure, if it's important,' his dad replies with a shrug. 'I've got a few business connections I'd like to check up on in London anyway, so I can drive you. What library is it you need to go to?'

'The British Library,' Kieran replies.

'Yeah,' confirms Robert. 'They've got what we need.'

Kieran glances at him, suggesting his addition had been both unnecessary and pathetic, but their dad doesn't seem to notice. He has his brow furrowed as though he's thinking about something, then says, 'That's near King's Cross… Yes … yes, I can take you tomorrow. What time?'

The two boys wait until their father's car has disappeared from view before they change their direction. They had been walking towards the doors of the British Library, but now he's gone there's no need to continue with the pretence.

'Come on,' says Kieran, leading them in the direction of St Pancras Station. From there they catch the Victoria line to Pimlico. Upon alighting, Robert takes out a piece of paper containing scribbled-down road names, in case they get lost. 'We need to find Rampayne Street,' Robert says, trying to read his own spidery writing.

'We're *on* Rampayne Street already. It's this way.'

'And then we need to find Bessborough Street, and then onto Lupus Street, and then—'

'I know, come on,' says Kieran impatiently. He's doing his best to appear calm, but Robert suspects he's nervous. Or excited. It feels like they're heading towards something bigger than they've encountered so far, and with each step closer towards St George's Square, he feels as though something is hanging in the balance. As though they're in the process of leaving their old lives behind and are striking out, doing something new. Something important.

St George's Square turns out to be an exceptionally long garden square opening out onto the banks of the Thames, much larger than it had appeared from the maps they studied online. The house they need is down towards the water. Robert feels as though his heartbeat is competing with his footsteps in volume and impact. Perhaps this was a mistake, he thinks. At fourteen and sixteen they are just kids – surely the adults attending this meeting will laugh at them? Or maybe they'll turn them away. Perhaps they've gone through all of this preparation and suspense for it to end in anticlimax and disappointment.

'This is it,' Kieran says, stopping in front of one of the last houses before the line ends. They notice a black BMW stopping just ahead, where the road ends. They hadn't clocked it coming down the road behind them, so intent had they been on finding the right house. The back door opens and a suited man – around middle-age with glasses and a black tie – gets out. He says nothing to whomever is driving the car, just steps onto the pavement, walks to the very house the boys have been aiming for, and presses the doorbell. The front door opens instantly to let him in. He says something to someone just out of sight, pausing so his frame blocks their view of what might be beyond. Then the door closes again. The briefest glimpse Robert manages to get before it shuts completely shows a dark hallway with a tiled floor and movement indicating there are people at the end of it.

'Should we ring the doorbell too?' Robert asks his brother in a hushed voice. He suddenly feels hot and flaps his T-shirt, trying to cool himself. He realises with a jolt that his brother is much smarter than him, in a shirt and dark trousers. He has clearly chosen this outfit in the hope that whoever they might meet will take him seriously. Robert should have done this too, he thinks, and curses himself for not thinking of it. He looks down at his default summer outfit of shorts, T-shirt and trainers with a mixture of embarrassment and regret. And why hadn't Kieran said something? He's about to mention this – suggest that perhaps they quickly find a Debenhams or John Lewis where he might get hold of something smarter – when Kieran marches forwards, up the small step to the front door. He presses the doorbell.

Oh shit, it's happening, Robert thinks, hurrying over to stand behind his brother, that huge beating drum of his heartbeat back once more.

The door opens and a man of around thirty, dressed in a black suit with a skinny matching tie, looks at them both.

'This is a private house hosting a private meeting,' he says bluntly.

'We know,' Kieran says. 'That's why we're here.'

The man cranes his head to look around Kieran, his eyes meeting Robert's.

'How old are you both?' the man asks, his expression hard to read but his eyes narrowing.

'We're eighteen,' says Kieran without hesitation. Robert surreptitiously starts to raise himself up onto the balls of his feet, hoping to appear taller and older.

The man's eyes grow narrower still. Another man appears at his side – older and wearing a dark brown coat over his shirt, in spite of the warm weather.

'Is there a problem?' he asks the man blocking their way.

'I hope not,' Kieran says. 'We've come a very long way and have been travelling for a long time.' This isn't entirely true. Rettendon isn't exactly the Highlands.

Robert thinks the older man looks a little amused and is trying to hide a smile. 'Stand back, Hamish. Let's give our young visitors the chance to be part of our … er … little gathering this afternoon.'

The other man stands aside. Kieran hesitates just for a moment, then nods and walks in. Robert stays close behind his brother.

The interior of the house is dark, or at least the hallway is, with a row of closed doors. Any movement at the end of the corridor that Robert spotted from the street seems to have passed through. Where to, though, remains a mystery. The younger man, Hamish, shows the boys through a door on the right-hand side. Inside is a desk and upon the desk is a sheet of paper.

'Sign this,' Hamish says.

Robert looks down at the sheet of paper. Kieran appears to have scanned it and is already reaching for the dark red fountain pen at the edge of the table, but Robert pulls the paper towards him and says, 'Wait a moment.'

'It's fine,' Kieran says. 'Just sign it.'

'Shouldn't I read it first?' Robert hisses. 'Dad says you should never sign something without reading it. He says—'

'Well, Dad's over in Bloomsbury with one of his women, so forgive me if I don't always go with his way of doing things,' Kieran snaps back.

Robert stares at him, unable to hide his astonishment. 'What did you say?'

'Is there a problem here?' says Hamish from behind them.

'No problem,' Kieran says, offering the man a smile, then turning back to Robert. 'Rob, just sign the sheet of paper.'

Robert tries to push what his brother has just said to the back of his mind, if only temporarily, and concentrate on the words on the page before him. He looks at each one, forcing himself to take them in.

MEETING DECLARATION: WESTMINSTER, LONDON,
26 JULY 2004

AS A FOLLOWER OF THE DARK CORE TRUTH
COLLECTIVE, I PROMISE TO HOLD CLOSE WHAT I SEE
HERE TODAY, BE SELECTIVE IN WHO I DISCUSS THE
GROUP'S BELIEFS, AIMS AND PRACTICES WITH, AND
AVOID ANY ACTION THAT MAY RESULT IN ADVERSE
COMPLICATIONS BEFALLING THE GROUP OR ANY OF ITS
MEMBERS.

PRINT NAME:_____
SIGNED_____

Robert frowns at the page. There's something about the odd phrasing of the sentences that feels a bit off to him – clunky and opaque, as if the form is avoiding spelling out what it really wants to say. *May result in adverse complications…* Does that mean something might happen here today that people might want to tell others about – and not in a good way? Report to the police, even?

'Just sign it,' Kieran hisses in Robert's ear.

He's taking too long, he knows it.

'If I do,' Robert says, 'you promise you'll tell me about Dad. About what you just said.'

'Christ, this is the wrong place and the wrong time,' Kieran says, barely audible, his teeth gritted. He gives Robert a look of quiet fury. Eventually, Robert nods and reaches for the pen and signs the paper.

Kieran turns back around to the man in the room.

'We've done it,' he says.

Hamish nods. 'Good. I'm going to need any mobile phones you may have about your person.'

Kieran pauses for a second. Then he takes out his Nokia and hands it over.

'You too,' the man says.

Robert doesn't like the idea of giving up his phone but doesn't feel he can object after Kieran surrendered his so easily.

'You're going to have to submit yourself to a search,' Hamish says. Something about the boys' expressions seems to make him smile. 'Don't worry,' he says. 'No rubber gloves are involved or anything too major, just your arms out at your side.'

Robert frowns. 'Why…?'

'I need to make sure you don't have any covert recording devices.'

Kieran steps forward and raises his arms, holding them outwards from his sides, as one would at an airport. Hamish runs his hands along him, pausing to look around the collar of his shirt, then moves down to his trousers.

'You're all fine,' Hamish says, then rounds on Robert. 'Now you.'

Robert goes through the same search, thinking how weird it feels to have this stranger running his hands on him, looking down his T-shirt, feeling all over him, presumably on the lookout for wires taped to his skin or a small Dictaphone hidden in his pockets. No such offending items are found, and at last, they seem to be cleared.

'Follow me.'

The boys are led back into the corridor. More people are entering at the same time, shown in by another suited man. The two new arrivals are a man and a woman, young but not as young as Kieran and Robert, perhaps in their twenties. They look like students, Robert thinks, catching the young man's eye as they're shown into the room they've just left, presumably to sign fresh copies of the declaration form.

Hamish opens the door at the far end of the hallway and says, 'Go in and take a seat.'

They do as they're told. The room appears to be a large dining room, or perhaps a function room, but with no large table, just rows of chairs lined up facing the wall on the right-hand side. There is a small table, or desk perhaps, similar to the piece of furniture they used to sign the form in the other room. Daylight streams in from tall windows that overlook a very small garden, with blocks of flats visible beyond. Robert's surprised – even though the little room they came from hadn't been shrouded in darkness, he had presumed the area destined for the meeting would be atmospheric, theatrical even, far closer to the aesthetic and vibe of the videos featuring The Raven.

The lines of chairs are only about a third full, with a lot of space still at the front, and the boys take their seats on the front row. 'Maybe we should go at the back, in case they realise we're … you know … not eighteen.'

'Shut up,' Kieran hisses. 'Nobody cares we're underage. They're not about to phone Dad and tell on us, or report us to the police. But you don't need to shout about it.'

'I wasn't shouting,' Robert says, then can't help thinking, *underage for what?*

While his imagination is starting to race, wondering not for the first time what he's got himself into, his attention is diverted by the reference to their father. 'Tell me what you meant about Dad. About him having a woman.'

Kieran's expression grows even more surly. 'I shouldn't have mentioned it.'

'Well, you did,' Robert says. 'You think Dad's having an *affair*?'

Kieran looks around him, seemingly embarrassed. There's a man at the far end of their row, and two older gentlemen behind them having a hushed conversation of their own. Robert notices the two student-looking types walking in and heading for seats on the far-left of the room near the windows.

Robert's about to prompt Kieran for an answer when a voice says, 'Excuse me, boys, but I wondered if I may sit with you?'

It belongs to the older man in the brown coat who convinced the man at the door to let them in. Up close, Robert finds it difficult to determine his age. He could be anything from forty-five to a well-preserved sixty-five – it is impossible to tell. His hair is flecked with grey, but there's still a striking handsomeness to him. There is something unusual about his voice, too. A lyrical, calming quality, slightly accented, that makes Robert feel both relaxed and alert at the same time. Robert opens his mouth to answer him, but Kieran gets there first.

'Yeah, sure,' he says, not smiling exactly, but nodding at the man in a familiar way as though trying to make out they're already firm acquaintances. Robert recognises his brother's attempts to appear more grown-up than he is, although Robert admits that Kieran's much better at it than he is. He is blurring the lines between childhood and adulthood, already very tall and muscled. Robert suddenly feels very small and weedy in comparison and wonders if this man is about to tell them that this meeting isn't for teenagers and it's been decided they both must leave after all.

But the man doesn't do this. He smiles at them, his dark eyes twinkling, focusing first on Kieran and then Robert.

'Is this your first meeting?' he asks quietly.

They nod. 'Yes, we couldn't make the others, but this one was fairly local,' Kieran says. If the man notices this contradicts what he told Hamish at the door, he doesn't say. He just nods slowly, watching him.

'Do you work here?' Robert asks.

'In a sense,' the man replies. 'In a sense.'

'Do you know The Raven?' asks Kieran. His attempts to appear grown-up and relaxed are betrayed by a quiver of excitement in his voice. Robert looks quickly at the man. His smile remains and he inclines his head.

'Yes, I do.'

Robert looks around, then leans closer and half whispers, 'Where is he? What's… What's he going to say to us?'

The man raises an eyebrow. 'Well, I don't want to spoil the surprise. Let's just say I think you boys will find this an afternoon to remember.'

As though on cue, darkness descends. One moment the room is light and the next it's plunged into blackness. Robert looks over and sees black drapes being pulled across the windows, almost entirely blocking out the daylight. Then in front of them, there are sparks and the sound of matches being struck, followed by three lit candles, which are carried by unseen helpers and placed on small tables around the edge of the room.

This is more like the kind of thing Robert expected, and to see it starting to become real in front of him – especially the creaking door in the centre of the wall before them – sends a shiver down the back of his neck.

'Prepare yourselves,' the man next to them says very quietly in the darkness. Robert wonders if he's enjoying unsettling them or if there really is something coming for which they should brace themselves.

From the darkness beyond the doorway, Robert sees movement. Then *he* walks in. The Raven. He wears his metal mask with the ornate golden leaves glinting in the candlelight. He isn't wearing the black cloak but Robert recognises the three-piece suit as the one he wore in the video about pathway visualisation. He doesn't say anything as he walks in and places two more candles on the small table in front of him. Then he takes one of the two chairs from the table and pulls it out, moves it forwards so he's nearer his audience, then sits down.

'Hello and welcome,' he says. Robert finds it strange hearing this voice he feels he knows so well now talking to them, barely two metres from him, right here in real life. It feels as if he has fallen into a TV show and is sitting in front of a well-known fictional character. It gives him a giddy, confused feeling, as though reality and fantasy are swirling together in an uneasy, intoxicating mixture.

'We are going to start with a pathway visualisation,' he says. With his right hand, he gestures to the floor and Robert notices he is barefoot.

'If you would like to participate in this visualisation, please remove any footwear and lay your feet upon the carpet.'

Robert glances at Kieran and sees he is already bent forwards and unlacing his brogues. Robert hurries to pull off his trainers and his socks. He's interested to see the man sitting with them doesn't move, apparently choosing not to participate.

The Raven then talks them through the pathway visualisation they are familiar with from the videos. He says they should feel the vibrations of the Dark Core through the soles of their feet. Robert wants to look behind him to see what the other attendees are doing but doesn't want to draw attention to himself so he keeps facing forwards as The Raven starts to guide their visualisation. He tells them to picture their pathway, picture the obstacles and see the details as if they are there to see in front of them. Robert tries, he really does, but just like at home he feels like he's making details up. He wants to tell Kieran that all this time his attempts at visualisation haven't exactly been successful. And this, the main reason he wanted to come, isn't working out how he hoped.

'See each obstacle. Focus on every little detail, for each detail is particular to you. And then imagine that pathway cleared. Imagine that pathway opening and widening so that you can walk down it free from delay or irritation or consequence.' Then a lower, quieter note creeps into The Raven's voice. 'Today, everyone will have the opportunity to experience secondary effects from an act in this room. An event that may well affect the pathways of those watching.' He claps his hands suddenly. Robert jumps and hears others intake their breath after the sudden sound. 'Open your eyes,' The Raven says, although Robert suspects many eyes opened after the clap. His certainly did.

'This isn't the end of the meeting,' The Raven says, standing up. 'This is only just the beginning of what we're here to do today.'

The door behind him hasn't been closed. It has remained open during the visualisation, though whatever room lies beyond is in darkness. But now, in the distance, a flame becomes visible, getting nearer. It's a woman holding a candle. Young, probably in her early twenties, dressed in what looks like a white flowing nightdress of the kind women wear in historical dramas or films.

'This is Collette,' The Raven says, stepping aside to let the woman pass and gesturing with his hand to the other chair by the table.

'Hello,' says the young woman, briefly looking around the room, then looking back to the masked man offering her a seat. She's smiling but looks a little afraid and disconcerted. her eyes dart about and the hand carrying the candle shakes slightly as she sets it down.

'Collette has agreed to join me in a séance.'

On the table is a small rectangular shape Robert presumes is a mat. The Raven starts to unfold it, and quickly it becomes clear it isn't a mat, but a board. The Raven reaches into his pocket and pulls out an object – a stone, a small pebble perhaps – and places it in its centre.

'Collette, are you ready?'

The woman nods hesitantly. Her smile is fading fast and she now looks worried. Or afraid. She glances around again, as though she isn't sure about what she's about to experience. Not entirely sure what she has agreed to.

'Are you ready to experience the vibrations of the Dark Core through the spirit world? If you are, hold out your hand.'

The woman nods and speaks this time. 'Yes. I... I am.' Her voice is small, probably only audible to Robert as he's so close in the front row. He gets a sudden, overwhelming feeling to stand up and help the woman, to tell her she doesn't have to go through with this if she doesn't want to. But then she offers out her hand and The Raven takes it and lays it on the stone in the centre.

'Close your eyes,' The Raven says.

She obeys.

Then The Raven stands and starts to pace slowly behind her. 'I am going to guide you through a visualisation, Collette. A very special visualisation that will allow you to gain access to the spirit world. The vibrations will become focused around the stone and I want you to keep your hand there no matter how strong the feeling becomes.'

Collette inclines her head to show she understands.

'Stay very ... very ... still...' The Raven says, dropping his voice even lower.

There's silence in the room – a silence that feels so tense. Everyone is waiting. Everyone is watching the woman in the flowing white nightdress. Expecting something to happen.

And something does happen.

Calmly and slowly, The Raven takes another item out of his pocket. And as it glints in the candlelight, he knows where he's seen it before.

It's the knife. The knife The Raven uses in his videos, the ones in which he takes a rabbit out of its little hutch. Robert realises this a second before it happens. He realises what they're actually watching. This isn't a séance at all. This woman isn't here to contact the dead. She's about to join them. She *is* the rabbit. And all they can do is watch as The Raven steps closer behind her.

'Keep your eyes closed,' The Raven whispers to her through his mask.

Then he leans forward.

There's a gasp and then a scream. A scream that's muffled by his hand as he clasps her mouth with one hand and pulls the blade across her throat with the other.

The blood.

Robert's never seen so much blood. It cascades down her white clothing, pouring down her front, splashing onto the table as she gargles and chokes. The Raven's movements become more violent as he cuts and saws at her neck until eventually the twitching and jerking of the legs stops and she goes limp in his arms, her head lolling forwards.

There could be silence in the room, or there could be a roaring, thunderous applause, or a thousand screams. Any of these make sense to Robert in that moment. He isn't sure what is the truth. He just knows that he feels shocked and panicked and confused and he isn't sure what he should do. He also knows his brother doesn't look shocked or panicked or confused about what he should do. There's a chance, of course, that he looked shocked when the act of violence began, had Robert looked at him at that moment. But now, as the body lies dripping blood on the floor, Robert turns to look at his brother and sees him looking not horrified or stunned by what's just happened.

He looks impressed.

Mesmerised.

Excited.

Chapter Twenty-Two

ROBERT

2004

'This is no spirit world. There is no afterlife.'

The Raven is talking again. His voice is so strong and terrifying that Robert starts to feel his hands shake. 'Collette was foolish enough to think that she would be contacting the dead this afternoon. But it is only this life that matters. Once our soul leaves our body after death, it's gone. Nothing matters other than being alive. And by sacrificing the life of another, a life so infested by such deluded, trivial beliefs, we send vibrations down to the Dark Core of our world and help clear the pathway before us.'

Robert looks around him. Some audience members look shocked; others seem delighted. At least two or three are clapping their hands. One of the young men who looks like a student is actually whooping and calling out 'YES!' Many others are nodding their heads, grinning, or with their arms stretched out, as though they're able to touch some invisible energy or force coming off the brutal scene. All of it looks completely insane, Robert thinks. Like a bad dream. The most disorienting, unsettling nightmare of his life. And it's real. It's all real.

He isn't sure if it's the sight of the corpse being lifted up by two suited men behind The Raven that makes him run, or if it's his brother's expression – that entranced, alarming glint in his eye, still clearly visible on his face. Whatever it is, he knows he needs to get out.

Standing up suddenly and feeling himself swaying, as though the ground is moving, he says weakly, 'We need to leave this place. Now.'

He then stumbles off towards the door. For one terrible moment, he wonders whether he'll find it locked and turn around to see The Raven standing behind him, announcing that he will be the next sacrifice. Or perhaps the whole audience will have suddenly donned golden masks and be closing in on him, ready to drag him screaming back to his seat. But no such thing occurs. The door opens and he finds his route through the hallway unobstructed. He opens the front door and is out on the street, taking greedy gulps of the warm London air as though it's the freshest and most revitalising oxygen he's ever breathed in.

The silence is wonderful. No, actually, not silence, but rather sirens and car horns and conversation from a couple coming out of the garden in the middle of the square and a man calling to his dog. But all of it is comfortingly normal. The reassuring effect of it all is like an anaesthetic to the rush of horror he felt back there in the house. Then there's another sound added to the mixture, much closer this time, and not quite as comforting.

'You made us look pathetic, back there.'

He turns to see Kieran standing on the small step in front of the door, his jaw jutting out as it always does when he's angry.

'You saw what they did,' Robert says. 'You saw what they did to that poor woman. How can you stand there so calmly?' He raises a hand to his head. He isn't sure if he wants to scream or cry or hit something – perhaps all three, and the something would be his brother.

'I'm not sure why you're so surprised. That was a sacrifice. What did you think he was going to do? What did you think we travelled here to see? Another rabbit being killed?'

Robert can't believe what Kieran's saying. His calm – or pretence of calm – is both repulsive and maddening to him.

Kieran walks up close to him. 'Just pretend, for a moment, that you're not, I don't know, restricted.'

Robert frowns. 'Restricted?'

'Yeah. Restricted by this whole, "Oh isn't violence awful" business that we're told to believe. We are so … so'—he looks up for a moment as though the answer might be written in the clouds—'so lucky. We're so lucky that we're being set free, Rob. We don't have to be boring and go through all that predictable stuff. We know what that was for and we need to get used to seeing moments like that as a necessary step towards what we're trying to achieve. That's what The Raven just showed us. Freedom.'

Although he's not entirely sure what he's going to say in response to this, Robert is just opening his mouth to respond when he sees movement behind Kieran's shoulder.

'Excuse me,' the man says, stepping down from the doorway and onto the pavement. 'But I thought you might like these.'

It's the man in the brown coat who had been sitting next to them. And he is holding a pair of grey trainers with red Nike ticks on the side, white socks sticking out the top of them. Robert looks down at his feet, surprised he hasn't noticed he's been barefoot this whole time.

'Oh, er … thanks,' Robert says, stepping forwards and reaching out to take his shoes.

The man smiles, then reaches into his coat pocket and pulls out two phones. 'And these?'

They take their devices. The man waits in silence for a moment while Robert pulls on his socks and shoes, then says, 'I was concerned you're both disturbed by what you have seen today.'

'We're not disturbed,' Kieran says immediately. 'My brother just ... needed some air.'

His smile widens, clearly aware Kieran's not being entirely truthful. Then he uses his right hand to beckon and says quietly, 'Come over here.' He looks behind him, directing his gaze down over the railings to the steps leading down to the entrance to the underground basement below.

Robert glances at Kieran. His brother steps forwards and Robert follows, and both of them peer over the railings to the ground at the bottom of the steps.

A young man is standing in the doorway of the basement entrance to the property. He has money in his hand and appears to be putting it into an envelope. 'Three hundred, as agreed,' he says. He holds it out and the package is taken by someone just out of sight, still inside the house. Then he steps aside and someone comes into view. Robert can't help but gasp.

It is a woman. Young, blonde-haired, smiling.

'Yeah, that's right,' she says, tucking the envelope into a small black handbag. It's her. The woman they just saw being sacrificed. Murdered. She's brushing something around her neck and jaw – either a tissue or a wet wipe perhaps – and she's no longer wearing the white nightdress. Now she's in a baggy T-shirt and denim shorts.

'That blood stuff gets everywhere,' she mutters, holding out the wet wipe to Hamish.

He takes it, not looking too impressed, but doesn't object, then nods at her and says, 'Until next time then.' She smiles and begins to climb the basement steps.

The boys come away from the railings before she can see them. The man in the brown coat is still standing there, watching their faces. Robert can see Kieran is surprised too, and he thinks he can see disappointment in his eyes. Robert hears the gate of the basement stairs make a metallic squeak as the woman comes through it. She doesn't say anything to them or seem particularly interested in their presence, too busy taking out a phone from her bag and starting to press at its buttons. She walks along the last part of St George's Square and onto the road towards the street overlooking the Thames, turns left and disappears out of sight.

'I think,' the smiling man says, 'you boys could do with a drink.'

Robert takes his eyes off the road where the woman was seconds before and looks at the man.

'A drink?'

He nods. 'Would you like to accompany me to a nearby pub? Then we can have a little talk. I'm very interested to hear what you both think of the day's events and what you hope to take away from our little gathering today. Will you come with me?'

For the first time since arriving, Robert notices his brother hesitating. Perhaps he's still dazed by finding out that the big, bloody moment of violence was a sham. A trick. An illusion. He'd had the wool pulled over his eyes and had been made to look foolish. Robert turns back to the man and decides to speak up first. 'Will a pub let us in? Surely we can't, you know, *drink* drink?'

The repetition of the two words sounds childish after he's said it. The man lets out a little laugh, although it sounds more like a brief, polite cough.

'Well, you are both eighteen. Right?' he says, a knowing smile on his lips.

The boys accompany the man to a small pub on the corner of a street, only a few roads away. As they go through the door, Robert notices the barman look over and give their chaperone a nod. He buys them both a cider without asking what they would like. No objection is voiced by the man behind the bar, nor does the man order anything for himself. The two bottles are placed on the table they've settled at in the corner of the mostly empty pub. There's a dusty, old quality to the establishment and the table feels sticky under Robert's hands.

Kieran takes one of the cider bottles, lifts it to his mouth and drinks deeply. His bold movements and definite actions suggest to Robert he's regaining his sense of equilibrium. How strange it is, he thinks, that his brother should be unsettled now to discover a woman is alive, instead of when he thought he had seen her being killed.

'Why fake it?' Kieran says once he's swallowed his mouthful. There's a note of irritation in his voice. Anger, even.

The man looks at him, his eyes now narrowed, as if he's deciding how much to tell them. Then he says, 'Logistics. It's very dull, really.'

Robert takes up his own drink and has a sip. The man continues to watch them.

'Logistics?' Robert says after he's swallowed. 'Because … because of legal issues. That sort of thing.'

The man pauses a second, then nods. 'Yes. It's because of that. We live in a difficult period in history where our society has never been more obsessed with rules and laws and what people can and can't do.' His voice is quiet, only a few notches above a whisper, but there is a hypnotic quality to it. Even more so than that of The Raven, perhaps.

Kieran straightens up. 'I don't see that as a reason to fake it. Surely you have people who could … sort things out?'

The man smiles. 'Yes, there are ways. But we try to meet followers all around the country and if we were to leave a trail of dead bodies across England, The Raven's attempts to spread his message would be … interrupted. So I ask you to forgive him for having to rely on a degree of theatrics.'

Kieran opens his mouth, perhaps to challenge this further, but Robert gets in first with another question on his mind.

'How well do you know him? The Raven?'

The man raises his eyebrows. It seems he wasn't expecting to be asked this.

'I've known him all his life. I knew his mother. I was present when he was conceived, during a ritualistic sacrifice on a warm spring night in a large country house in Oxfordshire, about twenty-five years ago. It seems apt that he has chosen to continue in his father's footsteps and embrace the impact and nourishing energy that sacrificial violence can bring to the human soul. His father disappeared before he was born, but his mother told him stories. Stories of the things his father used to do. Stories that had a great effect on him. I've stayed present in his life, guiding his way. I am impressed with the following he's built up using new technology, like videos and chatrooms on the World Wide Web. So I try to be supportive when he hosts events like today's meeting.'

This was a lot of information for the boys to digest and Robert tries to unpick it all in his mind. 'You were there when he was born?'

Kieran tuts. 'Conceived, he said. Not born.'

Robert realises his mistake. 'Oh … oh I see.'

The man looks amused. 'It may seem shocking to someone as young as you, but such a thing isn't unusual in ritualistic ceremonies. You could say it's more common than the act of violence you saw – or thought you saw – earlier today. And the environment where it happened was a very relaxed, experimental one. We had taken over the country house we were in, and aside from a rather troublesome housekeeper, we more or less had the run of the place. But that was a different time. Things are different now. The Raven prefers a more ordered and established approach. He likes simplicity, rather than, um … group participation. He likes to be the one spreading the message so people can go forth and find their own route along their own pathway. He wants them to use the tools he has taught them in ways they think best.'

Kieran nods, as though all this is starting to make sense to him. Robert, however, has more questions.

'What's his name? His *real* name.'

The man shakes his head. 'If you mean the name he was given at birth, that's not something I'm prepared to say.'

Robert pauses, then changes tack. 'OK, what's your name then?'

To his surprise, the man laughs at this. 'My name? Well, that is also a difficult question. I have had more than one name during my lifetime. But I think you two boys can call me Gary.'

This isn't what Robert expects. He'd think someone so closely connected to a man called The Raven would have an equally enigmatic moniker, especially if it's true that he's a father figure to the young man. Something like The Eagle or The Elder or The Master would feel more appropriate. Gary is way too, well, normal.

'You look surprised. I don't blame you. It's not a name I particularly like, and I confess I usually go by another, but I think it's the best one to offer you.'

Robert sees Kieran looking annoyed. 'If you normally go by another, why are we getting special treatment? Do you not trust us or something, just because we're young?'

The man appears to think about this for a moment. 'That's a fair point. All right then, you can call me Argento. That's the name the people close to me call me. I'm not sure, however, if our acquaintance will last long. I think it's unlikely we'll ever meet again after this pleasant little drink on a sunny afternoon. And I dare say I will not be the most memorable thing about today for you both. I hope not, anyway.'

They drink their ciders in silence for a minute or two. Then Argento speaks again, leaning forwards, his voice even quieter.

'The question I would like to ask you both is this: what will you do with your experience? What will you do from this moment on when you've witnessed a very small and brief sample of the power that sacrifice can bring? You've probably guessed that what happened today won't have an impact on your pathways through life. It would need to be you wielding the blade and taking a life, and as you have seen, no actual life was taken today. But our hope is that meetings like the one you attended will inspire our followers. Give them the mental tools and inner bravery to act. So what paths are you going to carve out in life? Think of today as a dress rehearsal. What you do next won't be a performance, it will be real.'

Chapter Twenty-Three

KIERAN

2004

Kieran is aware his younger brother is shocked by the day's events. As they get onto the Tube at Pimlico station and take their seats, heading back to St Pancras, he watches Robert looking about him nervously. He looks pale – even more pale than usual – and he is juddering his right leg; a habit he's always had whenever he's nervous. Kieran reaches out and puts a hand on his knee, stopping the movement. Robert looks at him as though he's surprised to find his brother sitting next to him. Perhaps he has been so caught up in his thoughts that he's forgotten where he is and who he's with.

'You all right?' Kieran asks.

He wonders for a second if Robert's about to cry. His eyes look suddenly very red, like they might fill with tears at any moment. But no tears fall. He just looks at Kieran, then faces straight ahead at an elderly lady with a John Lewis shopping bag.

'Yeah,' he says eventually. 'Strange day.'

Kieran finds himself smiling.

'Yes,' he says, letting out a short laugh. 'Yes, it's been a strange day.'

Their meeting with the mysterious man came to an end relatively quickly. After suggesting they continue to embed The Raven's teachings into their lives, he looked at his watch and said he would need to leave them. He told them to finish their ciders and stay in the pub as long as they liked. They did as he said, then headed for the Underground, the alcohol making Kieran feel much calmer than he did when he'd walked into the pub.

They don't speak about the afternoon's activities when they alight at St Pancras and walk to the British Library. Nor do they discuss what they will tell their father when he questions them about the important homework they've allegedly been researching. Luckily for them, when their dad picks them up, he seems to be in an odd mood, asking if they had a good trip but not making any detailed enquiries. He drives them back home in near silence and as London starts to turn into Essex, Kieran briefly wonders what his father has been getting up to during his 'work meeting'. Whilst it's unlikely to have been up to anything anywhere near as unusual as his boys' activities, Kieran would bet it's not something he'd like to talk about in a hurry.

As the next couple of days pass and the family starts to prepare for their holiday, Kieran reconciles his thoughts and doubts about what happened in London. He thinks about what Argento told them in the pub. About how an element of theatrics – fakery, if he's blunt about it – is necessary if they want to keep the movement going. At first, when he saw that woman's throat cut, he thought he'd witnessed the moment the life left her eyes. He thought he'd seen a moment so extreme that it had unlocked something within him. Something he didn't previously know was there. And that feeling has continued since the meeting, despite the discovery about the theatrics. He expected the reveal to cause an unravelling of his commitment, but so far, no such a thing has occurred. Because he's just so sure. He's sure the overall message of the core is sincere. And he knows he believes in it, truly and wholeheartedly.

But when it comes to Robert, he isn't so certain.

The night before they are due to travel to Cornwall, he pays a visit to his younger brother once their parents have retired to their rooms for the night. Seeing the light on under Robert's door, he quietly opens it, ignoring his own principles about knocking, and heads inside before his brother has time to look up from the book he's reading.

'We haven't really spoken about London,' Kieran says, deciding to dive in straight away and tackle the subject head-on. 'I'm worried it's given you doubts.'

Robert looks at him for a few seconds, then sets down his book. 'Doubts about what?'

'You know … everything we've learnt. What… What we might be able to do with what we've learnt.'

Robert looks at the floor for a bit, then says, 'Were you hoping…? Were you *planning* … for us to do anything with what we've learned?'

Kieran frowns. 'Not planning … well, not exactly. But … don't you want to feel it again? Like, really *feel* it?'

Robert looks back at his brother and shakes his head. 'I was scared. I know you'll probably be disappointed to hear it, but I can't lie, I was scared when he killed that woman. Or looked like he was killing her. And I was relieved when I found out he hadn't actually done it.'

Kieran nods and steps closer to his brother. 'I can understand that, I can, but the whole point is that the act has to be extreme, has to be something extraordinary for it to unleash enough energy to shift our pathway. If it wasn't a big, momentous act, it wouldn't do anything, or wouldn't be enough to keep our pathways clear.'

Kieran is keeping his voice quiet, but he's unable to keep the passion from it. This itself excites him. He's never been one to feel enthusiastic or strongly about anything much. For all his life, school has bored him. Learning has seemed monotonous and dull, whereas now there is something that feels fresh and strange and dangerous and new and he wishes Robert could see that too. But he recognises his younger brother's inability to meet his eye as a bad sign. It's a sign he's losing faith, a sign he's withdrawing from him and this shared interest they've had together, albeit briefly.

'Forget it,' he says, standing up abruptly. 'I was wrong.'

Robert turns quickly. 'Wrong? Wrong about … about The Raven and the Dark Core?'

'No, wrong about *you*,' Kieran snaps. 'I should have known you wouldn't have been able to hack it. I should have known in the end it would fall to me to go forwards alone.'

'Go *forwards*?' Robert blinks. 'Go forwards with what?'

'I don't know yet,' Kieran says, heading for the door. 'But let's just say I'm unsurprised I'll be doing whatever it is alone. I can never count on you to step up, can I? You're too timid, Rob. Too eager to please everyone else that you're scared to set out and take control of your own path. I think I always knew it. I'm just disappointed to be proved right.'

He leaves the room. He doesn't turn to look at his brother's expression, though he knows he would look hurt. Upset. Betrayed. He doesn't like having to say these things, but honestly, what choice is Robert giving him? Sometimes people need a little push.

The next day, Robert doesn't speak to him. He isn't sure if he's receiving the silent treatment, or if his brother just needs space to think and to digest what Kieran's said and, hopefully, reassess his position on things. He very much hopes it's the latter, so he remains polite and civil towards Robert as they pack the car with their bags and obey their mother's instructions about fetching items and tidying things up before they leave. But he doesn't corner him or force him into any discussions. He thinks pushing Robert into anything now would be overkill. He's said what he needed to say and now he has to wait for the words to take effect.

While they sit in the back of the car during the long ride to Cornwall, Kieran tries to do some visualisations. He purposefully wore only slip-on sandals so he could take them off easily during the journey, then lie back and attempt to focus. This proves difficult, however, as the sound of his mother and father bickering about motorway turn-offs and when to stop for food becomes such a frequent intrusion that the process of clearing his mind is impossible. Every time he glances over at Robert, he sees him staring out of the window, his thick headphones on, his Walkman whirring away, an open box of *Harry Potter and the Order of the Phoenix* cassettes next to him. Something about this irritates Kieran. Although Robert's fourteen, there are elements about him that Kieran feels would be more at home with a ten-year-old. He takes out his own entertainment from his bag – a new iPod Mini he'd saved up for – and plugs in the white earbuds, feeling as though Robert might need some attention from him over the summer. Not just on the subject of the Dark Core and his wavering beliefs, but in terms of growing up, becoming less of a child and more of a man.

The last stretch of their journey, as the day edges into the late afternoon, is filled with the countryside. Their mother, well aware the boys are buried in their audio content, starts pointing things out to them, like unusual buildings, quaint villages or rolling farmland.

Whenever they grunt in acknowledgement, she tells them they should show more interest in the world around them, and whenever they ignore her – accidentally or otherwise – she starts raging about the evils of headphones and how she wouldn't have dreamed of plugging herself away as a child. She says she's very tempted to ban electrical devices on long journeys and gets into a bit of a terse exchange with Robert about this, who has moved on to his *Greek Myths* cassettes.

'Little Robby can't be without his story tapes,' Kieran says, aware he sounds snide but not caring.

Robert turns to frown at Kieran. 'Leave me alone,' he says in a small voice.

'Yeah, don't make fun of your brother, Kieran,' his father says.

'I think Robert needs to start standing up for himself,' comments his mother in a low voice. Kieran sees her eyes glance at them both in her mirror.

After a few seconds of silence, Robert mumbles, 'They're audiobooks. Not *story tapes*.'

His mother laughs. 'Well, consider us all floored by that riposte.'

This makes even Kieran feel uncomfortable. Although no stranger to jibes towards his brother, he isn't sure he likes it when his mother joins in.

His dad seems unsettled as well, since he says, 'You enjoy what you enjoy, Rob. Don't make any apologies for that.'

This doesn't stop his wife, though, from going deeper into one of her favourite subjects of complaint: the youth of today.

'I fear the western world is bringing up a generation of overstimulated young minds. Over-parented, too. Coddled. Vaccinated up to the eyeballs for any and every unlikely virus or infection, practically talked into having allergies. Any excuse to cram their bathroom cabinets with a buffet of pills which parents now dole out to their offspring like Smarties. They have to be entertained at every second of the day through computers and devices and the internet. I heard that very soon most people will be accessing the web from their mobiles. How very depressing.'

Kieran begins to tune out his mother's voice. He looks instead at the road leading to Hill Valley, the large trees offering the long road a tunnel of shade. Kieran finds it a relief, welcoming the cool effect of the sudden lack of sunlight, even if temporarily.

'You'll be able to go for walks and runs around here,' their father says. 'Maybe meet up with the children at some of these houses.' He nods to their left where, through the trees, a cluster of large properties are nestled.

'I don't think we'll be hanging out with any *children*,' Kieran tuts.

'Or there might be young people down in the nearby village,' his dad continues, unfazed. 'There's a relatively new housing estate around there. Must be some kids for you both to talk to and hang around with.'

Kieran's about to reply with a grunt when his mother cuts in.

'I don't think we want to encourage our sons to go out of their way to befriend undesirable types from nearby housing estates,' she says icily as she steers the car around the bend, the country path becoming more winding as it goes on. 'I also don't like phrases such as "hanging out" and "hanging around". It makes me think of youths smoking near bus stops in the rain with nothing to do.'

'That's a bit hypocritical,' Kieran says. 'You smoked up until about five minutes ago.' This isn't true. His mother stopped smoking properly three years previously, although Kieran knows she occasionally has what she called 'a stress cigarette' whenever something difficult occurs with her work.

'Yes, but I didn't do it at bus stops, and certainly not in the rain,' she says evenly. 'And that makes all the difference.'

Robert glances over at Kieran, a ghost of a smile on his face, then turns back to the window. Kieran's encouraged by the action and sees it as a potential thaw between them, in spite of his ill-advised dig towards his younger brother earlier.

The car slows and his mother brings it to a halt outside some iron gates. 'Get out and open those, will you,' she says commandingly, without specifying who she's talking to. He stays where he is until his dad gets out of the car with a sigh. They watch him struggle with the gates until his mother tuts and says, 'Go and help your father, Kieran.'

Between the two of them, Kieran and his dad get the gates open and they drive through and then up to an impressively large lodge house.

'It's very nice, isn't it?' his dad says. 'Very nice.'

'Yes, you were so clever in picking it,' says his mum as she parks the car neatly outside to the left of the front door. As is often the case, it isn't clear if her words of praise are meant sincerely or sarcastically.

Inside, there is a fresh scent of pine mixed with a comfortingly spicy smell. Kieran doesn't know enough about trees or associated scents to be sure if it's coming from the wood of which the lodge is made, or the reed diffuser placed on a unit of drawers in the living room area. The kitchen is separated from the hallway by a wall with a wide doorway, and along with the living room, there is a smaller room to its left with bookcases that resemble a small, if understocked, library.

'Head upstairs and choose your rooms, boys,' their father says. Kieran heads for the stairs without waiting for Robert to follow.

'Not the master bedroom, though,' came his mother's shout from the kitchen area.

Upstairs, Kieran selects a room overlooking the garden, which slopes down to a mass of trees that appear to blend in to some woodland that stretches across the visible part of the valley. He had wondered if he'd be able to see the sea, but apparently not. Their dad announced to them on the way that they were only a few miles from the coast, but thinks it likely he'll need to consult a map – or Google – before he sets off to find it.

Kieran never bothers unpacking when on holiday. He opens the cupboard door to chuck in one of his travel bags still full and unopened and as he does so, the full-length mirror on its door offers him a different view of the garden from the one he saw seconds before. It is a view that gives him a glimpse of something in a tree, down at the end of the lawn, just before the main woodland. It's the same colour as the wood, but has a straight edge, only just about visible.

For a moment, Kieran is confused about what it could be. Perhaps it's a treehouse, he thinks, closing the wardrobe door and trying to crane his neck out of the window. The angle of the house makes it impossible to see it properly, but he thinks he can make out the edge of something in that large oak tree. Yes, he's fairly sure there's a treehouse down there. Interested, he comes away from the window and heads downstairs.

He's going to explore.

Chapter Twenty-Four

ROBERT

2004

The lodge is quite nice, Robert thinks to himself as he unpacks his clothes, books, cassette tapes and CDs. The room is large – larger than his one at home – and has a very big floor-to-ceiling window, although considering most of the view is of a tree quite close to the house, he isn't too sure of the point of it. To the left, he thinks he can just about see a farm, maybe a tractor and barns, and the edge of some woodland at the bottom of the lawn. Then he spots movement. Kieran is making his way along the lawn with long, determined strides. He watches him until he disappears from view, then decides to join him. The previous night's altercation, if one could call it an altercation – perhaps more of a one-sided personal attack – has wounded him, but he doesn't want to keep up the animosity for the whole summer.

After Kieran left the room with his harsh words hanging in the air between them, Robert thought a lot about what might have caused his brother to say such things. He wonders if it was less about himself and more about Kieran's own doubts and conflicting emotions coming to the surface. He's aware Kieran likes to think of himself as the strong, silent type, but he also knows that everyone, deep down, has a need for approval and permission, a yearning to be told their thoughts and actions are right, are OK. Perhaps Kieran was simply panicking. Panicking that his brother, who had been his companion through this exploration into the Dark Core's teachings, was about to abandon him. Robert hadn't exactly decided to leave it all behind and stop following The Raven's videos or believing in it all, but that was how Kieran had taken it. And now, after getting his thoughts in order throughout the long journey to Cornwall, he's more confident with his position. He has doubts and he has fears, but he isn't turning his back on it all. He has loved having a project that involves his older brother and can't deny that the dangerous edge of the videos they've watched and the shocking experience of their trip to London have all been rather exciting for him. And in spite of some misgivings, he doesn't want that to end.

He can't see Kieran at first when he gets down to the bottom of the sloping lawn. Nor does he initially notice the treehouse. But when he does see it, he can't believe he walked past such an impressive structure without noticing. When he turns around and sees the building sitting in the midst of the branches of the enormous oak tree, he's struck by how perfect it looks. It's as though it has been placed there by magic. The wood is polished and gleaming. The ladder leading down to the door on the left looks smooth and brand new. There are windows in the front of the house and even a little balcony running around two sides, with French windows opening out to it. As he notices these details, he realises all the doors and windows are already open. Then he sees Kieran appear on the balcony, looking outwards.

When he spots Robert standing on the grass below, he gives him a small smile and says, 'Come up. This is amazing.'

Robert does as he says, climbing up the rungs of the ladder until he's on the balcony and looking around. Although the treehouse looked high up when he was staring up at it from the ground, he's now surprised by how little view it provides. It is, after all, situated halfway up a tree rather than at the top of the branches, securely nestled in the thicker parts near the trunk and away from the weaker, thinner tips. Its position at the end of the garden, in a small alcove-like pocket before the woods, places the treehouse in total shade. Robert wonders if it ever gets full sunlight, or if it remains hidden away in permanent darkness even when the summer sun is burning bright.

'This is brilliant,' Robert says, going inside to explore. There are two single beds placed at right angles up against two walls, along with a comfortable-looking chair and a table complete with a fruit basket filled with apples and pears that look fresh.

'The people or company Dad's renting this from deserve full marks for preparation,' Kieran says, taking a pear. 'I was pissed off at first when he decided we weren't going to the villa in Portugal this year. I liked having the pool house away from them, but this will do nicely.'

'You planning on sleeping here?'

Kieran shrugs. 'Why not?'

Robert thinks for a moment, then nods. 'Yeah, I could stay here too.'

He sees Kieran frown.

'What?' Robert asks.

'Nothing,' Kieran replies, though he's still frowning.

'You don't want me staying here, do you? You want me back in the house. Too *eager and timid*, am I? Do you know, I've been thinking how fucking contradictory that sounds. How can someone be eager and timid at the same time?'

Kieran looks regretful. 'Look, I feel bad about what I said.' Kieran takes a step towards him and for a second Robert thinks he's going to hug him – something they don't usually do – but then he comes to an awkward stop.

Though Robert has been planning a forgive-and-forget attitude to their disagreement, he now doesn't want to let Kieran off so lightly. He turns away and says, 'It's a shame. This would have been the perfect place for us to talk about … things.'

'What's a shame?' Kieran says. 'What *things*?'

Robert heads out onto the balcony as if he's about to leave. 'A shame you clearly don't want me here. And you know what things. Things about the Dark Core. About our pathways. And what we can do to clear them, ready for our future.'

Even though he isn't exactly lying, Robert becomes aware that he's manipulating his brother. It's a feeling he isn't used to. Usually, it's the other way around, but now Robert rather enjoys the feeling of control and power; he likes being able to see the cogs of Kieran's mind turning. His brother doesn't want to be in this alone, Robert knows this. And now Robert has dangled a carrot in front of him – a continuation of their partnership – and he's certain his words are having an effect. Still, he drags it out, going over to the ladder and positioning himself as though he's about to climb down.

'Wait,' Kieran says.

Robert pauses, leg stretched out ready to be placed on one of the top rungs.

'I never said I didn't want you here,' Kieran says. 'I never said that and I don't mean it.'

Robert brings his legs back around and stands up straight on the balcony. 'I want us to carry on as we were. But don't say shit like that – the things you said last night. That wasn't nice.'

Kieran nods. 'I agree. I'm sorry. Come back inside. You can choose which bed you want. Then we'll go and explore the woods or go down to the sea. OK?'

Robert returns the nod, reassured by the earnestness he can see in his brother's eyes. 'OK.'

They sit and chat in the treehouse for a bit, selecting a bed each and talking about what stuff they'll move in. Back at the house, their mother is impressed to learn of the treehouse but not interested enough to go down to the end of the lawn to see it. Their father, however, is intrigued and accompanies them up the ladder for a tour, saying how he would have loved such a thing when he was a kid.

'Well, we're not kids,' Kieran says, sounding a bit offended, as though he's been caught out showing enthusiasm for something childish.

'Of course not,' their dad says kindly, smiling. 'At your age, I'd have been bringing girls back here and getting wasted.' Then he appears to check himself and says hurriedly, 'Not that you two will be doing either of those things this summer.' Then he lowers his voice, as though there were a danger of being overheard and says, 'Or at least, if you do, don't let your mum find out.'

Robert suggests they go and explore the beach. 'It'll be quite a walk,' his dad says. 'Come back up to the house and we'll look at a map.'

They discover the beach is about an hour's walk if they follow the road, although only half an hour if they go in a straight line through the woods and the farthest stretch of the nearby village, down to the coast.

'Tell you what,' their dad says, 'you head down on foot, then I'll pick you up later before it gets dark. Then your mum and I can unpack in peace and we'll get a late supper sorted.'

Robert suspects that his mum, who is currently having a lie-down after the long drive, might have something to say about that plan. The thought of them being excused from unpacking the car or helping out with food probably won't go down well, so both boys quickly agree with the plan and make their exit before anything delays them.

They cross the lawn and climb over the fence that's set back a little way behind the treehouse oak. Their walk through the woods feels pleasantly cool at first, but by the time they emerge at the little village, blinking in the bright sunshine, both of them are very hot and thirsty.

'Do you have any money?' asks Robert, looking down the quiet street for any sign of a shop.

'A bit,' says Kieran, in a way that suggests a full stop to the subject.

'I want to find a shop. Get a Coke or something.'

But the only buildings stretching off into the scorching distance look like small, dated, rundown houses, flats and bungalows – an untidy mixture unlike anything one would find on an idyllic Cornwall postcard. A group of children becomes visible at the bend in the road, one of them with their arm in a sling, the other kicking an old car tyre.

To the left, a woman comes out of one of the bungalows, apparently in tears, and yells back at the open doorway, 'Screw you, I'm going to my sister's, you prick! You knew she was my best friend, you bloody knew it!'

A male voice yells back, 'Good riddance!' and slams the door. The woman walks to a rusty old car outside the property, gets inside and drives away in a cloud of exhaust. Robert feels like he's just landed in a Cornish-accented episode of *EastEnders*.

'You two lost?' says a voice behind them. Robert turns around and sees someone sitting on the pavement in the shade. A girl. Around their age, or slightly older perhaps. She appears to be in the midst of painting the crumbling old wall separating the street from one of the more dilapidated bungalows.

'Er … yes,' says Robert at the same time as Kieran says, 'No, not really.'

The girl laughs. 'Well, make your minds up.'

'What are you painting?' Robert asks, stepping forward.

'It's a mural,' she says, getting up off the gritty ground and dusting her knees. She surveys her work and as she does Robert notices that there's a clear outline of a woman's face with her mouth open and a teardrop falling from an eye. It isn't good, exactly – it's too basic for Robert to marvel at any artistic skill being displayed – but he finds the fact this girl is doing such a thing at all in a street like this on a summer's day an interesting thing in itself.

'She's screaming,' the girl says pleasantly, admiring her work. 'I'm pleased with it. Don't you think it's got something…? You know what artists say, when they think they've *got* something. Right?'

Robert nods politely. He glances at Kieran, who seems to have more practical matters on his mind. 'We're looking for the seafront,' he says. 'Can you direct us?'

Just as he says this, a shout comes from their left. Robert sees a bespectacled teenage boy on a bike cycling on the other side of the street. He's waving and shouting, 'Hey, Chloe! Chloe!'

Robert looks back and notices embarrassment in her face. She gives a wave and the boy waves back even more enthusiastically, which causes him to wobble almost comically on his bike. For a moment Robert thinks he's going to fall off, but he steadies himself and carries on down the road.

'Friend of yours?' Robert asks.

'No, not exactly. He's an odd boy. I went on a date with him once. It was a bit awkward, to be honest. Hands everywhere.'

Robert turns back to see the boy disappear into the distance down the end of the long road.

'Not that I mind some eager hands now and then,' she says, her eyes very much on Kieran. 'Provided they know what they're doing.'

Robert notices his brother's eyes widen. 'Well,' he says, 'now we know your name. So, Chloe, the seaside?'

She turns to look at him with a dreamy smile. 'The sea? Yes, it's near here. Just carry on down this street until you come to some bushes down there. Then there's a pathway. It's a bit overgrown, but it's there. Next to the hedge that looks like Hagrid. I love it when plants look like things, don't you? Anyway, just carry on following it. You'll see that the ground stops being grass and becomes sand. Then you'll know you're almost there.'

Robert can see that something about this rather specific set of directions surprises his brother. He wonders if the girl's playing with them. Her comment about hands was definitely flirty. Or perhaps winding up the tourists is a local tradition around here. Nevertheless, Kieran nods and says, 'Thanks', and starts to walk in the direction of the beach. Robert says goodbye, then goes to follow Kieran, offering the girl a wave as he does so. She waves too, then wipes some of the paint on her hands on her bright yellow apron before settling back down onto the pavement and picking up her brush.

'Bit odd,' Kieran says once they're out of earshot.

'She seemed nice,' says Robert. 'Didn't you think so?'

Kieran makes a 'Hmm' sound as though he's not convinced, so Robert drops the subject.

The girl's directions prove to be accurate – right down to the hedge that Robert has to agree certainly has a Hagrid-like shape to it. When the ground starts to turn into sand, sloping steeply downhill, Robert remarks to his brother that he can smell the sea.

'I reckon we were up on the cliffs, and now we're going to the bottom of them,' Robert remarks.

'We were and we are,' says Kieran. 'I think that was clear on the map.'

Robert ignores this and strides ahead. Less than a minute later they're on the beach and Robert breaks out into a run, heading towards the sea. He's amazed at how empty the beach is – if this were Brighton or Southend it would be packed, but not so here, and he's delighted to see it. He suddenly has a lot of free energy, as though it's been pent up inside him over the past week since finishing school. Since discovering all those strange things online. Since their troubling trip to London.

'Come on, let's swim!' he shouts over his shoulder.

'We're not here to swim. We haven't got our trunks. We're just here to see the sea,' Kieran calls after him.

'*See the sea?* Where's the fun in that?' Robert shouts, throwing off his top and kicking off his sandals.

'We'll swim tomorrow,' Kieran says. 'I'm not in the mood today.' But it's too late. Robert's sped off into the water. There aren't waves as such – the weather's too calm for that – but the water makes a welcoming sway towards him, the temperature enjoyably cool against his hot skin.

'Come in, it's great!' Robert calls back, but Kieran shakes his head. He squints in the sunshine and pulls on his shades, sitting down on the sand. There's a moody edge to him that Robert finds annoying and he turns away from him and swims further.

He amuses himself for a bit, swimming about, going out further, then heading back closer to shore. He's aware currents can creep up on people and doesn't want to end up being swept off to the Isles of Scilly. He's about to call out to Kieran again, to try to convince him to reconsider and come in, then he sees it. A figure striding across the sand towards his brother.

For a moment the late-afternoon sun gets in his eyes and he can't make out anything other than the outline of the person walking towards Kieran. And in his mind, he imagines it's a tall, dark man in a golden mask, holding a long, jagged ceremonial knife, about to strike.

Then his vision shifts. As he swims closer, the light becomes dappled and then blocked by the trees on the cliffs. And he can see it's not a tall man walking towards Kieran. It's a female figure. A girl. Even before he's close enough to confirm, he knows it's the girl they saw earlier. Chloe. She stands next to Kieran for a few seconds, then sits down in the sand next to him, in conversation.

'Hi there,' she waves at Robert as it becomes too shallow to swim and he starts to walk towards them both.

'Hey,' Robert says. 'Nice to see you again.'

'Nice to see you,' she says. 'I'm pleased you've found the beach. This is my favourite place. And people don't often come here.'

'Why not?' Robert says, coming to a standstill.

'There are superstitions. That's what my Auntie Janey said before she died. People think this little stretch of the beach is cursed. But my mum thinks it's because our last bit of the village is the shit part and nobody wants to come near it. They all squeeze close together on the sand up near Port Bowen. You'd struggle to get an ice cream without a queue there. Although you wouldn't find anywhere to get an ice cream around here, apart from the freezer cabinet of the dodgy off-licence. And even that's probably an out-of-date Fab lolly.' She shrugs, 'But I don't care, you know? I'm not fussed. I like my cursed beach. The only thing about this place I do like.'

Robert is trying to take it all in. He doesn't know quite how to respond. After a few seconds' silence, Kieran says, 'Come and sit down, Rob. You'll need to dry off before we go home.'

Robert ambles over, trying not to feel self-conscious. But the girl's eyes aren't on him – they're staring out to sea, as though her thoughts are far away.

'What are you thinking about?' Robert asks her as he sits down next to Kieran.

'That's a bit personal,' Kieran mutters.

'Oh I don't mind,' she says. 'I'm thinking about the future. I don't know what it holds, but I know it doesn't include me. Not here. I'm going to go away. Far away from this place.'

'What about your cursed beach?' says Robert, trying to make it sound light, but her tone continues to sound wistful. Perhaps even a little sad.

'I think I might go to London. Or Edinburgh. Or America. Especially America. New York would be the best.' Silence falls for a moment. Robert starts to think how uncomfortable the wet sand is on his thighs. He wishes he had a towel to get dry. Perhaps Kieran was right. Perhaps it was a mistake to have gone in the sea.

'We're from London,' Robert says, then when Kieran frowns at him he hastily corrects himself. 'Well, near it. Essex.'

'Is it very busy?' she asks. 'I've never been. Never really been out of the village, apart from to Southampton when I was a child, to my auntie's funeral.'

'Umm … it is busy, yes,' he says. 'Or it can be. Depends where you go and at what time of day.'

She glances over at him. 'You think I'm weird, don't you?' Her smile is more knowing and self-aware than he expects. 'Don't worry, I'm not crazy. Just a bit stuck. Stuck in this place. Stuck in this life. You probably think it's strange I'm telling you all this stuff and you've only just met me.'

This is exactly what Robert thinks, but he doesn't want to say it. Instead, he tries to think of an ordinary thing to ask that would get them onto safer, more regular small-talk topics and realises there's a key piece of info he can ask for.

'Sorry, we haven't introduced ourselves,' he says. 'I'm Robert.' For a second, he's about to offer his hand out to her, then decides at the last minute this might seem too formal. His little jerk of the arm as he changes his mind doesn't seem to have been noticed by her, but he sees Kieran clock it – and the slight smirk that touches the corners of his mouth.

'I'm Chloe,' she says, smiling at him, then laughs. 'But of course, you know that already. And you?'

'Kieran,' he says.

'Enchanted,' she replies with a laugh. 'I saw someone say that in a film once during an introduction, one of those old things where the people wear bonnets and shit like that. *Enchanted*. I've always wanted to say it, so I should be grateful you boys have given me the chance.'

Robert laughs. 'We're glad to be of service.'

Kieran shifts uncomfortably next to him. He can't work out if his brother is bothered by Chloe's presence, or by Robert's reaction to her presence. Or if he's just in one of his moods regardless. He can often be relied upon to go into a bit of a silent mood – even more silent than usual – when strangers are introduced to him, so this isn't entirely a surprise to Robert. But even so, he feels there's a fine line between reserved shyness and rudeness and if they'll be spending most of the summer here on this beach and in the nearby area, they might as well be friendly.

After chatting for a bit more on the beach, Chloe suggests they go for a walk along the sand. She wants to show them a cave she particularly likes. 'Other parts of Cornwall get all the attention for their caves because of some Merlin or King Arthur stuff, but we have a good one here. I do chalk drawings on the walls.'

Sure enough, they quickly come to an opening in the rocks and Chloe leads the way inside. It has a relatively small opening, although the space beyond is bigger than it appears from the outside. The ground is dry, with some rocks strewn around that look as though they haven't seen water in centuries, so Robert assumes the tide never floods it. He drops the damp sandy ball that his T-shirt has become and goes over to stand on one of the large rocks. 'There's a ledge up there. Wow, a lot of space.'

'There is,' Chloe says. 'I've done a chalk drawing up there. It can be a bit tricky to get to. I've only been up once.'

'Give me a boost, Kieran,' Robert says. Kieran looks for a moment like he's going to refuse, as though he isn't into this whole cave exploration jaunt, but then sighs and walks over. With the help of a push, Robert is able to clamber onto the ledge and look at the chalk sketches Chloe has apparently daubed. They aren't as pictorial as her painted wall mural of a woman screaming, but Robert can see right away what they are: a castle, similar to a fairytale castle from a picture-book or animated film; a star, with some smaller stars floating around its points; a skull.

When Robert climbs down, he asks her what they mean and why she chose those three pictures.

She shrugs and says, 'Ah that would be telling.' Robert feels embarrassed, as though he's asked her something deeply intimate.

'Let me see,' Kieran says, scrambling up to the ledge. Robert goes to help him but he pulls himself out of reach muttering, 'I can manage.' He's proved wrong a second later when his foot slips and he almost loses grip on the rock.

'Careful,' Chloe says. She lets out a quiet laugh and steps past Robert to support Kieran, laying her hands on the back of his shorts to help push him up. Robert frowns as he sees her hands cover his brother's buttocks. Even though he was supported in his climb in much the same way, Kieran's hands on him had just naturally felt supportive and practical. Watching Chloe touch Kieran, however, he can't help but feel something else is going on in the way she holds tight onto him as he grunts, his hands scrabbling to take hold of the ledge. He finds himself wishing she had been the one to come to his assistance moments earlier.

'It's OK. I'm up,' Kieran says, pulling himself out of her reach. When he returns, he says, a little awkwardly, 'Yeah … um … the drawings are good.'

Chloe nods, as if she doesn't doubt this. 'I was happy with them. When I was younger, I used to do a lot more art. My auntie, the one who died, used to buy me things. She'd arrive with bags, saying, "Here I am with the craft supplies." She bought me a book once about modern art. It was about a famous gallery in New York. I loved it. But Mum … I don't know… She just doesn't understand why I'd care about things like that.'

Robert is surprised by how candid she's being with them. 'But you've carried on with the wall painting, like we saw earlier? And these cave drawings. That's cool, just in itself, I suppose. Are they symbols? Like, ancient runes or something?'

She throws her sandy blonde hair over her shoulders and says, 'Sort of. They're my life trajectory, as I see it. My auntie once told me the special people in life are at some point given keys to a very special castle. In this castle, they're taken to a high tower and given the chance to become a star – as in a star in the sky, not a pop star. When they become a star, they die. But it's not a sad thing. It's a nice thing. Because stars shine brightly for many years even after they die. Then the skull shows what happens to your body. Not in a scary way – bones and skulls aren't scary. It's just that our physical form remains while we float up high above us. Always as stars, never really gone.'

The two boys stare at her. Of all the things she's said so far, this one surprises Robert the most. Then she makes a sound and for a worried moment he thinks it's a sob, but it turns out to be a light chuckle and then she raises a hand to her face.

'Oh my God, you both look so serious.' She then walks over to

Robert and kisses him on the cheek. Then does the same to Kieran. 'There, that should put smiles back on your faces. It's a friendly kiss, mind. I don't want to give you ideas about this being some kind of summer romance for you boys. You're too young for me, anyway,' she says, laughing again.

'How old are you?' Robert asks, his hand going unconsciously to his cheek where she'd kissed him. He dimly notices Kieran frowning at him, as though this is something he shouldn't ask, but Chloe just smiles and says, 'I'm eighteen. And you are … let me guess … thirteen?'

Now it's Robert's turn to frown. 'I'm fourteen. Fifteen in the autumn.'

'I'm nearly seventeen,' Kieran says. 'Eighteen next year.'

'So this is your last summer of youth,' she says, looking at Kieran as though sizing him up.

'Er, well, not quite,' he says. 'I suppose that will be next summer.'

'I had one of those last year,' she says, almost wistfully. 'It wasn't very eventful. I wanted to go away. To New York, perhaps. Find that modern art museum. But that costs money.' She shrugs. 'I hope yours is better.'

'I hope it will be,' Kieran says. He looks back at the cave entrance and suggests they go back out to the beach. 'I think we should walk down to the main beach, the busy part. I think that's where our father is going to pick us up from.'

'*Father?*' Chloe says, imitating Kieran's accent. 'Gosh, you're posh, aren't you.'

Robert can see Kieran isn't happy with this observation. Chloe must have noticed it too, as she then says, 'I like your voice. I knew a posh man once. He used to come to the village as his daughter lived in a cottage there. He used to wear a suit and bow tie and smoke a pipe. Like a posh person from a storybook. Does your father wear a bow tie and smoke a pipe?'

'No, he doesn't,' says Kieran flatly.

'Only on every second Sunday of the month, when we slay all the pheasants,' says Robert, trying to diffuse any tension there might be.

Chloe laughs as they come out into the early evening light. 'You're a funny one, Robert. Well, I'll have to round up any pheasants I see and protect them from your very smart dad. That's if that mad farmer up at Hill Valley hasn't shot them all first.'

'Mad farmer?' Robert asks. 'I can see a farm from my window. We're staying in Sunshine Lodge in Hill Valley. Is the farmer there mad?'

'Yes, he's known for his madness,' Chloe says. 'The postman, Ned, he's my friend and he told me the farmer once growled at him. He has dogs. Ned's scared of them, and he once thought they were snarling at him, but it was the farmer, literally standing at the window making growling noises.'

Robert's about to ask something about the farmer when Kieran says, 'The postman is your friend?'

Chloe nods. 'Yes, why not? Postmen have friends. And he's a very good-looking postman, I'll have you know. He wears shorts.' She says this last fact as though it settles the matter.

They walk along the beach, Robert chatting easily to Chloe about school, and how he wants to study History at university whereas Kieran is hoping to do PPE at Cambridge. She says she doesn't know what PPE is, but doesn't wait to find out, looping back to her life at school and how unhappy it had been. She's fascinated about the minutiae of their school life and asks questions about everything ranging from where they keep their toothbrushes ('Do they all get mixed up with each other's?') to what they call 'homework' if it isn't being completed at home. She even expresses doubt that there'd be 'any space for a school in Westminster', saying how surely the whole district is taken up by the Houses of Parliament, Big Ben and Buckingham Palace.

'It can't be very private,' she says, 'having all those boys crammed in together. But at the same time a bit lonely, maybe? Do you miss your parents when you're away at school?' she asks. 'I wouldn't miss mine, although I've only got one of them. Maybe it would be different if I had two.'

'Er, yeah, I suppose,' says Robert at the same time as Kieran answers, 'Not really.'

Chloe looks interested and turns to look at Kieran. 'Aren't they nice to you?'

He shrugs. 'It's not a question of them being nice; I just don't find them very interesting.'

'What an odd thing to say,' she says, looking thoughtful.

'What does your mum do?' asks Robert as they change their course across the sand so as to avoid a cluster of rocks.

'Drugs,' Chloe says simply. Even though the subject is evidently a serious one, something about her flat tone and lack of hesitation in delivering this answer makes Robert laugh. Chloe doesn't, which makes him feel instantly bad. He decides he should change the subject and asks Kieran what the time is ('Time to get a watch' comes the answer) and wonders aloud about how long they have until their dad will arrive at the main seafront area of Port Bowen.

'He'll be there soon,' says Kieran.

'I'll have to say hi,' says Chloe.

'To our dad?' asks Kieran. 'Why?'

Chloe shrugs again. Her outlook on life seems like it could be summarised by the words *why not?*

'I'll just say hello and be friendly,' she says, as though it was the most natural thing in the world.

'Well, if you want, I suppose,' Kieran says.

Their father turns out to be there already. After being shown a set of steps leading away from the main beach, where a group of families seems to be having an evening picnic, they arrive on a street featuring shops and restaurants. Down the street, Robert can see signs pointing to a hotel situated on a hill, and a church in the distance, and to the right, overlooking the water, a 'bar and cinema' establishment that looks both modern and complementary to the local architecture.

'This is great!' Robert says. 'Nicer than—' He stops himself, but Chloe seems to know what he had been going to say.

'Yes, it's so much nicer down this end, unlike the shit end where I live. Hard to believe it's the same street.'

Robert looks down the road. 'So where we came out, before we headed to the sea, is down there?'

'Yep,' Chloe says. 'That's the way I'm heading.'

Kieran nods at the red car parked in a layby on the other side of the road. 'We shouldn't keep Dad waiting.'

Robert feels, not for the first time that night, that his brother is being a bit rude, so he says, 'We should meet up again. Tomorrow, maybe? If you're around?'

Before Chloe can reply, they hear a car door open and a shout. 'Boys, over here!'

'Coming!' Robert shouts back to his dad.

'I'll come and say hello,' Chloe says, and starts to lead the way across the road over to the car.

Robert was not expecting her to follow through on her promise, but here she is, saying hello to their father, remarking about how she's had a nice walk with his sons. He can tell his dad is a bit taken aback, but he smiles and is friendly to Chloe, telling her things she already knows – that they drove down from Essex earlier that day and are staying up at Hill Valley for most of the summer.

'Do you live nearby?' he asks.

'Yeah, just half a mile down the road,' she says, gesturing with her braceleted hand.

'Oh we'll give you a lift,' he says. 'Get in.'

Without any sign of hesitation or declining the offer, Chloe says, 'Thanks!' and opens the front passenger door and slides into the car.

Robert and Kieran exchange a look, then get in the back.

Their dad drives them down the road in the direction of Chloe's home. As he drives, he asks her about the town, and she mentions how it only really comes alive during the summer and how during the winter the community is like a sleeping beast waiting to stir. From his position in the back of the car, Robert can see his father's expression when he hears this and finds it almost funny. It's clear he's just as taken aback by Chloe and her strange way of putting things as he and Kieran have been during their afternoon in her company.

'I like this song,' Chloe says, turning up the volume button without asking. 'It's odd, but good odd. Floaty and fuzzy. Do you know what I mean?'

'Yes, I do. I certainly do.' Robert can tell his father is both impressed and pleased by her comments. 'It's called "Willow's Song". It's by an American named Paul Giovanni, composed for a film—'

'Dad,' Kieran cuts in, 'I'm not sure Chloe wants to hear about your old-person music.'

'Your dad isn't old,' Chloe says, mildly. 'And I like the music. I sometimes listen to songs while I do my drawings. I'll have to find a copy of this song. It makes me think of fields and swaying trees. I could paint it in a picture very easily, I just know it.'

The street is turning into a more suburban area, the houses

becoming smaller and more rundown. 'Just on the left down here,' Chloe says.

'Is your, um, mum waiting for you?' their dad asks awkwardly. Perhaps he's imagining her passed out on a bed of hypodermics and bags of white powder.

'Depends what you call waiting,' Chloe says. 'I think it's unlikely beans on toast and a mug of tea are on the cards. She's often out in the evenings anyway.'

Their dad nods, then says, 'Here, take this.' He ejects the CD from the machine. 'To help with your artistic endeavours.'

Chloe takes it without any sign that she intends to decline the gift. She doesn't even seem surprised. 'Thanks. I will.' She looks around the seat into the back of the car and says, 'Right, I guess I'll see you boys tomorrow.'

Robert leans forwards. 'What time?' he asks, a little too quickly.

Chloe seems to find this funny. His dad raises his eyebrows. Robert's pleased the sun has gone down behind the trees, hiding his blushing.

'Oh, any time, I'll be around,' she says. 'Goodnight.'

She then closes the door and heads towards the bungalow. All the windows are in darkness and Robert watches as she lets herself in with a key under a plant pot on the front step.

'Nice girl,' their dad says as he puts the car into drive and heads down the street. 'Just be careful about being too eager, Rob.'

Robert continues to burn with embarrassment. 'You're the one who gave her a CD.' His father doesn't reply to this. Robert glances at Kieran. It isn't unusual for him to be the quietest one in a car, or indeed within any group of people, but there's something about his silence during this moment that catches Robert's attention. He looks as though he's thinking deeply about something.

Throughout supper, Kieran keeps up his silence, allowing Robert to tell their mother about their trip to the beach and the interesting girl they met. His mother remarks how it will be nice if they make friends, so long as they 'aren't picking up any waifs and strays'. This barely veiled snobbery annoys Robert and he sets his knife and fork down with a clatter on top of his unfished risotto and says Chloe is a person, not a feral spaniel.

'I don't think feral spaniels are very common in Cornwall,' his father says, looking amused. 'Although I've heard those dogs over at the farm barking. I hope they don't keep us awake at night.'

'Well, the website we booked this place on has a page for reviews,' June says, reaching for some water. 'You can leave a negative review if you're not happy.' She glances over at Kieran. 'You're not eating much. Is there something wrong?'

Kieran doesn't reply. His eyes are on the dark green tablecloth, as intently as though he were counting the stitches. After a few seconds, he seems to realise everyone's looking at him and he looks up. 'Pardon?'

His mother sighs. 'Don't say "pardon", darling.'

Kieran looks even more confused. 'What?'

'That's better,' his mother says, nodding.

'I don't understand,' he says.

'Pardon comes from the French – as in *Je vous demande pardon*, and it ended up in the English language due to the lower classes trying to make themselves sound more educated than they were. They perceived the French language to have social-climbing properties and utilised certain words, like "pardon". So really, if you hear someone saying "pardon" rather than "what", it is a rather obvious warning sign.'

Kieran drops his cutlery with even more of a clatter than Robert did moments before.

'Oh I've had enough,' he snaps and leaves the room, stomping loudly up the stairs.

'Did I say something?' his mother asks, pouring herself another glass of Acqua Panna.

Before he goes to his room, Robert looks in on Kieran.

'Are you OK?' he asks.

Kieran has his laptop out. 'Can you believe that this place doesn't have broadband? It has dial-up internet.'

Robert shrugs. 'Well, it's a country lodge retreat, isn't it. I don't think that's much of a surprise. What are you trying to do?'

Kieran closes the computer with a snap. 'What do you think?'

Robert understands. He comes into the room properly and closes the door. 'The Raven?'

He nods. 'I managed to download some of his videos. I found a programme that meant I could save them to my hard drive. Which means'—he gets up and takes his bag out of the cupboard—'we can go to the Treehouse. Come on.'

Robert grabs some things from his room then the two boys head downstairs. Robert calls out into the kitchen area, 'Just going to the treehouse!' then they leave before any questions can be asked or protestations raised.

As they cross the lawn in the darkening late-evening light, Robert says, 'Maybe we should see her again,' as though they were already mid-conversation.

'What?'

'Chloe,' Robert says. 'She was nice. A bit, you know, weird, but nice.'

'Yeah, I think we should,' Kieran says.

His expression remains blank, so Robert deliberately walks into him, nudging his shoulder. 'Are you being strange about her because you fancy her? If so, I think it's me she likes. Sorry to be competitive, but girls always struggle to resist me.'

Kieran doesn't laugh. 'That's not why I think we should see her again,' he says. They've reached the ladder of the treehouse. He drops his bag down for a moment and looks at Robert.

Robert stares back. Then he understands his meaning.

Even though the air is still very warm, he feels goosebumps running up his arm and a chill descending around his shoulders.

'Come on. Pass my bag to me once I'm up there.'

Robert passes his brother the bag, then climbs up himself, all the while wondering where their new friendship with Chloe is going to lead.

Chapter Twenty-Five

ROBERT

2004

They spend the night in the treehouse. Kieran is keen to just climb into the beds and sleep there but Robert insists on going back to the house and telling their parents of their plans. To his surprise, their mother raises little objection, saying to make sure they come up to the house for breakfast in the morning and say hello before they disappear off to the beach the next day. Their father has little to add other than, 'Have fun!'

Robert gets a strange sort of thrill from delving back into the world of The Raven, although after a few minutes, he finds himself growing sleepy. Whilst the subject matter isn't calming, The Raven's voice has a quality to it that causes a floaty, spaced-out feeling in Robert and after the third video, with Kieran saying little in between, he finds himself nodding off. The next morning, while Kieran is up at the house showering, Robert looks at the laptop and notebooks scattered across his brother's bed up against the other wall. He's aware his brother has been taking notes about The Raven and the Dark Core ever since he discovered the pages on his desk in his dorm at school. But there's something different about these. There's a page divided into two sections, laid out far more neatly than the other scribblings. One has the heading 'Arranged ceremony'. The other says 'Opportunity'. They are two phrases The Raven used in one of the videos the night before. Under the first, there's a bullet-pointed list. A list that includes words like *Séance*, *Meditation*, *Orgy*, *Incense Burning* and *Healing Ritual*. The second column, under 'Opportunity' contains the words *Nighttime swim*, *Clifftop walk*, *Sleeping* and *Busy road*.

A noise on the ladder makes him start. 'Hey, that's mine,' Kieran says, coming through the open doorway, now fully dressed with his hair damp. He walks over to Robert and snatches the paper out of his hand.

'What is it?' Robert asks.

Kieran doesn't answer.

A few seconds of silence pass between them. Then Robert looks away.

He grabs his T-shirt and says, 'I'm starving. Need some, um, breakfast…'

He's having trouble with words, perfectly simple words, but they just won't come to him. Perhaps it's because different words are stuck in his mind. Words like *Séance* and *Clifftop walk*. Images of a woman being sat down and told she's about to contact the dead. Or walked along a clifftop on a stormy night, taken too near the edge, then falling … falling.

'Yeah, Mum's cutting up fruit and stuff over at the lodge,' Kieran says, snapping Robert back to the present. He watches as Kieran calmly takes the page of notepaper and tucks it inside the writing pad it came from. He puts it away with his laptop under the bed.

Robert thinks of all the things he could say. Things that worry him. Things that scare him. And things, if he's honest with himself, that excite him. But he doesn't. He just goes up to the house with Kieran for breakfast, trying to leave all those thoughts behind. He'll think about it later, he tells himself. There's time. Time to get all this straightened out in his head. Think about how he feels. And what it might mean for their summer in Hill Valley.

To Robert's surprise, Kieran doesn't reference the list or anything to do with The Raven once they're alone. He was certain it was the prelude to something, and that on their walk down to the seafront they would have discussed and debated the implications of what he had written and the things he was thinking when he imagined such scenarios. Because that's what they are – it's obvious now to Robert. But Kieran doesn't bring it up again that day. Nor the day after. Or the day after that.

Meeting up with Chloe becomes part of a daily routine. After breakfast, they walk through the woods to Chloe's street, where they call for her. They never see her mum, but they sometimes hear her shouting, 'Get the bloody door!' or something similar. Other times, Chloe comes to the door and the house is in silence and she says her mum's been out all night. She sometimes seems happy to talk about this in her floaty, carefree way, mentioning that she likes having the bungalow to herself. This means she can do what she wants and see who she wants. Other times, especially when they can hear her mum shouting from one of the back rooms, Robert thinks he can see a sad look in her eyes. On one of the days, towards the end of their first week in Hill Valley, the boys arrive to find a red post van parked outside the bungalow. Robert's about to ring the doorbell when Kieran takes hold of his arm.

'Wait a second. Can you hear that?'

Robert pauses. 'Hear what? I can't hear anything?'

'Wait here a sec,' Kieran says. He walks off around the back of the bungalow. Robert's confused. He backs away from the front door, onto the pavement, and looks down the side path to see where Kieran's gone. He's about to disregard his brother's request that he stay when Kieran reappears with a knowing grin on his face.

'Where did you go?' Robert asks. 'Is there nobody home? Maybe she's meeting us down near the beach today.'

Even before he speaks, Robert knows this probably isn't true. The look on Kieran's face makes it clear he's seen something during his brief trip around the back of the building.

'She's home,' he says.

'Right…' Robert says. 'So…'

Kieran sighs and rolls his eyes. 'Isn't it obvious?' He looks at the post van, then back at Robert. 'You know she said her postman wears shorts?'

Robert nods.

'Well, let's just say, from what I can see through the gap in the curtains, he isn't wearing his shorts right now. Or anything else for that matter.'

For a few more seconds, Robert's still confused. Then he realises what Kieran's telling him.

'Oh…'

'Uh huh,' Kieran says.

Robert has questions that part of him would like to ask – details of what Kieran saw. But he worries they'd either make him sound weird or *too* interested, which he fears in turn would make him seem childish. Unworldly. So he decides to take it all in his stride and waits with Kieran in silence on the front porch wall until the door opens and Chloe appears. As expected, she isn't alone. A man in a red postman's polo shirt and khaki shorts is with her, laughing about something. When he sees the boys waiting on the wall, his laughter stops and he suddenly looks embarrassed. He walks quickly to his van while Robert and Kieran watch. When Chloe mentioned the local postman, Robert imagined a middle-aged man, overweight, puffing and wheezing as he dragged a heavy postbag along the rundown street. By contrast, this man looks around thirty. He's slim and handsome – or at least Robert supposes women would think him so – with close-cut hair and tattoos over his muscled arms.

'I'll be out in a minute,' Chloe calls after the boys.

She comes out of the bungalow after another five minutes have passed, not meeting their eyes.

'He was delivering a parcel,' she says, looking at the pavement. She adds in a quieter voice, 'Needed a signature, couldn't find a pen.' She then stops still for a moment, raising a hand to her head. 'Oh, I forgot to give him his fairy cakes.'

'You baked him fairy cakes?' Robert asks.

'Yes,' Chloe says, looking forlornly down the street in the direction the red van went, now out of sight. 'For all his hard work. Delivering packages and letters, I mean. I didn't bake them – I got them at the local shop.'

Kieran makes a scoffing sound. 'You don't have to do this.'

Chloe frowns. 'What?'

'This pretending. That he was just delivering a parcel, or you were giving him fairy cakes. You don't have to act all innocent with us. It's clear what's going on.'

Robert can't tell from her face if she's offended or not. She looks back at Kieran, then says quietly, 'All those things are true, actually. More than one thing can be true at the same time, you know.' She shrugs, brushing her hair away from her face, and then says, in a much stronger, brighter voice, 'Let's do something different today.

I don't feel like going to the beach. The overcast sky makes me think rain is coming.'

Robert is about to tell her rain isn't forecast – he heard his parents comment on it that morning – when Kieran says, 'Why don't you come with us to our lodge? We could show you the treehouse?'

Chloe had shown interest when Robert told her about the treehouse briefly during their first meeting, so in some ways, it was only natural for her to eventually visit. But Kieran didn't warn him he was about to offer an invitation, and part of him wishes he had. He likes Chloe, more than he suspects Kieran does, but can't help but feel the treehouse is *their* thing, not somewhere to casually bring guests. It's a place for them to watch videos of The Raven, discuss his meanings and lessons, and make notes and come up with ideas. And plans.

He suddenly realises there might be another reason for Kieran's invitation. He looks closely at his brother's face, but as ever it isn't giving much away. His eyes are on Chloe, evenly and without a large amount of enthusiasm, as though the idea of her visiting their little hideaway is just a casual, carefree suggestion. But Robert's mind winds back to the lists he found in Kieran's notes. Lists about 'opportunities' and seizing the moment when it arises.

He feels cold. He wonders if he should think up a reason why Chloe shouldn't come to the treehouse. Why they should go to the beach as planned or perhaps feign illness. He wants to delay, buy time, time that would enable him to discuss this properly with his brother. Before it's too late.

'Yes! Love to,' Chloe says. 'Lead the way.'

Kieran does lead the way and Robert gives Chloe a distracted smile before striding up to Kieran and looking at him, not daring to ask any questions with Chloe so close, but trying to convey to him with his eyes how he isn't sure about this. Kieran keeps his gaze forwards and increases his pace deliberately – or so Robert suspects – and avoids looking at him.

'Are we in a hurry?' Chloe asks with a laugh, the hurried patter of her mint-green trainers ringing out in the empty street.

'No,' Kieran says. 'No, sorry, I just … thought we should get out of the rain before it begins.'

Robert thinks this sounds ridiculous, but Chloe chuckles and says, 'Oh that's the kind of thing I'd do. It's nice to reach a place of safety whilst dry, then you can shelter and feel all cosy. Though sometimes I go out in the rain just to feel the droplets pattering my skin. When I was a very young child, my aunt, the one who died, had a trampoline in the garden and when it rained, I'd lie flat and imagine the hundreds of drops of water were bullets fired by fairies. Have you ever done that?'

If Robert weren't feeling so uneasy, he would have laughed at this, especially when coupled by the baffled look on Kieran's face. 'No. No, I haven't,' Kieran replies.

'Well, I bet you have, Rob,' Chloe says, and to a mixture of horror and delight, he feels her arm go over his shoulder and give him a playful squeeze. 'I don't mean the fairy stuff. I know fairies don't fire down bullets at children. I'm not *that* mad!' She laughs and pulls her arm away from him. 'I just mean, I bet you've enjoyed the sensation of the rain on your skin.'

Not for the first time, Robert isn't sure if she's flirting, or if this is just one of her eccentric ways of making conversation.

Regardless, he just says, 'I don't mind the rain,' and leaves it at that.

His brain is too full to make conversation. He feels as though he sleepwalks back through the woodland and up to the treehouse, as though his movements take ten times the effort they normally would. By the time they reach the end of the woods, he isn't sure if he'll be able to clamber over the fence separating the public ground and the lodge's garden.

'Keep up, Rob,' Kieran calls back, not looking at him.

Robert slowly crunches through the twigs and fallen frazzled leaves, watching as Kieran and Chloe climb over the fence and into the garden. Robert does manage to follow, reaching the treehouse in time to see Chloe starting her journey up the ladder and Kieran watching her.

'Be careful when you get to the top and pull yourself up,' he says. 'Wouldn't want you falling backwards on top of me.'

Rob reaches his brother's side and whispers, 'What's going on?'

Kieran raises his eyebrows. 'Chloe's visiting the treehouse. What do you think's going on?'

He doesn't whisper back, just says it in a calm voice, as though he's unafraid about their visitor hearing. There are no signs she does because she turns to look at them as soon as she's reached the balcony above them and waves.

'I made it. And it's wonderful!'

She walks the length of the balcony, then the other side, then returns to go through the French windows at the front.

'You're up to something,' Robert says. 'I know it. Whether it's with me or her, you're ... playing games.'

Kieran turns to look at him, his neck moving quickly, his eyes flashing with anger.

'Shut the fuck up or go home,' he says very quietly. But the impact of the words is the same as if he had screamed them in Robert's face.

Kieran stares at him for a few more seconds, then climbs up the ladder himself, leaving Robert on the ground feeling confused and anxious. To his embarrassment, he feels the prick of tears in his eyes. He can still feel the sting of Kieran's harsh words, and the fact they were whispered makes them hurt more than if he'd shouted them. Not wanting Chloe or Kieran to see him upset, he starts to walk away from the treehouse in the direction of the main lodge. He doesn't want to talk to his parents so he sneaks upstairs, first to the bathroom and then to his bedroom. Even though it isn't cold, he fetches a jumper that he always wears when he needs comforting. He doesn't wear it, but carries it with him as he makes his way through the lodge and back into the garden. Just having it in his hands makes him feel a bit better.

When he reaches the treehouse, he can hear voices floating down from above. Chloe's voice. And something makes him stop for a moment before he steps up onto the ladder.

'I saw you watching, you know,' Chloe says. Her voice is soft, but still full of an energy that makes the hairs on the back of Robert's neck stand up. Without hesitating a moment more, he climbs up a few rungs of the ladder.

'We just wanted to see if you were home,' Kieran says. His voice sounds casual, but Robert can tell he's putting it on.

'Did you like what you saw?' she asks.

Even though it's not directed at him, and neither of them knows he's there, Robert feels a jolt run through him. He is embarrassed and excited at the same time.

'Why?' Kieran asks.

'I just wondered,' Chloe says. 'It's OK, you know. I didn't mind you … taking a look through the curtains.'

Robert waits a few seconds, wrestling with his limited options. He feels a mounting sense of guilt listening to this, not knowing where it might be leading. Unsure if he's making a wise decision or a foolish one, he pulls himself up the final few rungs and onto the balcony of the treehouse.

He sees Kieran sit up abruptly from his reclined position on one of the beds. Chloe, who is sitting on the floor opposite him, the small coffee table between them, stays exactly where she is.

She doesn't look flustered by Robert's arrival. Kieran, however, doesn't look impressed by the interruption.

'Thought you'd gone off to bed,' he says, as though he wishes this were the case.

'Well, I didn't,' says Robert, glaring at his brother.

Robert glances over at the pile of A4 notebooks on top of the white laptop. Then he looks back at Kieran, whose eyes are fixed on the rug on the floor. Chloe begins a monologue about how she had a storybook as a child that had a treehouse in it.

'My mum doesn't approve of books and shit – she says reading is for tossers – but my auntie used to read stories to me when I was a kid. One of them had a treehouse, with lovely green pictures.' She gets up off the floor and starts walking around the small space, looking at the polished wooden walls and reaching out to touch them. 'I imagine it looked a bit rougher and more unusual than this one.'

Robert sits down on his bed and tries to appear more at ease than he feels. Kieran still doesn't look at him.

When Chloe gets to the end of her speech, Kieran asks quietly, 'Have you ever been part of a séance?'

Later that evening, after their dad has dropped Chloe back home, the boys have dinner up at the lodge while their mother asks them questions about Chloe – about her home life and living situation and whether she's destined for university. Robert feels his irritation start to rise once more.

'Is this about you discovering how much of a *waif and stray* she is?'

His mother raises an eyebrow at him. 'There's no need to be in such a rush to take offence, Robert. I hope you're not going to start seeing outrage as a form of social currency. Those types of people are never popular, you know.'

Robert has nothing to come back with so stays silent. He glances at his father, wondering if he'll say something in defence of their new friend, considering he seems happy to give her lifts. But he just swallows his lasagne in silence.

Robert doesn't look forward to returning to the treehouse that evening. He worries that, after being careful to mend whatever fractures had been growing between him and his brother after the meeting in London, his attempts have been undone by his behaviour that day. He even thinks about just staying in the lodge, leaving Kieran to whatever it is he's planning. Then he remembers the look his brother gave him just before he followed Chloe up the ladder. A look of challenge. A look of excitement. And somehow the thought of not being part of whatever journey that look has to offer feels like the worst thing. So he climbs the ladder to the treehouse and braces himself for whatever reaction Kieran is about to greet him with.

To his surprise, Kieran is relatively mellow and calm when Robert pulls himself up onto the balcony and steps through the French windows. He tells Robert to come inside, then starts talking about Chloe's reaction to his suggestion of a séance.

'She seemed up for it, didn't she?' he says, Robert once again seeing that eager glint in his eyes.

'I suppose,' Robert says. Chloe had seemed interested, in a noncommittal, vague sort of way. Like with most subjects, Chloe had used the topic of séances as a gateway to memories from either her childhood ('Someone tried to do a séance in the PE cupboard at school when I was in Year 6, and Mrs. Hope *wasn't* happy') or things she'd seen on TV or film ('There was a movie about a séance – a video my mum picked up from a charity shop for her boyfriend at the time, and there was an old lady in it with scary teeth'). To say she was 'up for it' in terms of participating in one is, Robert thinks, rather stretching the truth. Chloe seems to have such a free-spirited approach to life that it wouldn't surprise him if she says yes to anything and everything by default. His mind briefly takes him back to the postman's van outside her house, and then a little while later, her arm around Robert's shoulder, giving him a squeeze.

Robert's less-than-enthusiastic tone seems to put Kieran off the subject – for that night, at least. They don't discuss his list or any plans to do with the Dark Core for the rest of the evening. They end up watching a film instead of a video featuring The Raven, although the laptop battery cuts out near the end.

'We could go back to the house? Plug it in?' Robert suggests.

Kieran shakes his head. 'Nah, I'm tired. Let's leave it for tonight.'

Robert agrees and says he's going to head back to the lodge to do his teeth and say goodnight to their mum and dad.

When he gets to the ladder, Kieran calls out quite casually, 'Oh, I was thinking Wednesday.'

Robert lowers himself down onto the first step, preparing for descent. 'What?'

'For the séance,' Kieran says.

Robert almost falls off the ladder. He grips the top end of the handles and looks back at the interior of the treehouse. Night has properly fallen and the boys didn't turn on the battery lamps during their film viewing. He can barely see Kieran sitting on the edge of one of the narrow beds, but he knows he's watching him. He knows that Kieran means something else with that word.

He pauses for a few moments, then he says, 'Don't you think we should...' He doesn't know quite how to put it in a way that won't risk annoying his brother.

'Don't you think we should *what*?'

Robert takes a breath, then says, 'Slow down?'

Kieran stays very still. Then he says quietly, 'If you're not ready for the step we're taking, you've had plenty of opportunities to step back.'

Robert sways a little, wishing he'd voiced this when he was inside the room with Kieran. He decides to backtrack.

'Yeah, no, sorry … I just meant … perhaps we should start a bit smaller. Work our way up.' He shrugs. 'Just a thought.'

Kieran doesn't say anything for what feels like a long while and Robert's hands ache from holding on to the top of the ladder.

Kieran says, 'Run along and brush your teeth, Rob.'

There's something in his voice – a sense of hard superiority – that Robert doesn't like. He opens his mouth to respond, but he can't think of anything to say. So he just nods, then starts to lower himself down the ladder, his feet shaking a little as they find each rung.

Robert wakes the next morning with that thick, heavy feeling of someone who's slept deeply. He can hear sounds – a rustling, then footsteps – like someone trying to move quietly. He looks around at his surroundings. Something doesn't feel quite right. There's a difference, but he isn't sure what. There's no clock in the cabin and his mobile is out of battery, but he can tell it's very early. And Kieran is missing. This isn't worrying in itself – he may have just nipped up to the house to use the bathroom or to get breakfast. But in those vague, waking moments, Robert has a feeling that Kieran left by stealth, rather than with his usual bold, uncaring thuds.

He gets up and stretches, then immediately sees what's wrong – a stark difference to how the treehouse was the night before.

The small coffee table, usually in the centre of the room, has been moved away from the beds. It's now near the door.

And there's something on its surface.

Robert takes a step nearer.

'Jesus!' he exclaims aloud.

Because on its surface is a bloodied mass. A mass of fur and gory, slick internal organs.

It's a rabbit. And it looks as though it's been ripped apart.

Chapter Twenty-Six

KIERAN

2004

In spite of Kieran's determination, Robert's words play on his mind.

Don't you think we should slow down?

Perhaps we should work our way up…

He tells himself they've done enough preparatory groundwork through their extensive watching of The Raven's videos, along with the pretty big step of attending an in-person meeting. But even so, he has to accept that he is thoroughly inexperienced. In all his life, he hasn't killed so much as a spider. He's never seen the point, since he isn't scared of them. He may have swatted a fly, but that's probably it.

With all this going around his head, Kieran is unable to sleep. Too hot and mentally exhausted yet finding it impossible to switch off, he eventually gets out of the narrow bed and walks quietly out onto the treehouse balcony. When he sees the rabbit on the grass, near the trunk of the tree below the treehouse, it's as though it's a gift. As though the universe is providing him with the tool he needs to get over this little hurdle. He keeps his eyes on it for a few moments before making up his mind. His watch tells him it's 1.30am. Unlikely his parents would still be awake. Robert's been sleeping soundly on his bed for over an hour. Kieran goes inside and picks up the sports bag he used to bring some clothes down to the treehouse, which is empty apart from a few loose socks. He leaves these on the floor and then very slowly climbs down the ladder, placing each of his bare feet very carefully on one rung at a time. When he reaches the ground, he half expects the rabbit to have run away, but it's still there, moving, but limping. It's injured. Must be why it didn't run, he thinks as he treads softly through the grass towards the little animal.

He bends down, lowering his body and reaches out a hand. He then makes a kissing sound – he's seen people doing this when approaching small animals to make themselves seem less threatening, smaller, a friend.

But of course, he isn't a friend. He doesn't mean this creature well.

The rabbit tries to escape, but its injured leg stops it getting further than a couple of bounds. Within a few seconds, Kieran's caught it and he stuffs it wriggling and writhing into his bag.

'Well, well. What are you doing with that?'

The voice makes him start. He drops the bag on the floor and looks around. It isn't Robert – the voice didn't come from above. Someone is down here, on the ground, with him.

Then he spots it. The glint of metal.

'I said, what are you doing with that?'

Kieran walks towards the fence and looks at the boy in front of him. The handlebars squeak as the boy turns them to steer his bike closer.

'Who are you?'

'I asked you a question first,' the boy says. As he gets closer,

Kieran can see the boy is around his age, perhaps a little younger, with large, old-fashioned glasses and light blonde hair. He looks familiar.

'I … don't have to explain myself to you,' Kieran says. 'Now please leave. You're trespassing.'

The boy laughs and belligerently leans over the handlebars. 'Oh, piss off. You don't own these woods.' He nods at the fence that separates them, a dividing line between the two boys as they stare at each other. 'I'm on public land, here. So what have you got in that bag? I saw you putting something in it.'

Kieran has no plans to answer and decides leaving would be the best thing to do. He doesn't want to act cowardly, doesn't like the idea of running away, but at the same time he isn't keen on conversing with less-than-friendly strangers on the edge of a dark forest in the middle of the night. He bends down to pick up the bag, but then he realises something. He looks back at the boy.

'Oh, it's you. You're that weird kid bothering Chloe.'

Even in the darkness, he can see the boy's face change. His body language shifts. He draws himself upright.

'You don't know Chloe!' he snaps.

'Is that so?' Kieran says. 'Well, it's been lovely to chat, but I need to get to back.'

'Stay away from her,' Sean says. 'Or I'll—'

Kieran shrugs. 'You'll what?'

'I could fuck you up, you know. I've done … weird shit.'

Kieran scoffs. 'Yeah? Weird shit? Mate, you really have *no* idea.'

This confrontation ceases to unnerve him. It's even mildly amusing. Because for all his talk and threats, this boy has no clue about what Kieran's going to do with the living creature inside his bag. Or what he plans to do afterwards. Ignoring the fact there isn't much to stop the boy hopping over the fence and murdering him and Robert in their beds, Kieran walks back to the oak tree and begins to ascend the ladder. When he reaches the top, he looks back down. The boy has gone.

'Prick,' Kieran says. He spins around, worried he's spoken too loudly, but Robert is still asleep on his bed, mouth slightly open, clutching his pillow like it's a teddy bear. He's slept through the whole exchange with the boy outside. And will hopefully sleep through everything that's about to happen. Very quietly, Kieran goes inside, picks up the small coffee table and sets it down away from the beds by the French windows.

Then he picks up the bag, sets it down on the top of the table, and reaches inside.

Kieran's in the bathroom shaving up at the house when he hears his brother thudding up the stairs. He bursts into the bathroom without knocking.

'Why did you leave that *thing* there?' he says.

'Good morning to you too,' says Kieran, glancing at his brother via the mirror in front of him, then swishing his razor in the cloudy water.

'Did you … kill it?'

Kieran frowns. 'Watch your words,' he says, keeping his voice very low. 'Mum's downstairs and Dad's in bed only two rooms away.'

'Why did you do it when I was asleep?' Robert asks. 'And then leave it for me to find when I woke up. It was … horrible. You'll need to clean it up, you know. I can't believe you just left it there.'

Kieran doesn't say anything. He just rolls his eyes, annoyed at his brother's reaction, even though it isn't entirely surprising. He had meant it as a bit of a statement after his brother's comments that he was too eager, too keen to go full-on with a human sacrifice.

The opportunity to prove he has it in him to kill arose and he took it.

'Answer me,' Robert hisses, reaching out and giving Kieran's shoulder a nudge.

'Ah!' Kieran lowers the now bloodied razor and looks at the cut on his face. 'You dick. Look what you've done.' Kieran spins around to look at him. 'What do you want me to say? You said we should raise the game. I did exactly that. You're just jealous.'

He stands there, feeling a trickle of blood run from the small cut down his neck and onto his chest. He sees his brother's eyes follow it. He's looking at Kieran as though he doesn't know him. As though he's a stranger.

Well, good, Kieran thinks. It's time Robert learns that change is afoot here. He's evolving as a person, with every step down this path he takes. And it excites him.

'Did you ... feel anything?' Robert whispers. 'As in, did you feel ... the vibrations? The Dark Core?'

Kieran looks his brother in the eye and allows a slow smile to spread across his face.

'Oh yes,' he says. He turns back to the sink and washes off the blood and any residual shaving foam. Then looks back at his brother in the mirror. 'It went beyond visualisation. Beyond anything I've ever felt. And when we go all the way, it's going to be incredible. I'm sure of it.'

Chapter Twenty-Seven

KIERAN

2004

Kieran's never thought of himself as a creative person, but over the next few days, he becomes skilled at imagining various scenes in his head. He saw once on a DVD extra how a director approached each film he made with a storyboard of the screenplay, getting scenes and shots planned out and visualised before an inch of celluloid has been shot. Kieran's been doing this himself entirely in his mind, imagining each and every variation of sacrifice he can think of. The way he might do it. The lead-up, the execution, the aftermath. And the instantaneous and incredible effect it will have on his future.

Her presence in their lives feels so immaculate, so perfect. Like a gift. And he's keen to seize this gift and accept it as fully and enthusiastically as possible. He thinks all the time of the two columns he's drawn in his notebook, with lists underneath them. Even though he's settled on the séance idea, because it mirrors what The Raven did at the meeting they attended, he can't help going through each idea on his list and imagining what that might look like. A meditation sacrifice feels too simple. Asking someone to meditate before Kieran takes his or her life feels like a bit of an anticlimax and not enough of an 'event' – not 'major' enough to honour such an important occasion. He's read about sacrifices occurring during orgies and finds it all very interesting, but since the participants other than Chloe will be him and his brother, he decides this option is unrealistic and inappropriate. Incense burning and healing rituals feel more doable, but the ceremonial air of a séance appeals to him more, though he decides to keep the idea of a healing ritual in his back pocket, so-to-speak, should the proposed séance end up being vetoed.

But the suggestion hasn't been vetoed. In fact, Chloe's been talking about how much she's looking forward to it, and even suggests they try and stage one immediately. Kieran's tempted when he hears this, but he wants a proper lead-up to the evening's activities. There are practical considerations too that he needs to consider, along with some last-minute research he wants to undertake.

So on a bright Tuesday morning, a couple of days on from when the topic was first broached, he wakes up very early, dresses quietly so as not to wake his brother, and walks as silently as he can over the creaking floor to the ladder, lowering himself down to the grass below. In under a minute, he's walking through the woodland. Some research online up in the lodge the night before has furnished him with bus times and directions to the nearest large public library. From there, he will be able to access an internet connection that is, he desperately hopes, capable of showing him videos without buffering every couple of seconds. It's a bit of a long shot, and he may not even be able to play them, but he wants to at least try. He feels he needs to hear The Raven's words about sacrifice one last time before he attempts it himself. He needs to hear him relate once again the benefits that will be made available to Kieran as soon as he carries out the process and removes all obstacles from his life pathway. He has some research to do too – research he doesn't want to risk doing on his laptop – along with one or two shop purchases he wants to make.

The town of Cresham is five miles away and boasts, along with the library, many shops in both the high street and a relatively new shopping centre. Kieran's confident he can get there by bus before 9am when the library opens, do his research for an hour, then swing by the shops he needs to visit before returning to the lodge before lunchtime. He plans to text his brother to tell him he's just 'popped into town' once he's got there, so to put paid to any fears that he's gone missing.

He's just composing a draft of this message in his mind, wondering how to word it without making Robert upset that he hasn't been invited along, when a voice behind him says, 'Going somewhere?'

He turns around to see Robert walking towards him. He's been so wrapped up in his thoughts that he didn't hear that he was being followed. But sure enough, here's Robert, standing between two trees, wearing yesterday's shorts and the crumpled red T-shirt he slept in.

'I saw you leaving. I wondered why you were trying to sneak out so quietly, when normally you just get up and stomp out of the treehouse without caring.' He gets closer to Kieran then stops. 'I knew something weird was up when I saw you moving about like a bomb was about to go off. That made me think you didn't want me to follow.'

'So after deducing all that, you just followed me anyway?' Kieran says, annoyance starting to take hold.

'Why are you cutting me out?' Robert says.

'Because I doubt your commitment,' Kieran says simply.

Robert says nothing, just bites his lip.

'You see,' Kieran says. 'Hesitation. That's you in a nutshell, Rob.'

'Well, is it any wonder, when you talk to me like that?' Robert says, looking offended. 'If I wasn't committed, I'd have tried to stop you. But I haven't. And I'm still here. Just... You have to let me get my head around what we're going to do. It's not easy, you know. I want to believe in it all, but it's...'

'A big step,' says Kieran, softening his tone, 'I know it is.' He moves towards his younger brother, putting a hand out and resting it on his shoulder. He feels the heat of him after his run through the woods to catch up. He feels him shift under his palm. They're not usually tactile – they've never been the sort of back-slapping, high-fiving, hugging sort of siblings that never stop touching each other – so there's something in the simple action that makes Robert pause and think. He looks down at Kieran's hand.

Then he says, 'I just want you to include me. And I'll do my best to stay committed. OK?'

Kieran nods slowly. 'Just promise me something. Part of what I'm heading out to do today is really important. Really, really important. It's one of the biggest steps in this whole process. If I bring you along, you have to promise that no matter what happens, you'll never tell anyone about what we're going to do. Or warn anyone.'

Robert looks shocked by this request. He says nothing, his eyes wide, staring into Kieran's.

'I need you to promise,' Kieran says.

Eventually, Robert says in a quiet voice, 'OK.'

———

Neither boy has ever caught a bus more than a handful of times. Their mother took them on one once when they were children, but that was in Munich during a visit to a distant relative. Her attitude to public transport in the UK has always been unsettlingly contradictory: some days London buses and the underground are referred to as 'one of the best things about this country' but on other days 'only used by people determined to catch SARS'. Regardless of their lack of experience, the journey goes smoothly. It takes them around twenty-five minutes to get to their destination, and they get off outside the large Marks & Spencer on Cresham High Street.

'The library should be only a short walk,' Kieran explains. 'There's a Boots and a Superdrug but look out for any other chemists. There's probably an independent somewhere. More than one if we're lucky.'

'Why?' Robert asks, frowning.

'Because we need to buy things,' is all Kieran says, striding ahead.

They get to the library just as it's opening and wait to the side of the door while the locks are undone. Kieran watches as two very keen studenty-looking young people with rucksacks and folders under their arms head in first.

'Is there a university near here?' Robert asks.

'No idea,' says Kieran. 'I mean, I suppose there's Exeter University, but that's over in Devon.'

For a moment, Kieran wonders about Chloe. About how in another world she might have been one of these students, home on summer break, researching for a dissertation maybe, or whatever students do in the holidays. He feels a pang of something at that moment, as they walk into the dark, surprisingly chilly hallway of the library foyer. Is it a twinge of regret, perhaps? Regret for something that hasn't yet happened. Something they are going to do. Then he shrugs it off. Whatever downsides there are to all of this, it's going to be worth it. He's sure of it.

'I can see some computers up here,' Kieran says.

Getting to use them isn't simple, however. Kieran had suspected they might need to pay to use them, or at least have a library card, but he'd hoped they'd be able to do a one-off session. But the young woman behind the counter looks apologetic and says, 'I'm sorry, you have to be a member to get online. I can sign you up if you have a permanent address here and some proof of ID?'

They have no such thing, of course. Kieran's about to try to bribe the woman with the little cash he has when Robert tugs on his T-shirt and whispers, 'Come over here.'

He frowns at him, but his brother's eyes tell him there's something important he needs to know. After quickly muttering, 'Thanks, no worries,' to the librarian, he follows Robert over to the computers.

'Look,' he says, holding something out for Kieran to see in his palm. Kieran looks down to see a small card. A library card. It has a Cornwall Libraries logo on it and a name printed in block capitals underneath. VIN TAKO-SMITH.

Kieran's eyes light up. 'Come on,' he says. They head for a row of three computers that are relatively hidden behind a stretch of shelves labelled 'Home Gardening and Allotments', and Kieran begins to key in the library card number into the login screen. Thankfully, the system only seems to require that and a name, which he adds into the box next to it and clicks 'GO'. A homepage, similar to a regular desktop layout, arrives, offering four labelled icons: 'WEB', 'CATALOGUE', 'NOTEBOOK' and 'PRINTER'. He clicks on 'WEB' and MSN Search arrives on the screen with encouraging speed. He heads to the website the two boys have become very familiar with over the past couple of weeks. The Raven's videos are uploaded and presented in a specific order, following a coherent thread to his teachings, although one of the forum members has made things a bit easier by organising lists of his videos into themes and groups. Kieran finds this post within one of the forum threads and selects a video under the list header 'Sacrificial Preparation'. He reaches into his rucksack. 'I've got headphones.'

Afterwards, Kieran looks at Robert and says, 'So what do you think?'

Robert looks taken aback, perhaps surprised Kieran's asking his opinion.

'In terms of…?' he says, blinking.

'In terms of what The Raven says about a "preparatory moment". What do you think ours should be? What should we do before the séance to help prepare the ground and become properly in tune with the energy of the Dark Core.'

Robert looks both confused and worried. 'I don't know. I suppose you've already written down midnight swim, so I guess that's the nearest to the moonlight bathing he mentions. What were the other options?'

Kieran sighs. 'They're not options. We're free to think up our own, but the ones he mentioned are carnal enjoyment. Carnal means—'

'I know what carnal means,' Robert snaps. 'I'm not a child.' Kieran notices him going red.

'Don't look so embarrassed,' he says, grinning. 'I've seen you looking at her.'

Robert looks even more uncomfortable.

'Is that why you've been so … well, so reluctant with all this. You fancy her?'

'You're the one who was flirting with her.'

Kieran seems surprised. 'When?'

'When she came to the treehouse and I went to the house. When I came back, I heard her flirting with you.'

Kieran nods. 'Exactly. *Her* flirting with *me*. Not the other way around. I'm focused, Rob. I'm just not sure you are.'

Robert falls silent again. Kieran folds his arms.

'Are we going to have a problem?' he says, still keeping his voice low but talking more firmly.

'With what?' Robert says, a belligerent note creeping into his voice now.

'With your feelings about Chloe,' Kieran says.

Robert's expression becomes pinched, as though he's biting his tongue. Kieran waits for a moment, then eventually grows impatient.

'Well, leaving that aside,' Kieran says, 'I think we can dismiss carnal enjoyment. So if we are just keeping to the suggestions The Raven mentioned, that leaves the sharing of bread and wine. I think that's probably the simplest.' He taps his hands on the smooth, shiny surface of the table, thinking. Then he says, 'Perhaps we combine two of them to really up our chances. We could suggest a moonlight swim, then return to the treehouse and share some bread and wine before we begin the séance.'

Robert nods, slowly, still looking unsure, then says, 'But how … how are you … we … going to actually…?' He trails off, concern evident in his eyes.

'That's one of the reasons we've come here – as in, into the centre of town. We have some shopping to do. And I need to check some things first.' From his rucksack, Kieran pulls out his notebook and flicks to the back where he's made a list.

'What's that?' Robert says, leaning over to look at the page.

'Isn't it obvious?' Kieran says.

He sees Robert scanning the notebook. It's a list of drugs. Not illegal or even prescription drugs – rather, medications people would expect to find in bathroom cabinets or available to buy over the counter, provided the purchaser is over sixteen. Robert recognises most of the items on the list, ranging from paracetamol to codeine to antihistamines.

'I was trying to research this back at the lodge, but the websites I wanted to use kept crashing,' Kieran says, navigating to a site titled Check Drugs Now UK, with a subheading 'Interaction tracker and checker'.

'I don't understand,' says Robert, pulling his chair closer to the screen.

'There are many medications easily available in the UK that can be fatal in relatively small quantities if combined together, especially with alcohol.' Kieran starts to type, entering the names of the drugs in two adjacent boxes on the site's homepage. 'You just have to find the right combination. Like a recipe, if you see what I mean.'

He continues to enter different drugs, switching up mixtures and amounts, checking the results that come up when he clicks 'Enter', then trying again. At last, he hits on something and writes it down, then another piece of information, underlining things he wrote previously and re-ordering his list, crossing things out. Then he navigates off the page.

'Are we done?' Robert asks.

'I think so,' Kieran says, strangely out of breath, as though he's been dashing around rather than typing things into a computer.

'What now?' Robert asks, adjusting his position in the uncomfortable school-like plastic chair. He doesn't sound bored or even worried. Instead, Kieran's interested to see there's something of the excitement he's also feeling burning bright in his brother's face, replacing the unease that was there minutes before.

'We go shopping,' he says.

He closes the notebook and drops it into his bag. He's about to exit the account on the computer when a voice behind them says something that makes Kieran freeze. And instantly go cold.

'I know exactly what you two are up to.'

Chapter Twenty-Eight

ROBERT

2004

Robert and Kieran turn around. Even though the voice is clearly male, Robert half expects to see Chloe standing there. But instead, his eyes settle on the surly face of a boy around their age.

'Er … sorry?' Robert says, confused.

'What do *you* want?' asks Kieran.

'Who is this?' Robert says, looking at Kieran, then back at the boy.

'You know who I am,' he says. 'And I'm here to say I know what you're doing.'

'Er … we don't know you,' Robert says.

'We do,' Kieran mutters out of the side of his mouth.

'What?' Robert is confused. He looks back at the boy. It takes a few more seconds to place him, and then it clicks. It's the boy who called out to Chloe when he was cycling in the street. The one she said she's been on a date with. The awkward one.

'Oh, yes, I remember,' Robert says.

'Yeah,' says Kieran, 'it's the weirdo.' He laughs, and it's either this or the word 'weirdo' that prompts what happens next. The boy seizes Kieran by his T-shirt and pulls him to his feet. A couple of the other computer users in the same row stop what they're doing and start watching avidly.

Robert gets to his feet too, both worried and half hoping this is going to descend into a full-on fight.

'You're planning to steal her away from me,' the boy says, his voice quivering with emotion. Although his act of tugging Kieran to his feet was bold and gave the appearance of strength, Robert spots the nerves in his delivery, the sweat on his brow and the trembling of his arms as he lets them drop to his side, his hands balling into fists.

Kieran laughs. 'As if you have any claim on her. She's not some prize to be passed between men. Is that how you see women?'

'*Men?* You're not a man; you're a little boy,' he says back at him.

'Oh yeah?' Kieran says, straightening up to his full height, which is a good inch taller than his opponent.

'And she told us she doesn't want you,' Robert says. 'She made that very clear.'

'Yeah, she said you were one of the weirdest losers she's ever had the misfortune to speak to,' Kieran adds, stretching the truth. 'She said she's embarrassed to be seen with you.'

'She didn't,' the boy says. 'And don't act like you know her. Just because you've managed to get friendly with her in that treehouse of yours. You've made her into some … some kind of whore. Some kind of dirty whore and it's all your fault.'

'Have you been following us?' Kieran says, sounding outraged.

'And that isn't what she's been doing,' Robert clarifies. 'You shouldn't say stuff like that. Nothing's been happening and we don't want it to either.' Even though there's something a bit thrilling about this confrontation, he feels the need to be the sensible brother here and de-escalate the situation. 'Plus, I don't think it's nice to use words like that about a girl.'

'Oh, you *don't think it's nice*?' the boy says, parroting the words with an exaggeratedly posh voice.

'Oh just fuck off, OK?' Kieran snaps, giving the boy a shove.

'Don't you touch me,' he says back, almost shouting now.

Robert becomes aware of someone else joining the scene now.

The figure to their left marches up to them and says in a carrying hiss, 'Boys! This is a *library*.'

Robert turns to look at the bespectacled lady, who looks about seventy, and feels a jab of admiration for her dedication in trying to preserve the peace of this place of reading and learning. It doesn't work, however, as it's the boy's turn to have his T-shirt seized. Kieran lifts him up so he almost falls out of it, struggling and choking as it bunches around his neck.

'Put him down!' the elderly lady says, making an admirable effort to keep the volume out of her voice. 'Or you'll be banned from this library.'

'Listen, mate,' Kieran says, keeping his eyes on the boy in his grasp, 'there's a reason Chloe doesn't want to see you, and that's because you're a timid little pussy. A weak little cunt.'

This causes the librarian to gasp theatrically. 'Such *language*! Right, that's it. Out! All of you.'

Robert watches as Kieran and the boy descend into an awkward scuffle. The boy uses whatever strength he still has to pull himself free, the force sending Kieran toppling to the floor. He aims a kick at him, but Kieran grabs his foot and pulls him down too.

'Shall I call the police?' a woman from one of the other computers says, standing up and brandishing a mobile phone as though it were a weapon.

'Yes, phone them!' the librarian shrieks, abandoning all pretence at keeping quiet. 'Phone them and tell them some louts are ruining this place for everybody else. I've never known the like, not in all my time—'

'You don't need to phone the police. We're going,' Robert says, stepping over to the struggling mass on the floor, both boys locked in an embrace and grunting muffled expletives at each other. He finds purchase around his brother's stomach area and pulls, managing to break Kieran away.

'Let go of me! I'm going to finish him!' he shouts.

'Finish me? *Finish me?* Don't make me laugh. You wouldn't last a minute if I really started on you,' the other boy sneers, though Robert sees how he clutches at his nose where a drip of blood has started to become visible.

'Out!' shouts the librarian again. When none of them moves, she clearly decides a more hands-on approach is required. She starts to nudge Kieran and Robert with her hands in a shooing motion, as one would treat an unwanted cat. The other boy gets to his feet, still clutching his nose. 'You too,' the librarian says, looking back at him, stretching one of her fingers into a point and aiming it at the doors.

Not waiting for further encouragement, the boy joins Robert and Kieran in heading for the exit, pushing past them so that Robert is knocked up against a book display near the door, sending a cascade of Jackie Collins paperbacks tumbling to the floor.

'Oh for goodness' sake,' the lady says, steadying the display unit before that goes over too. 'Needless to say, all of you are barred,' she calls after them, sticking her head out of the doorway before slamming it shut, reminding Robert of a pub landlord in a TV soap rather than a librarian.

Robert glances at his brother, whose face is flushed red. He has a cut on his lip, presumably from where one of the other boy's nails caught him. His assailant, however, has tears in his eyes as he struggles to unclip his bike from the railings to the left of the library entrance. For a moment, Robert feels a little sorry for him. He watches him become more flustered as he tries to get his wheels straight so they'll carry him away from this place, the watery eyes giving way to actual tears. But when he speaks, all pity vanishes from Robert.

'You're just two stuck-up posh pricks,' he says with venom. 'And I know you're planning on getting off with her. Just know that even if she does stuff with you, like she does with other blokes, in the end it's me she loves.'

His voice breaks into a sob on the last word.

'We're not *planning* anything,' Kieran says. 'Now just fuck off, OK?'

He heads off down the street. Robert looks over at the boy on the bike one last time, his face a mixture of tears and fury and blood from his nose, then hurries to catch up with his brother.

'Dick,' Kieran mutters. 'And he's deluded. Absolutely deluded.'

Robert nods. But he can't help thinking about what Kieran said.

We're not planning anything.

Because of course, they are. He wonders how horrified that boy would be if he knew the real truth.

It isn't seduction they're planning.

It's murder.

Chapter Twenty-Nine

ROBERT

2004

To Robert's surprise, the procurement of the medications Kieran listed goes relatively easily. In only one instance is ID required, in the branch of Boots, but since Kieran is sixteen that doesn't pose any problems. But by the end of their little tour of the chemists (apparently, different shops are necessary to avoid suspicion and because there are legal limits on the amount of certain drugs they can sell to one customer), Robert feels dazed by how far along they've progressed in their plans without being caught. How could they be planning what they're planning without the police suddenly pulling up beside them, throwing on the handcuffs and carting them off to a police station? He imagines his mother looking up from whatever German-language novel she's in the process of translating, to find two police officers at the door telling her that her sons are currently in the cells because of a crime they were about to commit.

'Rob, get on,' Kieran prompts.

They had been standing at the bus stop outside Argos, waiting to be taken back to Port Bowen, with Robert so lost in his thoughts he hadn't noticed its arrival or Kieran getting on board. He hurries to get on and Kieran leads the way to the back, dropping his rucksack down on the spare seat to his left. Robert hears the rattle of the boxes of pills as he does so. The sound makes him feel a bit sick.

When the bus arrives in Port Bowen, they remain sitting until it comes to a stop near the rundown part of the road where Chloe lives.

'Maybe you should text Mum where we are if we're not going back to the lodge first,' Robert says, feeling uneasy. 'Also, shouldn't we take the … um … stuff back?'

He hurries to keep up with Kieran as he crosses over the road, walking purposefully towards Chloe's bungalow.

Kieran shakes his head. 'She's not going to search my rucksack,' he says, giving his brother a brief eyeroll. Rob isn't so sure. Chloe is curious in a floaty, relaxed sort of way, and rummaging in someone else's bag and taking objects out, examining them and asking about them, is exactly the sort of thing he can imagine her doing.

But he need not have worried. The door isn't answered by Chloe when they knock. Instead, they hear a woman's voice shout, 'It's on the latch, Derek!'

Kieran pauses, then opens the door, sticking his head into the gloomy hallway. 'Er … Chloe?' he calls out.

'Derek?' the voice calls out again. 'Come up to the bedroom, you lazy fucker!'

Again, Kieran looks hesitant. 'I think it's her mum,' Robert whispers to him.

This earns him another eyeroll. 'Yes, I've worked that out, you know,' he mutters. He calls out, 'It's not Derek. It's … we're here to see Chloe.'

'What? Oh, she's out.'

Kieran is clearly unsure whether he should go inside uninvited or continue to hold his half-shouted conversation on the doorstep. Robert knows that Kieran would prefer to politely introduce himself properly – usually with a handshake – and continue any further communication face-to-face. Robert's eyes linger on the brown, fraying, stained carpet, the mass of junk mail pressing up against the door, takeaway pizza flyers and envelopes with words like URGENT: FINAL DEMAND on the front.

Kieran waits for a moment, perhaps hoping for more information, then he says, 'Will she be returning soon?'

A tutting sound followed by wheezing and coughing follows, then a louder shout, 'How should I know? Clear off and shut the fucking door while you're at it!'

Kieran pauses again, then leans away from the open door and closes it.

'Her mum sounds nice,' Robert says with grim sarcasm.

'Hmm,' Kieran replies.

They walk back through the woods in silence and when they reach the treehouse they climb up to deposit the bag and its contents under Kieran's bed. Back at the lodge, they find their mother in a bad mood. She's sorting out papers that seem to have become disordered, arranging them on the main table in the kitchen as she sorts them into piles.

'What's all this?' Robert asks as they stroll through the open glass doors of the kitchen.

'A manuscript I'm translating. Or I was until your father accidentally knocked it off the table,' she says, not hiding her irritation. 'So I'm having to waste my time getting it back into page order when I should be working on it.'

She lifts a neat stack of sheets and Robert sees 'KAPITEL 9' at the top of one of them before she places it onto another very thick stack. She lets out a sigh, then looks at them with narrowed eyes.

'Where have you boys been? Nobody was here for breakfast. I was worried, but your father said I shouldn't clip your wings when you're on holiday.'

'Where is Dad?' Kieran asks, avoiding her question.

She shrugs – a tense, jerky movement that makes it clear she's far from happy with the situation.

'Urgent business in Bristol, of all places. A firm that owns clothing factories needs him to follow up on something. Apparently they make anoraks. Why they can't find another business consultant while he's on holiday, I don't know. But I guess some people don't know how to switch off and leave work at home.'

The irony of this comment, as she continues to sort through the papers in front of her, echoes loudly in the room, although neither of her sons comments on it. Robert thinks they should leave her to her annoyance as quickly as they can, in case she starts to scrutinise their activities and gives them tasks to do. Kieran clearly feels the same, saying they're going to shower and grab something to eat, then head out for the day.

'Well, we're halfway through the day anyway,' his mother says, 'and I imagine I'll be working on this over lunch'—she casts a hand at the table—'so you might as well amuse yourselves.'

Once they're settled back in the treehouse, the boys start to talk about the sacrificial ceremony properly. Kieran now seems keen to discuss and explore, as though his silence and mysterious demeanour has finally worn away. Perhaps, Robert wonders, their trip to the town cemented his loyalty in his brother's mind. Robert, however, has never felt so conflicted. He knows the idea of what they are planning excites and appeals to him, and this itself is unsettling to acknowledge. Disturbing, even. But he can't deny that it's there.

He's also starting to face up to another inconvenient fact: he's attracted to Chloe. In the past, the whole subject of attraction and fancying the opposite sex has seemed like a terrifying prospect. He has been resistant to it throughout his teenage years so far because it feels like an element of complication that his life could do without. A very adult complication. He puts it off, even whilst his friends hook up with girls or try to sneak them into the dorms. Now, faced with a different sort of uncertainty – an uncertainty that threatens to take him down a sinister path of no return – the whole 'dating girls' thing seems refreshingly wholesome. But even though Kieran may have his suspicions, Robert doesn't dare tell him about it outright. Especially not when Kieran seems so enthusiastic about his plan, sorting through the boxes of pills he's bought and talking about how he's going to steal some vodka from the lodge.

'We should have bought a Ouija board when we were in town,' Robert says, hoping this sounds like a valuable contribution to the conversation.

Kieran doesn't seem to think so. He laughs and says he doubts they sell them in Woolworths. 'We'll make one,' he says, shrugging. 'It doesn't really matter how it looks.'

He goes off to the lodge and comes back with some sheets of printer paper and pens.

'Dad's still not back,' Kieran says darkly. 'Mum's pissed off. She's taking it out on her laptop. I fear for those keys she's punching.'

He starts to cut out parts of the paper, drawing on some areas with a black felt-tip pen.

'I know I'm the younger one and you're the … um … big brother,' Robert says cautiously, 'but I can't help thinking Chloe will take one look at this and think it's a bit childish.' He watches as Kieran begins to stick pages of paper together with a roll of Sellotape, the letters he's drawn on the edges starting to form a circle when joined together.

'It doesn't have to look good,' Kieran replies, not looking up. 'And she seems to like hanging out with us, so we just need her to stay long enough for it to work.'

Once he's finished, he leans back on his knees, observing his handy work.

'I think this will be OK.' He pauses for a few seconds, stroking his chin with his hand, then says, 'Right, we need to get the unifying event sorted, like The Raven said in the video.'

'I thought you said about the bread? And the wine?'

Kieran nods, slowly. 'Yes. But it doesn't feel like enough. I feel we need something else. I'm thinking the midnight swim we spoke about. A unifying event under the light of the moon.'

Something about the words *under the light of the moon* makes Robert shiver, even though it's still very hot and the air is close and muggy.

'I did think about drowning. As in, drowning as a form of sacrifice,' Kieran says, sounding like he's musing about plans for a party or a casual meal. The ease with which he says this still stuns Robert, even after everything they've discussed. It still feels unreal. He just stares at him. Robert isn't sure what to say.

Kieran shakes his head, as though replying to something his brother has said. 'But I think the midnight swim is best as the unifying event, so we're all bonded together as a group – a shared experience, like The Raven said. Then we can go back to the treehouse and perform the ceremony.'

He then looks at the boxes of pills, gathered in a pile.

Robert follows his gaze. 'How…?' He leaves the rest of the question unspoken, hanging in the air. But Kieran understands.

'It will be a potion. A potion to help us contact the spirits on the other side. She'll like that, I think.'

'I doubt she'll like the taste,' Robert says.

Kieran sighs. 'I think you need to get into a more positive frame of mind. It will be fine.'

'You don't know that,' Robert says quietly. 'She could just refuse.'

Kieran shrugs. 'We'll just have to see. This is our first time. It doesn't have to be perfect. So long as we don't lose our nerve, I think it will work.'

Some seconds of silence pass between them. Then Robert says nervously, 'Don't you … well … feel bad?' Robert says. 'Because … she seems quite nice…'

The sudden movement that follows takes Robert's breath away. Kieran lunges at him, knocking him backwards so that he's backed up against the wall. The force is such that it causes the whole wooden structure to reverberate. The push starts on his shoulders, then Kieran's right hand takes hold of his neck, clasping tight.

Robert has never been scared of his brother. He's been annoyed with him, confused by him, even unsettled or troubled by him, but never scared. Yet in that moment he is. He finds himself reeling from the force and shock of the sudden violent action.

Still holding him by the throat, Kieran moves his face closer and says through clenched teeth, 'Are you going to ruin everything?'

Robert can see the perspiration on his brother's lip, the stubble on his cheek lining his jawline from skipping shaving; he notices the anger burning in his eyes, feels the strength of him – a quality he's never truly appreciated before now.

'Answer the question,' Kieran says.

Robert shakes his head. 'I won't,' he says, feeling his hands tremble as he brings them up and rests them on Kieran's wrist. He doesn't want to use too much force, doesn't want to turn this into a proper physical fight like the one they had with that local boy in the library, but at the same time he needs to free his neck from Kieran's tight fingers. Using all the strength he can, he tightens his hold on his brother's arm and tries to push it away. To his relief, Kieran relinquishes his hold. Robert feels himself wilting, dropping forwards. Even though he was still able to take in oxygen, he gulps at it as though he's been holding his breath beneath the surface of a deep, terrifying ocean.

They look at each other.

Then, for the second time in the space of a couple of minutes, Kieran surprises Robert again, moving towards him quickly – this time not with violence, but with a big, almost desperate hug. He pulls him in tight and presses his head into his shoulder. Robert is so astounded and confused by this sudden change that he just stays still, limp, like a ragdoll in his brother's arms.

'I'm sorry,' Kieran whispers into his ear. 'I just want you to be committed. I want it to work for you too.'

He pulls back and stares at Robert again. A shaky quality in his voice makes Robert think he may have started crying, but he sees that Kieran's eyes aren't red and his cheeks are free from tears. With a tremor in his words, Kieran clutches Robert's shoulders, his expression earnest. Intense.

'We're doing this for our futures, you understand? Like The Raven says, the Dark Core of the Earth is pleased by every sacrifice. We're making sure our path through life isn't paved with obstacles and trials and suffering. We'll live rich lives filled with good fortune. Who wouldn't want that?'

Robert wipes away the tear that's running down his cheek.

'You'll see, Rob. You'll see. I'm going to be rich. I'll buy a lottery ticket later this week and I'll win. I promise you. I'm going to be so fucking rich, it will astonish you all. You, and Mum and Dad, will all be coming to me for money. That's what I want. And that's what I'll get. This is your chance to be part of that.'

Eventually, Robert nods. 'OK,' he says, his voice feeling weak and scratchy.

'Promise me you're with me. One hundred per cent.'

Robert tries to hold his gaze. He knows Kieran will doubt him even more if he doesn't. It's hard, seeing something close to mania writ large in his brother's eyes, but he manages it.

He keeps eye contact.

He takes a deep breath.

'I'm committed, I promise,' he lies. 'One hundred per cent. I'm with you.'

Chapter Thirty

ROBERT

2004

Planning to commit a murder isn't how it looks in movies or TV shows. Robert thinks this to himself as he lies awake in the treehouse that night, his thoughts becoming even more suffocating than the rising summer heat. In films, people always seem to know what they're doing, and he's aware that in spite of the pretence Kieran keeps up, neither of them really knows how the next day is going to go. But perhaps that's because in films murderers always seem to have a very clear motive. They all tend to kill because someone has wronged them in some way. Women kill their husbands because they've walked in on them shagging a woman from work or because they've discovered he secretly has another wife in another city. Men kill their wives because they're after money or life insurance, or they're just awful misogynists. Gangsters kill people because they've cheated them or stolen from them or some other dispute, probably involving mountains of cocaine and wodges of banknotes in briefcases. Then there are all the people who kill simply because they are insane, lashing out with a weapon because he or she truly believes voices have instructed such an act.

Are he and Kieran insane? he wonders, turning over in the thin bed, unable to get comfortable. He's too warm and the bed is too short. How would Kieran feel if Robert left the treehouse and went back to sleep in the lodge? He doesn't want to give his brother any further reason to doubt his commitment, or make him worry that he's telling their parents about their plans. Perhaps, then, he *is* insane: surely someone would have to be, to turn down the chance to stop a crime in its tracks, not to take up every opportunity to stop it.

You haven't tried to stop it. Not properly.

He presumes these thoughts are coming from his conscience. He thinks about the little cricket in *Pinocchio* who reminds the puppet of right and wrong when he takes the wrong path. Is that the same as hearing voices? He isn't sure. But he knows the statement is true. He hasn't tried. And the thought that follows next is true too: *you don't want to stop it.*

He sits up, swings his legs off the edge of the bed and leans forwards, putting his head in his hands, but still he can't stop the voice. It's like a horrible little echo, reverberating off guilty walls.

Because you're scared your brother's right. You're scared he'll secure a future free from difficulty and hardship and you'll be left behind, with your life getting steadily worse, filled with stress and worry.

He moves his hands from his head to his knees and clutches at the material of his pyjama trousers. He thinks about all these things, each thought leading to other thoughts. What will happen when the dawn arrives? What choice will he make? And all the while, a face is present in his mind, never far from the surface, floating in and out of focus, no matter what he's thinking about. A girl's face. Chloe.

He knows instantly what he must do. The thing that he must find out before anything can continue.

As quietly as he can, he gets dressed and pulls on his trainers, all the while keeping an eye on the sleeping Kieran. He has his face turned to the wall so Robert can't properly see him, but in the darkness he can just make out his shoulders rising and falling in a rhythmic way that suggests he's fast asleep. He hopes he is. After the sudden shock of his brother's aggression, Robert definitely doesn't want to upset him further.

He exits the treehouse and climbs down the ladder without being discovered. Then he begins to pick his way through the last stretch of the garden and over the fence into the woods. The night sky above is clear and some of the natural light makes its way through the leaves. But even so, he's still rather daunted by the darkness around him. He's determined to press on, determined to do what he's come out here to do. But he can't lie to himself: he is more than a little afraid.

He's only been walking for five minutes when the sound causes him to jump and clutch hold of a nearby tree. A shriek, loud and piercing. And it wasn't a human sound. He then hears the impact of fast movement upon the forest floor – something running. Then two barks.

'Get over here, you idiotic beasts!' a man shouts. A whistle sounds, followed by more running.

With the sound of his heart pounding in his ears, Robert slowly peers around the trunk of the tree in the direction of the sound. He sees the dogs then, running towards the upper end of the slope where the nearby farm backs on to the woods. They must have escaped, he thinks. Well, he's pleased they seem to have gone now. He doesn't fancy walking through the woods at night with those vicious-sounding animals running wild. After he's sure both animals and the owner have gone and the more peaceful sound of the woods at night descends, Robert peels himself away from the sanctuary of the tree trunk and continues to walk down the slope in the direction of the village. In the direction of the row of rundown houses and bungalows. In the direction of Chloe.

He reaches Chloe's street a little while later. The whole place is deserted and his watch tells him it's just gone two in the morning. He walks up to her home. The whole place is in darkness. He wishes Chloe had a mobile so he could text her, find out if she is awake. But instead, he has to improvise. He has no idea if she's at home, but he remembers the sound of her mother's voice shouting out from the back of the property, and he's fairly sure the sound came from the left-hand side. That means it's very likely that Chloe's bedroom is on the right. He doubts the bungalow has more than two bedrooms, and it makes sense for them to be at the back. At least he thinks it does. Not that he's ever been in a bungalow before.

Worried that his trainers will make too much of a sound on the hard path that leads around the back of the building, he silently slips them off and walks in his socks, hoping nobody sees him.

This is mad, he thinks to himself as he tiptoes. What if she mistakes him for a burglar and phones the police? What if she's not even home? What if he gets her mum's bedroom by mistake? What if she has her curtains drawn, like most people would, and he can't even see anything?

But the night is so hot that his gamble pays off. The bedroom to the right side of the bungalow has both curtains and window open so wide that Robert is amazed at the security risk. If he wanted, he could hop up onto the window ledge and climb into the bedroom.

Perhaps he does want to. He pauses, peering in. He's fairly sure he can make out a shape on the bed. He's also fairly sure it's Chloe, sleeping peacefully. Then she moves, gently and slowly, still asleep, she rolls over and Robert sees her hair fall over her front, part of her face hidden. But it's definitely her. She's wearing what looks like a large T-shirt with a picture on the front he can't make out, her bare legs wrapped around the lower end of the bed covers.

Suddenly, she opens her eyes.

Robert panics. He tries to step back, but his feet come into contact with something sharp that makes him cry out. At the same time, he drops his trainers and they make a clattering sound on the stone patio. He falls onto his backside, landing on a dry patch of grass. He can see, in the midst of his disorientation, that he has trodden on some garden implement – maybe a trowel or something similar with prongs – and he feels a searing, burning pain in his right foot.

'Who's there?' a girl's voice calls out. Chloe's voice. She's at the window, climbing out of it, brandishing something in her hand. Then she stops and lowers her arm.

'Oh … Robert? Is that you? What are you doing here?'

'Sorry,' Robert says, trying to pull himself up. He wouldn't be surprised if he's bruised his coccyx, and the searing pain in his foot feels more like skin trauma than a sprain. He touches his foot and the sole of the sock feels damp. He can make out a dark patch on its white surface.

'Ahh…' He winces, the pain coming in waves. 'I think I've hurt my foot.'

Chloe looks at him. Even in the dark, he can tell she's frowning. He's not used to her seeming annoyed or displeased in any way. 'Can you stand?' she asks.

'Yeah, I think so,' Robert says, getting to his feet shakily. Chloe puts out an arm and takes his hand. 'Thanks.'

'Come inside. You can look in the light.'

Her tone is brisker and more businesslike than normal. Robert wonders if this is because she's just woken up, or because she's cross with him for scaring her. He also didn't bargain on being invited inside the house. In his head, he was going to throw a stone at the window to attract her attention, like boys do in the movies, and she'd sneak out to see him and they'd go for a romantic walk in the moonlight during which he would confess his burgeoning feelings for her, and she'd say she's been feeling the same way ever since setting eyes on him. Then they'd run away together, or at the very least tell their respective parents of their love and likely marriage in the future. All plans of séances and sacrifices would go out the window, because who needs the Dark Core to clear one's life pathway when one's life is already destined to be amazing anyway?

All this melts away very quickly when Robert is shown through the back door into the messy kitchen of the bungalow. Of course, the building being one level, there was never any hope of him throwing up small stones to attract Chloe's attention. Instead, he feels like a creepy, skulking figure at the window. The chance of a moonlit declaration of mutual attraction also seems unlikely, especially in a kitchen with harsh fluorescent lighting, open baked-bean cans, empty cereal boxes and stained surfaces. Chloe flicks the light on as soon as they enter and makes no apology for the state of the place. His eyes hurt in the sudden bright glare.

Robert looks around and asks, 'Won't we wake up your mum?'

'Oh, she's not in,' Chloe says. 'Off with Derek. Or Bernie. Not sure which. He swung by and picked her up earlier, just when I was getting home.'

'Where have you been all day?' he asks.

Instead of answering she looks down at his injured foot and says, 'You're hobbling. It must hurt. Come into the bathroom.'

He follows her into a small bathroom that looks like it could do with a good clean but is at least in a better state than the kitchen. She tells him to perch on the edge of the bathtub as she takes an ancient-looking first aid box down from a shelf, blowing off a layer of dust as she does so.

'I've always wanted to do a bit of first aid but don't usually get the chance,' she says, smiling and sounding a bit more like the normal Chloe. She inspects the cut on his foot and puts a bandage around it. 'So what were you doing at my bedroom window so late in the evening? Or I suppose I should say so early in the morning.'

Robert feels himself going red. 'I was just … missing you…'

Chloe nods slowly and smiles again. 'Well, that's nice,' she says. 'I was missing you and Kieran too. But it's only been one day, Robert. I'm sure you can both cope without me for one day. I'll soon be off to America, and what will you do then?'

Robert opens his mouth but can't get any words out. This is the first he's heard of any plan of hers to go to America, other than the vague intention she'd spoken about on the beach, but that had sounded so hypothetical and unlikely that he hadn't thought about it since.

'Oh, I haven't told you. I finally managed to convince Derek to help me pay for a ticket.'

'What? When? Who's Derek?'

'One of my mum's friends. Well, he's my friend now too. Or let's just say, I know him *very* well now, if you know what I mean. It wasn't easy to convince him to help me, but most men budge if you do them a few … favours.'

Robert is confused. 'I don't understand. He's taking you to America?'

She shakes her head. 'No, God, I just needed him for the discount. And the loan. I think he wants me out the way. He says I cramp his style, but he's trying to be all generous as he wants to move in with Mum. Anyway, his sister works at a travel agency and has got me a good deal on the tickets. The rest of the money Derek covered, provided I was OK with his *arrangement*.' Robert thinks he sees her shudder a little. Then she sweeps her hair aside in her usual casual manner and shrugs. 'I thought I'd go over there and travel around for a bit.'

Robert nods, even though he's struggling to comprehend everything he's been told. What he says next surprises even himself.

'Well, if this Derek's not going and you're going to be alone, maybe I can come?'

Chloe is in the process of putting away the bandage roll in the first aid box but pauses for a second before closing it shut.

'I … don't think that will be… I mean, I think it's only one ticket Derek can get me. And it's one way. I don't know if I'll manage to stay there, what with visas and working permits and shit, but I plan to figure out all that stuff when I'm there, but I don't know if you … I mean, you're still a child.'

Those last four words are like knives.

'I'm not a child,' he says in a small voice.

Chloe's smile is back, as though he's an adorable puppy who's just done a trick, or a kid who's made a cute mistake.

'Don't look at me like that,' he says.

'Oh come on, Robert. It wouldn't work, would it?'

'But I… I…' He tries to reach for her hand. He imagines it to be a romantic gesture to demonstrate how earnest and true his feelings for her are, but the movement causes her to drop the first aid box. It opens as it hits the tiles, sending the contents scattering across the floor.

'Sorry,' he says, trying to help her pick up the plasters and bandages but he loses his balance on the edge of the bath. 'Shit!' he shouts as he falls backwards.

Chloe laughs.

Even in the disorientation of the tumble – his second mortifying fall in her presence within the space of ten minutes – he can't help but notice the laugh and feel hurt by it. He's embarrassed, and furious with himself for behaving so stupidly and clumsily that he's caused her to laugh at him.

'Come on, take my hand,' she says, holding it out. 'God, you're in a bit of a state tonight, aren't you?'

She glances at him and apparently misreads his expression of humiliation and annoyance as one of upset and distress. 'Shall we phone your brother or dad to come and get you?'

He frowns. 'What? No. No, I'm … I'm fine. Chloe, I … I wanted to tell you something.'

He's standing in front of her now, steady on his feet. Or mostly steady. He didn't hit his head when he fell back, but his shoulders are sore where he jarred them and it hurts to stand up straight. He stoops a bit but tries to keep eye contact. He's aware he looks strange, but he doesn't think that excuses her second laugh. Again, she's amused by him. And not in a good way.

Anger flares in him. He isn't entirely sure what he'd planned to say. That he fancies her? That he wants to kiss her, to run his hand through her hair, across her face? Or other things. Things concerning a plan being hatched not far away. A plan with consequences so terrible, she probably wouldn't believe him even if he said it out loud. Not that he's going to, not now. The mixture of embarrassment and annoyance and the heat and a sudden rush of tiredness all tumble around inside him. In spite of the pain, he draws himself up to his full height, which is a little more than hers, and looks at her with unveiled scorn. All of a sudden, he can't imagine what he saw in her. He just wants to leave. He's desperate to get out of this horrible, filthy bungalow, filled with clutter and evidence of her and her mother's sordid lives. This isn't his world. It never was. He's an idiot to have ever thought there could be anything between the two of them.

'I'll go,' he mutters, transferring his eyes to the floor and heading to the door.

'Oh, OK,' Chloe says, not sounding disappointed exactly, more taken aback, but Robert doesn't stop to explain. 'I'll see you later, if you boys are around and want to hang out. I'm not free until the evening, around five or sixish, but we can do something then.' She comes with him to the back door. 'You can go out the front, you know.'

'This is fine,' he says, still not looking at her. 'And yeah, sure … er … I think we'll be around later.'

'Good,' she says. 'Kieran said something about a séance. Sounds fun. Is that still the plan?'

Robert pauses. He's out on the back patio, reaching down to pull on his trainers. When he looks up, he finds he can look her in the eye again. Without even being aware of it, he's made a decision.

'Yes,' he says. 'That's definitely still the plan.'

'Great, I'm looking forward to it,' she says.

Robert nods, still looking at her. 'Yes. Me too.'

Chapter Thirty-One

ROBERT

2004

Dawn is breaking when Robert gets back to the treehouse. He climbs quietly up the rungs of the ladder, carefully pulling himself up onto the balcony and is just getting to his feet when he sees something that makes his heart jolt. Kieran is sitting inside, very still, watching him through the open doorway.

'Nice to see you've returned,' he says. His voice cuts through the gloom, his expression surly, his eyes piercing.

'Er … yeah … I…' Robert stutters, trying to get his words out, hating how guilty he sounds. 'I went for a piss.'

Kieran frowns. 'And you needed to get fully dressed to go for a piss? Makes me wonder if it was more of an *excursion* than you're letting on, Rob.'

There's something odd about his tone. He doesn't sound cross, exactly, but there's a false, heightened quality to his low voice that Robert feels is there deliberately to unsettle him. Robert stays where he is on the balcony. It's as if he's an animal in the wild who's been spotted by a predator in the long grass. Even in his worried state, he's cross with himself for feeling like this with his own brother.

'All right, I went for a walk,' he says, entering the treehouse. Kieran doesn't move. He just sits there. 'I … couldn't sleep,' Robert says, sitting down. 'I went for a walk.'

Kieran doesn't reply to this. He watches Robert with a terrible look on his face. Eventually he says, 'You've been to warn someone, haven't you?' He says it very quietly – even quieter than before. 'Who was it?'

'What?' Robert says, looking confused and playing for time.

'Was it her? Or Mum and Dad?' He waits a beat, then says, 'Or did you go to the police?'

The word 'police' sends another jolt through Robert. 'I didn't… I haven't…' He takes a breath, then stands up and moves in front of Kieran, facing him properly. 'OK, I went to see her.'

He sees a widening of his brother's eyes as he stares back, perhaps a little triumphant that his suspicions are correct.

But before Kieran can speak, Robert holds up a hand and says, 'But not to warn her. I just … needed to be sure.'

Kieran's frown has returned. 'Sure?'

Robert nods, 'Yes, sure. I needed to be sure how I felt about her.'

Again, he lets some seconds pass before he replies. Robert gets a strange feeling, as though Kieran has the ability to see through his eyes and into his mind. Or into his soul.

'And are you?' Kieran asks eventually.

Robert nods. Once and firmly, still holding eye contact. 'I am. We continue with the plan. I told you yesterday, I'm committed. That's the truth. There's nothing else to discuss.'

An atmosphere remains between their parents at breakfast, with their mother choosing to eat alone on the veranda while the boys and their father sit at the kitchen table. In spite of this, their dad's mood seems otherwise buoyant, saying that after his busy work trip the day before he plans to go for a swim and asks the boys if they want to join him. Kieran says they have plans already and Robert nods along.

'Do you want a lift down to the seafront?'

Kieran says they'll go down to the beach later so they'll walk through the woods.

'I'm not sure I like you walking through those woods,' their mother says, coming through from the veranda into the kitchen.

'Why not?' asks Robert.

She places her plate in the sink, then says, 'I saw an odd-looking boy wheeling a bike, loitering near where the trees back onto the garden, here. And then there's that farmer, who I've seen from my window drunkenly wandering around, shouting at those savage-looking dogs of his. There seems to be no shortage of unsavoury types around here.'

Robert notices Kieran roll his eyes. 'Because Essex, on the other hand, is completely free from unsavoury types. You do know what Rettendon is internationally famous for, right?'

His mother ignores this. 'Perhaps you should spend the day playing in your little treehouse.'

'We don't *play*. We're not children. What's the point of coming on holiday to the sea if we don't enjoy it?' He gets up and pushes his chair back under the table. 'Come on, Rob. Let's play some tennis on the lawn. Then we'll go down to the beach whilst remaining on the lookout for anyone remotely dodgy.'

The rest of the morning and afternoon passes with achingly slow speed. The boys play tennis down on the expanse of grass at the end of the garden near the treehouse. Each time Robert checks his watch he expects to see hours have passed, but with dismay discovers it has only been a few minutes since he last looked.

He isn't sure if Kieran wants to talk about their plans for the moment they've been building up to, or if he's avoiding the topic. When Robert makes a reference to 'later' and whether everything's prepared, Kieran changes the subject or starts remarking about something unimportant, like their made-up scoring system for their tennis game or how the temperature is even hotter than it was the day before. Before they go to the beach to meet Chloe, however, he fetches his laptop from its charger in the lodge and beckons Robert up into the treehouse. Together, they rewatch one of his downloaded videos, one they've seen multiple times before, and yet it still holds a strange, unsettling power. The Raven talks about visualising their pathways, about the power of sacrifice, and emphasises how the change in one's life going forward is so profound that one will be able to feel the vibrations lasting for years later through their visualisations.

'Let's do it one last time,' he says, taking off his sandals. 'Let's do a visualisation one last time. Try to see our life pathways, then we'll repeat it later – after the sacrifice. Then we'll be able to see the impact it's had.'

They sit very still. Robert tries, as before, to make his mind go blank then he tries to see his pathway in his mind's eye. And for the first time since the start of everything they've discovered, he thinks he sees something. An image arrives there without the effort of creation, without any doubt about what it is. He knows what it is.

A gravel path, snaking through a wood. Not like the woodland outside, this one is more like the one in The Raven's videos – autumnal oak trees, leaves falling, rustling, scattering about, great drifts of them blocking the pathway. Hiding things. What things? He tries to look closer but isn't sure how to. He's there, standing on the path, but at the same time he's distant from it. Too distant to see properly. Then he realises what one of the hidden shapes is. It's a hand, poking out from the leaves. Then another. Body parts litter the pathway, some of them no more than bits of severed flesh, like meat. Others are whole limbs. Arms. Legs. Bones sticking out, grisly, charred, gnawed, as though damaged by both fire and teeth. He tries to go forwards but he can't move. Barbed wire is stopping him, snagging on his feet, making him bleed. He feels a sharp pain in his right foot, feels the razor edges of the wire rip into him, damaging tendons and muscle. He tries to hop on one leg but he can't. He falls, headfirst into one of the mountainous drifts of dead leaves. The contents are both dry and damp – cold with decay, dust and mould filling his lungs as he tries to breathe. He tries to stand, to pull himself free, but each time he does his foot snags on another loop of wire until at last, the pain becomes too much and he cries out.

'Rob!' someone shouts.

It's Kieran. His brother is crouching in front of him, staring at him. But he doesn't look worried. He looks excited. Pleased, even.

'You did it, didn't you?' he says in a hushed, awed tone. 'You saw your pathway.'

Robert is breathless, panting, perspiration gathering on his hairline and around his collarbone, aches in his hands and arms where he's been clenching. He has a rush of a weird, dizzying feeling – déjà vu, yes, he's sure of it; it's déjà vu. Kieran crouches before him, except this is the reverse of what happened before – back home in Essex, in the living room, with Kieran breathing fast as though he'd run a race even though he hadn't moved from the dining room chair he'd been sitting on.

'Rob, I think I've known you hadn't truly *seen*,' Kieran says. 'I get why you wanted me to think so, but I knew it wasn't true. I knew it would take time.' He places his hands over Robert's and grips them tightly. 'And I'm so pleased it's happened today,' he says. 'This is a very good sign. I just know it.'

A food delivery to the lodge, organised by their mother, provides Kieran with the opportunity to claim – or rather steal – a sourdough loaf and a bottle of red wine. Robert watches as Kieran wraps the bread in a tea towel and places it on the table in the treehouse, next to the paper séance apparatus. Next to it, he places another item he's taken from the house: an ornate, patterned blue bowl which had, up until very recently, held potpourri. Kieran looks up and sees Robert watching.

'Don't worry,' he says, as he sets down the bottles of vodka and wine next to it. 'This is all going to go to plan.' Then he takes out the boxes of tablets from his rucksack and begins to open the blister packs.

They set off through the woods in the early evening. If they'd been able to spend the day with Chloe, perhaps Robert wouldn't have been able to go through with it. But the distance of two days without her has helped dilute his sense of their friendship. Absence, in this case, has made the heart grow weaker. And last night's visit to her made him see how wrong he was about her.

He considers telling Kieran about this, as they pick their way down the slope, wandering around the thick tree trunks, Kieran pressing ahead with determination. He feels the pain in his foot where he injured it on the trowel outside the bungalow and decides against it. Sneaking around the windows of a girl's bedroom seems pathetic to him now. After his assurance that he is committed to the evening's plans, Kieran hasn't pressed him on details of his nighttime visit. He hopes it will stay that way, and Chloe will keep quiet for the remainder of the evening. Or rather, the remainder of her life.

The dogs come seemingly out of nowhere. Unlike the night before, when he heard their approach as they crashed through the undergrowth, this time they arrive unbidden, barking, snarling and biting, snatching at the bag Kieran's carrying containing their beach towels. One dog, white with a boxy face, tears at the bag with savage haste, throwing it aside, then rounds again on Kieran.

'Fuck!' he shouts, as the dog lunges towards him.

He backs away but knocks into Robert, who falls onto the dry woodland floor, straight into the path of the second dog, a large Alsatian. He cannot get to his feet before the dog reaches him. When its jaws clench, he's convinced for a second that it has hold of flesh, but it's only his T-shirt. He does his best to kick out and push the dog away and for a second he succeeds, his sleeve coming away as he rolls onto his side, trying to reach for Kieran. The dog then bites again, this time at Robert's backside, although again misses his skin, only tearing off his pocket and the back of his shorts, the ripping sounding harsh and violent. It makes Robert's blood go cold, thinking how any second that might not be a pocket, but his flesh.

'Kieran!' Robert shouts, reaching for his brother, but he's in the process of dodging the continued lunges of the white dog.

'Stop, now!' A shout sounds through the trees, followed by a sharp whistle. The same whistle he heard last night, from afar. The dogs, miraculously, do as they're told and run away from the boys and off back up the slope in the direction of the farm.

'Sorry about that,' says the voice, and the figure of the old farmer wanders into view, accompanied by the thick scent of alcohol. 'But it's your own fault, trampling around the woods, upsetting them.'

'*Upsetting* them?' gasps Kieran, rubbing a grazed elbow. 'This is a public wood, isn't it? It's not like we're trespassing.'

The old man furrows his thick, grey eyebrows, squinting at Kieran as though he's never seen anything quite like him. 'You're one of the holiday folks, aren't you?' he says. 'Don't know what you lot are up to, wandering these woods at night.'

'It isn't night,' says Kieran.

'I think he's talking about me,' Robert says, coming to stand close to his brother. 'I heard the dogs during the night. They were running about.'

'Not just you, others, people making noise at night,' the farmer says, his words slurring, his feet stumbling as he points first at Robert then away off into the trees. 'There was a man…' he says, pausing to scratch his wild hair. 'I've seen a boy on a bike, too…'

'Well, we don't have any bikes,' Kieran says. 'And if you can't keep those dogs under control we might have to inform the police.'

This causes a laugh. 'Police? What, little Jimmy Galbraith, the local constable? Why, he's only about twelve years old. What's he going to do, throw the cuffs on me because my dogs bark a bit loud?'

'They nearly killed us I'll have you know!' Kieran says, growing angrier. 'Look at my legs!'

Kieran's knees are indeed bleeding, although from what looks like scuffs from falling to the ground rather than teeth. He had already changed into his swimming trunks and the usually white material is now covered with dirt and bits of leaf.

'*I'll have you know*,' the man says, rocking his head and exaggerating Kieran's accent. 'You'll survive. They didn't actually get you. Just piss off and don't come crashing through here again.'

He begins to wander away. Kieran looks like he's tempted to go off after him and continue the argument, but Robert shakes his head and says, 'Come on, leave it.'

Kieran looks at him, frowning. 'Are you hurt? Your clothes…'

Robert looks down at his torn shorts, then to the side where his right T-shirt sleeve is hanging by a thread. He rips it off and casts it aside. 'We haven't got time to go back for me to change. Chloe will just think it's a weird new fashion choice.'

Kieran nods and they continue their journey down the slope in the direction of the village.

Chloe's waiting for them in the street. She's painting again, only this time appears to be covering up the mural she was working on the first time they met her. She has a rather ancient-looking rusty pot of paint with the word 'Cloudless' in big letters on the side, and is slathering it on the low front wall with a large brush. As the boys approach her, the hairline of the woman's face she had painted previously disappears under a liberal rush of blue.

'Oh there you are,' she says, dropping the brush, apparently unbothered by the flecks of paint she's getting on the public pavement. 'I wondered if you were coming.'

'We were attacked by dogs,' Kieran says, as though such an occurrence were a common cause of delay.

Chloe gets up off the floor and looks at Kieran's knees and then at Robert's clothing, bits of leaf and dirt still clinging to him. 'Yes, you look as if you were.'

'Why are you painting over your creation?' Robert asks.

Chloe turns back to look at the plain blue wall and sighs. 'Well, if I'm to leave this place, I don't want to leave things untidy. And that painting of the screaming woman did look a bit rough and unfinished. I couldn't get her expression quite right. Mum won't care, but I thought I'd paint the wall a nice blue for her before I go.'

'Go?' Kieran asks. He looks confused. Robert understands why; if he hadn't already been told of her plans to go to America, he too would have found the unintentional prescience of her words unnerving.

'Let's go to the caves,' she says, 'and I'll tell you as we walk.'

They walk down the little pathway through the bushes and down towards the steps in the cliff, and Chloe explains to Kieran about her US plans. Or lack of plans, Robert thinks as he listens, since although Chloe talks at length about the things she's going to do on arriving in New York City – most of these revolve around the museum she has previously mentioned, along with bagels and shopping in vintage clothing stores – actual concrete arrangements still seem thin on the ground.

Kieran is quiet while she says all this. Robert glances at him from time to time, as he listens to how her mother's friend will subsidise her travel and how she's always yearned for a new life.

Kieran says in a quiet voice, 'Perhaps, in a way, you were never destined for this world. Perhaps you were always meant to leave it.'

He says this as they step onto the beach, facing the expanse of the sea. A breeze runs over them, both warm and cool at the same time. Robert feels it ruffling his hair and invading the back of his shorts that've been left open after being torn by the dog's jaws. Memories of that recent brush with death, mixed with the elemental nature of the sea air and sound of waves that surround him now, cause Robert's skin to prickle. Excitement rushes through him.

'Let's go in the sea now,' he says.

'We dropped our towels when the dogs— And we were going to wait—'

Robert knows what Kieran is trying to say. They were going to wait until the moon was in the sky. A moonlight swim. That was going to be their unifying event before the sacrifice. But the thought of waiting is unbearable to him now. 'Let's not wait until the moon is out. Let's go in as the sun is setting. As the light disappears. That will be better.'

Kieran's looking at him – he can feel his gaze. He can see it in his peripheral vision. Robert doesn't know if Kieran's angry at him for changing the plan, for overruling him, or encouraged by his brother's bold approach. Whichever it is, Robert doesn't wait to find out. He kicks off his trainers, throws off his ruined T-shirt and ripped shorts and runs into the waves.

He hears Chloe laughing behind him. He hears someone crashing through the water nearby. He thinks it's her, for a second, but turns to see Kieran swimming up to him. Chloe's in the process of pulling off her baggy yellow T-shirt on the shore. Before she's in the water and near enough to hear, Robert moves close to his brother and says, 'I don't want to wait. If we're doing this, I want to do it soon. I can't wait until midnight.' He stares at Kieran, waiting for him to react.

Kieran gives him a rare smile and nods. 'OK.'

The waves make them rise and fall. The motion pushes them together, and Robert floats towards Kieran.

'This is the start, isn't it?' he says, and is surprised to find tears in his eyes. 'The start of our new lives. It's going to work. It's really going to work.'

Kieran grasps Robert's shoulders and holds tight. 'It will,' he whispers into his ear. 'It will.'

They're still just about able to stand in the water, but a wave comes in too quickly and strongly and splashes over their heads. They're thrown off balance, and come spluttering up to see Chloe, now nearby, giving them an odd expression.

She laughs. 'Am I interrupting some sort of brotherly bonding experience?'

'No,' Kieran says simply. 'We were just saying how perfect this holiday has turned out. We weren't keen to come here. We wanted to go to Portugal like we did last year. But this is great. It really is.'

Chloe starts to swim around them in a rough circle, then turns and heads out towards the horizon.

'Well, at least the water's warm. Probably not as warm as Portugal. But if you'd gone there, I'd have never had met you both. You've all brightened this last week here for me.'

She curves back around, swimming confidently towards them. She comes to a stop in front of Robert, leans forwards … and kisses him on the cheek. Then she does the same to Kieran. There isn't anything flirtatious to the kisses, or at least Robert doesn't think so. Instead, it feels like a full stop.

Like her way of saying thank you.

Her way of saying goodbye.

Chapter Thirty-Two

ROBERT

2004

They lie on the sand until the air dries them. The sun disappears and a deep blue-grey light fills the sky. Chloe ties her top around her shoulders and seems content to walk back in her bikini. When they reach her road, Robert wonders whether she'll make some excuse – perhaps say she's tired or needs to get back because of her mum or something like that. But she doesn't. She passes her home without a mention or hesitation.

The only pause in their walk occurs when Robert stops in front of the stile entrance to the woods. It's by far the quickest way back, and he'd like to retrieve the bag containing their towels and his trunks. But at the same time, the memory of the snarling Alsatian going for him is a hard one to shake. Kieran seems to be thinking the same thing.

'Oh come on,' Chloe says. 'You two strong lads aren't scared of some puppies, are you?'

'They weren't puppies,' Kieran says.

'I'll protect you both,' she says with a laugh as she marches ahead.

'We could go along the road,' Robert says, looking to his right, down the long stretch that winds up the hill and out of sight.

Chloe comes to a stop. She lets out a sound somewhere between a sigh and a huff. 'Maybe we should call it a day,' she says. 'I was supposed to be seeing a friend later anyway and … well, the road will take ages. I liked the idea of a séance but it might get too late.'

She climbs back over the stile.

'But … it won't get too late,' Robert says. 'We were supposed to be swimming when the moon came out, so we would have been doing the whole thing later anyway. Why are you seeing a friend when … when we…?' He trails off.

Robert sees a flicker of irritation on Chloe's face, similar to how she looked the night before when she found him outside her bungalow.

As though this incident is on her mind as well, she raises her eyebrows and says, 'Oh come on, Robert, you know I don't like set plans.' She walks over to where he and Kieran are standing. 'If you're going to get all jealous, maybe it's best.'

'I'm not jealous,' Robert says.

'You sure?' She smiles and chuckles. 'Because if I'm not mistaken, little Robbie, you were outside my window last night declaring your love for me.'

Robert feels his face growing red. It feels as if he's been plunged headfirst into a pan of boiling water. He dares not look at Kieran. He's mortified Chloe's mentioned it. He feels this revelation is an unnecessary distraction – one that risks destabilising their plans. They are so close, and he is so ready, so keen. His biggest fear is that if they wait even a minute too long, his courage and resolve will weaken. They need to act now, while he has the strength and will to do so.

'Oh come on,' Kieran says. 'We're wasting time.'

Relieved his brother seems to feel the same, Robert climbs over the style and drops down into the woods. Kieran follows.

Chloe pauses, just for a few more seconds, then she joins them. They make their way through the woodland without talking much. Neither Chloe nor Kieran refers to the subject of Robert's nighttime visit. He hopes there won't be any further mention of it. The night is complicated enough without that.

When they reach the treehouse, Chloe goes first up the ladder. For a moment, Robert worries about what may have been left out. He imagines an open laptop with The Raven's figure on the screen laid out on the table, or Kieran's notes detailing everything they're planning to do. But of course, nothing of the sort greets them as they all walk into the interior. The boys left it exactly how they wanted it to be found: the makeshift Ouija board; the cloth-covered bread; the wine; and, hidden under the bed, the 'potion'.

'God, I feel quite tired,' Chloe says, sitting down on the edge of Robert's bed. 'So glad you've got wine.' She points at the bottle. 'I do like wine, but my mum mostly does vodka. Or whisky. Derek got her into whisky. You don't have any whisky, do you?'

Kieran shakes his head. 'No. But we do have a rather strong concoction for the séance. It will help us conjure the dead.'

Robert's impressed at how easily this lie seems to slip off his brother's lips. Chloe responds encouragingly, nodding and grinning at him.

'I'm hungry,' she says. 'We should have got some chips.'

Kieran starts to unwrap the bread. 'Well, we don't have chips, but we do have this,' he says, breaking the loaf into rough pieces.

'I think people would call this "rustic",' Chloe says with a chuckle, taking the clump Kieran passes her. 'Well, if it's what's on offer, why not?'

She eats the bread. Kieran pours her some wine. He's kneeling on the floor as he does this and glances up at Robert.

'Er … Rob? Do you want to sit down, perhaps?'

It takes a second or two for Robert to respond, then he realises he's been standing near the doorway, staring at the *mise en scène* starting to unfold in front of him. He can't quite believe it's happening. That the moment has finally arrived. They are about to cross the threshold of one of the most important moments of their lives.

'Sorry,' Robert says, eventually snapping to attention and going to sit down, opting for Kieran's bed so he can face Chloe. He wants to be able to see her reactions. He's worried that any second she'll decide she's had enough, that she wants to get back to her bungalow to see whatever friend she's planned to meet. But she seems quite content to eat the bread and drink the wine, and she doesn't hesitate when Kieran sets up the Ouija board and takes out a stone – a perfectly formed pebble – from his rucksack by the bed and sets it on the board.

The more wine she drinks, the more relaxed Chloe becomes. Within minutes, she's reclining on Robert's bed, eating more bread than either of the boys and talking about all the deceased people she'd like to try to contact.

'Hmm … let me think. There's my grandma, who was a total witch, and not the spooky nice Halloween type. I'm talking about a nasty old hag who kicked my mum out when she became pregnant with me.'

'Why would you want to contact her, then?' Kieran asks.

'To tell her she's a bitch,' Chloe says. 'Obviously.' She laughs, then goes on. 'And then there's my dad – I don't actually know if he's dead as my mum got pregnant with me when she was eighteen at a party and doesn't know which bloke it was. There were a few around at that time, but it was really tragic, as it was some lifeboat volunteer meet-up and she got off with quite a few of them, and then three of them drowned soon after, before I was born. Isn't it awful? A local tragedy, that's what people call it. And one of them was probably my dad and he never found out. So we'll see if we can speak to all of them tonight. I want some answers. I reckon their spirits will be able to tell if I'm their daughter or not.'

Robert listens to all this, surprised at the extent Chloe to which is embracing the whole séance process. He knew she was a bit 'ethereal' and floaty, and it doesn't shock him to find out she believes in spirits and the afterlife, but he had presumed her taking part in the séance was, at least to some degree, down to her humouring the boys. Having a laugh. Nothing too serious. Whereas now it seems like she actually hopes to make contact with the dead.

'Before we start,' Kieran says, 'we should swap the wine for this.' He moves the bowl over to the centre of the little table on top of the Ouija board. 'Give me your glass.'

Chloe hands him the little glass and Kieran carefully pours in some of the mixture. 'I love the blue,' Chloe says, her words already showing signs of alcohol consumption. 'So … so swirly and dreamy.'

Kieran looks pleased. He then pours out two other glasses and hands one to Robert with a meaningful look. He knows what to do. They aren't to drink, but instead pretend to take small sips. Kieran also has something else up his sleeve. He acts as though he's taken a sip but then coughs and sets the glass down. 'Actually, don't drink it, that's too strong. You should stick with the wine.'

Chloe scoffs. 'Too strong? Oh come on.' She rolls her eyes and then raises her glass to her lips.

Kieran's strategy had been a risky one, but it works.

Chloe determinedly downs the whole thing, coughs herself a bit and says, 'God… OK, I see what you mean, but it's not *that* bad.

Takes like very sharp lemony vodka.' She makes a sound with her mouth, moving her tongue as though she's tasting something. 'Ugh … the aftertaste, though. Oh that's … not nice.' She reaches for the wine bottle, not bothering to pour any out, just lifting the neck to her lips and drinking deeply. 'That's better,' she says. 'Now, let's start trying to … to…' She's trying to get the word out. '…*communicate!* Yes, that's it… Let's try to communicate with the *other side.*'

She raises her eyebrows playfully and smiles at them both. Robert can see her gaze is dreamy and lacking in focus, her eyes wandering, her lids closing and then opening. She gives herself a shake and then gets off the bed and kneels in front of the coffee table, like Kieran is. Robert does the same.

'Place your hand on the stone,' Kieran says quietly. 'You have to properly be touching it for it to work.'

Chloe does as he says. Robert follows suit.

'Now ask a question,' Kieran says. 'You can go first, Chloe. Ask a question. Anything.'

She nods. 'OK. I want to know … if the drowned men are here?'

The stone moves. Robert presumes Kieran's driving it to offer the best and most involving outcome and feels it slide across to the word 'YES' printed in capital letters in one of the corners.

'Oh super,' Chloe says, 'I'm glad. It means my father's here.'

'Maybe that should be the next question,' Kieran prompts.

'Yes,' Chloe says, nodding. As she does so, her hair falls over part of her face and she doesn't try to brush it away. 'Yes… Are you… Is … one of you… Is my dad here?'

She seems to be having trouble stringing words together now. Robert shifts his eyes over to Kieran. They share a glance, then move the stone back to the centre, and then once again to 'YES'.

'I'm pleased … pleased he's … he's here…'

Whether it's tiredness or the wine or the bitter concoction taking

272

effect, Chloe seems to be already struggling to stay awake. She yawns, bringing her hands to her face and rubbing at her eyes.

'I'm… I think I might need … just a few minutes… Can I lie down over here?'

She crawls over to Robert's bed and, with what seems like considerable effort, pulls herself up onto the thin mattress.

'Just a few minutes,' she says again.

'No problem,' Kieran says.

He's watching Chloe with a fixed expression. He looks mesmerised by what's happening to her. Robert can feel his heart beating fast. He suddenly feels all trembly and for a second wonders if it's the potion working on him too, then remembers he and Kieran didn't drink any of it. Perhaps it's just adrenalin, he thinks. Then Kieran puts something else into his mind.

'You can feel it too, can't you? The vibrations?'

Chloe shifts on the bed. She murmurs something. Robert thinks she might have thought Kieran was speaking to her, but she then goes quiet, properly closing her eyes and nestling into the pillow.

As he watches her, Robert nods slowly. 'Yes,' he says, 'I can. I can feel it.'

Kieran moves over to Chloe on the bed.

'I think you need some more of the potion,' Kieran says, reaching for it on the table. He pours some into the glass and tries to get Chloe's hand around it, but she bats him away. Kieran has to lean back to avoid the liquid going everywhere. 'Have a drink of this, Chloe,' he says, his voice quiet but still firm, again trying to get her to grip the glass.

'Oh … yeah, thanks…' she says, taking the glass. She manages to tilt her head and he tips up the glass. She takes a sip and swallows, but then makes a gasping, groaning sound. 'Ugh … no … not that again. Not … that… It's horrible.'

Robert thought he was prepared. He thought he'd committed,

that he knew what he was part of. But what happens next makes him realise, in an instant, how naïve he was to think that. How out of his comfort zone he really is.

Kieran places a hand around Chloe's jaw and forces it open. He then proceeds to pour the liquid into her mouth. 'Drink,' he says. 'Drink it.' She moans and splutters as the liquid flows into her. She starts to writhe.

'Get hold of her, Robert,' Kieran says, his voice filled with an intense urgency.

Robert, at a loss as to what else to do, does as he's told without stopping to think about it. It's as simple as that, as simple as following an instruction from someone in authority. And his brother has authority here, his strong arms holding Chloe's top half as Robert leans in and grabs her legs. He pushes her away from the edge so she doesn't fall. Yes, that's what he's doing, he tells himself; he's helping her. So she doesn't fall.

And he carries on helping her.

And carries on. And on.

Holding her down.

All the while, Kieran continues to pour the liquid into her mouth. She chokes and coughs. He fills the glass again, then carries on, in spite of her protests, in spite of her struggles, which with every passing second grow weaker and weaker. Until at last, she stops struggling.

Eventually, the boys stand back. Kieran has splashes of the liquid down his front. The scent of alcohol is strong in the air. It makes Robert feel sick. As does the sight of Chloe, lying motionless.

'Oh … God…' Robert says. He can't believe they've done it. Can't believe they've actually gone through with it. That *he* has actually gone through with it.

No. No, *he* didn't do it.

Kieran was the one forcing her to drink … making her, even though she said…

He feels his vision swaying.

The terrible truth causes a flood of dizziness.

Because it wasn't just Kieran, was it? His own hands are still aching from where he gripped her, holding her on the bed.

He looks at his older brother. Even in this terrible moment, he finds it hard to read his expression. He watches as Kieran sits down on the other bed. He then closes his eyes. Robert knows what he's doing. He's checking to see if it's worked. He can't believe his brother has the composure and sense of stillness to do this. Within seconds his eyes are open again. And for the first time that evening, concern crosses Kieran's face.

'It hasn't worked.' He stands up. His hands are trembling, his jaw clenched.

'What do you mean?' Robert asks.

'I mean it hasn't worked. I can't see… My pathway, it isn't clear. We've done something wrong, we…' His gaze settles on Chloe. 'I'm so stupid!' he says. Then he laughs out loud. He actually laughs. 'Ah, that's a relief.'

'What's a relief?' Robert says, taking a step towards him. At the same moment, Kieran moves back to the edge of the bed where Chloe is lying and says quietly, 'She's not dead.'

Of course she isn't, Robert thinks, realising this in a mad, wonderful rush. Of course she isn't dead. She must have just passed out due to tiredness or maybe even sunstroke or something, something unrelated. Healthy young girls don't die in an instant. Surely it would take hours for that poisonous mixture to harm her – to actually do serious damage to her internal organs? People don't die immediately from drinking something, not in real life. That sort of thing only happens in movies, doesn't it?

'I think … yes, there's a pulse,' Kieran says.

'Thank God,' Robert says.

Kieran stands up and gives Robert a quizzical look. 'Thank God? Are you saying that because it explains why my pathway hasn't cleared? Or are you thanking God because of something else?'

Robert just blinks at him. He can't believe it isn't obvious.

Kieran moves around the table and stands close to him, his face right near his.

'I think you need to prove yourself, Robert.' He reaches down to his right and picks up the pillow from the bed. 'Here.'

He pushes the pillow into Robert's chest.

Robert closes his hands around it. He knows what Kieran wants him to do. He looks back at him.

'No,' he says, as firmly as he can, although his voice is hoarse and strained. As though he's been shouting. Or screaming.

'Come on, do it,' he says. 'It will help. Trust me. It's time for you to play your part. I've put her to sleep. Now you can finish her. Finish everything.'

Robert feels his heart rate increasing. He feels the prickles down his back develop into needles. His skin is painful. His eyes are burning. For a second, he thinks he hears a noise somewhere close – a creaking, beyond what's normal for the interior of the treehouse. As if there's movement nearby. But he can't focus on that.

He holds his brother's gaze and says again, 'No. I won't do it.' He drops the pillow.

Kieran opens his mouth to speak, but Robert never finds out what he intends to say because his eyes widen at what he can see over his brother's shoulder. The reaction causes Kieran to turn to see what he's looking at.

Chloe has woken up. She is sitting up on the edge of the bed and is trying to stand.

The boys stand frozen, watching her.

'I'm … I'm going to be sick.'

She vomits, copiously, over the red carpet.

'Lie back down,' Kieran says quickly.

'Fuck off,' she says. She doesn't seem to have the energy or strength to shout, but there's still force in her words. And anger.

'You need to sleep,' Kieran says. He goes to put an arm around her, but she hits it with the flat of her hand.

'I said fuck off. You're … you're both horrid … both…' She succeeds in getting to her feet and Robert sees a trail of vomit fall from her mouth down onto the makeshift Ouija board, staining the word 'NO' in one of the corners.

'Sit back down,' Kieran says, trying to manhandle her and also dodge her flailing arms.

Robert had thought the worst was over but he's wrong. It happens in just a second. Kieran gives her a sharp shove. Perhaps he means to push her back onto the bed. Maybe he's just become frustrated by Chloe's attempts to fight back – by her refusal to do as he says, to just be quiet and die.

The thud of her head on the back wall of the treehouse is like a gun going off. The sound of it ripples across time, touching their past, present and future. Robert feels it inside him. It's impossible for this *not* to affect their future, to remake it and reshape it. How can it not send them both spinning down a new path, transforming them into different people?

The noise causes Robert to raise his hands over his face, as though someone really has used a firearm or set off an explosive. As if there is something physical that might fly into his face. Shrapnel, perhaps, or flames. It's a ridiculous thought, really, but at that moment, his mind isn't clear enough to distinguish the absurd from the probable. He lowers his hands when he realises what's happened. He watches as Chloe slumps down, no longer speaking. No longer fighting to get away.

He notices the mark on the wall, then. It's small – faint, but visible. Is it blood? Or a scuff in the paint? He doesn't know. He just watches as Kieran once again leans over the body on the bed and feels for a pulse.

'Has she gone?' Robert asks. He can't say 'dead' or 'die'. He just can't bring himself to use those words.

Yes,' Kieran says. 'Her soul's floating away now. I can sense it.'

Robert suddenly feels a rush of reality – the façade of the whole sacrifice and his brother's talk of souls is starting to feel truly insane, and the horror of what's happening is becoming clear.

'Oh God,' he says. 'Oh God… What have we done?'

Kieran puts his fingers to her throat. 'I can't feel a pulse. I can't feel one.'

Robert expects – hopes – Kieran is as shocked as he is, but he looks back at Robert apparently delighted.

'She's dead. It's worked.'

Chapter Thirty-Three

ROBERT

2004

Robert is panicking. He feels like he's slipped into a strange dream. Or maybe Kieran and Chloe have invented all this. Perhaps, like the meeting they attended in London, this is all a sham in order to convince the uncertain of the power of the Dark Core. Well, he had been uncertain, so maybe this really is what's happening.

But had he *really* been uncertain? With a stab of guilt, he remembers his resolve, the feeling of excitement and power that had burned so brightly within him just hours before. He didn't feel uncertain then. He felt determined. Thrilled. Alive.

Kieran isn't saying anything. Robert realises this as his attention snaps back to the present. With a mixture of disbelief and fury, he sees that Kieran has again settled himself down in a straight-backed sitting position on the empty bed, eyes closed, bare feet flat on the floor. He sees that the edge of one of his feet is touching some of the vomit on the carpet, but he doesn't seem to care. His expression is serene. Calm.

'Kieran!' Robert cries out. 'Stop it!'

He shakes Kieran by the shoulders. He expects this to anger his brother, but he doesn't care. He's had enough of all this. They need to talk about what they're going to do next. How they're going to cope with what they've done. But to his surprise, when Kieran opens his eyes, a grin spreads slowly across his face. He stands up and embraces him, tightly, warmly. It's a hug like the one they shared in the water earlier. Only now, they're in a different world. A terrible world.

'It's worked,' Kieran whispers into his ear.

Robert can't cope with this. He pushes his brother away. 'Stop it, Kieran,' he says. 'Just … just stop it.'

'Rob, calm down. It has. It *really* has,' Kieran says. He's still grinning and the sight of it is maddening to Robert. 'Here, sit down,' Kieran says, trying to manoeuvre Robert into the same sitting position on the bed he occupied moments before.

'What? No! Get off me!' Robert yells. 'I'm not—'

'It's all gone, Rob. It's all gone,' Kieran says. He reaches out and clasps Robert's face. He's never done anything like this before. The feeling of Kieran's hands on his cheeks is so strange, the action so alien in its bizarre intimacy, that he finds for a moment his will to fight back leave him. He stares at Kieran and sees tears in his eyes. He hasn't seen him cry for years – not since he was a small child. He can't even remember the last time. But the tears fall and Kieran does nothing to brush them away. He just holds on to Robert's face and whispers, 'It's beautiful. I saw, Rob. I saw it. The pathway. It's paved with these golden stones. There's nothing blocking it, nothing nasty. And it's, like, dawn, with this glowing orange light, everything sparkling and shimmering.'

'You're mad,' Robert says, breathlessly. 'You really are mad, Kieran.'

'Don't resist it,' Kieran says. 'Embrace it now and it will be amazing forever. I know it. I honestly do.'

Robert extricates himself from Kieran then. He doesn't push him or shake him. He just steps away.

'I don't know what to do,' Robert says, looking at the slumped body on the bed. *Chloe*. It's amazing to him how quickly he's able to think of her as a 'body' rather than as a person. 'What are we going to do? Should we tell Mum? Dad?'

Kieran shakes his head, although he doesn't look cross or annoyed by the suggestion.

'We don't need to do anything. We'll put our trust in our pathway.'

Robert can't accept this as an answer.

'We have to tell them. They'll see us trying to lift her down the ladder. I can't believe we didn't think about these things...'

He looks at the splashes of vomit on the floor. Even if they did, somehow, remove the body, this will take some explaining. Their parents will have to pay for it to be cleaned or lose whatever deposit they've paid for the holiday home. It's amazing to Robert how, before this point, their plan seemed so simple, and now, in the dreadful aftermath, it seems fraught with difficulties. Difficulties that paled into the background when they were caught up in the excitement of the whole thing, now seem painfully obvious. Thousands of problems and complications seem to unfold before him. They'll never manage it. They'll never be able to fix this. They'll never be the same again.

'I promise you it will be fine,' Kieran says. 'Now, we're going to go back, back up to the lodge. We're going to say nothing to Mum and Dad. *Nothing*, you understand? There's no need to. And we'll worry about all this'—he gestures to the room around them— 'tomorrow morning if we need to. Nobody will come up here before us. There's nothing for us to do now. Come on.'

And so Robert follows. He follows because he can't think what else to do, especially not on his own. He feels completely powerless and at a loss. Who should he turn to? How should he go about it? As he climbs down the ladder, he imagines his parents' disbelieving faces if he said, *'Kieran and I have killed a girl and we need help covering it up.'* They'll phone the police. Perhaps their father will try to think up some solution, but their mother will probably hand them over to the police herself. She likes things to be neat and tidy. That's what she always says. And everything that's happened is the opposite of neat and tidy.

They hear the TV on in the living room in the lodge when they reach it. Nobody comes out from the room and they don't look in to see which of their parents is still awake. Instead, they go up the stairs as silently as they can. In the bathroom, Robert spends some time gripping the sink, wondering if he's going to be sick, but nothing comes up. The nausea comes in waves, with the peaks occurring every time he remembers details of what happened. Of the killing. Of what they have done. How she kicked as he held her legs. The sounds of her spluttering and choking. Her words of protest, becoming less clear and audible as the seconds ticked by.

He gets into the shower and turns it on. He's aware his parents will hear the water going. He knows it's a risk, that they might ask questions, but he doesn't care. He feels like he's coated in Chloe's vomit – or worse, her blood – as if it leaked through the pores of her skin when he held her down on the bed.

He scrubs himself until his skin feels raw, then shuts off the water. He lets himself slide down the wall and onto the floor. It's as though every spare reserve of energy has been drained out of him. All his strength is swirling down the plug hole with the water, never to return. He can't imagine a time when he'll be able to do anything again. How will he carry on with this holiday? How will he go back to school in the autumn? How will he do his A Levels?

How will he go to university, get a girlfriend, marry, have children, live a full life? That's all gone. Washed away. Deleted.

'You all right?' Kieran's voice comes from behind the closed door. Robert doesn't answer.

His brother tries the door handle. In his confused state, Robert forgot to lock it and it opens very slowly and quietly. Kieran looks in and sees him huddled on the floor of the shower.

'Come on, Rob. Let's get you into bed.'

He wants to say that he's not a child and that he doesn't need his big brother to act like this, especially when they've both done something so terrible. He hates the way Kieran's behaving, as though everything's fine – better than fine. As though everything's brilliant. Perfect. Couldn't be better. But there's no fight left in him. So he takes the hand offered to him and allows himself to be pulled up. He towels himself dry with weak arms that feel as though they're made of damp paper, like they might disintegrate at any moment.

He allows himself to be led across the hallway to his room. He gets into his bed, but he can't stop himself occasionally giving voice to things that are floating through his mind.

'The body... The treehouse... We can't... We need to...'

Kieran shushes him, sounding more caring and soothing than he's done in years. Robert relents and rests his head on his pillow. He closes his eyes, and before sleep takes him, he thinks about how comfortable and large this bed feels compared to the thin single one in the treehouse. How different things might be if they'd spent their nights here in the main lodge. If they'd never discovered the treehouse in the garden. If they'd never come on this holiday. How different their lives would be.

During the night, he doesn't dream. He doesn't wake. He falls asleep quickly and sleeps deeply. But when he wakes, he knows straightaway that something's wrong. He sits up in bed and looks out of the window at mist and rain. This change alone is enough to unsettle him. It's so far removed from the burning sunshine of the past week – has it only been a week since they arrived? – that he feels as if he's been transported to a different place and time. The memory of the killing the night before doesn't hit him in a rush – it isn't a memory or a moment of realisation. It's with him immediately, as though the knowledge of what happened has become a physical part of him. A growth on his brain, an abscess that can never be cut away.

He's only been awake a minute or two when the door opens, very slowly at first, and Kieran comes into view. He's already fully dressed and has his shoes on. They look damp, probably with morning dew.

Robert knows what it means. It means Kieran's been outside.

The words that follow confirm it, though he never would have guessed what those words would be. Not in a million years.

'She's gone,' Kieran says.

His expression is no longer the mixture of joy and excitement it was last night. Now he looks stunned, and worried.

'I've just been down to the treehouse. I got up early. I didn't want to wake you. But when I got there, the treehouse was empty. She's nowhere to be seen.'

Chapter Thirty-Four

ROBERT

2004

R obert wants to run through the woods, but Kieran tells him to slow down.

'We have to go about this calmly,' he says as they walk through the forest. 'There's no point in panicking.'

'No point in panicking?' Robert snaps, wincing as he scrapes his leg on the branches of an old fallen tree. 'She could be phoning the police right now. They might be there at her home.'

'Which is why I think we should have stayed back at the lodge,' Kieran says, sighing. 'I promise you, Rob, we don't have anything to worry about.'

Robert stops and turns to look at his brother, anger flashing in his eyes. 'If you mention your fucking "life pathway" again and how free from obstacles it is, I'll scream. And in case it has escaped your attention, if Chloe is alive, we haven't sacrificed anyone. If she's at a police station, or in a hospital getting treatment, she isn't dead and therefore no Dark Core wizard magic shit has been conjured.'

Kieran shakes his head, looking disappointed. 'Don't pretend like you don't know how it works. You know nothing is "conjured". This has nothing to do with wizards. Don't be so insulting.'

'What I'm saying is,' Rob says, glaring at Kieran, 'even if all that bollocks was true, it all counts for shit. Because sacrificed girls can't get up and walk away.'

A sound reaches both their ears causing them to freeze. Although it comes from further off into the trees, it's clear to them what it is. The bark of a dog. Then another.

'Oh Jesus, that's all we need,' Robert says, feeling himself go cold. He looks around him, does a full turn, but can't see any sight of the dogs. But as his eyes scan the woods, something does catch his eye. Something light amidst the forest floor, lying at the dip in the hill by the nearly dry stream that runs through its centre.

'What's ... that?' Robert says, walking towards it.

He has a suspicion, but he doesn't want to believe it to be true.

He hears Kieran following behind him, but other than the sound of their footsteps, everything seems to have gone silent. The whole world stops. All Robert can do is stare down at what's in front of him.

It's an arm. A pale, bloodied arm. A jagged spike of bone is visible from its end. Fingers are broken back. Some of the nails are gone.

Then Robert looks further ahead, in the only damp part of the stream. There's more to see. He doesn't want to see, but he can't look away. Even if he can't make out what it is he's looking at. Even if he can't make out which body parts are which. Where the flesh ends and the bones begin. The parts that are skin and the bits that should be on the inside, not the outside. There are smudges of things across the leaves. Things that might be internal organs mixed with hair.

It's a horrifying sight. Eventually, after what feels like an age, Robert looks over at Kieran and sees him watching. Before he has a chance to make out his brother's reaction, though, he hears a shout.

'Oh my God!'

Then before he knows what's happening, there are people with them. Two of them. A man and a woman, both middle aged. The woman looks horrified at the dismembered corpse in front of them.

'Jesus, we're too late,' the woman says.

Robert looks at her, wondering what she means. Why are they too late? None of it makes sense to him.

'Don't look, lads,' she says to them.

'Christ, you can see the teeth marks,' the man says.

'My God. I can't believe this,' the woman says, turning her back to the grisly sight.

The man raises his phone to his ear, waits a few moments, then says, 'Police.'

'We've only just phoned them,' the woman says, looking at Robert. 'We saw the dogs. They were running up to the farm, but the white one – it was covered in blood.' She turns back to the body, briefly steals another glance, then closes her eyes. 'Good Lord, I think it's a girl. Or a young woman. It's hard to tell, though.' She reaches out for Robert's arm. 'Don't look at it, love. Come on. Let's go and wait over there, further up the slope.'

The boys follow her.

'Just came across her, did you?' she says. This is the truth, after all, so Robert nods. 'Must be a terrible shock. Are you local? Did you both know her? Well, I suppose it's hard to see who it is, isn't it? Were you out for a morning walk? Such an awful thing to come across during a walk in the woods. That's what we were doing. We're renting a cottage not far from here – well, actually, it might be a few miles. We've been walking for quite a bit, or were, until we saw the dogs. Marauding, I think that's the word. And the blood on them, especially the white one… Horrible. Of course, with the other, an Alsatian I think the other one was, it's harder to see, isn't it, when the coat is dark, but I reckon it had blood on it too and now seeing what we've seen it's probably covered in it. After we spotted them, I got very worried and made Geoff phone the police, saying someone or something must have been hurt. And now, poor lass, it seems to be true.'

She says all this as though she never needs to draw breath, words just flowing from her without need of thought or pause, filling the otherwise quiet morning air. Neither Robert nor Kieran interrupts her. For Robert, her words are oddly comforting, as if having a stranger provide this commentary and take control in the way adults do helps distance him from the horrors that lie just feet away on the forest floor.

A minute or two later, her husband, Geoff, comes up and says, 'The police are on their way. They said to stay here if it's safe to do so.'

'Well, is it?' the woman says, looking around her. 'What if the dogs come back? Did you ask them that?'

Her husband shakes his head.

'Oh, bloody hell! What… Where…?'

'Calm down, love. I think they've gone back home. They looked pretty determined when they were running off.' He gives his wife a pat on the shoulder. 'You boys OK?' he asks, looking at them. Like his wife, he seems concerned for their welfare, but settles for saying, 'Not a nice thing,' and leaves it at that.

Kieran says, 'We're fine. We'll wait for the police.' Robert looks at him. In his own state of shock, he's surprised Kieran is so happy to wait for law enforcement, considering the part they've played in what's happened here. But whatever part they have played, Kieran doesn't volunteer any more information – he just gives Robert a look, a look he knows means, *let me do the talking*.

That's what Robert does when the police arrive. Before they speak to the boys, the two uniformed officers talk to the married couple.

During that time, Kieran says very quietly, 'Don't you see? This is how it's supposed to be. She was killed by the dogs.' He smiles, briefly, and says, 'Everything's going to be fine.'

Then he replaces his smile with the look of a concerned, worried teenager rather than a confident, calm young man. It makes him look instantly young, as though he's an innocent bystander in all this, a distressed member of the public, not one of the architects of whatever's happened here. Robert wonders if such a thing can be pulled off – if they really can melt into the background of this case. Because that's what it's now going to become. A murder case. Or, if they're lucky, an accident. He watches the two police officers – two young men – as they go down to look at the body. The younger-looking of the two doesn't look much older than Kieran and he visibly backs away when he sees the bloody mess on the ground by the stream.

When they come to talk to the brothers, Robert stays silent while Kieran answers the questions calmly. He says they were walking through the woods when they found the body, and the man and the woman came across it at about the same time, then the police were called. Short and simple and Kieran delivers it with the occasional pause and tremor in his voice to indicate a degree of distress. It sounds convincing. If Robert didn't know the tone of the whole thing is laced with affectation, he'd have bought it completely.

Another police officer arrives, this one in a light brown suit and a little older than the uniformed constables. He introduces himself as Detective Constable Holton and asks the ages of the two boys. He says his boss will want to talk to them but they'll need one of their parents present and he asks if they live nearby. Kieran explains they live up at one of Hill Valley's lodge holiday homes, Sunshine Lodge – their family are renting it for the summer.

Although he's already mentioned this to the uniformed officers, DC Holston looks pleased by this news, saying, 'That's convenient. Tell you what, I'll ask either PC Smith or PC Galbraith to walk back with you to your lodge and talk to your parents, tell them what's going on. Then when we're ready, we'll come and have a proper chat and get a statement. That OK?' He doesn't ask if they're all right, but Robert feels like it's part of the question at the end.

'Yeah, that's fine,' Kieran says.

DC Holston goes off to talk to the younger policemen. Robert feels something on his arm. It's Kieran's hands, gripping him tightly.

'Remember what I said,' he says very quietly. 'Let me talk, follow my lead, and everything will be fine. No confessions. No dramatics. This is a good thing, Rob. A very good thing. You'll see.'

Robert shakes his head. 'They'll find out,' he says, equally quietly. 'They'll find out we killed her. I don't know how she got out of there for the dogs to do that to her, I don't know what happened after we left, but they'll trace the whole thing back to us. They will. I just know it.'

Chapter Thirty-Five

KIERAN

2004

They go back to the lodge. Their mother's in the kitchen, sitting at the table reading an enormous book with a cup of coffee next to her. The police constable explains what's happened – that a body has been found, and the brothers, along with two other walkers, were the ones to find it. He says his superior officers will want to talk to the boys but because of their age, they need an adult present.

Their mother looks surprised for just a few seconds, then says, 'You'd better sit down. I'll make you some coffee.'

Kieran sits down as she gets up out of her chair. He doesn't expect her to start comforting either of them. She's never been that sort of mum. He thinks it's likely they'll get more checks on their emotional welfare from the police than from her. Seconds later, he hears a noise out on the stairs. The police officer turns to look and says, 'Ah, is this another of your sons?'

Kieran has to hide a smirk.

'No,' his mother says, her voice taking on an icy edge. 'That's my husband.'

He sometimes finds people's reactions to his parents' age difference funny to witness, although he takes care to hide his amusement now. He needs to give the right impression.

His father wanders into the kitchen, rubbing his eyes. He's in a T-shirt and boxers, and blinks blankly at the police officer standing in front of him. Then he looks absolutely horrified. For a second, Kieran wonders if his father's going to faint.

He says to the room at large, 'What's … going on?'

Kieran looks first at the police officer, then at his mother, waiting for one of them to explain. The young officer hesitates a beat too long and Kieran's mother gets in first.

'Go and get dressed. The police are here,' she says curtly, as if her husband should have known this already. 'I'm just making the constable a cup of coffee.'

'But … why?' he replies, staring at his wife as though he can't properly compute what she's saying.

'A body has been found, sir. Down in the woods. Your sons, along with a couple who were out walking, were the first on the scene.'

Kieran listens with interest to the clunky, stilted way the young officer says this. He wonders if this is the most serious thing he's ever had to deal with. Perhaps his days are usually spent sorting out traffic disputes and kids stealing chewing gum from the village shop. This is out of his league, he thinks. And at the moment, he appears to believe the whole thing is just a tragic accident. A dog attack. If only he knew the truth. Then he really would be out of his depth. So would his superiors. And most other people in this dull, unenlightened world.

But Kieran knows the truth. He sits there observing everything unfold, feeling as if he was watching a play. He may not know the ending, but that doesn't disturb or worry him. He doesn't need to know how the play ends, because his job is to sit back and let it all happen. He doesn't need to avoid any obstacles, doesn't need to get himself in a tangle about timings and alibis and coming up with outlandish plans with Rob to cover up what they did. None of that is necessary. He knows this, like a precious jewel of truth buried deep within him.

Kieran sees his dad look over at him, then at Robert, who's sitting opposite, looking at the floor. Kieran can see his knee jerking up and down – a nervous habit when he's stressed.

'What…? Who…? Do you know who the body is?' his dad asks hoarsely. Kieran sees him glance at the sliding glass door, out to the grey drizzle of the garden.

'We don't at present,' the PC says. 'Can I ask, is there anyone else here on the property?'

'No,' his mother says. 'The cleaners were here a moment ago but they've gone.'

Kieran looks up. He hadn't realised the lodge had cleaners. The PC seems satisfied with this and gets handed his coffee, then takes a seat at the table too. Kieran looks over at his dad, still standing there looking shocked by the whole situation.

'Martin,' his mum says eventually, 'perhaps you should get ready. The detectives will be here soon.'

He blanches, looking at her with alarm in his eyes. 'For what?'

'To speak to the boys,' she says slowly, as though talking to a small child. 'Now go and put on a shirt and those new jeans I ironed. The use of a comb, too, wouldn't go amiss.'

He nods and absent-mindedly raises a hand to his head as though surprised to find hair there. Then he wanders out of the room without saying anything else.

The detectives, when they arrive, don't include the detective constable they spoke to down in the woods. Instead, it's a much older man and a young woman. They hear them before they enter, talking outside on the veranda for a bit while the younger officer flicks through a notebook, then shows the older man something on it. He nods and Kieran hears him say, 'Makes sense. Yes, of course, you're right. Christ, this is bloody typical. Just days away from my retirement and a bloody dead girl goes and puts a spanner in the works.'

He hears the woman say something about 'sensitivity' and puts away her notebook, looking at him disapprovingly.

'Yes, yes, don't nag me.'

Then he looks to his left and sees them all staring. The man lets out a long, weary sigh and tries to open the sliding glass door, fails, and there follows an awkward moment during which his colleague, PC Galbraith, and Kieran's mum all try to assist. Eventually, he gains entry and introduces himself as DI Oldman and his colleague as DS Lock. His tone is gruff, bored and suggests he sees the interview with the two boys as nothing more than a routine that has to be observed for the sake of due process, rather than because anything interesting might be gleaned from it.

'I know it's hard to tell, given the state of it, but did you recognise the body when you saw it?' DI Oldman asks them.

Kieran nods and answers before Rob has a chance to. 'Yeah, she's a girl we've spoken to a bit down on the seafront. We didn't know her well.' He wonders if his father will interject and show surprise at the downplaying of this, considering Chloe has been in his car and he knows his sons have become friends with her over the past week since they arrived. But he says nothing. No frustrations, dangerous moments or obstacles present themselves throughout the rest of the interview. Formalities are observed, boxes are ticked, the police seem happy.

'Sorry you've had to go through all this. It must have been upsetting for you both,' DS Lock says kindly.

'Yes, yes,' DI Oldman says, waving his hand as though the concept of emotional distress is a time-wasting distraction. 'Well, we'll take details in case we need to contact you again, but I think we're done here.'

When the police are gone, the family sits in silence for a bit. Kieran notices his father still looking shaken. His mother's expression is neutral and she says something about having to get on with some work and she'll do it in the living room.

Before she leaves, Kieran says, 'I didn't know we had cleaners.'

She pauses and looks over at him. If she thinks it a strange thing for him to mention, after such an extraordinary morning, she doesn't say. She simply replies, 'Yes, they'll come at the end of each week that we're here. They weren't very impressed by the state of the treehouse, by the way.'

In his peripheral vision, Kieran sees Robert flinch, but he keeps his eyes on his mother. 'Oh yeah?' he says calmly, raising his eyebrows.

His mother nods. 'Yes, they mentioned vomit on the floor. They've worked their magic apparently, but said to be more careful if we don't want to risk our deposit. If you're unwell and feeling sick, you can come and tell us, of course. But if such moments of illness are the result of alcohol abuse, any deposit deductions will be coming out of your allowances. Keep that in mind throughout the remainder of our stay.'

Then she leaves.

The stillness and silence in the room continue after her exit. Kieran looks at Robert and then his father. Eventually, the latter says, 'I don't think we'll be staying here much longer. Not after this … terrible thing.'

'But…' Robert says, looking worried, 'will we be allowed to go?'

'We're not people of interest, I don't think,' Kieran says.

'We're certainly not,' his dad adds quickly. 'And besides, the detective has our home address. We're not prisoners.'

Robert appears to be about to say something, but Kieran looks at him and he closes his mouth.

Then his dad says, 'I'm … going to go back to bed for a bit. I think it would be good if you boys stayed in today. Not … not nice weather out there, anyway. Maybe summer's fading sooner than we expected.'

'Yes,' Kieran says. 'We'll stay in. Might catch up on some sleep. I think we both need a quiet day.'

The two boys go to their separate bedrooms. Robert seems to be content not to talk and Kieran doesn't initiate discussion. It's probably best to leave him be, he thinks. And besides, he's keen to be alone.

As soon as he's closed his door, Kieran kicks off his trainers, takes off his socks, and sits on the edge of his bed. He feels the wooden floor beneath the soles of his feet, closes his eyes, and begins to visualise. It barely takes a second for him to see it, his mind serving him the images he saw the night before: a clear pathway; the golden paving; a route through life that looks not just easy, but wonderful. It wasn't just a fluke. It's worked. Regardless of how Chloe ended up dying, whether by poison or during the dog attack, it's still worked.

Robert may have lost his commitment – maybe he never was

committed, not fully – but Kieran is committed. Kieran has remained faithful to everything he's learnt. And now it's going to pay off. Leaning back on his bed, he puts his arms behind his head and smiles. This is going to be a great summer. Not just a great summer, a great life. He can feel it.

Chapter Thirty-Six

ROBERT

2004

Robert finds the next few days excruciating. He barely comes out of his room and Kieran doesn't come to find him.

Where is he? Why isn't he talking to me? What's going to happen to us?

All these questions crowd his head, even though he knows Kieran's in his room just across the hallway. Even though he knows he can go and talk to him if he wants to. But he can't. He doesn't know what to say and even if he did, he's afraid of the reaction that would greet him. He'd get annoyed and tell him he was panicking for no reason. Or, worse, he would be in that weirdly calm, happy mood, which Robert would find even more disturbing.

His parents also keep their distance. At meals, his mother occasionally alludes to the body in the woods, referring to it obliquely as 'the incident' or 'the unfortunate discovery', remarking how she hopes it hasn't spoiled their holiday without ever properly enquiring if her sons are OK. Kieran usually fields these remarks by saying how he isn't too bothered and 'life goes on'. Robert wonders if his dad will pick Kieran up for being too callous or flippant about such a serious, tragic thing. He does not. He just carries on eating his mushroom-stuffed pork in silence.

On the fourth day after that terrible night, Robert wakes to find his mental anguish and mounting anxiety seem to have taken on new physical symptoms. He feels completely shattered – even worse than he did the morning after the killing. He spends the day in bed, interrupted only once by his mother, who comes in to check on him. She implies he should get up and 'do something functional' with his day. He grunts in response and goes back to sleep. In the night, he feels feverish. He staggers to the bathroom and drinks two large tumblers of water. It takes some time because his throat feels tight, making swallowing very difficult all of a sudden.

The next day he's worse. The high temperature continues and eventually it becomes clear to the rest of the house that this isn't teenage laziness or him just being unproductive. There's something actually wrong with him.

They think it's flu. They tell him as much, his mum laying a hand on his head and remarking, 'Just a fever, it will pass,' and his dad bringing him warmed orange juice with honey and some lozenges for his throat. He knows they're wrong. He knows this isn't a virus. This is guilt. This is the ravages of guilt, tormenting his body, poisoning him from the inside out. In the midst of his awful state, Robert is grateful the summer heat has passed – how much more unbearable this would be if it was still bright and baking outside. But something about the drab, grey, drizzly days outside saddens him. He feels like he and Kieran killed the summer. They committed an act so elementally evil that it has literally blocked out the sun.

It starts to become hard to keep track of time. He doesn't know what number day he's on or how long it's been since that horrific night. He doesn't know whether it's late evening or early morning. Whether the grey twilight is dusk or dawn.

At one point, he wakes up during the hours of complete darkness and reaches for his glass of water. Try as he might, he can't open his mouth to pour the water in. It's like his jaw is clamped shut. He can only get small amounts of water in through the edges of his mouth.

Here, let me help you.

Chloe is sitting on the edge of his bed, taking the glass from his hands.

'You … can't … be … here…' he manages to say with great difficulty.

Of course I'm here, she says softly, laying a hand over his. *I'll always be here, you know. Whether you're poorly or well, happy or sad, young or old. I'll always be with you. Forever.*

She raises the glass to his closed lips.

Drink.

He struggles. She tilts it more and water splashes down his chin. He tries to voice his protests, but he can't get the words out, whether it's because of his immovable jaw or the flow of water, he doesn't know. More water follows, and it has a horrible taste now. The drops that fall into the gaps between his lips taste bitter and sharp. He feels tears in his eyes and his body shakes, tense and out of his control, as though he's having a seizure. Then he sees Kieran is there. His brother's pulling back the duvet and taking hold of Robert's legs, preventing him from struggling, just as he did to Chloe, in the treehouse, on that terrible night. The night from which he'll never be able to escape.

'I'm sorry,' he manages to say in a sob. 'I'm so, so sorry.'

The glass, now apparently empty, is taken away from his mouth and placed on the bedside table.

Oh, well, if you're sorry, I'd better be on my way then, Chloe says, in her usual relaxed, floaty way.

And she leaves. She walks out of the door, not making a sound, and Robert is alone on his bed, dripping wet, with no sign of Kieran.

'Wait,' he tries to say, but he can't get the word out.

He stumbles from his bed, thuds across the floor and out onto the landing. He thinks he can still see her, disappearing down the stairs.

He tries to call after her again, but he can't. He wills himself to move faster, but his feet are slow. He's at the top of the stairs now, looking over the banisters to the hallway below. Trying to see.

Then there's nothing. Nothing but a freeing, weightless feeling of nothing. Followed by a split second of pain. Then nothing again.

Robert wakes to the sounds of a hospital around him. He hears it all before he sees it. He knows it's a hospital because the sounds are unmistakable: voices, peeps of machines, the sound of wheels, perhaps a medicine trolley. It's as though someone is playing a stock sound effect in his head, but when he opens his eyes, he finds it isn't an effect. It's real.

'Oh God... Oh son, you're awake!' His dad is by his side. He's laughing, smiling, holding Robert's hand. 'Oh, thank Christ.'

Robert's head hurts. He tries to lift his arm, the one his father isn't holding, but he can't. Then he looks down and sees it's in plaster.

'You broke your arm in the fall,' his dad says.

'Fall?' Robert croaks back. The word triggers something in his mind. The feeling of falling. Yes, he can remember that. Of falling through the air. Then the pain.

As he thinks the word 'pain', it hits him. He is in pain. Quite a bit of pain.

'You fell down the stairs,' his dad says. 'You've been asleep for over two weeks. You broke your arm during the tumble, but really, son, it was a blessing.'

'Don't … I don't understand,' Robert mutters. 'Water … I need water.'

His father pours him some and helps him drink. The action gives him a sudden memory. A memory of water pouring down his chin, his mouth unable to open. And something else. A missing detail about the memory. Something nasty he can't quite put his finger on.

'If you hadn't fallen, we may not have got you to the hospital in time. You didn't have flu, Rob. You had tetanus.'

He tries to frown, but the muscles in his brow hurt so he stops. 'Tetanus?'

His dad nods. 'Yes. You could have died.'

His mother arrives at his bedside then, closely followed by a middle-aged man in a checked shirt with a kind smile.

'Oh my gosh, he's awake,' his mother says. She and his father swap places and she stands close by Robert's side. 'I'm … I'm so pleased, my dear,' she says, in a somewhat stilted voice. 'It's been stressful.'

He feels as though she's leaving space for an apology, as though he should be saying sorry for becoming unwell and falling down the stairs. As it turns out, though, from what the doctor says next, it should really be her saying sorry. Not that she does. Which doesn't surprise him.

'It's quite rare for anyone to die from tetanus in the UK, but you nearly did,' the doctor says, his smile fading into a stern expression. 'That's because this country has a highly effective vaccination programme.' He opens his mouth to say something else, but he's interrupted.

'Let's not go through all that again,' Robert's mother says, reaching into her handbag and withdrawing a tissue. 'He's awake now, so we'll say no more about that.'

The doctor looks awkward. Robert glances up at his mother, who dabs at her eyes then stuffs the tissue away and clips her bag shut. 'I wasn't vaccinated,' he says, realising what's actually being said here.

The doctor's expression is grave. 'Correct,' he says.

'Because you', Robert says, looking directly at his mother, 'apparently know better. You know better than scientists and doctors and every other parent.'

Tears now fall from her eyes, causing her to reopen her handbag and perform the same eye-dabbing as before, this time with shaking hands. 'I shouldn't have to apologise for having principles,' she says, not looking at him. 'I was just doing what I thought was right. It's what every parent should do.'

Robert transfers his gaze to his father, who also looks embarrassed. 'I'm so sorry,' he says again. 'I should have… Your mother seemed better read on these subjects than me.'

'Well, it seems mother doesn't always know best,' the doctor says bluntly. 'When you came into contact with the bacteria, the result was very dangerous and could have been lethal. There were points when it looked like we were going to lose you. I believe the route of infection was the wound in this foot.' He lightly taps the big toe of his right foot. 'It can be found in soil, so if you've been wandering around outdoors, it's likely you picked it up that way.'

'Just bad luck,' his mother mutters, but Robert isn't really listening. All he's now thinking about is the wound in his foot. And the night he got it. Outside a girl's bedroom, falling backwards onto the grass. Injuring himself on a trowel or shovel. Probably coated with flecks of soil impregnated with bacteria.

Up until this point, the heavy weight of Chloe and her death and what he and Kieran did hasn't been on his mind. The mystery of his illness and hospitalisation has given him a distraction, acting like a dam, holding his thoughts and memories at bay. But now the dam is breaking and the horror is unleashed.

'I want to sleep,' he says.

'That's one of the best possible medicines,' the doctor says, nodding approvingly. 'Rest as much as you can.'

Kieran comes to see him later that day. Robert is awake when his brother wanders in. It can't be possible, but Robert thinks he looks taller. He moves with a swagger, a straight-backed confidence that feels new and rather inappropriate for a hospital ward. When he gets to Robert's bedside, he moves the chair closer and sits down with bold confidence.

'Hey.'

Robert stares at him, trying to work out what else is different. Then he realises it's his hair. Whilst it has never been long, he's now had it cut close to his head on the sides, with a fashionable flick to his fringe styled with product. He smells of expensive aftershave, and his clothes are different. He's wearing a brand-new jacket and a shirt Robert has never seen. When he takes the jacket off and places it on his lap, Robert sees a Hugo Boss logo.

'Pleased you're awake,' Kieran says with nod.

'I nearly died, apparently,' Robert says. Then he adds, 'Part of me wishes I had.'

If he said this in the presence of his parents, who have shuffled off to the hospital café, they'd probably be both confused and alarmed. But Kieran's reaction is to roll his eyes and sigh.

'Oh God, you're not still going with the whole guilt thing, are you?'

Robert tries not to feel angry hearing this, but he can't help it.

'The whole *guilt thing*? Is that what you call it? Don't … don't you feel anything?'

Kieran smiles. 'Yes, of course. I feel fucking *incredible*. I have ever since it became clear that all our work has paid off. It went beautifully.'

Robert thinks back to the sounds Chloe made as Kieran forced more of that poisonous liquid down her throat. Of the gargling sound, the jerking and kicking of her legs as Robert held her down. There's nothing beautiful in the images that haunt him. They're ugly. The whole thing was cruel, vicious and ugly.

'It was horrid,' Robert says.

Kieran sighs again and rubs at the side of his chin. Robert notices a coating of designer stubble – another change. It is as though, during the relatively short time he's been in hospital, Kieran has transformed into a different version of himself.

'Robert, surely even you can see the proof with your own eyes,' he says. 'We didn't get caught. She wasn't even found on the property. She was found on public land. The body was in a condition that messed up the forensics and so thoroughly confused the situation, that the police never connected us to her. To them, we're just the boys who found her. The farmer has been arrested for manslaughter and something to do with the Dangerous Dogs Act. It couldn't be better. Even the cleaners turning up and tidying the treehouse, removing any evidence – it's all so perfect. It worked. The sacrifice worked. The pathway is clear, the obstacles have gone. All we have left to do now is enjoy life.'

Robert sits in silence for a bit, digesting all this. Then he thinks about what he wants to say and the best way to say it. At last, he speaks, keeping his voice as calm and neutral that he can.

'I realise we may have to give evidence or answer more police questions. I hope we won't, but I'll do that. I'll say what you want me to say. It's going to be awful carrying on knowing what we did, but I might as well feel awful at school and university rather than in prison. But I want you to promise me that aside from any official stuff, neither of us will ever talk again about what happened this summer. I never want to discuss it. I never want to talk about The Raven or the Dark Core or all the things you want me to believe. You can think what you want to think, I can't stop you. But this is the last time we talk about it. Agreed?'

Kieran looks at him for a long while. Robert is surprised to see something like sadness in his eyes. Or disappointment, perhaps.

'OK. If that's what you want. We'll never speak of it again.'

Robert nods. 'Thank you.' He swallows, feeling like he's made the right decision. He doesn't expect things to be easy. His anguish and guilt aren't going to be vanquished so easily. But at least he feels like he's going in the right direction. Kieran takes out his phone. A new phone. A black and red Motorola, not his cheap brick of a Nokia.

'Kieran, what's going on with all this new stuff?'

His brother looks up. He grins, looking excited, like someone who's been waiting to tell the punch line of a joke or reveal the twist in a story.

'Oh yeah, didn't Mum and Dad tell you?'

Robert blinks at him. 'Tell me what?'

Kieran's smile widens. 'I won the lottery. I promised you, didn't I? Do you remember? Before we did it, I said I would buy a lottery ticket and win. Well, I did it. Got a full line of matches. Bought the ticket while you were ill back at the lodge. I won the day after you were brought in here. Mum and Dad said they didn't want to tell you until they knew you were going to be OK. I wondered if Dad might let it slip, but I guess not.' He shrugs. 'And now you're fine, we'll be able to enjoy my winnings. Don't worry, I'll give you some.'

Robert is stunned. 'How much?' he asks.

'Twenty-five and a half million.'

Kieran stands up, preparing to leave.

'See, told you. Life's good, Robert. Everything's going according to plan.'

Chapter Thirty-Seven

JUNE

Present day

June has always been quite good at listening to her sons. Both in person and when they're not aware of it.

It's eavesdropping, of course, but a mother has to do these things. That's what she tells herself, anyway. It's her business to know what her sons are thinking and what they're doing; what mistakes they've made. Everyone makes mistakes, of course. She's made her fair share over the years – like the whole business with the vaccinations when the boys were younger. She thought she'd been right to go with her instinct on that. She'd thought she knew better. But that moment when her boy was near death in hospital taught her that nobody can be right one hundred per cent of the time.

All those years ago, when she stood in that kitchen watching her boys being questioned by police, she'd known they weren't being entirely truthful. They left things out – things about their friendship with Chloe. She saw the girl going up into the treehouse with them. She made a lot of presumptions – presumptions that, now, she has to accept may have been incorrect. She'd presumed the girl was *involved* with the boys in some way. Whether with one or both of them, she didn't know, but she suspected drink, drugs and sex were involved. At the time, she decided to watch from afar and take a liberal approach, aware that teenage boys wouldn't want their mother intruding into such things, as they explored and experimented. Her main concern was about heartbreak, about what would happen if both boys fell in love with the girl and competed for her affection, ruining their sibling relationship. So she'd presumed they were economical with the truth with the police because they were embarrassed their parents were there, listening to every word.

But listening to them now, twenty years on, during Robert's sudden flurry of random visits to the family home, she has to accept she was quite wide of the mark when it came to the full story. But of course, her sons didn't know the full story either. They hadn't known, when they were sitting in the kitchen at the lodge that day, downplaying their role in Chloe's death to the police, that there were two key players in what happened to her, present in that room. Two people they'd mistakenly thought were at the periphery of the whole tragic tale: their parents.

But time has passed. Robert had his brush with death and needed to be nursed back to health. Kieran had his lottery win and that brought with it financial security for them all. It seemed best to let the secrets stay in the past. But then this recent crisis arose. June became aware that something was happening between her two sons – something to do with a television drama. She overheard Robert mention it to Kieran, back when his series of visits first started, when they thought they were alone. She later saw the programme crop up on the 'recently viewed' on the TV, so she watched it. And everything slotted into place. Things started to make sense to her. A picture began to form in her mind about what had happened, and why her boys – or men, as they are now – are so alarmed. She understands why they've been acting as if there's this big disaster happening around them that only they can see. What a private hell they must have been in, she thinks to herself. And how well she knows what that can be like. But the key thing is to press on. Don't stop and ruminate. Don't give any of the thoughts power over you. Keep going. That's all anyone can do.

But when you choose to just carry on and not admit defeat, things can get tricky. Decisions have to be made. Hard decisions. She's about to make one of those hard decisions now, as she hovers out of sight in the hallway beside the room where her sons are talking. She's about to let her guard down. She's about to welcome them into the secret world she's been inhabiting for twenty years. And, as a result, the world in which their father has been residing. She's talked it over with him. It's been distressing to see his already frail face computing everything that's happened. She hated having to explain to him the context, the recent developments, and the consequences that might follow. But they are both in agreement that they need to keep their sons out of prison. No matter who's died, no matter who's to blame, no matter who carries the most guilt.

With more precision and calm than she feels inside, she opens the door. Her sons stop their conversation at once and turn to look at her. She stands in the doorway for a few seconds, watching them.

'Shit,' Kieran says quietly.

Robert's guessed that she's heard and starts to say, 'Mum, I'm so sorry,' but tears flow from his eyes and a sob rises in his voice.

'Enough, both of you,' she says, holding up a hand. She has to take control. She's good at this. She's always been good at this part. She's the figure of authority. She's the person who identifies an issue and gets it sorted. She needs to take on that role now, in this hardest of times. If she doesn't, chaos will ensue.

Robert stops talking, but his tears are still flowing. He's always been the one more liable to tears, to a more open display of emotion compared to his brother. She looks at her eldest son and sees a frown creasing his brow. He looks more confused than distressed. Turning back to Robert, she sees the phone in his trembling hand and decides that needs nipping in the bud immediately. Walking over to him, she takes the phone from Robert's hand. He lets it go without protest. He doesn't look as though he's in a fit state to argue. Understandable, she thinks, considering he was close to phoning to police and confessing to a murder. She sets the phone down on the coffee table in front of Kieran and looks at them both.

'Before anyone phones the police, you both need to come with me.'

Robert says nothing. He just blinks his teary red eyes at her. The mixture of confusion and emotion seem to have made speech impossible for him. But Kieran frowns and says, 'Where are we going?'

June takes a breath, then says, 'We're going to your father's room. We're all going to have a little chat. There's something you both need to know.'

She leads them to their father's bedside. Martin is sitting up and he looks awake enough to talk, although June wonders if he'll make it through the whole story and the inevitable discussion that will follow before he has to sleep again.

'Hello, boys,' he says. He's always called them that. He didn't stop when they reached their twenties and it's carried on into their thirties. It's like he's holding on to their youth; they're still his little men. Two miniature versions of him, though with slightly different attributes. Robert's blonder; Kieran's taller. But you can still see Martin in both of them. June feels tears coming to her eyes and she blinks them back hurriedly. She needs to keep a clear head for what's about to happen next. In some ways, she feels the past two decades have been leading up to this moment. She doesn't want to ruin it now with too much emotion. It's going to be hard enough as it is.

'Has your mother told you why I need to speak to you both?' he asks. His voice is hoarse, raspy but steady.

'She just said there's something we should know,' Kieran says.

Robert nods.

'Yes,' Martin says. 'You see, I've had … a secret, I suppose you could call it. I kept it to myself for a while, but eventually told your mother. It was too big for me to keep alone. It was seriously impacting any sense of happiness I had, ruining any quality of life, and I told her everything. And to my astonishment, she's stayed by my side.' June sees him reach out and she moves to his side and takes his cold hand, feeling his weak clasp, and bundles his fingers up with hers.

'OK. I'm just going to come out and say this. I killed Chloe. All those years ago. It was me. It was my fault.'

June sees the effect this has on her sons. Kieran opens his mouth, as though he's trying to speak but no sound comes out. Robert, on the other hand, starts shaking his head.

'No, no,' he says in a tremulous voice. 'It wasn't… It can't… *We* did it. Kieran and I. It's awful and terrible and I regret it so much, but it was us. We gave her pills… We made her drink … and then she hit her head. If she hadn't, she may have been able to outrun those dogs or fight them off. I've been trying to tell myself for years that we didn't kill her, that the fact that the dogs attacked her means that we weren't really to blame, but we were.'

Martin waits for his son to stop, for his words to peter out, then he says. 'Let me explain. And in telling you this, I'm aware you'll never be able to think about me in the same way again, but it's important I tell you everything. The sad, sordid context to it all.' He takes a deep, slow breath, then says, 'I was having an affair with Chloe.' Silence greets this. June feels her pulse rate quicken as he says the words. She can't help but loosen the grip on his hand ever so slightly. 'I was … *involved* with her,' he clarifies, as though the meaning isn't already clear.

'*What?*' Robert says, looking utterly shocked, as though this is the last thing he expected to hear. Kieran, meanwhile, doesn't say anything, but his frown is back, furrowing his brow and making his smooth, handsome face look older than he is. She wonders if he's guessed this, over the years. She's not sure how much he knew about his father's affairs when he was younger. June always turned a blind eye and let him have his dalliances, going along with the pretence that he had a lot of work. So long as the boys didn't know, she could cope with it. That's what she'd told herself, but she found her ability to cope was tested when he moved on to a teenage girl. A girl almost the same age as one of his children. As she thinks about this, she takes her hand out of her husband's and moves over to the window.

'I know this must be a shock. I'm so sorry it happened,' he says, his voice thick with embarrassment and regret.

'*How* did it happen?' asks Robert.

'When I picked you boys up … from the seafront, that first time and gave her a lift back. I felt … I don't know how to put it … a connection with her. It was instant. I knew I had to see her again. And I knew, if I saw her, what would happen. One day, when your mum was doing some work and you were in your treehouse, I went down to the bungalow where we'd dropped her off. I watched and waited until I saw her. I'm not proud of it. I knew it wasn't great – but I was still in my thirties. I still felt *young*. I hope, now you're at similar ages, that you understand. I didn't feel like a … well, like a dirty older man. I felt like I had this amazing connection with a girl. So I followed that feeling just to see where it went. I'm not asking you to excuse it, and I'm not trying to dress it up as something it wasn't, like some tragic love story. It was infatuation, not love. But even so, I hope you can find it in your hearts not to judge me too harshly.'

Robert still looks horrified. Kieran's expression is blank. Neither boy rushes to absolve him or even to say that they sympathise. Eventually, Martin carries on.

'As I'm sure you know, her mother had her own … activities, involving men and drugs and things like that. Not a nice home life for a girl of Chloe's age. But it meant her bungalow was sometimes empty at night. Or during the day.'

'So, when you went off for work that just couldn't wait…' Robert says, an edge of anger to his voice.

Martin nods slowly. 'I drove to the nearest train station, parked my car and got a taxi back to her place.'

'Jesus Christ,' Robert whispers, shaking his head.

'I know. And I'm sorry. But…' He pauses. June watches as he appears to be gathering all the strength and courage he has left to say the next bit. 'This is very difficult to say, but that's not the worst of it. Not by a long shot.'

Robert seems to be struggling to stay calm. June comes forwards and lays a hand on her son's arm.

'Do you need to sit down?' she asks, gesturing to the chair beside his father's bed.

He shakes his head and wipes away his tears. Then he turns back to his dad and says, 'I get that you having affairs with teenagers isn't great, but it still isn't comparable to what we did. What Kieran and I—'

'Wait a moment,' June says. 'Listen to what your father has to say.'

Robert nods and waits, his eyes on the floor now.

'The purpose of this little … confession, for want of a better word, isn't to excuse myself or mount some kind of defence. And with no disrespect to your mother, being the younger person in a marriage by some mile does something to you. I'm not saying it's bad or good, but it … it sets you apart, especially if it's the man who's younger. So it was refreshing to feel like the older one. The worldly, wise one. I liked that. It's probably wrong of me, but I did. However, I would like to say there weren't *affairs*, plural, with teenagers. She was the only one younger than me. The only one *that* much younger.'

Robert grimaces. 'Well, that's all right then,' he says sarcastically.

'Can you stop interrupting, Rob?' Kieran says quietly. 'I want to hear what Dad's trying to tell us.'

Martin looks at his eldest son. 'Thank you. As I said, this is very difficult. It saddens me that I'm probably nearing my last days, and the fact that this is what we have to go through… This will be one of our last conversations. It breaks my heart. But it's necessary. And you'll see why.'

'Get to the point,' Robert mutters.

'OK, I will,' he says. 'I planned to meet Chloe the night that she died. I was going to go down to her home late at night, then come back very early in the morning. She was intent on going to America with some cheap tickets a friend of her mother's had managed to get her. I'd only just met her and thought she was going to be around all summer. Again, I know this sounds sordid, but now you're adults, you boys may know that once a certain part of your brain is engaged – or rather, not your brain, but well, you know, you end up making stupid decisions. And that part of me was very much engaged; engaged and excited that I thought I'd be able to see Chloe frequently. And then she just casually announced she was leaving, that she was going to the US, and didn't know when she'd be back. If ever. So my hopes of a summer spent … seeing her changed. And that led me to do something … very stupid.'

June sees the rapt attention on her sons' faces. She wishes this could be different. Wishes there's another way, but this really is the best. The way it has to be. They need to hear about this. And after so many years keeping their father's sins to herself, making sure they didn't know, she's surprised to find that part of her is glad. Glad that, at last, they're getting to know what type of man their father is, what sort of marriage she's had, what sort of compromises she's had to make. But everyone makes compromises for love, and she still loves him. In spite of everything, she can't help it. Without saying a word, June takes back her husband's hand and grips it tightly within hers. He'll need her for this next bit. It's going to be the worst part of the evening.

Well, one of the worst.

There'll still be more to do after he's said his piece. She's not looking forward to that.

'Your mother and I have always had separate rooms, as you know. You boys were ensconced in the treehouse. I've always suffered from insomnia and regularly wander out at night so it was easy for me to sneak out and come back in the early hours. Everything was fine. Until, of course, it wasn't on that night. The night of Chloe's death.'

He pauses for a moment, and for a second, June wonders if her husband is about to cry. But he doesn't. Just blinks quite fast and carries on.

'That short stay in Cornwall was both incredibly exciting and absolutely terrifying, even before what happened to her. I spent most of the time planning to see her again whilst simultaneously worrying she might tell you boys about what we were doing. It skews your thinking, that mixture of desire and fear. Replaces rational behaviour. It taints and obscures everything. So, on that awful night, I was desperate to get to Chloe's bungalow to see her, for what would perhaps be the last time. We'd only been involved with each other for a week, but it felt like a lifetime.

'I was, of course, surprised to find her walking through the woods too, on her way home. I'd presumed she'd have been in her bungalow, waiting for me. I asked where she'd been. To my shock, she told me to piss off or something along those lines. I'd never heard her talk like that. It was awful, like she'd shot me. She just carried on walking slowly through the woods, swaying a bit. I assumed she was drunk. Then something occurred to me. Since we were walking in the same direction, I asked if she'd come from the treehouse. If she'd been seeing you both. I … I'm not proud of this, but I … I realised I was jealous.'

He stops to cough. He looks to his left, and June pours out a fresh glass of water from the jug on the little table near his bed and helps him drink. Once he's swallowed, he dabs at his lips with the back of his hand, then carries on.

'I'm sorry, boys, I know how pathetic it sounds. Feeling jealous of your own sons … it's quite a shameful thing. But the thought of you being young and carefree in that treehouse, still in the midst of youth … I found it too much to bear. I asked if she was involved with one or both of you, if she was messing with us all, if her aim was to make me hate my own children. I had no evidence of that; it was my anger talking. But something about it touched a nerve. She looked at me with disgust. Even in the darkness, with chinks of moonlight shining through the trees, I was horrified at the expression on her face. It's imprinted onto my memory.

'She said something along the lines of "Your sons are psychos" and how she never wanted to see either of you again. She started to say something about going to the police about what you'd done. I was appalled. I didn't know what she meant by it, what she was accusing you both of, but I … I got a bit aggressive with her.

I started shaking her, demanding to know if she'd told you about us, about what we'd been doing ever since that night I dropped her home. It suddenly felt like the most important thing in the world to know. She slapped me and the surprise of it made me let go of her. She set off walking away from me, but called out something about the police, about telling everyone about me, about you boys…'

He stops. He looked at his sons as he spoke, but June watches as he lowers his gaze to the bed covers in front of him.

'What I did next will sound like it was only motivated by self-interest. But it wasn't. I … I felt like I was acting for all of us.' His face looks pained, more pained than usual – not with the physical discomfort of his illness, but with an inner, deeper pain. A torment of his soul. 'I know that's no excuse … but it's true. Or at least … I think it is. I hope it is.'

Silence.

Then Robert says in a trembling whisper, 'What did you do, Dad?'

Martin pauses, then he says, 'The worst thing I've ever done. By some mile. I was walking back home when I heard the dogs. They were barking and running around. At first I thought they'd escaped into the woods already, but as I climbed the hill through the woods I saw them running around the stretch of fenced ground. It … it was so simple. Such an easy thing to do. I unlatched the gate to the farmer's land, and then I walked away. I returned to our lodge and went to bed.'

A stunned silence follows this. Then Kieran speaks for the first time in a while.

'So you're the reason why the dogs attacked Chloe? They ran off into the woods and savaged her as she was walking home?'

His father nods. 'Presumably so. I managed to go to sleep that night telling myself I wasn't that culpable. I knew, from what you boys had said, that they occasionally got free. I knew the farmer would be blamed if anything happened. And because I didn't know if anything would, I didn't actually feel like I was … well, you know … killing her. I just felt I was helping even up the scales a bit. I figured she must have known the risk of walking through those woods. It felt like … like I wasn't really changing anything, just…' He leaves the sentence unfinished.

June watches a single, solitary tear roll down his left cheek.

'I don't know what you boys did, or tried to do, to Chloe in that treehouse,' he continues, 'and I never want to know. I don't want to be in the position of trying to excuse or justify it in my head. I've had a difficult enough time doing that with my own demons. And that's why I've never told you what I did. So you didn't have to carry my sins along with your own, whatever they are.'

June watches her two sons digest this news.

Robert says, 'But this doesn't change anything. Not really. I need to go to the police. Someone knew what Kieran and I did. I know you said you don't want to know about it, and I'm sorry, but'—he raises a hand to his face to rub at his eyes—'but someone did know. Someone overheard what happened. He tried to blackmail me and I killed him. So I *am* a killer. Even if Kieran and I didn't exactly kill Chloe, I can't get out of that one. I didn't mean to, but it was still me. I did it. I killed him.'

June interjects. 'No, Robert, you didn't.' He starts to protest, but she stops him. 'No, really. Please be quiet. I heard you boys the afternoon before it happened, in the house, talking upstairs. I listened and I was worried what you might do.'

Robert looks at her. She sees the realisation in his face. 'You heard everything? So when I came downstairs, you knew…'

'I knew I needed to do something. I was struggling to digest it all in that moment, I confess. I think you noticed.'

He nods slowly. 'Yes. I was worried you had dementia or something. You seemed weirdly distant.'

'Well,' she says, folding her arms, 'I hope you understand now why I was like that. To hear your children discussing murder isn't something a mother expects to come home to.'

Robert's shaking his head, still crying. 'I don't see—'

'Listen to me. You didn't kill Sean Smith. *You* weren't to blame. I am one hundred per cent certain about that.'

'How?' Kieran asks, frowning at his mother as Robert struggles to control his sobs.

'Because I killed him,' she says simply.

Chapter Thirty-Eight

JUNE

Two days earlier

June is alarmed to see her son's car parked outside the house of Sean Smith. She'd hoped she could get there first and talk to the man – and hopefully pay him off – before her son could speak to him. It was a slim chance, and she feels at that moment like she's failed him. It didn't take long to look up R.R. Dread's address. She has a contact at the agency that represents him – she's done some translation work for the literary side of the business – and it took only a quick phone call and some creative lies to get the address. She had a pen and paper ready to write it down, but of course didn't need them as soon as she heard it. She should have guessed, really. Perhaps she'd always been destined to return to Hill Valley. Not that she believes in destiny. People make their own luck, that's always been her view. She likes to be 'in the know' and quietly sort out any issues before they become full-blown crises. It's usually possible to turn even the trickiest of situations around. Through action, thought and dedication, she's always been one to take up the reins and steer the course of her own future. And this is what she's doing now.

She parked her car a couple of minutes' walk away in a layby and walked down to the front gates. How very strange it is to be back at this place, she thinks to herself as she moves her gaze from her son's car to the front door. Then the front door opens and she moves back around the brick pillars, watching through the gaps in the gate as her youngest son emerges from the front door. She instantly knows something is very wrong. His face makes that clear. He's pale and unsteady as he opens the car door, and his car screeches and crunches as he turns around on the gravel and speeds too fast towards the gate. She has to back into the side of the hedge so as not to be seen as he zooms past her. Even so, she wonders if he'll suddenly come to a halt on the road having seen her in one of his mirrors. But the car just carries on.

Going quickly through the gate before it closes, June walks up to the house, unsure of what she's going to discover. The door isn't swinging open, so there's no hope of getting in that way. She peers in through the windows at the front, but there's nothing to see, the reflections from the sun making it hard to focus on what or who might be inside. Someone must be, she thinks. The image of her son's face as he fled is imprinted on her mind. There has to be someone inside. And, with a rising sense of anxiety, she feels she might have an idea as to what has transpired between Robert and Sean Smith. She just hopes she's wrong.

June decides to walk along the side of the lodge around the back. She can see alterations and modernisations have been made to the building since she was here, including a sizeable extension which looks to be still in progress. There are no builders in sight, though, nor is there any sound coming from inside. She sees the sliding glass doors of the kitchen are open as she comes around the back of the house. Tentatively, she walks up to them and looks in.

A man is standing in the kitchen. He reaches out to a sink embedded in a beautiful kitchen island in the centre and turns on the taps. That wasn't there when they stayed here, she thinks, wondering whether this man has made these alterations himself during the recent building work or whether he bought it like this. The man runs a kitchen towel under the tap, but he shuts it off as soon as he sees her.

'Who the hell are you?' he asks, turning to look at her. The twisting of his neck makes him wince and he raises the wet cloth to a spot on the back of his head.

'Hello,' June says, crossing over the little grove in the floor.

'Er … hello? I asked what the fuck you're doing in my house.'

She smiles and says, 'Well, actually you didn't.'

'What?' he says, frowning at her.

'Your first question was about who the hell I am. Then you asked what I'm doing in your house. Whilst I understand you'd like both questions answered – I would if I were in your position – I'm sure you'll agree with me that they are, in fact, two separate questions. Connected, I grant you. But still two questions.'

The man watches her, blinking. He looks both in pain and annoyed at the same time. 'What… Who…? Are you with him?'

'Him?' June repeats, raising her eyebrows. 'We're the only people in this room.'

'*What?*' he says again. 'Are you fucking messing with me? The bastard who just tried to kill me.' He pulls the cloth away from the back of his head and looks at it, then shows it to June. 'Look. Blood! He's a murderer, you know. You must have seen him. If you did, you can be my witness.'

June shakes her head. 'But I haven't witnessed anything. I can't be a witness if I haven't seen anything, can I?'

The question looks as if it's causing Sean Smith actual physical pain – or at least exacerbating whatever pain is already there.

He starts to sway, moving to the side and knocking over a knife block and two bowls drying on the side. One of them smashes to the floor and the other falls into the sink with a crack.

'I need to sit down,' he says.

'Perhaps you should,' June says, stepping forwards.

'Clear off! I still don't know who the fuck you are,' he says. 'You're trespassing, you know that. You're…' He trails off, squinting at June as though something's just occurred to him. He raises his hand to his head again and closes his eyes. She wonders if he's going to faint, but when he opens them again, she thinks she can see triumph blossoming within them. 'Holy shit, I know who you are.'

She feels a prickle of panic then. There's something about the low, quiet voice in which he says it that causes her to feel suddenly very vulnerable and unprepared. She'd wanted to offer this man money, wanted to buy him off, to tidy everything away so she could tell her son he had nothing to worry about anymore. But that reality now feels remote and naïve, especially when Sean Smith starts to laugh.

'Are you his mum? What are you, a family double act? God, this is good. Has he sent you in here to clear up his mess? Well, after today you can tell him the price of my silence has gone sky high.'

'The price?' queries June. 'So you and my son reached an arrangement, did you?'

He smirks back. 'So I'm correct then? You're the killer's mother?'

She feels her hands tense, her unease replaced with anger. 'Don't call him that,' she says.

'Why not?' he says belligerently.

'Because it isn't true.'

This causes him to laugh. 'Oh, *as if*. Like you'd be here if he wasn't. I'm getting déjà vu here. Are you sure you two didn't work out a script together before coming here? And his little temper tantrum has messed stuff up for you both? Well, it *has* messed things up, because like I said, price rises are on the way. It's going to take a lot more than what I told him to keep me quiet now, make no mistake about that. I'm just impressed he told you. But it makes sense. Snivelling little pricks always go running to their parents at the first sign of trouble.'

The anger is burning even stronger within her now. 'He hasn't told me anything.'

Sean laughs again. 'Oh yeah? Are you sure? I take it you've watched my series on TV? I take it you've seen what the boys do? Newsflash: it's all true. They did that.'

'Be quiet,' June says in a whisper.

'They held her down and forced her to drink their own sick little potion. Probably got some perverse kick out of it as they did it.'

'Be quiet,' June says again.

'I watched them do it. Both of them. Your baby boys are two vicious killers and it's because of them that she wasn't able to outrun those dogs. Because of *them* that we're here right now. Tell me, what does a mother have to do to her children to fuck them up that badly? Were they made like that in your womb or did you twist their little brains when they were kids and mess them up good and proper? Which is it, nature or nurture?'

June doesn't waste a second thinking about what she does next. She just does it with two quick movements. One movement to reach forwards and pick up the knife, the next to plunge it into the man's chest. Although she uses a lot of force, the knife doesn't go fully in. It reaches something hard that stops it and she lets go.

But in shock at what's happening, Sean Smith loses his balance.

He yells out, a noise of surprise and pain, then makes a movement with his hands, perhaps to steady himself, or perhaps an attempt to pull the knife from his chest. Whatever the purpose, June doesn't know. She watches him fail to pull the knife from his chest, and then she watches him slump forwards. She watches him fall against the kitchen island, the knife sliding deeper into him before he comes to a stop with a half grunt, half moan sound. Then there's silence.

June doesn't plan to keep the murder weapon. She almost vomited when she lifted Sean Smith's torso by the shoulder to pull the knife from him. She wasn't entirely sure what she was doing – she was acting on impulse when she did that, which isn't like her. Now, she's driving home with the knife wrapped in a Waitrose carrier bag in the boot of her car. She considers throwing it off a bridge – she's seen people doing that on television dramas not dissimilar from the one that kicked off all of this. *The Treehouse*. She went down to look at the treehouse in the garden of the lodge one last time before going back to the kitchen to remove the knife. It looked new and very modern. She never went up in it, back when they stayed here twenty years ago, but she could tell it wasn't the same structure as before. Again, she wonders who built this one. Was it Sean Smith, as part of his little obsession with what happened that summer, or was it any of the owners in between? She doesn't need to know. She only knows she never wants to see any part of this place again.

She drives without any plans to stop and rest, just keeps going. Each time she sees a bridge over a river or a roadside bin or a skip, she thinks about disposing of the knife, but something tells her it might be wise to keep hold of it. She doesn't quite know why, but she has a feeling that it may be necessary, at some point, depending on what her son does next. She hopes he won't do anything stupid. She hopes he'll be sensible. She hopes he'll go home and leave things to play out by themselves rather than trying to confess to anything. He's always been a reassurance seeker, Rob. Not like Kieran, with his quiet, confident swagger and his easy, carefree life filled with money and limited responsibility.

Sean Smith's words – some of the last he ever uttered – come to her as she exits the motorway, heading towards Rettendon, tiredness threatening to overwhelm her. *What does a mother have to do to her kids to fuck them up that badly?* She thinks about her choices as a parent and some of the more controversial decisions she made throughout their youth.

Her insistence that smacking them when they were naughty was good for them.

Her stance about vaccines that proved to be so perilous for her younger son.

Her insistence on always knowing best. Better than anyone else. Facts, not fiction. Certainty, not ambiguity. *Her* facts. *Her* version of certainty.

She knows little about the strange sacrifice ideology her boys were swept up in, save for a few snatches of overheard conversations, but she does wonder if maybe she inadvertently laid the foundations for that sort of thing to take over their lives. She discouraged them from reading fantasy novels like *Narnia* or *Harry Potter*, was critical of any belief in ghosts, described followers of religions as deluded, and drew parallels between the devout and those with mental health issues. Perhaps she helped create a vacuum where belief in unscientific fictions could flourish. All these thoughts keep her company until she pulls the car to a stop outside her home. In the end, she has to accept the uncomfortable truth that she'll never really know the whys and hows of the whole thing. She'll just have to live with that as best she can. After all, there's plenty both her sons and her husband don't know. There may come a time when she has to tell them what she's done. Some of it perhaps, but not all of it, if she can avoid it. Everyone has their secrets. And what she did to Sean Smith today is her secret.

Or one of them.

Chapter Thirty-Nine

ROBERT

Present day

The two brothers wait in the living room. Robert was grateful for a reason to leave when his mother said she wanted a moment to say goodbye to their father. She'd phoned the police more or less immediately after telling them what she'd done. Now it was just a question of waiting for them to arrive. He'd made an attempt to stop her. He told her they should all say nothing, keep quiet, wait for the police to catch them, if they ever did. But she said no.

'There's been too much of that in this family already,' she said, looking at him with sad eyes. 'We've spent decades looking over our shoulders, wondering when all of this was going to unravel. Let's put a full stop to it. Finish it for good.'

In need of fresh air, Robert goes out into the garden. He hears Kieran follow him. He feels emotionally drained and very anxious, and for the first time in a while he isn't sure he wants to share his discomfort with his brother. After all this time feeling like they were bonded by this ordeal, he now feels like they were actually oceans apart, for years. He just didn't realise it.

Robert takes a seat on the garden bench at the side of the house and Kieran sits himself down next to him. They'll see the light of the police cars when they come up the driveway. But for now, they have the deep blue darkness of the summer's night. It feels like the night before they attempted their sacrifice, as though they're about to tip into another realm, another way of life. This feeling of teetering on a precipice has a nauseating familiarity and Robert isn't sure he can bear it.

As though guessing how he's feeling, Kieran says quietly, 'I hope now you can see why I didn't want you to confess.'

Robert turns his head to look at him. 'Please don't tell me you're happy with how this has turned out. Don't tell me you're happy that both our parents are murderers. It doesn't let us off the hook. I've spent my life trying to atone for it all. Why else do you think I work in the charity sector, trying to do good? Hoping that if I can help other people's lives, it will somehow rid me of the guilt of the one I helped take? Nothing we've heard today changes any of that. It was still terrible. What we did to Chloe wasn't just misguided or a mistake. It was horrific.'

'You're looking at all this the wrong way,' Kieran says. 'This frees us. Yes, it's unfortunate that Mum will probably end up going to prison—'

'*Unfortunate?* Christ, can you hear yourself?'

'But,' Kieran says firmly, carrying on, 'her actions have helped secure us our freedom.'

'God, you sound just like how you did back then, back when you were obsessed with the Dark Core nonsense. And worst of all, it sounds selfish. As though our lives – *your* life – is all that matters.'

Kieran lets out a slow breath. 'Rob, mate, I've always tried to be honest with you, but there are things I haven't told you. Things about me. Things I … like to do.'

Robert is suddenly afraid of what he's going to hear. Part of him wants to press his palms against his brother's mouth, to stop him speaking. But he can't help listening. He knows he needs to hear it. But their conversation is brought to an abrupt end by the sound of crunching gravel, followed by the sight of a police car coming up the driveway.

They go back inside. Robert wants to be with his mother while she confesses to the police officers the murder of Sean Smith. He feels he owes her that.

'I wanted to look around the house, you see,' she says, surprisingly calmly. 'I'd stayed there previously, many years ago, when it was a holiday rental. He welcomed me in at first, but then … well, he tried to attack me. I managed to push him over and he hit his head, but then he got up and tried to stop me leaving. There was a knife on the countertop. I used it to defend myself. I didn't mean to stab him, not really, I just acted very quickly, but he fell onto the knife. I shouldn't have fled the scene. I'm sorry. I understand you'll need to arrest me. I'm willing to come and make a full statement.' She holds out her hands, wrists together, as though expecting to be cuffed on the spot. The police officer looks at her, clearly surprised by all this. Then she tells her she can lower her hands. They won't be using handcuffs.

'Will I be taken to Cornwall?' June asks.

'We'll be taking you to Chelmsford for now,' the police officer says.

Robert watches his mother nod. She turns to look at him, and then Kieran. 'May I say goodbye to my sons before we go?'

She's told she can. She kisses Kieran on the cheek, and then Robert. She looks him in the eye and for a moment he thinks she's going to say something else, as though there's something more she wishes she was able to tell him. But she only says two words. 'Stay strong'. Then she leaves, and the boys go to be with their father, feeling like they should all be together during this strangest of evenings.

Robert watches his father sleep. He tracks his slow breaths, rising and falling. He thinks about how frail he looks. How different from when they were children and he was still a young man. Still with looks that caused girls like Chloe to turn their heads and offer him their time and affection. The thought of it makes him feel ill. The lies, the secrets, the betrayal of a girl who never harmed anyone – unlike the three of them, sitting there, years of regret echoing around them like ghosts.

Robert feels his phone vibrate in his pocket. It takes him a while to muster the energy to fish it out, and once he does he's missed the call. It was Albie. A WhatsApp message arrives a minute or two later.

Rob, I tried to call. Long story, but I'm out of the London version of Chicago and am taking a role in the touring production instead. Won't bore you with the details but basically I'll be away for a long time so I think it's best I move out. Hope you're OK.

Robert locks the phone without responding. He'll reply in the morning, perhaps. It doesn't matter anymore. There's an emptiness within him that encompasses everything. Friendships, connections, human interactions, all these ordinary human things seem off limits to him now. It's like he's exempted himself from ordinary life and will forever be floating in a guilt-tinged vacuum.

'Maybe we should go to bed,' Kieran says, taking Robert out of his thoughts. 'It's three in the morning.'

Robert stays silent for a moment. Then, when he speaks, he asks a question that's been on his mind for a while. 'When did you stop believing in the Dark Core and all that nonsense? When I think back to it now, I can't believe I was captured by it. So I wondered … when did you let it all go?'

The light from the lamp at the side of the room throws Kieran's face into shadow. Robert can't see his face, can't read his expression. He's just a blank silhouette in front of him.

Eventually, the silhouette says, 'Why do you think I've stopped?'

Robert feels a horrible, prickling feeling on his neck. At first, he thinks his brother is joking. It's a sick, inappropriate joke, considering what's happened that evening. But then, when Kieran doesn't say anything further, Robert realises he's serious.

'I don't… I don't understand,' Robert says.

But he does understand. It now seems blindingly obvious to him. Kieran's reaction to the crisis involving the television series, R.R. Dread, Robert's wish to visit him; Kieran's cautions; his insistence on doing nothing. All of it fits into his brother's trust in something else. Something *other*. A deeper, darker force neither of them can see.

'Think about it,' Kieran says, his quiet voice pulling Robert back to the present moment. 'I got to enjoy my youth untroubled. We were never arrested. I won a large sum of money that means I've never needed a career. I've never needed to do anything I don't want to do. And it looks like we're going to get away with it once again. The police don't seem interested in us. It looks like Sean Smith's threat about audio recordings was an empty bluff. Either that, or nothing has been found. And it never will, because we're untouchable, Rob. Untouchable. So *of course* I still believe in it.

Don't you see, we've had easy lives *because* we were brave enough to make that leap when we were young? Surely you can see that from your own life. You've benefitted from my money; you've had flash jobs, a lot of flings with beautiful women, a gorgeous flat in Central London – all of that's been possible because we helped clear our pathway. We cultivated and curated a smooth road through life. We did something extraordinary.' He draws himself up, putting his hands on his knees, looking taller. More imposing. 'All we need to do now is carry on. Go with the flow.' He pauses for a moment, then says, in a harder tone, 'In case that's too cryptic for you, Rob, I'll simplify it. From now on, do as you're fucking told. OK?'

Robert can't speak for a few seconds. He glances at his father who continues to sleep in front of him, blissfully unaware of what his sons are talking about.

'What did you mean, earlier, about … urges?'

Kieran stares back at him, his eyes narrowed. Then he smirks and says, 'Let's just say the Dark Core, the concept of sacrificing, it appeals to urges I've always had. The whole concept of killing … I don't know, it's just always had an appeal for me.'

Robert sits up, suddenly tense. 'But you're the one who tried to talk me out of killing Sean Smith.'

'Because I knew you'd screw it up. You weren't going to do it to benefit your life or nourish your soul or appeal to an inner love of power, the beautiful, enriching power that comes from violence. That wasn't your motivation, Rob. You were acting out of panic and fear. That's not enriching. To be frank, that's just foolish. Childish, even. What I'm talking about is quite different. Controlled killing in controlled environments. Sacrifices in properly managed settings.'

Robert's heart is pounding now, realising what Kieran is telling him. 'You mean … you've … done *more* … more since Chloe?'

He rolls his eyes. 'Bless you, Rob. You're so naïve. Of course I have. You remember that man who took us for a drink after we went to that meeting in St George's Square?'

Robert nods. 'Yes. Although I can't remember his name. It was so long ago.'

'Argento,' Kieran says. 'And it wasn't that long ago for me. I mean, I've stayed in touch with him. Over the years. And others who are like me. Like-minded individuals. He understands our desires, you see. He's good at supplying what we need. And in return, I help him by finding others who may wish to explore that part of themselves. People who want to have what I've managed to have: wealth, freedom, the chance to explore that true part of oneself that usually remains buried.'

Robert swallows. 'What … what do you want me to do with that information?'

Kieran shrugs. 'To understand, I suppose. If that's not too much to ask. I live a truly extraordinary life, Rob. Honestly, you don't know the half of it.'

Robert stands up shakily. He swallows and wonders for a second if he might be sick. But he takes in a few steady breaths and manages to return his eyes to Kieran, who sits there, looking at him.

'I think I already know more than I'd like.' He turns away and walks slowly towards the door. Before he leaves, he looks back. 'All these years, us being brothers, after everything we've been through,' he says, trying to keep his voice steady, 'I still believed that, in spite of what you did, in spite of what you encouraged me to do, I still believed you were good inside. That you were a good person who did a bad thing. But now,' he says, shaking his head, his eyes fixed on Kieran who refuses to look away, 'now, I wonder if I ever knew you at all.'

Epilogue

The church is surprisingly full. Even though the friends drifted away during his long illness, Robert is still impressed by how many have turned up to mourn his father's death. He nods in greeting at some of the people he recognises. Old family friends from the past. People he recognises as his dad's former colleagues. But as he watches people take their seats on the varnished pews, winter coats brushing against the fraying hymn books, he can't help wondering if these people are here for another reason. Here, perhaps, to catch a glimpse of the convicted killer who is rumoured to be arriving with a prison escort.

To Robert and Kieran, of course, this is no rumour. It's a plan, a fact, an arranged detail of the service of which they have been part. And here she comes now, taking her seat at the back of the church, a stony-faced uniformed woman of about forty sitting next to her. Robert wants her to come to the front, to sit with him and Kieran, but when he gets up she shakes her head. She wants to be at the back. Not on display. She probably feels like too much of an exhibit already, he assumes, as he sits back down, turning his gaze to the light brown coffin at the front, waiting for the service to begin.

On the way home, less than an hour later, Robert finds himself thinking more about his mother than about the funeral itself. He exchanged some brief words with her, promising to come and visit her soon. She'd only been inside a matter of weeks before his father passed away and he'd only visited her once in that time, accompanied by Kieran. During that visit, he couldn't quite work out if she was glad of their presence or embarrassed by it. She was in a grey tracksuit with her hair tied back and no make-up. So completely different from how they'd always seen her before, as though she were impersonating a teenager out for a jog. During that visit, he once again had the feeling that she was holding something back. There was a moment when Kieran went to the loo when he was sure she was going to tell him something, just like in the seconds before she was taken away by the police. Something in her look. Not dissimilar from her look at the funeral, her eyes silently communicating something.

Robert lets himself into his flat. Part of him wishes he'd stayed at the family home with Kieran, but the two of them haven't spoken much in the months after the night of their mother's arrest. They haven't had a falling out, exactly. It's more that Robert isn't sure if they ever really fell-in. If his brotherly admiration and sense of kinship with Kieran isn't, in the end, just a mirage.

The flat feels empty and cold, even though he's got the heating switched on. He wonders if it's because Albie's moved out, something that happened almost without him noticing, back when he felt as though his life was falling apart. Has it fallen apart? He isn't sure. It's hard for him to think of his mother sitting in a jail cell as a just end to whatever sorry story they've all been caught up in. But it does, at least, lend the whole thing an air of finality.

Finality. That's it. That's the thing he can't dismiss. It should feel like the door is closed on the whole business. But it isn't. He just knows it. There is something else, some key detail his mother isn't telling him. After a sleepless night, he opens his iPhone and looks at the next date in his calendar he has marked with the word 'Mum' as a scheduled event. His next visit to the prison. The day he plans to get some answers.

It's a decision he will end up regretting for the rest of his life, but he doesn't know that, a week later, when he takes his seat in the visitors' room and his mother walks over to the chair in front of him.

To his surprise, she looks more confident than before. She's still in the tracksuit, still with her hair tied back, but she no longer has the gaunt, tired look she carried throughout the trial. She even seems noticeably improved since the funeral, even though that was only ten days before. 'You look well,' he says truthfully.

'Thank you,' she says, giving him a thin smile. 'I'm settling in.'

She makes it sound like she's away on an extended cruise, not in prison for murder. But Robert doesn't waste the limited time they have making small talk. Instead, he dives straight in. 'I still feel like there's something in all this you haven't told me.'

She looks at him, saying nothing, but a slight frown creases her brow.

'I may be wrong, but I think there's something else – some other aspect in the death of Sean Smith that you left out. Some detail that might change everything.'

Her expression alters. Her eyebrows rise. 'This takes me back to marking your homework when you were a child before you handed it in at school. Sadly, in this instance, your score is low. Only one out of three.'

Robert stares back at her, feeling his pulse rate quicken. 'Which bit is correct?'

She takes a deep breath, then says, 'You've got this the wrong way around. I don't have anything further to say about the death of Sean Smith. There's nothing new to be found there. I told you the truth about that. Of course, I lied in court about it being self-defence, but you know why I did that. I did it to protect you. And, of course, to reduce my sentence. Nobody else has drawn the connection between his screenplay and the death of a teenage girl in Cornwall all those years ago. I can't promise nobody ever will, but I think if those dots were ever to be joined, it would have come out around the time of the police interviews and trial. Of course, it helped that I pleaded guilty. That kept things … tidy. People like things tidy, I've found. The police, the lawyers. It keeps the system ticking over.'

'So it's something else, then?' Robert prompts.

She nods slowly. 'Yes. In short, you've got the wrong murder.'

It's Robert's turn to frown. 'What?'

'You were wrong about there being any further secrets regarding my killing of Sean Smith. You were wrong that there was a hidden secret that would change everything about that case. But you're right that there are things that you don't know about Chloe's death. If you switch your focus to that, then, well…' She tilts her head, as though she's weighing something in her mind. 'I suppose everything does change. Everything your father told you, at least.'

Robert's mouth falls open. 'Dad was *lying*? Why … why would he lie about something like that?'

'He wasn't lying,' she says. 'He was telling the truth. The truth as *he* saw it.'

Robert feels himself getting frustrated. 'You're confusing me and talking in riddles.'

She nods. 'I know, I'm sorry; I don't mean to. I just … haven't spoken about this to anyone. But I think it's fair I tell you. I think you might understand.' She pauses, clasps her hands together, then says something that changes Robert's world. 'I killed Chloe.'

Robert feels a chilling effect rippling across his skin. 'No,' he says very quietly.

'Yes.'

'But ... how? He said it was him? He unlatched the gate. It was because of him the dogs escaped the farmer's land and ran off into the woods.'

She shakes her head. 'He presumed that was what happened, and I let him think that. It was just simpler. And it's true, he did unlatch the gate. I watched him do it. I watched from the window of the rented holiday home. I saw the girl walking in the distance. I saw him going into the woods. I knew he was going to meet her. When he came back sooner than expected, I presumed something had gone wrong. And when I saw him walk up to the top of the hill to the farm and unlock the gate and leave it open, I guessed what he was trying to do. So I watched and waited. I heard your father come in and go to bed. The dogs were visible in the farmer's field, but the gate was still too closed for them to run free. So I made a decision. I didn't stop to think about it. *Get the job done*, that's what I've always thought you need to do when you have a difficult task ahead of you. And this was an unexpected chance to get this particular job done. A job your father had started. I just finished it. I walked out into the night and went over to the farm. I opened the gate wide. A bit risky, of course, but the dogs shot out into the darkness of the woodland. And as I walked back to the house, I heard a scream. I could have been imagining it, but I'm fairly sure I heard the moment the dogs got her. She probably didn't stand a chance.'

Robert is stunned. '*You* did it? All these years, I've thought I was responsible for Chloe's death. Dad's been thinking he's the reason she's dead. But all this time, *you* were the one who did it. The one who wanted her dead.'

She stares back at him, as though waiting for him to compute all this.

'Why? Because Dad was screwing her? Couldn't you have just divorced him like a normal person?'

Again, she looks as if she's weighing something up. Testing out a mental problem she finds mildly interesting. 'Hmm, yes, I could have done. But I must confess, that would have rather spoilt the fun.'

Robert's eyes widen. 'Fun? You had *fun* killing Chloe?'

She smiles. 'No, my dear,' she says. 'I had fun killing *all* your dad's women.'

Robert is sure he must have misheard her. Sure he must have thoroughly misunderstood what she said, his brain inventing inconceivable, preposterous things in order to fill in the gaps.

'Yes, you did hear that correctly,' she says. 'It became … sort of a little game.'

'A game?' he says weakly.

'Yes, a game of chance. A game of power. I don't know, I'm sure a psychologist would have an opinion on it. All I know is, I enjoyed the challenge and liked the sense of completion it gave everything. It felt like I was making things tidy in the world.' She looks up, as though accessing a distant memory from the archives of her mind. 'It began not long after your brother was born. Your father was having an affair with one of his colleague's girlfriends. I heard she had an extremely severe nut allergy, so I brought some peanuts with me to a wedding, added some to her plate of food, then conveniently hid her handbag out of sight. Nobody could find it or access her EpiPen. She died before the ambulance arrived.' She shrugs. 'So simple. I was surprised by how much I had enjoyed it. So I continued. Over the years, I killed three women, including Chloe. All accidents. Things that could have theoretically occurred by chance. The middle one was an overdose. Well, that's how the coroner recorded it. I had thought your father was classier than that, but apparently attractive opioid addicts weren't beneath him. It made things easier for me, in any case. So when it came time to remove Chloe from the picture, you could say I was quite the veteran.'

Robert is horrified. This is a mistake. He should never have come here, never have asked her to explain. Never have dared look into the darkness. It's like Kieran said. He just can't let things be. And now he knows all these terrible things and desperately wishes he could remove them from his mind. Go back in time. Return to ignorance.

'Don't look so appalled, darling,' his mother says to him now.

They're not supposed to touch, but after a glance at the prison guard, she reaches forwards and takes his hands in hers.

'I don't think either of us can judge the other on what we've done when it comes to murder. After all, you drove to Cornwall to kill Sean Smith, didn't you?'

She sees him open his mouth, but she continues before he can interrupt.

'Don't deny it, my dear. And thank goodness I was ready to sweep in and tidy up your mess. It's what mothers do.' She lets go of his hands and sits back, surveying him. 'We're complicated creatures, human beings,' she says, smiling. 'I think it's nice for us both to know that we're as complicated as each other.'

Acknowledgments

Huge thanks to my wonderful family: My partner Leno for his continued kindness and encouragement throughout the writing of each book, my parents, sisters, uncle, and to Rebecca and Tom and all my close friends. Special mention to my Gran, who passed away while I was writing *The Treehouse* and was always an enthusiastic supporter of my writing.

Thanks to agent Joanna Swainson, rights director Hana Murrell and everyone at Hardman & Swainson, and to my editor Jennie Rothwell and to Charlotte Ledger, Lucy Bennett, Kara Daniel, Chloe Cummings, Grace Edwards, Sofia Salazar Studer and everyone at One More Chapter and HarperCollins. Thanks to Lizzy Barber, John Boyne, Fiona Cummins, Simon Masters, Lauren North, Marion Todd and Michael Wood for all the WhatsApp chats during our writing days, along with joyful lunch trips! Massive thanks to the authors who so generously read early proofs of this book (with a really tight turnaround!) and offered such kind words.

I'd like to say thank you to all the readers and booksellers who have picked up my books and taken the time to recommend them, leave reviews online and post about them on social media. I'll always be extremely grateful.

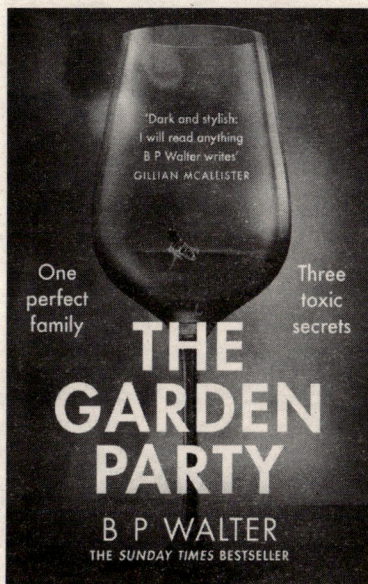

The absolutely gripping *Sunday Times* bestseller with a breathtaking twist.

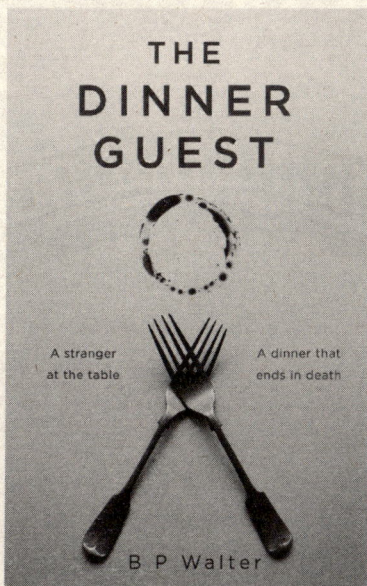

Matthew: the perfect husband.
Titus: the perfect son.
Charlie: the perfect illusion.
Rachel: the perfect stranger. Charlie didn't want her at the book club. Matthew wouldn't listen.

And that's how Charlie finds himself slumped beside his husband's body, their son sitting silently at the dinner table, while Rachel calls 999, the bloody knife still gripped in her hand.

Available in paperback, eBook and audio now!

Everyone is capable of murder. Are you?

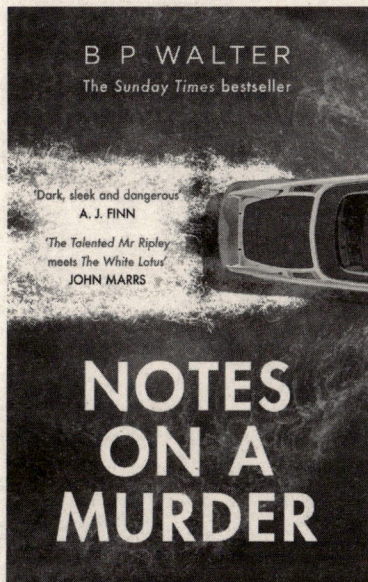

It started with an invitation to dinner. An evening of good food and good company at a luxury villa. But as the night progresses, the party takes a dark turn.

The host makes you an offer, a party favour he calls it: another guest has committed a heinous crime, you can end their life, stop their terror. He tells you there will be no consequences; do you believe him?

Your decision will change your life. Choose carefully.

Available in paperback, eBook and audio now!

ONE MORE CHAPTER

YOUR NUMBER ONE STOP

FOR PAGETURNING BOOKS

The author and One More Chapter would like to thank everyone who contributed to the publication of this story...

Analytics
James Brackin
Abigail Fryer

Audio
Fionnuala Barrett
Ciara Briggs

Contracts
Laura Amos
Laura Evans

Design
Lucy Bennett
Fiona Greenway
Liane Payne
Dean Russell

Digital Sales
Laura Daley
Lydia Grainge
Hannah Lismore

eCommerce
Laura Carpenter
Madeline ODonovan
Charlotte Stevens
Christina Storey
Jo Surman
Rachel Ward

Editorial
Kara Daniel
Charlotte Ledger
Federica Leonardis
Lydia Mason
Ajebowale Roberts
Jennie Rothwell
Sofia Salazar Studer
Helen Williams

Harper360
Jennifer Dee
Emily Gerbner
Ariana Juarez
Jean Marie Kelly
emma sullivan
Sophia Wilhelm

International Sales
Peter Borcsok
Ruth Burrow
Colleen Simpson
Ben Wright

Inventory
Sarah Callaghan
Kirsty Norman

Marketing & Publicity
Chloe Cummings
Grace Edwards

Operations
Melissa Okusanya
Hannah Stamp

Production
Denis Manson
Simon Moore
Francesca Tuzzeo

Rights
Helena Font Brillas
Ashton Mucha
Zoe Shine
Aisling Smyth
Lucy Vanderbilt

Trade Marketing
Ben Hurd
Eleanor Slater

**The HarperCollins
Distribution Team**

**The HarperCollins
Finance & Royalties
Team**

**The HarperCollins
Legal Team**

**The HarperCollins
Technology Team**

UK Sales
Isabel Coburn
Jay Cochrane
Sabina Lewis
Holly Martin
Harriet Williams
Leah Woods

**And every other
essential link in the
chain from delivery
drivers to booksellers
to librarians and
beyond!**